Mistletoe Christmas

"I'm cold," Cressie said, though it wasn't true. The room was small enough that the lanterns took the chill from the air.

"May I kiss you?"

Cressie couldn't believe her ears. "What? Why?"

"Surely someone has told you that you have beautiful lips?"

Her lips opened to say "No," but no sound emerged.

"Perfectly shaped, and a remarkably erotic color," he said thoughtfully. "I've been thinking that, by the way, ever since yesterday's soup course."

Words reeled through her mind but none of them seemed to connect into sentences. He wanted to kiss her? *Elias?* It was impossible. It was—

"Cressida?" he asked, bending closer. "May I?" His breath warmed her cheek. Even though every ladylike sensibility should rebuff him, she couldn't. But she couldn't speak, either. She felt as if she were turned into one of those frozen instruments, waiting to be woken.

She managed a nod.

Also by Eloisa James

The Wildes of Lindow Castle series
Wilde in Love
Too Wilde to Wed
Born to Be Wilde
Say No to the Duke
Say Yes to the Duke
My Last Duchess
Wilde Child

Desperate Duchesses series
Desperate Duchesses
An Affair Before Christmas
Duchess by Night
When the Duke Returns
This Duchess of Mine
A Duke of Her Own
Three Weeks with Lady X
Four Nights with the Duke
Seven Minutes in Heaven

Fairy Tales series
A Kiss at Midnight
Storming the Castle (a novella)
When Beauty Tamed the Beast
The Duke Is Mine
Winning the Wallflower (a novella)
The Ugly Duchess
Seduced by a Pirate (a novella)
With This Kiss (a novella in three parts)
Once Upon a Tower
As You Wish

Essex Sisters series
A Fool Again (a novella)
Much Ado About You
Kiss Me, Annabel
The Taming of the Duke
Pleasure for Pleasure
A Gentleman Never Tells (a novella)

Duchess in Love series
DUCHESS IN LOVE
FOOL FOR LOVE
A WILD PURSUIT
YOUR WICKED WAYS

Ladies Most series
THE LADY MOST LIKELY (with Julia Quinn and Connie Brockway)
THE LADY MOST WILLING (with Julia Quinn and Connie Brockway)

Standalone novels
MY AMERICAN DUCHESS

Also by Christi Caldwell

All the Duke's Sins series
Along Came a Lady

Heart of a Duke series
In Need of a Duke (a novella)
For Love of the Duke • More than a Duke
The Love of a Rogue • Loved by a Duke
To Love a Lord
The Heart of a Scoundrel
To Wed His Christmas Lady
To Trust a Rogue
The Lure of a Rake
To Woo a Widow
To Redeem a Rake
One Winter with a Baron
Beguiled by a Baron
To Tempt a Scoundrel

The Heart of a Scandal series
In Need of a Knight (a novella)
Schooling the Duke
A Lady's Guide to a Gentleman's Heart
A Matchmaker for a Marquess
His Duchess for a Day

Lords of Honor series
Seduced by a Lady's Heart
Captivated by a Lady's Charm
Rescued by a Lady's Love
Tempted by a Lady's Smile
Courting Poppy Tidemore

Scandalous Seasons series
Forever Betrothed, Never the Bride
Never Courted, Suddenly Wed
Always Proper, Suddenly Scandalous
Always a Rogue, Forever Her Love
A Marquess for Christmas
Once a Wallflower, At Last His Love

Wantons of Waverton series
Someone Wanton His Way Comes
The Importance of Being Wanton

Sinful Brides series
The Rogue's Wager
The Scoundrel's Honor
The Lady's Guard
The Heiress's Deception

The Wicked Wallflowers series
The Hellion
The Vixen
The Governess
The Bluestocking
The Spitfire

The Theodosia Sword series
Only for His Lady
Only for Her Honor
Only for Their Love

Scandalous Affairs series
A Groom of Her Own
Taming of the Beast
My Fair Marchioness

The Brethren series
The Spy Who Seduced Her
The Lady Who Loved Him
The Rogue Who Rescued Her
The Minx Who Met Her Match

Brethren of the Lords
My Lady of Deception
Her Duke of Secrets

Regency Duets
Rogues Rush In (with Tessa Dare)

Also by Janna MacGregor

The Widow Rules
A Duke in Time

The Cavensham Heiresses
The Bad Luck Bride
The Bride Who Got Lucky
The Luck of the Bride
The Good, the Bad, and the Duke
Rogue Most Wanted
Wild, Wild Rake

Standalone Novels
Bachelors of Bond Street
The Young and the Ruined: Compromised

Also by Erica Ridley

The Wild Wynchesters series
The Governess Gambit
The Duke Heist
The Rake Mistake
The Perks of Loving a Wallflower

The 12 Dukes of Christmas series
Making Merry
Once Upon a Duke
Kiss of a Duke
Wish Upon a Duke
Never Say Duke
Dukes, Actually
The Duke's Bride
The Duke's Embrace
The Duke's Desire
Dawn with a Duke
One Night with a Duke
Ten Days with a Duke
Forever Your Duke

The Rogues to Riches series
Lord of Chance
Lord of Pleasure
Lord of Night
Lord of Temptation
Lord of Secrets
Lord of Vice
Lord of the Masquerade

The Dukes of War series
The Viscount's Tempting Minx
The Earl's Defiant Wallflower
The Captain's Bluestocking Mistress
The Major's Faux Fiancee
The Brigadier's Runaway Bride
The Pirate's Tempting Stowaway
The Duke's Accidental Wife
All I Want (short story)
A Match Unmasked

The Gothic Love Stories
Too Wicked to Kiss
Too Sinful to Deny
Too Tempting to Resist
Too Wanton to Wed
Too Brazen to Bite

The Magic & Mayhem series
Kissed by Magic
Must Love Magic
Smitten by Magic

The Wicked Dukes Club series (with Darcy Burke)
One Night for Seduction
One Night of Surrender
One Night of Passion
One Night of Scandal
One Night to Remember
One Night of Temptation

MISTLETOE CHRISTMAS

An Anthology

ELOISA JAMES
CHRISTI CALDWELL
JANNA MacGREGOR
ERICA RIDLEY

AVONBOOKS

An Imprint of HarperCollins*Publishers*

This is a work of fiction. Names, characters, places, and incidents are products of the authors' imaginations or are used fictitiously and are not to be construed as real. Any resemblance to actual events, locales, organizations, or persons, living or dead, is entirely coincidental.

First Avon Books mass market printing: October 2021

Print Edition ISBN: 978-0-06-313969-5
Digital Edition ISBN: 978-0-06-313970-1

Cover design by Amy Halperin
Cover illustration by Anna Kmet
Cover images © Dreamstime.com
Author photographs by Bryan Derballa (Eloisa James); Kimberly Rocha (Christi Caldwell); Hilary Hope Photography (Janna MacGregor); Roy Prendas (Erica Ridley)

FIRST EDITION

21 22 23 24 25 CWM 10 9 8 7 6 5 4 3 2 1

Contents

MISTLETOE CHRISTMAS

A MISTLETOE KISS

by Eloisa James

Prologue

Lady Elizabeth Childe to her American cousin, Mrs. Sarah Darby

November 25, 1815

My dearest Sarah,

I'm so thrilled to tell you that after years of hoping, Lord Childe and I have finally received an invitation to the Duke of Greystoke's Revelry! 'Tis a magnificent Christmastide house party featuring every amusement and wonder. I've heard there are plays, dancing, a magical grotto . . . His Grace has a genius for bringing together the finest in England: the aristocracy mingles with artists, politicians, commoners—even journalists and opera dancers!

As you can imagine, such a Revelry does lend itself to scandalous behavior. For mothers, though, it's as important as the Season: a girl who has failed to attract a husband might find success in its less formal atmosphere. We shan't discover the other names on the guest list until it is printed in the Morning Chronicle.

My husband grumps that Greystoke thinks too highly of his party, but the Revelry has been labeled a cornerstone of British society. Now that the duke is on his deathbed, though, no one knows what will happen next year. If this is to be the final gathering, I've no doubt it will be a Revelry to remember.

On a topic closer to home, you would be thrilled by my hothouse peonies . . .

Chapter One

The Duke of Greystoke's annual Christmas Revelry
Greystoke Manor, Cheshire
December, 1815

The Duke of Greystoke would likely be dead by Epiphany, but he counted that as a triumph.

"Only a week left in the Revelry . . . I'll make it to the end, won't I?" He gasped for breath because his heart no longer supported bold statements. Back in the fall, his doctors had advised him he'd be gone by All Hallows. "Proved them wrong. Made it to my party," he added.

His youngest daughter, Lady Cressida—known to most as Cressie—said, "So you did, Father." She was seated at her father's bedside, pretending to listen dutifully, but actually scribbling a list of niggling problems springing from the presence of so many guests in the manor.

"Going well, isn't it?" The duke had only come downstairs once since the house party began a week ago, but sounds of raucous cheer had filtered to his bedchamber, and he'd entertained a stream of visitors.

"Yes, indeed. The cast has arrived for the pantomime, and Isabelle is working with them."

"Isabelle?" the duke asked uncertainly.

"Your granddaughter, Lady Isabelle Wilkshire," Cressie said.

"That's right. Never married, obsessed by the theater. Unsuitable, very." He nodded, satisfied. "What else?"

"The Prime Minister told me in confidence that he is feeling much better about the outcome of the farm bill in Lords."

Her father scoffed. "Nothing more exciting?"

"The lead opera singer at the Theater Royal had chosen Lord Bennett as her new protector," Cressie offered. "Last night Lady Bennett tossed a cup of mulled wine at his head."

"That's more like it," the duke said, smiling. "Wouldn't be the Revelry without scandal."

There were seven days to go in the duke's annual Christmas festivity—if His Grace's death didn't cut the party short. Cressie was fairly certain that her father would refuse to accompany the Grim Reaper until the last carriage had rolled away.

"The Revelry must go on," the duke said, as if he heard her thought. "We've only missed the one year, when your mother passed. We must have at least another decade! Damn it, Cressie, he has to carry on my legacy."

He was the duke's heir.

The Duke of Greystoke and his wife had been blessed with five daughters but no heir, a tragedy underscored by the death of his brother. The title and estate would devolve to his nephew, Valentine Snowe, Viscount Derham.

Valentine, or Val to his family, was pleasant enough, although Cressie had to admit that she scarcely knew him. He dutifully attended the Christmas Revelry on the express command of the duke, but he eschewed the ballroom and closeted himself with a group of men as reclusive and rakish as he.

"A few months ago, Val had the gall to tell me that he wouldn't carry on with the Revelry," the duke barked.

Cressie didn't think that Val *could* carry on. The truth was that the work of throwing the complicated series of parties and events that made up the annual Revelry was hers. For more than a decade, she had created the invitation list and designed all the elaborate entertainments.

Yet much as she had enjoyed the creative license her father had given her, she wanted to do something else with her life. She longed for a house of her own, and someday a family, rather than an existence consumed by an annual party.

"Changed his tune now," the duke said, his voice triumphant.

"How did you do that, Father?" Cressie asked.

"I made him an offer he can't refuse."

"Indeed?" Cressie murmured, wondering if she should turn the evening's quartet into a trio. One violinist hadn't made an appearance.

"I am giving him the Scottish estate," her father announced, darting a glance at Cressie. "For foolishly sentimental reasons, he wants that estate. But I told him that he couldn't have it unless he swore to hold the Revelry for the next decade."

Cressie straightened and her heart gave a sickening thump. The list slid from her hands to the floor. The Scottish estate had long been promised as her dowry, or if she didn't marry, a place for her to live once the ducal estate passed out of her father's hands.

"Pick that up!" her father ordered. "You're always dropping things."

Cressie's stomach clenched into a knot. She loved designing and running the enormous machinery of the Revelry. But she didn't want it to be her life's work.

"Why should you mind?" her father demanded. "The Revelry is my legacy, all I leave behind, since I had no sons." He didn't meet her eyes, because he knew perfectly well how unfair he was being.

"I do mind," Cressie said hotly, bending over to grab the list.

"I'll make Val promise to take care of you. He *has* to take care of you because you're key to the whole thing."

"I refuse to be that key!" Cressie retorted, springing to her feet. "You presuppose I will agree to continuing the work involved in the Revelry—and I will not! You promised me Morley House years ago, Father."

Her father turned his head so their furious eyes finally met. Cressie held her ground, staring back at him. "I want to marry and have a house of my own. Future Christmas parties I plan will be mine, not yours. To be absolutely clear, Father, I refuse to live at Greystoke Manor, nor will I continue planning the Revelry."

"I require you to do so," the duke growled, his thick eyebrows bristling.

Cressie gritted her teeth. Apparently, her father wanted her to spend her entire life in the castle, growing gray and old while hiring acrobats and arranging for the annual pantomime, watching other people kiss under the mistletoe—and never being kissed herself.

Her father's legacy would continue, and no one would ever know that it was really *her* legacy.

"You, Daughter, will do as I say!" The duke hauled on the velvet cord that hung beside his bed, and when a footman opened the door, spat at him, "Fetch my heir."

"This is unfair!" Cressie cried. "You promised me the Scottish estate after my debut was cut short. You could—you could give it to Val after my death."

"Ungrateful chit!" her father sputtered. "You can live a life of luxury here in the manor, a security that many old maids don't have. It's not my fault you aren't married. Every gentleman worth his salt has passed through this house. If you couldn't attract one of them, we all know why!" He cast a withering look at Cressie. "How could a daughter of mine turn out such a plain, dowdy creature, trailing scraps of paper in your wake like a rubbish barge?"

"I never said it was your fault that I'm not married,"

Cressie said. Her throat was tightening, and she had a horrible feeling she might cry. "I'm only twenty-three; I may still marry. I shall if you don't give away my dowry!"

The door opened again, and Val walked in, accompanied by his friend Elias, Lord Darcy de Royleston.

Her father didn't notice. "Your dowry is irrelevant. Not a soul has offered to marry you, dowry or no, and I've already changed my will!"

"Please forgive me. We were coming along the corridor," Val said, walking forward. His face was composed, but Cressie thought she saw amusement in his eyes. "I hope you don't mind that I brought de Royleston with me, Duke." He bowed. "Cressie." He bowed again.

Cressie didn't bother to answer, just brushed by and ran out of the room. She felt sick to her stomach, her heart pounding, tears pressing on her eyes.

She had had no debut Season because it took most of the year to plan the Revelry, and her father would spare her for only three weeks.

So now she was, at twenty-three, an old maid.

She wasn't precisely plain, because she had a wealth of pale yellow hair that had been particularly admired when she debuted. But she was short, and her mouth was a little too wide, and her nose turned up at the end. She did tend to scribble ideas on scraps of paper and leave them around the house. Her hair was forever falling from its pins. She wasn't neat, and tidy, and perfect.

All the same, Val had been *amused* by the mere idea that someone might to want to marry her.

Even worse, Elias had overheard it too.

Lord Darcy de Royleston was the sort of man who wandered about with no idea of the effect his features had on the female population. He had dark hair and a strong nose that combined with angled cheekbones and a square jaw to give him the air of a medieval knight. A French knight, because he had a delicious accent. He would look marvelous in a suit of armor with a liveried page or two in attendance.

Put that together with a large estate, even before he inherited a title and further lands from his father, and an absurd amount of time at the Revelry was wasted in gossip about him.

Cressie scarcely knew de Royleston, other than the odd formal conversation. She thought of him as Elias because . . .

Just because.

Which made it all worse that he had overheard her father's scathing comment about her marital prospects.

Likely, Elias had laughed at her as well. Probably, all three of them were chortling over her wish to wed, given what a lumpish fright she was.

She made it to her room before bursting into tears, which was a blessing.

Plain, dowdy, weepy—and undowered? No Scottish estate?

Her father was right. No man would take her.

She'd have to become a companion, fetching and carrying for one of her older sisters.

No. She was a duke's daughter, still Lady Cressida, even without a dowry. She wouldn't be a companion, but a wilted maiden aunt, sitting in the corner, gray hair poking out from under her ruffled cap, dropping crumpets instead of paper.

Wonderful. Just wonderful.

Chapter Two

"That was awkward," Elias said in a low tone.

His friend Val walked past him to stand at the Duke of Greystoke's bedside. "Why were you berating Cressie, Duke?" he asked.

"No one wants that chit," the duke retorted. The man was obviously on his deathbed but clinging to life with grim strength. "Besides, I cannot allow her to marry. You need her."

"What for?" Elias asked, walking to the other side of the bed from Val. He didn't like seeing anyone bullied, and he definitely didn't like the desolation he'd caught in Cressida's eyes as she rushed past.

"His Grace has demanded that I continue holding this Christmas gathering," Val said with evident disdain. "It seems Cressie plays an important role in organizing it, though I fail to see why I must continue that particular tradition."

"You could hire a secretary to organize the party," Elias suggested.

"The Revelry is *not* a mere party. It is the most important gathering held in all the kingdom," the duke snapped, pushing himself up on the pillows. His eyes were burning, as if he had a fever. "This manor has witnessed the seeds of constitutional change and great inventions, not to mention marriages between England's greatest families."

Elias couldn't argue with him about that; the Revelry was famously important.

"I've changed my will as we discussed," the duke said to Val.

Val stilled like a hawk that caught sight of a mouse.

"I've given you the Scottish estate, on your oath that you'll keep the Revelry going for ten years," His Grace continued, gasping for breath. "My solicitor is here, in the castle, so I made a new will this morning."

Elias looked across the bed at Val. "Is the duke referring to *the* Scottish estate? The one your father lost in a card game?"

"Yes. The estate that was won by Greystoke in a hand of cribbage," Val said in a clipped tone. "Your Grace, am I to understand from your conversation with Cressida that she was unaware that the estate is no longer her dowry? I didn't like the fact, but I had accepted it."

"Cressie doesn't need it," the duke replied with a rasping cough. "No man's offered for her. No call for a dowry. She can stay here in her childhood home and take care of the Revelry. Another decade, that's all I'm asking."

"Your daughter is plain," Elias said bitingly. "She fades into the background. And now you're taking away her dowry, the one thing that could entice a husband? Not to mention the fact that you have bribed Val with the estate that belonged to his father before you won it at cards?"

"Are you accusing me of cheating?" Somehow the dying duke managed to wheeze out a question that sounded like the preface to a duel.

"No," Elias stated.

There was no need to answer the obvious: the morality of winning an estate from one's brother on the flip of a card, and then using it to bribe his son, was obvious.

At least to a man who'd been brought up to treasure family, as Elias had been.

"As I told Val last month, if he didn't promise to hold the

Revelry, I had decided to give the Scottish estate to charity," the duke said. "For the good of my soul." He managed a pious look.

A pulse was ticking in Val's forehead, but he kept his mouth shut.

"Cressie doesn't eat much, and she's not extravagant about her clothing. You won't even notice her," Greystoke continued. "Damn it, every title comes along with pensioners and the like."

"A duke's daughter is rarely one of those pensioners, as they are dowried and married off," Val said, a sharp edge leaking into his voice. "I assumed that you'd offered her an equivalent dowry to the Scottish estate!"

"She'll be your right hand, better than my steward," Lady Cressida's father retorted. "She does it all. Invitations, entertainments, all of it. She's a marvel. She's run the whole thing, ever since she was fifteen years of age."

"Cressida is in charge of determining the Revelry list?" Elias asked, astounded.

All of high society waited for the day when the Duke of Greystoke's invitations were delivered, always by hand rather than by post, even if the recipient lived in the furthest reaches of Wales. Greystoke's grooms would spread out through London while people waited at home, twitching the curtains in the sitting room, desperately hoping to see a man wearing the duke's green livery mounting the front steps.

The following week, the *Morning Chronicle* would publish the list—on the front page. Reputations were made or lost depending on the names that appeared in that list; Elias had attended the Revelry for years, and while he disliked his host, he had reluctantly acknowledged the duke's brilliant ability to bring together the best and brightest, and to design thrilling entertainments for their pleasure.

Except apparently the duke hadn't done any of it.

His Grace nodded. "No one knows. Wouldn't do to let it out that a chit has that much power. Cressie scours the papers and gossip columns front to back, deciding who gets my invites. She'll be happy just buzzing around the estate, working on the Revelry. You won't notice her," he said again to Val before going into another series of panting coughs.

"On my father's deathbed, I promised him that I would reacquire the Scottish estate," Val said, meeting Elias's eyes over the bed. "I had hoped to buy it from Cressie."

"You can't buy it from a charity." Greystoke closed his eyes. "Tetchy fellow, your father. Rotten at cribbage."

Elias instinctively held up his hand at the look on Val's face. "He's dying."

Val's lips moved. Elias fancied he muttered something along the lines of "Can't be too soon," but such things were better left unspoken.

The duke appeared to have fallen into a doze.

Val narrowed his eyes. "You need a wife, Elias."

"So?"

"Why not take my cousin? You live next door, so she could offer a little help with the wretched party."

"So you do plan to continue the Revelry?"

"I swore an oath to that effect. For God's sake, I'm sure any decent secretary could run this party," Val snapped. "Cressie can glance over the invitation list or something. I'll dower her, if her own father won't."

"I don't need a dowry." It was true. His father had seen the way the wind was blowing in France years ago, sold everything, and moved to England to augment the already considerable estates in Somerset where Val had grown up, since his mother insisted he be sent to Eton.

"Cressie is a duke's daughter," Val said. He left it at that.

Elias had met Lady Cressida repeatedly, especially when she was a child, but for the life of him, he couldn't remember much about her as an adult. They hadn't danced together in years, to the best of his recollection.

"You don't want beauty and wit," his best friend said. "They lead to trouble. Were you in the room last night when Eloise Bennett threw wine at her husband? She was the most sought-after girl on the market two years ago."

"Bennett is an ass," Elias said. "He was flirting with an opera singer in front of his wife."

"But she's having an *affaire* with a neighboring squire, and everyone knows it."

"What's your point?"

"The more beautiful a woman is, the more men tempt her to slip away with them. The more elegant she is, the more her clothing will cost. The more witty she is, the more irritating she will be over the breakfast table." He paused. "Cressie is a good person."

That was Val's highest praise.

Elias felt desperately sorry for the young lady whose only value seemed to be her labor. Though he privately abhorred the trading of women like visiting cards, it was a fact of life or at least, life in the peerage. "I'll consider it."

"I'll make her dowry commensurate with her . . . her lack of attractiveness," Val said.

Elias glared at him with such disgust that his friend blinked. "You are talking about a woman who may be my wife, and you are bargaining like a swine-herder at market."

"I apologize. You are absolutely right. I was—I am torn between my late father's love for his Scottish estate, and my cousin's painful situation. She had a claim to it, and if things were different, I would honor it."

Elias turned to go.

Val met him at the end of the bed. "I meant it as a true apology, my friend. My offer was ill-phrased."

"Ignoble," Elias said, "and cruel to the lady, should she ever know."

"Your assessment wasn't much kinder than mine," Val pointed out. "We've both underestimated my cousin, since it appears that she runs the Revelry. She is . . . she appears to be a sweet mouse, and I mean that in the best of ways, or I would never suggest you marry her."

Elias hadn't thought of marrying a mouse. In fact, he hadn't thought much about marriage. But he knew that he had to. His younger brother had entered the priesthood in Avignon, and while his father was hale and hearty, Elias had to produce an heir at some point.

"I'll think about it," he said. "I suppose she'll be at dinner?"

"Of course," Val said. "I'll have a word with the butler and make sure that you're seated beside her." He frowned. "Did I understand my uncle to say that she not only makes all the decisions regarding invitations but manages everything else? He didn't tell me that when he bribed me to keep it going."

"She runs this monstrous party," Elias said. "Perhaps you'd better keep her. You could promise her a dowry in exchange for managing the Revelry for a few more years."

"You heard her tell her father that she wants a husband. Every time I'd look at her, I'd feel guilty about her single state, not to mention her dowry. Your estate runs beside this one; you'd be a good spouse, and if she would agree to help me with the confounded Revelry, I could fulfil my father's dearest wish without guilt."

"You could dower her so lavishly that she'd get a husband, mouse or no," Elias suggested.

"A fortune hunter," his friend said, his eyes even colder than they were by nature.

"Some of my closest friends are in need of a fortune," Elias retorted. "Decent fellows, who simply didn't inherit land. Don't be such a stiff-rumped ass."

Val gave him a wry smile. "She can't help me with the

damned party if she's married to a fortune hunter from Wales, can she?"

They began walking down the corridor, away from the duke's bedchamber. Behind them, they heard His Grace begin another of those exhausting series of coughs.

"It doesn't seem fair to the lady," Elias said.

"Marriage is never fair to the lady," Val replied.

True enough.

Chapter Three

Cressie walked into the drawing room only minutes before the gong would sound for dinner. She and the castle butler, Twist, had been able to recruit a violinist from among the guests and the "Evening of Bach" planned for the post-dinner entertainment would go forward.

She was exhausted, heartbroken, and aware that her eyes were wretchedly red. But she couldn't hide in her room, no matter how much she might wish to. Twist depended on her to cope with any problems, and given the mix of people in the house, there were always problems.

So she'd powdered her nose and allowed Nanny—formerly her nanny and still known as such—to pin up her hair in outrageous curls because Cressie wasn't paying attention. Little sausage-like ringlets fell all around her head from a towering topknot of curls.

Hopefully they would stay there; Nanny had stuck in so many pins that Cressie's head felt like a pincushion.

"I look like a children's toy," she pointed out, glancing in the mirror. Not that it mattered, because no one paid attention to her except to offer complaints about their chambers. Her father collected the praise; she collected the problems.

"Don't you dare touch your hair!" Nanny said fiercely. She had never gotten over the idea that she was in charge of a nursery, even though she'd been acting as a lady's maid for a decade. "It's taken me the better part of an hour to tame your curls," she added, folding her arms over her plump bosom. "You have more hair than any other lady here, and at least now everyone will notice!"

Cressie sighed, looking in the glass. "Perhaps I should cut it."

"I'd never allow that," Nanny decreed. "It's a woman's glory."

Cressie knew what she meant. When you had an unremarkable face, you couldn't lop off the only asset you had.

"You look a treat," Nanny said, darting at her with the powder puff again.

Cressie walked down the stairs blinking white powder from her eyelashes.

The butler met her in the hallway. "Lord Snowe requested a change in seating arrangements," he said anxiously.

Cressie rolled her eyes. What a marvelous time for Val to begin showing interest in seating. "What's he done?" She managed to bite back a speculation that he'd seated himself next to the oh-so-enticing opera singer that everyone seemed to want.

"Moved Lord Darcy de Royleston to the seat beside yours," Twist said.

Cressie narrowed her eyes.

Why was Elias suddenly seated beside her?

From pity, most likely. He had never paid the slightest attention to Cressie. No matter the speculation that Elias was finally looking for a wife at this Revelry, he certainly wouldn't look to her.

But he was kind. Kind enough to pity her, to want to say something sympathetic to a woman shamed by her own father.

She almost stopped walking. Could the day grow any worse?

"All right," she told Twist and entered the drawing room.

Greystoke Manor was widely known as one of the most elegant in all Cheshire, but the building itself hadn't been good enough for her father. The public rooms had been refurbished as if royalty might stroll in at any moment. The walls of the drawing room were covered in damasked silk, specially woven from a pattern used at Versailles. The ceiling and portrait frames were picked out in so much gilt that—to Cressie's mind—the room resembled the inside of an egg yolk.

To her surprise, it seemed that Elias had been watching the door of the drawing room, waiting for her. He moved directly toward her, ignoring the smiling invitations of several women who tried to block his path.

Given his supposed marital plans, the man no sooner strolled into a room before he was surrounded by chaperones, even though he rarely danced with their charges. He generally chose to circle the floor with married ladies and dowagers, even if all the eyes in the room followed them.

It was a trifle shameful to admit, but Cressie was one of the women who often found herself watching Elias move around the ballroom. He was so large and exquisitely dressed, with a negligent French air that put most gentlemen to shame.

"Crickets," Cressie muttered to herself. The last thing she wanted was most of the party wondering what Elias was doing with her. She looked about for one of her sisters, but they were partnered with their spouses, on the verge of making their way to the great dining hall.

It was too late. Elias was strolling directly toward her, and moreover, he was smiling. He was so handsome that even the happiest of married ladies broke into an involuntary giggle as he passed.

Cressie refused to giggle. She drew in a steadying breath and remained where she was. She wasn't pretty or particularly witty, but she could be dignified.

Now, if ever, was the time to remember that.

"Lord Royleston," she said, bending her head and dropping into a curtsey. To her horror, the heap of curls on top of her head swayed as if they were about to topple to the side. She'd have to curtsey shallowly from now on.

"Is it going to fall?" Elias asked, when they were both upright once again.

Cressie could feel pink stealing up her neck. "I gather you are talking about my hair," she said stiffly.

"I have sisters," he replied, with a charming grin. "I know about the difficulty of balancing extra swatches of hair and horsehair pads on one's head. My little sister once dropped a curl into a teacup, didn't realize, and handed it to the vicar."

Cressie puzzled for a second and realized that Elias thought she was wearing fake hair. "A topknot can be challenging," she said.

"Why do it, then?" his lordship said, apparently deciding it would be fun to chatter with her as if they were old friends. "I can't see that it adds much to have all that extra stuff on your head. Especially as everyone knows it's not truly one's own, if you see what I mean. You don't mind my saying that, do you?"

"No," Cressie said, untruthfully. She did mind being given beauty advice by a man who had never once had to question his own attractiveness.

"Were I a lady, I think I would leave it off," he said.

"Good to know," she murmured.

His eyes narrowed. "Irony, Lady Cressida?"

"Absolutely not," she said. "You misunderstand me. I agree that your face would not be well suited to additional swatches of hair."

"Especially ones curled to look like little sausages," he pointed out.

She didn't have to curl her hair: it formed corkscrew curls all on its own. Which was none of his business. Still, she couldn't stop herself from imagining him with similar hair.

Elias was incredibly *male*. His face topped with a bouquet

of curls, as she wore? She giggled before she could stop herself. "You would resemble a large poodle."

All too obviously, he caught back a grin.

"I suppose that I have some resemblance to that breed as well," she agreed, resigned.

His eyes could have been mistaken for affectionate, which suggested she was losing her mind.

"May I escort you to the dining room?" he asked.

Cressie took his arm, reminding herself that she was no object of pity. Through habit, she paused in the door, scanning the dining room to make certain that every table was gleaming with linen and silver. Silver bowls graced the center of each table, filled with hothouse roses and trailing ivy.

"Looks nice," Elias said.

"Thank you."

"Did you plan it?"

"Yes." She walked toward the table she'd assigned for herself, only remembering when she saw Val's back that she had seated herself beside him. Something eased inside her.

She hadn't been singled out for a compassionate conversation about her future. Likely, the two men just wanted to talk to each other, perhaps because they were disinclined to carry on regular conversations with the guests.

Elias hadn't switched to sit beside *her*; he'd moved to be seated at a table with her cousin—whom she herself had placed at her left hand. Why, oh why, hadn't she thought about moving Val to the other side of the room after that humiliating scene with her father? She knew the answer to that: she'd lost two hours crying bitterly, and then forgot.

In short, she was an idiot, and now she had to spend the meal next to the one person in the world—other than her father—whom she truly didn't want to see. Through no fault of his own, Val would soon have the estate that was meant to be her home.

"Good evening," she said to her cousin.

He had risen, of course, and was regarding her unsmilingly, doubtless noting her reddened eyes.

They seated themselves, and Elias turned away to greet the lady on his right.

"You look somewhat . . ." Val paused, obviously trying to come up with an appropriate adjective. "Diminished," he said, finally. "I am sorry."

Cressie decided to not waste time with pleasantries. "I want you to know that I do understand that the estate in question belonged to your father long before it was promised to me," she said, pitching her voice below the chatter of aristocratic voices. "I shall ask my father to provide me with a dowry from other funds. We needn't speak of it again."

"Your father informed me that you are entirely responsible for the Revelry," Val said. "Which no one in England knows."

Cressie couldn't stop a wry smile.

"Your father's legacy is truly yours?"

"The Revelry was originally his idea."

"When you make all decisions from invitations to entertainment to seating, you are doing far more than carrying out someone's wishes," her cousin observed. "Do you wish to continue the Revelry for another decade, Cressie?"

"Absolutely not," she stated.

"I shall take that into account." Val smiled at her, and his saturnine, angular features became charming.

The footmen placed watercress soup before each of their seats at precisely the same moment, as Twist had trained them. Cressie pushed the whole question of future Revelries out of her head. The soup was excellent, and a quick look around the room showed that every table was happily chattering.

"Lady Cressida," Elias said, from her other side.

She gave him a serene smile. "Yes, your lordship?"

"I have attended this party for years," he said, "and although I am always dazzled by the glittering entertainments, I feel I don't know you."

"True," Cressie agreed, taking another spoonful of soup.

"Do tell me about yourself?"

He had an eyebrow raised, and a smile on his face. She cast him a look that came dangerously close to real dislike, and said, "I don't see any point, do you?"

"Yes."

She narrowed her eyes. "Are you looking for a companion for an aged aunt or something of that nature?"

"Something of that nature," he said, his manner polite, and faultlessly impersonal.

She relaxed. "It's kind of you to think of me, or perhaps it was Val who suggested it?"

He nodded.

The footmen arrived and removed the bowls without spills, and then put down the next course—duckling with cherry sauce and an assortment of roast game—before Cressida was able to respond.

"What would you need to know about *me* in order to hire me as a companion?" Elias asked, rather surprisingly.

His smile was extraordinarily charming, so much so that she did all she could do to keep her expression polite and not melt into a girlish puddle.

"Men are never asked to be companions," she blurted out.

"Odd, isn't it? Elderly women are given companions, and elderly men are not."

"Because men generally have wives and daughters who fetch and carry for them," Cressie said.

"That is never wasted time for a loved one," Elias responded, which just proved he was male. "Would you like to know anything about me?"

"Why?"

"We agreed that we should get to know each other," he prompted.

The footmen intervened again, so Cressie had time to think that this conversation was very strange. "I don't remember agreeing to a friendship."

"We would need to know more of each other before we could live under the same roof," Elias said, his eyes amused.

The horrid thought occurred to her that he was teasing her for some secret reason, mocking her with an awkward version of courtship, but common sense squelched that idea. He was a decent man. Kind.

Perhaps too handsome for his own good, and prone to be arrogant, but what aristocratic male wasn't?

"The suggestion is irrelevant," she said, picking up her wineglass and discovering that it was empty. "I have no intention of becoming a companion to one of your elderly relatives, though I appreciate your kindness in thinking of me." She said it as firmly as possible.

Lord Darcy de Royleston flicked a look over his shoulder, and a footman instantly stepped forward to refill her glass.

"What is planned for tomorrow?" he asked, accepting her refusal without protest.

"Twist will give you the list of activities planned for gentlemen, or you may explore on your own," Cressie said automatically, having answered this question a million times in the last decade. "The snow grotto is open. I recommend that you explore it, if you haven't seen it. I believe that this year's grotto is the best we've ever constructed."

"Keeping this many people happy and occupied must entail an enormous amount of work," Elias observed.

"Twist is marvelous, and I have a large staff. In addition, a great many people are hired only to work on the Revelry."

"Seasonal labor? Or are they here year-round?"

"Some of them remain on the estate: the men who work

on stage sets and designs, for example. Mr. Blossom designs and builds the annual grotto, so he is with us all year, as it requires tremendous planning and preparation."

"Then why do it?" He didn't ask it aggressively. "I mean the grotto, not the Revelry."

"Have you never visited one of our grottoes?"

He shook his head.

Cressie had avoided looking at Elias's face during their conversation; he was too handsome, and she was a little afraid that she might start blushing. But now she saw nothing but curious brown eyes.

She couldn't help brightening. "They are marvelous fun, with a different theme every year. We've had the City of Troy, for example, with an enormous Trojan horse that people could climb into. Mount Olympus, with ten-foot-high gods sitting in state. King Neptune's palace, surrounded by truly astonishing fish and seaweed. That one was marvelous!"

Elias had attended the Revelry for years as an act of friendship to Val. They occasionally joined the boisterous group of men who hunted in the afternoons—or whatever other gentlemanly activity was offered.

He had never made his way to the grotto.

Lady Cressida's eyes were shining as she talked about turrets and burrows. He knew without asking that the ideas were all hers.

She looked suddenly alive, her smile transforming her face. Her hands flew through the air; her napkin slid from her lap and fell to the floor without her notice.

He'd been wrong about her looks.

Cressida was pretty with her head crowned by all that sunshiny hair, fake or no, and her brown eyes sparkling. Her lips were a dark rose color, and her bottom lip formed the most perfect dip and curve that he'd seen in his life.

"Will you bring me to look at it?" he asked, when Cressida paused to take a breath.

"What?"

"The grotto, of course," Elias said. "Your grotto. Tomorrow afternoon, perhaps?"

"Oh, I don't have time for that," she said, blinking at him. "I spend every afternoon in consultation. It's the only way to make sure that the Revelry proceeds exactly as planned." She accepted the napkin he handed her. "Thank you! I drop things all the time. My father finds my carelessness so bothersome."

"Remembering all the details of this vast party—not to mention designing the grotto—is a tremendous amount of work," Elias said. "How can anyone fault you for dropping the occasional napkin?"

She gave him a sudden, quirky grin. "I wish it was only napkins. I can't tell you how many cups of tea I've spilled. What's more, I scribble down ideas on scraps of paper and leave them around the house. Twist has to send a maid around in the evening to collect them."

They had eaten their duckling by the time Cressie finished telling him about the Herculean tasks that underpinned the Revelry. Her father was certainly right that Val would have difficulty planning the party by himself.

"Who attends the daily meetings?" Elias asked.

"All of us who lead the Revelry: me, Twist, Blossom, Mrs. Peters, who is in charge of the bedchambers, Fettle, who manages the stage and puts on the pantomime every year. Our head cook comes in to go over the menus for the next day, as do the head pastry chef, the head gardener, and the man who runs the hothouses."

"You solve problems?"

"Exactly," she said. "I probably should slip away now, as a matter of fact."

"We haven't had dessert yet," Elias protested. He may have missed years' worth of grottoes, but he had never left a meal in Greystoke Manor before dessert. The duke's pastry chef was famed throughout the British Isles. "That would be like ignoring a lovely woman." He gave her a direct look.

Cressida sighed. "Don't. Please."

"What?"

"Make syrupy comments. The sort you might make to . . . well, to a lady."

"You *are* a lady," Elias pointed out. He narrowed his eyes. "Does anyone speak to you as if you are not a lady in the midst of these consultations?"

"Of course not; we've worked together for years. I'm talking about gentlemen. I'm not the sort of lady whom a gentleman flatters." She caught Elias's gaze and held it. "I must ask you not to offer any false reassurances."

Elias didn't like it. But he could see the spark of rebellion in her eyes—and respect it. She was right. Lovely or not, he *had* ignored her for years. "There is nothing false about this statement: you are lovely, Lady Cressida."

She opened her mouth, ready to spar with him again, but he distracted her. "You didn't tell me about the theme for the grotto last year?"

"The Wild Wood," Cressida replied, her eyes lighting up again. "Snow-caverns and snow-castles, with terraces and ramps in every direction, and in the midst a witch's hut, because the wood was 'wild,' you see."

Her napkin slipped away, followed by a stray fork. Elias bent over to retrieve both of them. "And this year?"

"King Arthur's castle, with a portcullis and a drawbridge, and an archway leading to the castle. We reused some of the structures—"

"I thought everything was made of snow?" Elias asked, interrupting.

She shook her head. "Underlying stability is essential, if only to make sure that no one gets caught in a snowfall. Plus, some years we have sufficient snow, like this year, and others we build the grotto entirely from wood."

Elias couldn't stop himself. "You do realize that you are quite brilliant?"

She rolled her eyes.

"I'm serious. You have masterminded the most important gathering in all England, not just once, but annually." He leaned forward. "Perhaps more important, you design works of art."

She waved her hand. "Pooh! They are ephemeral. Beautiful, yes, but they melt with the snow and are gone."

"The more beautiful for that," Elias said, suddenly deeply sorry that he had never bothered to visit the grottoes, though he had repeatedly heard them referred to as one of the greatest wonders of England.

He was beginning to think that he was the biggest dunce in the western hemisphere, because he had overlooked the most important things.

Cressida gave him that quirky smile of hers, the one that had nothing to do with civility. "I will admit that I am very proud of the grottoes, perhaps even more so than if they lasted a lifetime. They must be *experienced*, if you see what I mean. No one can sell them, or hang them up on a wall."

"Of course," Elias said, understanding. "Your artworks can't be bought or sold."

Her smile deepened. "Yes."

"I feel like the greatest fool in the world for having missed any of them," he said. "Would you please do me the inexpressible courtesy of accompanying me to see your latest creation tomorrow after luncheon?"

"It doesn't open until two, so that the staff can eat. I'm afraid that I shall be unable to join you, as I previously explained." Cressida folded her napkin.

"The inestimable Twist can run the meeting tomorrow or, even better, Val can take his place," Elias suggested. "His Grace is insistent that Val carry on the tradition of the Revelry. Don't you think that your cousin should get an idea of its challenges?"

Cressida's brows drew together. "Val has been a help with planning entertainments this year. I don't know why it never occurred to me to ask him to join the afternoon meetings."

"Let's push him through the door and give him a glimpse of what he's taking on, shall we?" Elias leaned forward and caught Val's attention. "There's an organization meeting of sorts that happens every afternoon. You'll take it over tomorrow, won't you? I'm going to whisk Lady Cressida away after luncheon."

"Certainly," Val said.

Elias smiled at Cressida. "So tomorrow—"

"I'm afraid that I must leave you both," she said, standing up. "Twist just signaled a problem." Her napkin fell to the ground yet again, followed by a couple of pearl-topped hairpins.

"Send Val," Elias suggested, rising.

She shook her head and several long ringlets fell from her topknot and tumbled down her back. She didn't seem to notice. "That would be throwing him into deep water. Planning is not problem-solving."

Val bowed. "I am looking forward to attending tomorrow's meeting."

"I shall meet you on the front steps after luncheon, Lady Cressida," Elias said.

The two men stood shoulder to shoulder, watching as Cressida made her way to the door. She was stopped constantly, as guests greeted her or—Elias suspected—requested special favors. She was polite to each, curtseying, nodding, promising whatever they asked for.

"She's left a trail of hairpins," Val observed. "You would always be able to find her, unlike those children lost in the wood because their bread crumbs had disappeared."

"Hansel and Gretel?" Elias asked, seating himself. A

footman instantly removed Cressida's chair. "Your cousin is a bloody genius, Val. You didn't know?"

His friend shook his head. "The duke takes all the credit."

"You never bothered to look below the surface," Elias said. "Any more than I did."

Val bent over, picked up a piece of note paper from the floor, and read aloud. "'*Val: Sleeping Beauty? B and B! Bluebeard.*' The last is crossed out. And there's a few more sentences I can't read. What on earth?"

"Ideas for future grottoes," Elias guessed. "B and B is likely *Beauty and the Beast.*"

"No Revelry, no grotto," Val said firmly.

Elias took the paper from him. Cressida's handwriting was spiky and quick, speckled with exclamation marks, as creative as the woman herself. "I'll give it back to her."

"My uncle is a beast," Val said, dislike rumbling in his voice. "She should have received the credit for fashioning the Revelry. Instead, he made himself into a powerful figure in English society."

Elias tucked the paper away in his pocket, giving Val a wry smile. "I don't think she minded. It's my impression that she loved the challenge of running the Revelry, especially the more creative aspects."

"If she agrees to help me, I would make certain that all England knew that it was her work," Val declared.

"You might be able to convince her to help you with a new grotto, but the problems should be yours, Val."

His friend winced. "A decade of problems."

"In exchange for your father's dearest wish."

"A fair trade."

Chapter Four

The next day Elias was just beginning to think that perhaps Cressida wouldn't join him when she tore into the entry, Twist at her shoulder. She was dressed for cold weather, he saw thankfully.

"Lady Cressida, good afternoon," he said, bowing.

She glanced at him and then back at the butler. "Lady Elizabeth Childe wants rice water in the afternoon; Mrs. Perkins is complaining of indigestion, so please find her with a soothing draught; and don't forget that Isabelle is working in the music room on *Cinderella* and will need tea. She often forgets to eat."

"Yes, Lady Cressida," Twist said, opening the front door. "Your gloves."

"New snow!" Cressida exclaimed, trotting down the front steps. "I haven't even looked out a window since breakfast."

Elias looked down to where she had stopped at the bottom. Little snowflakes were twirling in the chilly afternoon sunshine.

She smiled, turning her head so that snow fell on her face, never mind the fact that most ladies would have done the opposite.

She must have removed all that extra hair she'd bundled on top of her head yesterday, because the hood on her pelisse fit close to her head. Even he, who knew little of ladies' fashion, could tell that her garment was several years out of date.

Perhaps *all* her hair was false? Perhaps she wore a wig and shaved her head. That might explain Val's insistence on plumping up her dowry.

Bewigged or no, she looked utterly fetching at the moment, her cheeks pink with the cold and a smile on her lips.

In fact, Cressida wasn't plain in the least, he registered, an odd tremor going through his body. Her lips were delicious and just now, as she closed her eyes, he saw that her lashes were luxurious, a darker color than her hair.

There was an almost audible click in his ears, the sound of a puzzle piece slotting into place, or a piece of carpentry sliding into alignment. She wasn't what he had pictured as his bride, but she was going to be his wife.

This brilliant, reclusive, creative woman whom no one seemed to know—including her own cousin—was going to be his.

"Forgive me," Cressida told him. He expected her to stop and take his arm, but she turned and walked away. "I haven't been outside in several days."

"It's not healthy to remain indoors for days," Elias said, catching up and taking her arm before she could speed ahead.

"I've had no time," she explained. "The grotto is down the hill to the east. Excuse me." She gently disengaged herself and picked up a scarlet ribbon that had fallen by the path. Then she kept walking ahead of him, looking about her cheerfully, as if he didn't exist.

Elias didn't think he was being vain to say that unmarried young ladies—and yes, married ones as well—generally didn't behave as if he were no more interesting than a footman. Cressida wasn't glancing up at him through her lashes. She didn't begin a conversation, giggle, or cast him a simpering look. In fact, by the time they rounded a curve and headed down a hill, he had the distinct sensation that she'd forgotten he was following her.

The paved path must have been recently shoveled, although snow was beginning to blur the corners of the paving stones. Cressida's indifference to him was prickling Elias's sense of self; he caught up and took her gloved hand in his.

Sure enough, she startled.

"You'd forgotten I was with you," he said, an involuntary smile curving his lips.

"It's only because I have so many things on my mind," she said, glancing at him. "The archery field, for example, needs to be swept again." She nodded to the right, and he saw targets standing red against the black tree trunks, but like the path, they had a softer aspect now, with snow clinging to the scarlet paint. "I designated it as the gentlemen's activity for tomorrow afternoon."

Elias nodded, determined to keep her attention on him. "Is the grotto always in the same location?"

"Oh, yes. On the other side of this small wood. Last year, Mr. Blossom used the far edge as the boundary of his Wild Wood."

They reached the grove of trees and walked under a festively painted arch that read *Tintagel Castle.*

Elias tried to shock her into paying him attention. "As I recall it, King Arthur's father disguised himself as his mother's husband in order to sneak into her bed. An unsavory parentage for a king."

"One that I'm hoping no one acts out back at the house," Cressida said, glancing at him. He was delighted to see the laughter in her eyes. "One never knows at the Revelry."

The snow was thicker in the woods, bunching under their feet. The grove was silent but for a bird call here or there and the muffled sound of their boots on the paving stones.

King Arthur's castle had to be eleven feet high, a tall icy structure cut with ramparts and windows that allowed light to go straight through the building. They walked over the drawbridge that crossed the moat, under a great arching door that led to a single room. Leaning against the wall were human-sized musical instruments carved from ice: a base viol, two violins, a pianoforte, three flutes.

Elias reached out and touched the dark string of a starkly white base viol. It let out a soft noise as he plucked it.

"Merlin turned the musicians into their own instruments when Arthur died," Cressida told him. "They wait for the master of the castle to return."

"Amazing," Elias murmured.

"We have guides who explain the story, but they're at luncheon at the moment," she added, more prosaically.

They peered into a moat swimming with creatures that looked like gargoyles or winged creatures.

"Who thought up those?" Elias asked, knowing the answer.

"Oh, I make up things," Cressida said. "It's Mr. Blossom who tackles the work of figuring out how to bring my rough drawings to life in ice and snow."

"I should like to meet him," Elias said.

"Yes, you must ask Val to introduce you," she said. She kept stepping away from him, testing the strength of a pillar, or poking at the underneath of a gleaming ice sculpture.

"What is that?" Elias asked, pointing.

"Head of an eagle," Cressida said.

If he squinted, he could recognize it. "Looks like a donkey," he commented.

She looked again. "Only if donkeys had beaks in Arthur's day. Over there is the king's favorite steed, with which he would 'beat back the cloudy skies'."

"A quote?"

"Yes. We write a description to go along with the grotto, and that is one of my favorite lines. Quite silly, really."

What Cressida meant was that *she* wrote the description.

Elias drew in a deep breath. He took self-confidence as a given; ever since he left Eton, ladies had simpered at him. But Cressida was different. She was uninterested by his title.

In fact, he wasn't certain what sort of man *would* interest her.

She headed through a different archway that led to a hole carved in a snowy hillside. "Every year this cave becomes something different," Cressida said over her shoulder. "One year it was King Neptune's treasure chest." She pointed to a signpost. "This year, Merlin's cave."

Elias bent his head and followed her inside, happy to find that he could stand once inside. He tapped the walls of the cave with a gloved finger. They were solid: rock that had been covered with layer after layer of shimmering ice and hung with glass balls enclosing tiny candles that bounced light around the cave. "It's beautiful, Cressida."

She cast him a look. He caught back a grin. Ladies angled for him to show the slightest interest in intimacy, and she was chiding him for using her name without her title.

"Doesn't Val call you 'Cressie'?" he asked.

"Val is a member of the family," she said coolly, turning to leave. "I see no reason why you and I should be so familiar."

"Because I'd like to marry you."

She froze, outlined in the bright light of the cave entrance. She had a curvaceous figure, Elias noted. Which he liked.

Cressida turned. "What did you say?"

She didn't seem to be greeting his proposal with enthusiasm, but Elias knew perfectly well that it would be a shock. He hadn't wooed her. But he didn't have time to woo her. The duke had one foot in the grave, and somehow, after ignoring the issue for years, Elias thought he'd quite like to have a wife now.

Not after six months or a year of mourning: *now.*

Cressida was staring at him, eyes round. "I asked for your hand in marriage," he said.

"No, you didn't. You announced that you'd like to marry me, which I gather you considered a proposal? In other words, the declaration of your desire, if it could be so termed, was good enough?"

She had a point. He gave her his most charming smile. "Will you do me the honor of your hand in marriage, Lady Cressida?"

"Absolutely not," she said, turned, and sailed out of the cave, her little nose in the air.

He followed her and realized that she was heading back to the manor. "Wait!" he called, to stall her. "What about that one?" He nodded to the last structure, a square house that seemed made entirely of snow.

Cressida put her hands on her hips. "Are you mocking me?"

"No." The sincerity in his voice had the effect of making her glower at him.

"We have only the merest acquaintance," she said, pursing her pretty lips.

"We've been acquainted for years," Elias protested. "We've shared a meal; you're here with me, unchaperoned. A marriage proposal is practically *de rigueur*."

"Nonsense! I suppose my cousin talked you into this."

He shook his head.

Her eyes watched him steadily. "Bribed you?"

"That is an insult, my lady," Elias said, his voice expressing precisely how offensive that suggestion was.

"I beg your pardon," Cressida said, looking taken aback. "I'm sorry, but I can't imagine any other reason for your farcical proposal, if one could call it that."

"You don't remember me, do you?"

"What are you talking about?"

"You don't remember when we first met?"

Chapter Five

It was humiliating to admit, even to herself, but Cressie knew precisely when they had met, at least, as adults. It was her debut ball, and her cousin had walked over to her and said, "Here, Cuz, dance with Elias; he'll be a marquess someday so he's good to practice society conversation that's not about that infernal Revelry."

She had looked up into the eyes of the most beautiful man in the ballroom and managed a wavering smile.

Elias hadn't said more than a few words to her and ignored her the rest of the evening.

They danced once again the following year, and although Elias had been entirely polite, he had engaged in exactly the prescribed amount of talk of the weather before he lapsed into silence, bowed at the conclusion of the music, and left. He likely didn't even remember.

For years, he had strolled the manor at Christmas, making all the ladies' hearts thump and their knees weaken, looking confident, arrogant, uninterested.

Make that deeply uninterested.

"Other than passing encounters as children, we met when I debuted," Cressie said now. She had the odd feeling that she had somehow wandered out of time and into a fairy tale, perhaps one set among King Arthur's knights.

One of the most objectively beautiful men in the British Isles was glowering at her because she had the temerity to suggest that he might have had to be bribed into offering her marriage.

It was a perfectly rational conclusion. He could have anyone: a delicate lady with auburn hair and a sweet laugh; a fairylike sylph who floated around the ballroom; a plain lady whose inheritance would fill Merlin's cave with gold coins.

She had nothing to offer, including a dowry. While she didn't believe in unnecessarily downplaying one's own charms, he scarcely knew her, so her intelligence played no part in his offer.

So his proposal had to have sprung from that pitiful scene in her father's bedchamber.

"Years before that," Elias said impatiently.

"In that case, I have no idea what you are referring to," she said, managing to make it sound as if she was uninterested.

"You were five years old," he said, rather surprisingly. "Do you suppose that you could call me Elias?"

"No," Cressie said, more and more certain that she had become the butt of a jest, and not a kind one. "I'm cold, sir. I should like to return to the house now."

He took a long stride and caught her right hand. "Show me the last structure? I already missed the other grottoes. I don't want to miss anything of this one."

Cressie didn't roll her eyes, but it was a near thing. "Right." She tugged her hand free, nearly losing her glove in the process, and walked over to Queen Guinevere's bower.

"We follow a pattern," she said briskly, ducking her head. "There's always a glittering chamber like the one we were just in—Merlin's cave, or Neptune's jewel chest—and there's always a bower. One year it was Queen Titania's; this year it is Queen Guinevere's."

Elias stopped short inside the door. Her eyes followed

his to the strings of fresh flowers crisscrossing the roof, and from there to the white fur thrown over elaborate fainting couches carved from snow and ice. All around the room, ice lanterns flickered, their light hidden behind more flowers and holly berries frozen in the ice. "How on earth did you achieve this?" he asked, turning in a circle and looking upward as well.

"Those are sugared flowers draping the lanterns," Cressie said, softening despite herself, as he looked genuinely interested. "They keep their color because the air is so cold."

"The lanterns?"

"A round glass container, with a smaller one inside, and water, flowers, and berries in the space between. We freeze them, and then add a small candle to each. The grooms light them in the morning, and they will burn well into the night. First thing in the morning, all the lanterns are replaced with fresh ones."

"I'm astounded," Elias said, bending to look closer at a lantern.

"People relax on the furs," Cressida told him. "We make certain the cave is always attended."

Elias was thinking to himself that likely Guinevere's bower had been the site of many a chilly kiss and perhaps more.

"What's this?" He stooped over a musical instrument lying in a small cradle. The flute was carved like those in Arthur's castle, from ice but much smaller, every hole painstakingly cut in a perfect circle.

"Oh, nothing much," she said dismissively. "Just another instrument."

"But it's here rather than Arthur's castle," he said. "And it's in a cradle." He straightened and looked back at her.

"Legend has it that Arthur had beautiful women playing instruments for his court," she explained. "I thought that perhaps one of them had a baby. And if she did, Queen

Guinevere wouldn't have left it lying about the castle, leaning against a wall."

Elias took another look at the little flute, realizing that the cradle was lined with fur, and turned back to her. "This is astounding, Cressida. You do know what a genius you are, don't you?"

She turned a little pink. "Nonsense. It's just . . . just entertainment, that's all."

"No," Elias said. "This is a work of art and I'm furious at myself for missing years of grottoes."

"We've only started the tradition seven years ago," she told him, a smile lighting her face.

Elias took a step closer.

Cressie tilted her head back to look up at him, which gave her a peculiar feeling, even if she wasn't already feeling a little dizzy from the warmth in his eyes. And his compliments.

"You didn't answer my question," he said.

She frowned. "If your question is about when we met, and you aren't referring to my debut, then I have no idea. If the question is about marriage, the answer is no. I refuse to marry you." She took a step backward.

"You were only five," Elias said, catching her hands in his. "Val and I would have been sixteen. We were going skating, and you desperately wanted to come. You got free of your nanny and followed us to the lake. Do you remember now?"

She shook her head. "My father does not countenance a lady on skates."

"You tried to run onto the lake, lost your balance, and slid straight into me," Elias said, holding her hands very tightly. "I crashed to the ice, and you laughed and laughed. I lay on my back, completely winded, and thought that your laughter sounded like music. Birdsong."

"Huh," Cressie said. "I'm afraid I don't remember that."

She'd had no time for laughter in years. Her father's

ambitions grew every year. He was never satisfied with the Revelry: he always demanded more and bigger: more spectacle, more scandal, more fabulousness.

The last three years he hadn't even come to view the grotto—but he had listened to his guests talk of it, repeating the slightest criticism to her, demanding ever greater heights of artistic beauty.

"You look tired," Elias said.

"I'm cold," Cressie said, though it wasn't true. The room was small enough that the lanterns took the chill from the air.

"May I kiss you?"

Cressie couldn't believe her ears. "What? Why?"

"Surely someone has told you that you have beautiful lips?"

Her lips opened to say "No," but no sound emerged.

"Perfectly shaped, and a remarkably erotic color," he said thoughtfully. "I've been thinking that, by the way, ever since yesterday's soup course."

Words reeled through her mind but none of them seemed to connect into sentences. He wanted to kiss her? *Elias?* It was impossible. It was—

"Cressida?" he asked, bending closer. "May I?" His breath warmed her cheek. Even though every ladylike sensibility should rebuff him, she couldn't. But she couldn't speak, either. She felt as if she were turned into one of those frozen instruments, waiting to be woken.

She managed a nod.

He bent his head and kissed her.

Elias's kiss was far more than the brush of lips she would have expected. He pressed his lips to hers, his hands on her back rather than politely at his side, his tongue . . .

His tongue begged entry.

Cressie opened her mouth without thinking, without any notion of how a kiss can change the world, how much it changed the fabric of the moment. One stroke of his tongue and she was aroused to the tips of her fingers.

She'd never felt anything like it. Her blood thumped through her body in a rhythm that made her off-kilter. Her tongue met his, timidly at first, then in more daring caresses, her breath coming quickly, his in little pants.

His hands were still on her back, but rather than lying flat, they were gripping her tightly, so that she was pressed against him. For the first time in her life, her curves made sense. She was soft in some places, and he was hard in others.

Elias breathed an oath, his voice harsh in the silence of the bower, and that woke her.

"Elias," she gasped.

"Please don't stop me," he breathed. "You kiss like an angel." His hands left her back and cupped her face. His broken groan matched the sound she made in the back of her throat, but she'd never—

"We shouldn't!" she said, gasping, pulling away so quickly that she almost fell over.

Elias pulled back immediately, looking down at her, his eyes fierce with need. She'd never seen that emotion before, but her body instinctively recognized it and swayed back toward him.

"Marry me," he said. "Marry me, Cressida. Please."

She blinked at him. "Certainly not. That was a kiss, not a courtship."

"I don't have time to court you," he said. "Your father is dying. If we don't marry, we'll end up with a baby out of wedlock."

His heady, presumptuous words sank slowly into her head because she was looking at him and seeing, for the first time, not a beautiful man, but a concoction of parts like anyone else's: a strong nose, a nice mouth with a firm set to it, eyes with laughter wrinkles spreading from the corners, hair showing just the faintest signs of silver on the temples.

Elias didn't look beautiful at this moment. He looked desirous. His eyes were scorching, the demand in them making her shiver and feel oddly hot. Her mind supplied her with another word: *lustful*. The concept made her feel dizzy.

Men didn't feel passion for her. Their eyes slid over her as she didn't exist, as if she were part of a wainscoting oddly dressed in a skirt.

"Why do you want me?" she asked.

"Damned if I know," he replied.

Her heart squeezed into a small ball, and before she could stop it, her mouth quivered.

"You misunderstood me," Elias said.

She shook her head, and her hood fell back. "It's been a long day. I think we should get back . . ." Her voice trailed off because he wasn't listening.

Instead he was staring at her head. "You didn't take your hair off."

"Well, no," she said, regaining a bit of her normal snappish manner. "Any more than you do, I assume."

Elias looked shocked.

She pulled up her hood back over her head, and he moved his gaze back to her eyes. And then to her mouth. He did seem to admire her lips, which was interesting. Cressie had never thought much about mouths, as they existed for talking and eating. She had to stop an impulse to touch her bottom lip.

"All that hair was yours? It's the color of barley sugar twists."

She sighed and turned to go. "This has been interesting, but—"

Long arms caught around her middle. "Please don't go."

Instinctively she knew that if she struggled even the smallest amount, he would let her go. But she froze, enjoying the feeling of a large male body flush against her back, his arms around her.

"Will you marry me?" Elias asked in her ear.

"No," she said flatly. "One doesn't marry someone on the basis of a kiss or two."

"I've kissed many women in my life."

She stiffened. "Am I meant to applaud?"

"No kisses felt like ours, Cressida. Not a one."

"You are exaggerating," she said, feeling horribly uncertain. She wished she could see his face. Of course, *she* hadn't, but then *she* had never . . . well, whatever it was that happened. With tongues and all.

That.

"No, I am not." Elias's voice was deeply certain and rather charmingly, his French accent strengthened. "You are so creative, Cressida. But you kiss like a woman on fire." His voice dropped to a lower key. "You have the most sensual bottom lip I've ever seen. You have a wealth of hair that would send Queen Guinevere into fits of jealousy."

"The queen probably had twice as much hair!" Cressie said, unable to think. The conversation was making her feel peculiar.

"No, she was bald," Elias said. "Completely bald. I've heard it a million times." He gently turned her about to face him, his hands still at her waist. "If I might raise an improper subject, may we discuss your bosom? So many women have no need for a corset, because there is nothing to hold up."

"That is a shocking thing to say," Cressie managed. Secretly she was enjoying it because she desperately envied slender young ladies who drifted around the ballroom like willow trees. Not needing corsets, because willows didn't.

"It would be shocking if I moved my hands so that they brushed the bottom of your breasts," Elias said. His voice was so deep and dark that he sounded nearly hoarse. "Do you want me to say aloud how I feel about your hips?"

Cressie thought about that.

The answer was *yes*. But on the other hand . . .

"When did you start feeling all of these emotions?" she asked. "Were you by any chance hit on the head? I've heard that irrational behavior can follow a head injury."

"No."

"You may not remember," she pointed out.

"I would know."

"If you didn't take a blow to the head, you must be drunk."

Elias shook his head. He traced the arch of her eyebrow with a gloved finger. "As delicate as if drawn with an ink pen, but a darker barley sugar, as if it were burnt in the making."

She blinked. "Eyebrows don't matter. *Eyes* matter. Mine are plain brown."

"So are mine."

He was right, but the rest of his face was chiseled and beautiful.

"I used to pray for blue eyes when I was little," she told him. "My sisters have blue eyes and I thought that perhaps the color would change overnight." Cressie had a sudden pulse of sadness, thinking of how hopeful she'd been.

"I am not drunk," Elias said, a touch of reproof in his voice. "I didn't know you then, or we would have married seven years ago, after that first dance we shared at your debut."

Cressie was used to judging truthfulness, thanks to hiring the hundred or so workers who joined the household for the Revelry. She searched his eyes and they seemed . . . truthful.

"What does it mean to 'know me'?" she asked.

"I see you." He backed up two steps and sat down on a fur-covered couch, bringing her with him so she found herself on his lap. "Is this acceptable?"

"No," she said, but she didn't move.

His arm was around her. Over the smoky candles, she could smell a spicy hint that belonged to him alone. "There is nothing *to* see." She took a breath and spoke the truth aloud. "I'm plain and clumsy. I'm not a very good dancer, and now I don't have a dowry." She didn't let any self-pity leak into her voice because she was well aware that she was lucky: born to a duke, always warm and fed. Not exactly loved, but valued.

"I know," Elias said. "Luckily, I needn't marry for money."

He had put his chin on top of her head and wrapped both arms around her. Cressie let herself enjoy sitting on his lap in his embrace. This was madness. Elias must be suffering from brain fever.

"I have to ask again: did my cousin ask you to marry me?" she asked, because she couldn't bear not knowing.

Elias hesitated.

Her heart sank.

"Val feels guilty because he wants the Scottish estate," she said, putting two and two together. "If you marry me, I will live next door and help with the Revelry, and that would keep the estate away from a charity." She put down her feet, and his arms parted, allowing her to stand.

Elias had risen when she did, of course. He was looking at her thoughtfully. "You do wish to marry someday?"

"Of course," she said crossly, turning to go.

"I have proposed," he said, following her outside.

"I want to marry, but not to a man doing so out of sufferance. I don't know what my cousin or my father offered you," Cressie said, making her way out of the grotto and heading for the woods, "but you should think very carefully before you agree to a devil's bargain. A wife is forever. She'll be the mother to your children."

"So?"

"You should pick a pretty lady so that your children are as beautiful as you are," she tossed over her shoulder, glad to be walking ahead of him. If he gave her a sympathetic look, the tears pressing on the back of her throat might spill over.

"I think you are very pretty," he said, unforgivably. She couldn't bear people who told untruths. She didn't answer, just sped up. She trod on the red ribbon that she'd picked up earlier and somehow let fall.

"Barley sugar twists are my favorite candy," Elias said behind her. "Your curls are different colors, from sunshine to barley sugar, more gold than yellow. Lovely."

It was nice that he liked her hair—and that he now realized she hadn't plumped it up with horsehair—but that didn't change anything. She walked even faster, but his legs were long.

He caught up with her, tucked the red ribbon in the pocket of her pelisse, and walked at her side. The light snowfall had crystalized, so sunlight danced as if on a bed of diamonds across the broad expanse of lawn before Greystoke Manor.

The path leading up the hillside had been broomed clear since they first walked that way; she made a note to tell Twist that the grooms were doing a good job.

"I want to marry you," Elias said, beside her.

She stopped. "Oh for goodness' sake! Haven't you ever been given a straight answer that you didn't like? I know you're going to be a marquess someday, but you must learn to listen to people. I don't want to marry you. I'm sorry about whatever my cousin or father is holding over your head. I'll have a word with Val about it."

She patted him on the arm.

"It's not easy to hear no," she said, forcing herself to use a kindly tone of voice. "The rest of we mortals learned it at an earlier age. Now I really must go. Goodbye."

Elias stared at Cressida, trying to figure out whether she believed that Val was holding something over his head.

Could she truly believe that he would *marry* someone to repay a debt? Or bow to blackmail? Or the rest of the nonsense she spouted?

"I just want to clarify," he said. "You are refusing to

marry me because you think our children wouldn't be beautiful?"

She wrinkled her nose—she had an adorable nose, he noticed. In fact, he was fast coming to the conclusion that everything about her was adorable.

"You make my reasoning sound stupid, which is unkind. I was merely giving you advice for your future choice of bride. I am refusing to marry you because I don't wish to marry a man who is forced to wed me. I think most women would agree with me on that front."

"I am not being forced."

Cressida ignored that. "You didn't play cards with Val, did you? His father lost that wretched Scottish estate in a game of cribbage, and I've noticed that Val can't bear to lose even a game of spindle sticks."

"Your cousin has not offered me anything in trade. Well, he offered me a dowry."

"You don't owe him money?"

"None."

"That's good," she said.

Elias saw the desolate look in her eyes and felt crushed for her. He stepped forward and wrapped her in his arms. "Your father will give you a dowry. He's just worried about his precious Revelry. Not that I want one from him."

All he could see was one of her cheeks. As he watched, a fat tear rolled down it. "Don't cry," he said. "Please don't cry." Elias fumbled about in his greatcoat pocket, found a handkerchief, and pressed it into her hand.

Cressida pulled herself away and wiped her tears. "Someone might see us through the window." She blew her little nose decisively. Though her face was white and tearstained, she met his eyes and managed a polite smile. "Good afternoon," she said. "Please forgive me for not curtseying. There is somewhere I have to be."

She turned and began walking briskly toward the castle, her shoulders straight and defiant, her head up.

Elias watched her go, thinking hard. Cressida didn't want him, and why should she? As far as she was concerned, he was just another useless aristocrat, trading people for estates, and perhaps even beholden to her cousin for a gambling debt large enough to force a marriage.

He walked into the house in the grip of deep thought. Cressida wouldn't want him to trot out details about his finances. He had a strong feeling that she wouldn't care. She would want a different kind of evidence about the man she agreed to marry.

She'd want to know whether he was a man of integrity, a man to whom ethics mattered. She'd want to know that he wasn't like her father.

He needed help.

Chapter Six

Cressie went to her room, called for a bath, and then cried until she felt sick. Nanny fetched a cup of hot chocolate and made her drink it.

"Is it your father, Lady Cressida?" Nanny asked sympathetically. "I'm sorry His Grace is failing."

"No," Cressie said, her throat scratchy and sore from crying. For a moment she considered telling Nanny the truth: that she had turned down a proposal of marriage from a future marquess. But the news would spread, and no one would believe it. They would pity her for having made up such a tale.

Still, Nanny deserved some portion of the truth. "My father changed his will, giving my dowry, the Scottish estate, to Val in return for keeping up the Revelry for another decade. He threatened to give it to charity if Val refused."

Nanny blinked. "I never liked the idea of going all the way to Scotland. Better that it goes back to the hands as was supposed to own it, because everyone thinks that your father marked the cribbage cards to win that estate in the first place."

"They *do*?"

Nanny nodded. "It has ill luck attached to it. You'll do better to have a dowry like your sisters."

"My father is not offering me a dowry at all. He—he wants me to stay here, on Val's sufferance, and keep up the Revelry because Val can't do it alone."

Nanny took such a deep breath that her bosom swelled alarmingly. She popped her hands on her hips and said, "He's a wicked old man, even as I say so as shouldn't!"

Cressie shook her head. "He loves the Revelry, that's all."

"He's turned you into a drudge for years, he has," Nanny snapped. "I've seen it, as has the entire household, my lady. We all agree, and I'm not saying anything that hasn't been said down in the Hall. Well, not in those words because Mr. Twist would never allow such language about His Grace. But in so many words, my lady: yes, that's exactly what everyone has said, and believes!"

"He didn't force me to put on the Revelry."

"Now there's another thing," Nanny burst out. "We all know that the Revelry has turned into such a grand party because of your ideas, none of his, not in the least. Dragging you about from pillar to post so that you can choose who to invite, even making you watch Parliament through that peephole in the attic."

"It's not Father's fault that ladies are only allowed to watch through a peephole," Cressie pointed out.

Nanny just snorted. "The newspapers going on and on about the duke's sagacity, and the way he shapes the future of England, and all the time, it's you that does it."

Cressie managed a smile.

The truth was that she had interpreted her father's need for her as affection, even parental love and caring.

It wasn't. All he cared about was the Revelry.

Her father had never loved her, and her siblings had married and moved away without appearing to give her a second thought. It was a bitter pill to swallow, but it was better to face it now than continue to try to dazzle her father with better and better Revelries, expecting him to love her for her efforts.

Especially given that he'd be gone and presumably no longer worrying about his legacy.

The thought made her feel exhausted and empty, but

it was true. And truth, no matter how demoralizing, was important.

She climbed out of the tub, took the towel that Nanny handed her, and began rubbing down her legs. By happenstance, the tub had been placed opposite the tall glass on her dressing table, and she caught sight of herself.

The current fashions for narrow dresses and high waists didn't suit her. She would have been fine in the 1600s, when Venus was painted as a curvaceous woman, her breasts full and tipped with rosy nipples.

Nanny left to fetch a fresh pressed petticoat, and Cressida did something she'd never done: she dropped her towel and simply looked at herself in the glass.

She wasn't ugly or plain without clothing. What Elias called her barley-sugar hair was drying in twists and curls that brushed the middle of her back and spilled over her arms. Her body was curved in the right places. It wasn't flattered by dresses whose waist began at the armpit, but that didn't mean her body wasn't seductive in its own way.

She ran a hand down her sides, and then more daringly, right over her breasts and around the curve of her hips. Her thighs were plump, but her body balanced, top and bottom.

She had always thought her only attributes besides her hair were delicate eyebrows and small feet. Curves didn't make her beautiful, but . . .

By the time Nanny popped back in the room, Cressie was wrapped in the towel, her hair drying in the warmth of the fire. Usually she bundled it away until it dried, but instead she was finger-drying it, combing through her curls.

"Your hair is the prettiest thing I've ever seen," Nanny exclaimed, pausing.

Cressie gave her an uncertain smile. "Lord Royleston said that it was the color of barley sugar twists."

Nanny's eyebrow rose. "A good man, from what I've

heard. His valet likes him, which isn't the case with many a man whom your father invites under this roof."

"I know," Cressie said, sighing. She allowed Nanny to drop a petticoat, still warm from the iron, over her head. As Nanny began lacing her corset, Cressie said, "If I planned a Christmas party for myself, it would be quite different."

"No one doubts that," Nanny assured her. "Lord Pendle wouldn't darken these doors if you had your way."

The duke always insisted on inviting the powerful lord, but the maids had to be protected from his roving fingers.

"He hasn't done anything this year?" Cressie asked anxiously.

"Not so far," Nanny said. "If he rings from his bedchamber, one of the footmen goes or Mr. Twist tells his valet to answer the bell."

She slipped a gown over Cressie's head that was in the very first style but didn't suit her. The mauve color clashed with her hair, but Cressie hadn't had time to choose the fabric herself. The bodice was adorned with ruffles *and* lace, and cloth billowed around her hips.

Suddenly her curves weren't delicious, but matronly.

With a sinking feeling, she realized that her unmarried state was at least partly a result of her own carelessness. She always paid meticulous attention to the smallest details of the Revelry; why on earth hadn't she given her clothing the same consideration?

She knew the answer. Her father had long ago decreed her dowdy and plump, and she had never bothered to fight his assessment.

His *unkind* assessment.

She allowed Nanny to do as she wished with her hair, which meant that in around an hour she had a great many curls down her back and only the smallest topknot on her head.

"Are you certain that I don't look untidy?" Cressie asked, as Nanny was pushing in a last pearl-topped pin.

"The ladies will eat their hearts out with jealousy," Nanny said. "All the gentlemen will think of you in a different way." She put her hands on Cressie's shoulders and met her eyes in the glass. "Unless you want to live your life here in the manor with that cousin of yours, you need a husband." She flipped open a little tin in her hand. "Lip salve," she said briskly, "and a little color for your cheekbones as well. Just the faintest pink, my lady."

"Goodness," Cressie said, looking at herself. She still hated the gown, but it was less noticeable with all her hair floating about. The lip salve definitely did something. She couldn't help thinking of Elias saying that her bottom lip was perfectly shaped.

Presently, she went to her father's bedchamber, but he was deep asleep, looking small and withered in the bed. She paused there for a moment, thinking about him. About the years she'd spent working for him, though he never paid her for it.

She would refuse to have anything to do with the Revelry and that included attending it. The party was her cousin's problem now.

If worse came to worst, she could go to London and take up a position in a shop. Ladies weren't supposed to work, but the truth was that she was used to it. Many a night she'd worked until ten, and then rose at the dawn to cope with unfinished problems.

Downstairs, she walked into the drawing room, moving from group to group to make certain that the right people were meeting and chatting. At some point, she turned her head and discovered Elias was on the other side of the drawing room, staring at her.

She shook her head at him without a smile and turned away.

No matter what Val was offering, Elias would have to move on to another young lady. He would forget her as easily as he had decided to marry her.

Whereas *she* was in danger of falling in love with a man whom she hardly knew, whose departure might crush her.

It was frightfully irresponsible, and hopefully the feeling would go away as quickly as it came.

Sometime later, Cressie walked into the dining room only to discover that her cousin had altered the dinner table arrangements again. She shifted the seated arrangements every evening. But tonight Val was again on her left, and Elias was still on her right.

In case she had any doubts, Val was obviously forcing Elias to propose.

"Moving guests about isn't a good idea," she told her cousin later, when the meal was almost over. "I should sit at a different table every night."

"Why?" he asked.

"Conversations are more successful when there is someone to steer the topic," Cressida explained. She nodded to the table next to them. "I put Mr. Stockbridge in the vicinity of Lord Xavier. Mr. Stockbridge has developed a new type of engine, which he would like to employ in a carriage that would move without horses."

"Unlikely and dangerous," Val commented.

"In my opinion, such a carriage is inevitable," Cressie said.

His eyes narrowed for a moment and then he said, "I shall take that under advisement, Cousin. What has Lord Xavier to do with it?"

"His lordship loves speed," Cressie explained. "He likes to invest in creative projects. Last year, he backed a mechanical umbrella." She gave him a wry smile.

"I gather that you would not have advised the umbrella," Val said.

"No," Cressida responded. "If I were sitting between them, I could ease the conversation in the right direction. You'll have to do it next year." To her right, Elias was chatting with his other neighbor, but Cressida was irritatingly aware of his broad shoulder next to hers.

"I shall practice," Val said. "Did you know that Elias already runs his father's estate? Along with extensive lands and the marquessate, he will inherit several business concerns, including one that makes steam engines for the new locomotives."

"I did not, and I haven't the faintest interest," she said. Their table was occupied by chatter, so she lowered her voice. "I will thank you, Val, not to plan my future. I recognize that my chance of marriage is slim, but I would prefer that any husband I take actually cares for me. I shall be happy without one."

Thankfully, Val didn't pretend to have nothing to do with Elias's proposal. "You are welcome to live with me." He gave her a lightning-quick smile that she'd seen only rarely. "Elias informed me earlier this evening that if I listen to you, I shall be as rich as he is within a year or two."

"How vulgar," Cressie said. She would love to turn away, but Elias was waiting to talk to her. She could feel his eyes on her back.

"I believe him."

She gave Val a level look that hopefully expressed contempt.

"Did you know that Elias's great-grandfather founded an orphanage, which Elias runs?" her cousin asked, showing no signs of registering her silent reprimand.

"Stop it," she said sharply.

Her cousin's eyes were limpid and innocent. "I'm attempting to steer a dinner guest in directions that will interest her and might change her future."

"You are playing some sort of game, Val."

His eyes kindled, but she raised her hand. "Please. You have never shown interest in making my acquaintance; I would be surprised if you knew much more about me other than my name."

"That is fair," Val said, after a pause.

"When my father passes away, I shall leave this house. You needn't worry about what I do or where I go," Cressie said. "I am of no concern to you."

"I see," Val replied. He looked over her shoulder. "I did my best, Elias."

"Your best is rubbish," Elias retorted, his voice deep with annoyance. "Were you never taught any oratory skills at Eton? I went to Harrow," he said to Cressie. "We were trained in the fine arts of oration, otherwise known as, *getting what we want*."

"Fascinating," she said, pushing back her chair. "I'll leave the two of you to practice your boyhood skills with each other."

She walked out, her entire body humming with annoyance at the burst of laughter that followed her from the room along with the sound of a thump, as if one had whacked the other on the back. "No better than schoolboys," she muttered to herself.

"That's true," Elias said at her shoulder.

She gave a little scream. "You oughtn't to creep up on a person!"

He smiled down at her. "You'll have to get used to me following you out of rooms. If you are determined to be exasperated with me, and I am determined to be with you, I shall probably become very familiar with your defiant back leading the way to a door."

That was so foolish that she found herself nearly smiling.

"I have things to do," she told him. "Please return to the table."

Her shoulders were prickling, because guests were surely watching her leave with one of the most desirable bachelors in London. They would never imagine she was setting her cap so far above herself.

"I too have things to do," Elias insisted, "and I need you to help me."

"Don't be absurd," Cressie said. "Please go back to the table."

Elias shook his head. "Not without you, darling."

"What did you call me?" Cressie asked, her voice little more than a whisper.

He took her hand and drew her across the corridor and paused before the door to the small study that Cressie used for paying bills and perusing the newspapers. "Come inside with me, please?"

If there ever was a moment to be brave, this was it. Part of Cressie longed to bustle away and go back to being the efficient organizer of the Revelry, running to and fro with no time to talk to anyone.

But another part, a small neglected part of her, was thrilled. And even bold.

She reached out, opened the door herself, and walked through.

"Finally," Elias said, once they were inside.

She frowned at him. "Finally?"

"We're alone again." He gave her a sunny smile.

"Don't smile at me," she said, feeling a flash of nervousness. "It isn't—you're not the smiling type of man."

"I am around you," he said.

He bent his head and began kissing her again. Cressida didn't mean to kiss him back. But he smelled so good, and he tasted good too.

And she loved him.

The fact presented itself *as* a fact in the middle of a kiss, and by the time they broke apart for air, she knew it was true. No matter what happened in the future, her heart belonged to Elias. Not because he made her feel beautiful, or admired her organizing skills.

But because he noticed the baby ice flute. Because he kissed her as if he could never get enough.

It wasn't until quite a long time later, after they had made their way to a couch and scarcely taken a breath before Elias began kissing her fiercely again, that Cressie finally managed to say something.

"We shouldn't," she whispered.

"We're going to be married," Elias said. His hands had stayed very properly away from her bosom, but she followed his gaze down to her inadequate bodice. "Your breasts," he growled, and stopped.

Cressie resisted the impulse to give her bodice a tug. It wouldn't make a difference, because the style in scanty bodices meant that her nipples were always on the verge of popping into the open.

"Marriage license," Elias stated. "Twist gave me one that your father bought for the use of guests at the Revelry—and how the duke managed that, since marriage licenses are strictly regulated, I don't know."

"Father knows a man at Doctors' Commons. He gives him one hundred pounds on top of the usual price for two licenses," Cressie said, trying to decide what to do.

She loved Elias. He didn't love her, and to his credit, he wasn't pretending that he did. On the other hand, his desire wasn't a deception.

As far as she knew, no man had ever felt desire for her before, but she felt the truth of his in her bones. She saw it in his eyes, and the way he cupped her face, the way he kissed her and then opened his eyes and met her gaze.

Yet it would be horrible if he grew tired of her bosom and wandered off to another woman. She would be left at home, loving him. She swallowed hard. That would be intolerable.

"My grandparents lived apart," she said. "They led separate lives."

"When I take a bride," Elias said, "I shall take her for the rest of my life. I will not look at another woman." He gave her a lopsided smile. "If she tries to leave me, or leave the room, I shall follow her. Wherever she goes."

"That sounds lovely," Cressie whispered. She couldn't

say again: *Why me?* It sounded as if she were fishing for compliments, as if she were self-pitying, sorry for herself.

"Marry me, Cressida," he said, taking her hands to his lips and kissing them deliberately, first one, then the other. "May I call you Cressie?"

She looked at his bent head and realized with a thump of her heart that she had to accept. Frightened though she was, she loved him. And love—love was worth the risk.

"Yes," she said with a gulp. "I'd need my father's permission." Then she lowered her eyes because she saw a flash of pity in Elias's face. He knew she had no dowry, and the extent of her father's lack of consideration. "He is not a perfect father. But I owe him that much."

His hand tightened around hers. "I honor you for it," he said quietly.

The door burst open, and a vivacious, laughing group of women entered. "Oh! This isn't the correct room, is it?" the lady in the lead cried. "Why, Royleston, what on earth are you doing in here?"

Cressie felt herself paling, but she rose. Elias stood up too, but he kept her hand in his. "I'm courting my future wife," he said.

She was in just the right position to see the surprise that crossed Lady Xavier's face and the glances the other young ladies gave each other. It made her feel sick, the way their eyes skittered over her from head to toe, asking without words what such a handsome man could be thinking to betroth himself to a frump.

In the burst of congratulations that followed, Cressida kept stealing glances at Elias to see his expression.

Was he embarrassed to be courting her? That would break her heart. But most of the time she found that he was actually watching *her*, and whenever their eyes met, she felt as if he was telling her something that could be summed up as, "Let's leave this room and be alone somewhere."

She actually shook her head at him.

"We must speak to His Grace now," Elias said, catching Cressie's hand. After the ladies left, he kissed Cressie until her hair had gone far beyond untidy, and tumbled down her back. Elias's response to this development was entirely satisfactory.

"I must return upstairs and put my hair up again," Cressie said, finally.

"Will you wear it down for our wedding? Tomorrow morning?"

She shook her head. "No."

"No, you won't marry me tomorrow?"

"I haven't accepted your hand yet."

"Please." He met her eyes and then sank to his knees, raising one of her hands to his lips. "Please marry me, Cressie."

Cressie blinked down at him, once again in the unnerving grip of a feeling that she had walked through a portal to another version of her own story, one in which Cinderella wasn't chosen by the prince because of the size of her foot, but because she kissed well, had a lovely bosom, and a nice lower lip.

She was in love with him. He'd promised to be faithful. Perhaps he could learn to love her later.

"Yes," she said faintly.

Elias was on his feet and pulled her into his arms scarcely before the word left her lips. Cressie kissed him, her heart skipping a beat at the low sound in his throat, the way he gripped her as if she mattered.

"Your father," he muttered later.

Cressie stepped back, startled by the reminder.

She was afraid.

It was one thing to realize her own sire did not love her. She had tried hard to love her father, with all his demands and criticisms, but she had failed. She knew nothing else. He was her parent. Wasn't it her duty to love him?

What she felt for Elias was deeper, fiercer. She would be destroyed if he left her.

"No," he said, taking her hands. "Stop worrying, Cressie."

"I can't stop." She pulled her hands away and began briskly winding up her hair again.

"I suppose putting your hair up will give me the pleasure of taking it down," Elias said, his voice dark with anticipation. "No other man should see your hair down."

She twisted it into a bun and haphazardly stuck in pins, fighting with herself not to run from the room. She was accustomed to sitting at the side of the ballroom and watching men like Elias bow before delightful ladies, the pretty ones who looked as if they were made from the finest French ceramic.

The lumpy girls sat by the wall, chatting with each other and pretending that they didn't care when a dance was announced, and no one disturbed their conversation.

But they did.

They cared so much.

"I don't love this gown," Elias said. "But I do love the way the drawstring behind your neck is untied." His voice dropped. "It makes me think of undressing you."

Lust, Cressie told herself, knotting the string at the back of her neck. *That's all it is.* But what a lovely dream she was in.

She and Elias walked to the ducal bedchamber together.

Her father was awake.

And that's when the dream shattered into a million pieces.

Chapter Seven

Elias hadn't had many close encounters with death. As an only heir, he was kept from the battlefield; his parents were not in the best of health, but not deathly ill, either. Yet it didn't take expertise to realize that the Duke of Greystoke was on his last legs.

The man was pasty white, his cheekbones standing out from his face, although his eyes still burned with the fierce energy that characterized him. He was propped up on the pillows sipping a cup of broth when they entered.

"Hello, Father," Cressie said, going to his bedside and dropping a curtsey.

He paid her no mind, Elias noticed, actually twitching away from her and frowning.

Elias rounded the bed so he could take Cressida's hand. "With your permission, I plan to marry your youngest daughter, Your Grace."

"I don't hold with public displays," the duke said, nodding at their hands.

"I can see that you are not feeling well, Father," Cressie said. "Perhaps we should—"

"Course I'm not feeling well," her father snarled. "I'm dying, you little twit. I'm dying and all I can do is lie here and fret because my work, the most important work of my life, is being left in the hands of my ne'er-do-well nephew. If you'd been a man, we'd be in a different place!"

"That was not something within my control," Cressie

said. Elias was glad to see her take a step away from the bedside. He wrapped his hand around hers more tightly.

"Don't you dare leave," her father said sharply. He glared at Elias. "What are you talking about with that absurd proposal? What did he offer you?"

"Your nephew and I made no bargain," Elias replied. "You gave the Scottish estate to Val, which is no concern of mine. Nor, since you recanted your promise to give it to Cressida as her dowry, is it any concern of my future wife's."

"Elias wants to marry me for myself," Cressie said, standing beside him, head high. Elias felt a bolt of pride. She had been treated abominably by her father but she had never lost her backbone. "He will take me without a dowry, if you won't offer one."

"I won't!" the duke snapped.

"That is within your right," Cressie said. "It is not ethical, however; I should have the same dowry as my sisters. Nor is it kind."

The duke's mouth curled in disgust. "You've bamboozled my daughter!" he hissed at Elias.

"No," Elias said. "I have been honest with her."

"I doubt that," the duke said, stabbing the air with a bony forefinger. "You called her 'plain and fading into the background.' You said that no man would take her without a dowry. And now supposedly *you* have taken her on for nothing? Of course, my nephew's offered you something."

Next to him, Elias heard a choked sound, and Cressida pulled her hand away.

He kept his eyes on the old fool in bed, willing him to be silent. "There was no arrangement."

"My daughter's got a good sense of what she's worth, and I'll warrant she doesn't believe that you've suddenly fallen in love with her, not after years of racketing around the place and hardly noticing she wasn't part of the wallpaper! Tell him, Cressida!"

"I asked the same question, Father, but Lord Royleston insists that there has been no bargain."

Cressie hadn't even looked at him: simply dropped "Elias" and turned him to "Lord Royleston."

"More the fool you, for believing him," His Grace said. His voice was audibly rasping, as if there wasn't enough air to keep sound moving from his mouth. "Anyway, he can't have you. My dunce of a nephew needs you to put on the Revelry. Val has to be bankrupting the estate to pay this scoundrel enough to take you on as a wife, which means the Revelry won't be funded. Tell him how expensive it is, Cressida!"

Cressie finally turned and met Elias's eyes. She was white, her eyes incredibly sad, but not angry. "He's right. Whatever Val offered to pay you is probably more than the estate can afford."

Elias felt fury rise up inside him like a flood at the idea that this lovely, brilliant woman had been taught that her planning skills were her only asset.

"I'm marrying your daughter," he snarled at the duke. "I'm taking her without a dowry, and I'll give her a jointure. There *is no bargain*."

"Stop lying!" the duke wheezed. "My nephew promised you a 'dowry commensurate with her lack of attractiveness.' I was in the room when he made the offer. The estate can't bear the cost, not given your low estimation of the girl!"

Cressida made a faint sound like that of a wounded animal.

"What was it that Val said in reply?" the duke continued. "Oh, 'The more beautiful a woman is, the more men tempt her to slip away with them. The more elegant she is, the more her clothing will cost. The more witty she is, the more irritating she will be over the breakfast table.' It's all true, I suppose. My wife was the exception to the rule."

"I withdraw my acceptance of Lord Royleston's hand," Cressida said, crossing her arms over her chest. She looked at Elias with no more emotion than if she had overheard that he preferred carrots to peas.

A flash of panic joined the rage surging through Elias's body.

"I brought up my daughter to face the truth," the duke said. He turned to Cressida. "You need to stay here, in the manor, working on the Revelry. Marriage is not for you. This is your place."

Her expression didn't change, but Elias knew instinctively that the duke had lost his daughter forever. Cressie would never help with the Revelry, whether she married or no.

"Damned right you shouldn't accept his proposal," the duke said, happy now that he thought he was getting his own way. "You've been a good daughter. Worked these years till all hours, sometimes half the night. Smarter than your sisters too."

Cressie opened her mouth.

"Don't you dare thank him for that preposterous compliment," Elias growled.

She glanced at him as if he were a complete stranger and turned back to her father. "Do you think you might sleep now, Father? You sound frightfully tired."

"Dying is hard work," the duke said. "Lying here, worrying about the Revelry . . . but I can rest easy, now that you've given up this foolishness. I understand that Val doesn't want the burden of a spare female on the estate. But he doesn't understand that he needs you. What's more, the estate can't afford to pay a man enough to take you on."

"Yes, Father," his daughter said.

The colorless tone of Cressida's voice chilled Elias to the bone. He'd never thought much about having children; he merely knew it was his duty. But at that moment, he vowed deep in his bones to love them to the best of his ability, and to put them before his estate and indeed, his own life.

Before everything but his spouse.

"I suppose I should speak to your sisters," the duke said. His voice was perceptibly lower, and he mumbled something they couldn't hear. "You'll tell them to pay me a visit, won't you, Marge?"

Who was Marge?

"Mother is no longer with us," Cressie said, her voice gentle. "I'll give them your message, Father."

"That's right," the duke said, closing his eyes. "She passed on and she's waiting for me. Maybe she'll be angry at me, but I did my best for you. Made sure that Val would keep you in good state here at the manor where you grew up. Didn't let you be used as a pawn in exchange for God knows what."

"Thank you, Father," Cressie said. She patted his hand and then bent to kiss his cheek.

Elias held open the door for her; it had scarcely closed behind them when he erupted. "Your father is a cruel bastard with no more concern for you than he might have for a hunting dog that he kicks away because it outlived its usefulness!"

"I would like to disagree, but obviously, I am unable," Cressie said, her cheeks a fine shade of parchment. "If you'll excuse me, Lord Royleston." She dropped a curtsey.

"No, I will *not* excuse you," Elias barked. "Where's your chamber? We can't talk here in the corridor where anyone might come along."

"I'd rather not discuss what just occurred," Cressie said. "My father's startling ability to repeat conversations verbatim revealed more than either of us would wish to hear spoken aloud, but what is done is done. I can't unhear what I heard."

"It wasn't like that—"

She cut him off. "Did you and Val not say those things? My father is never wrong. Over the years, I've found it enormously useful when dealing with tradespeople who try to change the terms of an agreement."

She said it quietly, with no inflection, but it stung all the more for that.

"There is no agreement between me and Val," Elias repeated. "I am not pretending that I didn't say those things about you. I didn't know you when I said them, but I haven't lied to you since. Val has offered me nothing, and he will confirm that I was deeply offended as regards his offer of a dowry. He apologized. Twice."

"I am actually happy to hear of Val's offer to pay a man to take me on," Cressie said, a trace of something in her voice making his heart twist. "It would have been interesting to know the precise amount that he would pay to rid himself of me. I suspect that Val drew the conclusion that, based on my appearance, I was worthless."

Elias choked back a rebuttal. She had the right to think that.

"I am *not* worthless simply because I am not beautiful," Cressie said, head high and eyes tearless. "You are fools, both of you, for making your determinations on such flimsy grounds. My father is equally stupid, for had he loved me even a little, I would have worked harder than I already did. The three of you are equally despicable, and if I end up working in a flower shop, I shall rejoice to be working with people who understand honest labor."

"I described you before I knew you," Elias said.

She curled her lip at that, an expression that he'd never seen on Cressie's sweet face. "I have known you for seven years, longer if one takes into account that charming little story you told me about my falling on the ice." She cocked her head. "You made it up, didn't you?"

Elias drew in a breath of air that seemed to burn his lungs.

Damn it to hell. He was in love with her.

He stared at her, telling himself again. He was *in love with her*. That wasn't supposed to happen. Not that he was opposed to love, but he had viewed it as something that happened to lucky people like his mother and father, who had come to love each other over years, had grown together like leaning trees.

Love didn't happen like this, at least not in real life. Not as if one was struck by lightning and woke up to a new world. He'd been contentedly planning to marry a fascinating woman whom he thought was damn beautiful . . . but that wasn't the same as being *in love*.

Cressie's eyes narrowed. "You made up that story about ice-skating to coax me into feeling comfortable with you, so you could—so you could *win*. Because if you really didn't accept anything from Val, then this is a game, isn't it? A competition."

"Do you think that of me?" he asked. His voice sounded queer in his own ears. He was used to being considered worthy. He took it for granted that women found him honorable.

"What I think doesn't matter, does it?" Cressida asked, turning away. He watched her as she opened a door, walked inside, and quietly closed the door.

It was over.

He'd found her—and lost her, all in one day.

This love of her, though? It wasn't going anywhere. It felt as if it had settled into his skin. Changed him forever.

He had to tell her. The prideful part of him wanted to rush after her and tell her that she had it wrong: there was no competition, no bribe, no dowry. But none of that mattered.

What mattered was the fact that he loved her.

Would always love her.

Chapter Eight

Cressie walked into her room, realized with relief that Nanny was not waiting for her, and sank down onto the bed. Her primary feeling was irritation at herself.

Why hadn't she listened to her own instincts? She *knew* there was something havey-cavey about Elias's proposal.

The evidence was overwhelming, even before Elias suddenly began smiling at her, kissing her hand, and acting as if he gave a damn what she thought or felt. She prided herself on being so intelligent, and yet she had acted as stupidly as any young girl in her first Season, swayed by a fortune hunter's smile.

Yet Elias wasn't a fortune hunter. She had no dowry. Her cousin obviously promised him one in the future, but he didn't need it.

Whatever his reasoning was, it didn't really matter, she realized dully. His courtship had been an act, a performance that few women could have resisted, let alone one who had never had the attentions of a gentleman.

She rolled on her side into a ball, crushing her gown in a way that would give Nanny fits. She did believe that Elias had rejected Val's offer of a dowry. Something else had taken place between her cousin and his old friend. Perhaps Elias owed Val a favor.

It must be a big favor. Perhaps Elias saved Val's life at some point.

With difficulty, she pushed the thought away. It was irrelevant.

She would leave the castle the moment her father passed away.

He had given her seed money twice a year that she had never spent, because when they went to London every moment of her day and evening was full as they attended parties, musicales, the opera, the theater . . . anywhere and anything where a person worthy of an invitation to the Revelry might be found.

With sudden decision, she got up and walked across the room to the enameled box where she tucked her allowance. There must be hundreds of pounds: not a fortune, but enough to go to London and establish herself.

Sure enough, there was a reassuringly thick roll of pound notes. She was just counting it when the door opened. She whirled around, Nanny's name on her lips—

But it wasn't Nanny.

It was Elias, his face set.

Cressie closed her eyes. "For God's sake," she said, the words tumbling from her mouth without conscious volition. "Haven't you done enough for the day?"

"I did say those things," Elias said. He walked in, leaving the door ajar. "I said them before we had lunch, before you showed me the grotto, before we kissed, before I asked you to marry me."

She sat down on the chair before her dressing table, exhaustion dragging her down. Rather than meet his eyes, she stared at the thick roll of pounds, her fingers curled around them like a lifeline. "I know that you feel sorry that I learned of your comments. I suspect you are a good person, and it would be painful to hear one's unkind words quoted in public." She managed a faint smile. "You fell victim to a common ploy of my father's."

"May I be seated?"

It took a moment, but she had control of herself now. She

wasn't going to cry. Elias had the look of a man who was determined to have his say: it was a failing of his sex, that inability to accept refusal.

"All right," she said. "You should close the door, though, and put on the latch. The staff knows not to knock if the door is latched."

Elias turned from the door and sat on one of the two chairs positioned before her fireplace. She remained where she was, although she tucked the money back into her dressing table.

"Your cousin Val offered me a dowry," Elias said, his dark eyes direct and serious. "He knows that given my father's uncertain health, I had thought of marriage. He suggested that you and I might be suited. I didn't ask why he thought that. My response was unconscionable and unpleasant."

"You were truthful," Cressie responded, thinking that this would be a nice moment to have a stiff brandy. She put flasks of brandy in all the guests' rooms; why on earth hadn't she done the same for herself?

"Then you and I spoke," Elias said, his mouth uncompromisingly stern. "I had long admired your father's brilliance. I wondered why he played the fool in the drawing room, portraying the jovial but stupid peer, but I thought that was a subtle strategy, a way of leveling the playing field so that brilliant people felt comfortable together."

"My father is a gifted host," Cressie said.

"No, you are the brilliance behind the throne, Cressie. On top of which, I knew nothing of your imagination, your curiosity, your creativity. And then . . . And then there's the way you kiss."

"Wonderful," she said, because he seemed to be waiting for a response. "Perhaps I shall consider selling kisses at Bartholomew Fair in one of those stalls." Then she flinched because no one would buy a kiss from a plain woman.

"You *are* beautiful, Cressie," Elias said instantly. He had an unnerving habit of guessing what she was thinking. "Yours is not a beauty that one sees immediately, especially not if you're a man like myself, who spends a great deal of energy trying to escape from women who are interested in being my wife. I'm putting that bluntly, because I will never lie to you."

"I see," Cressie said, wondering what she was supposed to say. Her impulse to tell him that he was an arrogant ass probably wouldn't be considered courteous.

"You think I'm a conceited fool," Elias said, unerringly reading her face again. "My only explanation—not an excuse—is that since the year I turned sixteen, I have exercised a great deal of ingenuity to avoid being trapped into marriage."

"I haven't had that problem," Cressie said wryly.

"You would, if anyone had looked closely at you."

She shook her head wearily. "Please go, Lord Royleston. Please don't stretch our brief acquaintance to the point of absurdity. I realize that you dislike accepting failure, but I am begging you to do so this time."

He closed his eyes. "Your hair is all the shades of sunshine, from winter light to summer warmth. Your eyes are mostly brown but with green flecks that are the color of fir trees in winter. Your bottom lip is perfectly the size of your upper, and the corners turn up just slightly, as if you're about to smile."

Cressida scowled.

He didn't open his eyes. "Your chin is sweetly rounded, and you have a graceful neck, with a small scar just where your right shoulder begins. Your breasts would bring any man to his knees. I have spent an inordinate amount of time thinking about your figure. I believe you have the joyful luxury of an Italian goddess painted in the 1600s, which has little to do with physical appearance."

Cressie swallowed.

"Those painters used their mistresses as models for Juno

and Venus and the like. The paintings put desire for the flesh into shape and form. You look like that, Cressida. Your body is warm and curved, and you will be a delicious bed companion."

"No," she said, though she stored away every sentence to treasure later.

Elias's eyes snapped open. "Why not? I *know* you. I may have once said that you faded into the background, but, Cressie, it must be obvious to anyone who knows you that you *choose* to fade. It's not fair to blame me for a brilliant piece of acting on your part."

"I didn't—"

"Yes, you did," he said uncompromisingly. "You could have been a brilliant hostess, but instead you let your father take the limelight. You allowed him to be the focus of attention, but if people had known, they would be looking to *you* for predictions about where the nation was going. Not to your father. Never to your father."

Cressida scowled at him again.

"Wouldn't they?" Elias asked, his voice gentling.

"People would never believe that a woman could come up with ideas," she pointed out.

"You could have proved them wrong. Instead you chose to fade into the background, to hide your wittiness, to dress inelegantly. You fostered and created the opinion I had of you, Cressie!"

"I did not choose to be plain and awkward," she retorted, fury marching up her spine. "You are blaming me for the face that I've had since I was a child."

Elias surged up from his chair and stood behind her, turning her chair to the glass. "Look at yourself."

Cressida raised her eyes, but instead of looking at her face, she looked at the reflection of the man who moved to crouch at her side.

"Your hair, your eyes, your lips, your cheekbones," he said softly.

She would sound like a pitiful, desperate fool if she pointed out the fact that disparate features didn't add up to beauty.

"I am not being kind," he insisted. "There is nothing *kind* about desperation. I am telling the truth, Cressie."

She gave him a lopsided smile. "I beg to differ. You are being very kind, and I assure you that your kindness now will assuage any sting I felt from the comments my father repeated. I suppose I did choose to fade into the wallpaper."

She did so because it was painful to be in a room and watch men turn to pretty girls and ask them to dance. It was easier to back away rather than stand in the group of women waiting to dance.

"Yet I won't marry you," she said. "We are ill-suited, Lord—" And, at the flash in his eyes, "Elias."

"I don't agree."

"It is a lady's prerogative to marry or no," she stated.

His hand was curled around the arm of her chair so tightly that his knuckles were white.

"Look at me and convince me that you don't love me, and I'll leave," Elias said, his words like staccato beats of a drum.

Cressida felt a stab of cold to her heart.

To reveal her love would be to give him everything. He was beautiful, wealthy, confident, desired by so many women. He had everything. Her mouth stayed firmly shut, her mind running in circles like a terrified rabbit.

Elias waited, and she saw the light fade in his eyes. Then his jaw hardened and he said, "You could grow to love me over time, Cressie. I am—I will *make* myself lovable to you. Tell me what you want in a husband, and I'll do it. Become it."

Cressida swallowed hard. She was back in the fairy tale, the one where a handsome prince knelt at her side—all right, crouched at her side—eyes passionate and direct, begging for her hand in marriage.

She'd never considered herself a courageous person, but now she summoned up everything she had. "I want to be loved," she said, the sentence hardly more than a thread of sound in the air. She paused and steadied her voice. "I want to be most important to someone." She finished defiantly. "I'd rather never marry than find myself married to a man who loved me as my father did: for what I can give him, rather than for myself."

She watched as fierce emotion swept over Elias's face. He stood up and drew her to her feet. "I can do that," he said, his voice exultant. "I'm in love with you, Cressie. My feelings won't change: you can ask Valentine or any of my other friends. I'm doggedly loyal and once I love someone, I never let them go."

Cressida's lips parted in surprise, her eyes searching his face. "There truly is no bargain? Not even a favor you owed to Val?"

"No. And by the way, I don't know a man who would accept a wife as a favor."

"Val could have saved your life?" Everything in her trusted this moment, this man, his truth. Elias was in love with her.

"I've never been in love before," he said, "so it took me half the day to recognize the feeling. I am in the grip of a ferocious, possessive wish to throw you onto that bed and never let you out of the room, not just to make love to you, but to talk. I want to know everything about you. You're—I never imagined a woman like you, Cressie. Never."

He meant it.

He thought she was . . .

Enough. More than enough. She saw that in his eyes.

"I find this hard to believe," she said honestly.

"Only because your father made you a drudge," Elias said. "I know you had a debut, but did you have a Season?"

"I was presented to the queen, but there wasn't time for many events," she said, her voice faltering.

"Did you have a new wardrobe?" His eyes searched her face.

She racked her brain, trying to remember. "A gown or two?"

"Who selects your clothing? Who selected this gown?" He nodded at her sadly crumpled attire. "Not that I don't appreciate the bodice, because I do."

Heat crept into Cressida's cheeks. "My father chose them from fashion plates. It—it saved me valuable time. He was happy to do it."

"I expect he was," Elias said, an edge in his voice. "This mauve-colored fabric is precisely wrong for your hair, Cressie. He hid you in plain sight, because you were his greatest asset. How often did he imply or straight-out tell you that you were unattractive?"

Cressida stared at him, unable to find words.

"Did he introduce you to appropriate gentlemen?" Elias asked. "Did he hire a chaperone for you, after your mother died? I don't remember seeing you dancing at any Revelry, for example."

"No, I'm sure you're wrong." Cressie took a deep breath. "I don't have the right figure, Elias. I don't look good in clothing."

His smile lightened his eyes. "I want to see you without clothing, I promise you that. But I also think that given an excellent *modiste,* you will be shocked to discover how beautiful you are." Elias's hands settled at her waist, making Cressie shiver. Deliberately, holding her gaze, he caressed the curve of her hips. "I am never wrong."

Even given the heated atmosphere between them, she laughed at that. "You may have done more to wound your chances of having me for a wife with that comment than you did with all of those about my appearance!"

He gathered her into his arms. "I'm an arrogant fool. But I know when I'm bested, Cressie."

She looked at him anxiously, but he was smiling. "I'm

going to have the smartest damn wife in all of the English isles. And the most beautiful too."

She emerged from his kiss shaking with desire and love, her fingers trembling as she ran them through his hair.

"Are you . . ." He took a deep breath.

Cressie was startled to see something that looked close to fear in his eyes.

"Do you think you could love me, Cressie?"

Her mouth curled into the happiest smile of her entire life.

"Yes," she said. "Yes, yes, yes."

Chapter Nine

"What . . . what now?" Cressie asked, an hour later. She was in Elias's lap, and they'd hardly stopped kissing to breathe. The warmth of his hand on her hip was burning through her clothing. Behind them the bed loomed suggestively.

He had managed to banish her fear. To the core of her being, she believed him: believed he desired her, loved her, wanted her as his bride.

"Marry me," Elias said, his eyes on hers. "Please. I want to take you away from here. I want you to be my wife. We'll go to my estate, and we'll mourn your father in whatever way you wish, in black and tearfully, or not."

Cressida blinked at him. "You want me to leave the Revelry? Just leave?"

He nodded. "Why not?"

"Why not? Well, my father . . . It's . . . I solve a hundred problems a day," she explained. "I keep everything running smoothly."

"And if it doesn't run smoothly?" Elias grinned at her.

Cressida gulped. She'd given years and years of her life to making certain that the Revelry went off without a hitch, that the acrobats were onstage precisely when called for, that the food was excellent—

"Dueling," she exclaimed. "I had to talk four different men out of duels last year."

Elias shrugged. "Val can do it. Though knowing him, he'll probably just let them hack at each other with swords.

Most duels come to nothing, you know. It's hard to swing a sword about, and even the most irascible fellow tires after a few minutes."

"'Val can do it,'" Cressida repeated.

"He might as well get used to it. You're not going to have anything to do with the Revelry ever again, are you, sweetheart?"

She looked at him anxiously. "Val is your best friend. He'll need help."

"You're going to be my *wife*," Elias said, his voice dropping. "Until we have children, you are everything to me. Val is just a friend. If you don't wish to, you will never again attend this wretched party."

Happiness permeated every bit of Cressie's body, from her toes to her fingers. "You are everything to me too," she said shyly.

This time, this kiss, Elias's hands wandered until Cressie's breath caught, and the bed no longer loomed behind her. It felt like a necessity, so much that she turned her head and looked at it. "Perhaps . . ."

Elias shook his head. "Not until we marry."

She colored. "I didn't mean . . ."

"Yes, you did, and I did too, but I won't. I won't dishonor you."

Cressie longed to say, "I don't care." She managed to stop herself.

"Will you marry me tomorrow?"

"No!" Cressie cried. "Absolutely not! Tomorrow my cousin Isabelle—well, she's really my niece, but she's my age—at any rate, she's performing a play that she wrote herself tomorrow. I couldn't possibly miss it!"

"The day afterwards," Elias said.

She gulped and nodded. Elias stood up and brought her to her feet, and then put his signet ring on her finger and clasped his hand over hers to keep it from falling off. "I haven't taken that off since my father gave it to me at fourteen. I'll replace it the day after tomorrow with a wedding ring."

Cressie blinked at him, but her hand clenched around the ring.

"I'd better go," Elias said, his voice gravelly with desire. "I'll find the vicar."

Cressie watched him go, and then uncurled her fingers. His ring was heavy gold, the symbol of a noble family that would now be hers.

Chapter Ten

The next day passed in a whirl of small problems, and all the time, in the back of her head, Cressie thought about Elias. About marrying Elias. About loving Elias.

Late in the afternoon, Nanny came in and bustled about her bedchamber. Cressie sat down and then blurted out, "Do you suppose you could pack my trunks, Nanny?"

Nanny stopped and whirled about. "What? You're never leaving Greystoke!"

"Yes, I am," Cressie said. "Tomorrow, as a matter of fact."

"What of His Grace?" Nanny asked. "The doctor believes he'll survive to the end of the Revelry."

"I made my goodbyes," she answered, peaceful with that decision. Her father had called her a twit; he wasn't likely to give her his blessing, as fathers did in sentimental stories.

Nanny put her hands on her hips. "You're off to London, aren't you? Well, I'm coming with you, Lady Cressida, and that's a fact. You're not going anywhere without me."

Cressie opened her mouth, but Nanny wasn't finished.

"Master Valentine hasn't any need for a lady's maid. I'm going to London with you."

"Oh, Nanny," Cressie said, her eyes misting.

But Nanny broke in again. "If you're setting yourself up in a shop, Lady Cressida, I'll be behind the counter. It isn't right that a lady should be talking to customers."

"You would do that?"

"I'm not the only one," Nanny said. "We all think downstairs that you'll be rich as Croesus within a year or two, so we'd do better to tie ourselves to your coattails."

A tear ran down Cressie's cheek. "I don't deserve that loyalty. But I am so grateful for it. I'm not going to London."

"Wherever you go, I'm going with you. There's no need to pay me, because I've saved a good amount of my salary and I can support myself. But you can't do without me, Lady Cressida. Just think of your hair!"

She looked so appalled that Cressie started laughing.

"Where will you go?" Nanny asked.

"Next door," Cressie said. Because Elias was their neighbor.

Nanny swung about. "Not—" she gasped.

"Lord Royleston has asked me to marry him, and I agreed."

Nanny's mouth fell open.

"It's unbelievable, isn't it?" Cressie said. Surprisingly, she didn't feel humiliated by the fact her own nanny was shocked. Why should she worry about the world's opinion, about the ladies who would whisper behind her back that she was a terrible choice for his wife? Elias thought she was beautiful.

"No, it is not unbelievable," Nanny stated. "I've told you and told you, Lady Cressida. If you'd just be yourself and let your hair show and all the rest of you, the men would be around you like flies on honey."

Cressie had always dismissed those comments as the supportive fibs of a loving nanny.

"Elias agrees," she said happily.

"I always liked him," Nanny said. "Even back when you were just a little girl, when I was your nanny."

"Oh, did you know him as a boy?"

"Certainly. Your father insisted that Master Valentine visit the estate after it became clear that your dear mother was ailing and couldn't bear more children. The young master began visiting when he was only twelve years of age, or so, and Master Elias was often sent over to play with him. From the very first day, they were thick as thieves, they were."

"Was Val a nice boy?"

"Naughty as the day is long," Nanny said. "Always on the point of plunging headlong into a trough of water and drowning himself. Master Elias was the more levelheaded of the two. He kept your cousin alive. Did as much for you as well!"

"What?"

"You don't remember?"

"How did Elias save my life, Nanny?"

"Well, you were like to split your head open, weren't you?" Nanny said. She began trotting around the room, pulling clothing from the press.

"Ice-skating?" Cressie asked, knowing the answer.

"You were a stubborn little thing," Nanny said, shaking her head. "Your older sisters listened to me. I wouldn't call them docile, exactly, but they were biddable. You would toss all that hair around, stamp your feet, and do just as you pleased."

"Really?" Cressie found herself oddly fascinated by the image of herself as a rebel.

Nanny turned around and leveled an elderly finger at Cressie. "Your father has used you something terrible, as I've told you. But you were never one to do what you didn't choose. If you'd wanted to marry, you'd be married by now."

Cressie nodded, and Nanny dropped her arm, satisfied, and turned back to smoothing the creases from a chemise. "You were four or five, I think, when you first realized that there was a way to glide over the lake. Oh, did you want to do it!"

"Skate?"

"Your father didn't think a lady had any business near a frozen lake, and neither did your sainted mother, bless her. You managed to sneak away from the nursery and made your way down there. I was just coming down the hill when you flung yourself onto the ice, hair and arms flying. Of course your little boots slid; you went across the skating patch like a bullet from a revolver. Likely to smash your head open, you were, but Master Elias saw you and nipped across the ice and cut you off."

"He didn't say that," Cressida said, sitting down. "He said that I knocked him down and then laughed."

"You did, so you did. He had a goose egg on the back of his head, but you laughed so hard that he did too, while Master Valentine just looked at the two of you as if you were mad. You were a great laugher in those days," Nanny said, a touch sadly.

Cressie almost told her that Elias said her laughter had sounded like birdsong, but she kept it a secret.

Nanny draped a gown on the bed. "For tonight."

"Red velvet?" Cressie said, rather startled. "I don't remember that gown."

"You've never worn it before," Nanny said. "His Grace said to get you something for Christmas, but he was feeling poorly and for once he didn't choose the color. I did."

Cressida frowned. "Elias is of the opinion that my clothing was chosen deliberately to be unflattering."

"I wouldn't go so far as that," Nanny said. "This gown, though, will suit you a treat. It's warm instead of all those light gauzy affairs that make ladies look like shivering elms. The waist is lower, which is all the fashion in Paris these days."

Cressida couldn't help hoping for a miracle as Nanny helped her put on a chemise, corset, and then the gown itself. The deep red velvet swirled down around her legs and the waist settled just above her own, which was much more flattering than below the bosom.

"Look at that," Nanny said, turning her gently. "Look at yourself, Lady Cressida."

The bodice was trimmed with shimmering swathes of silk in a pale rose echoed in a wide band at the waist. The neckline was low and wide, so that the top half of her shoulders were bare as well.

"You look just right," Nanny said with satisfaction. "Rounded in all the right ways, as a woman should be."

Cressida swallowed hard. The gown was lovely, especially in the way that it clung to her bosom and emphasized her waist. But that wasn't what made her look beautiful.

She wasn't experienced, but she knew what she saw in her own face. It was anticipation, the look of a woman who had decided to give herself to a man, and not because of vows or dowries or paternal approval, either.

She had *chosen* Elias.

She smiled at herself, and the woman in the mirror smiled back: a grown woman whose eyes sparkled with desire.

"You always were trouble," Nanny said, shaking her head. "You went sailing out on that lake as if I'd never given you a caution in your life, as if there were no rules saying ladies don't skate."

"I don't remember," Cressie told her. She picked up a box of lip rouge from the dressing table and put the faintest wash on her cheekbones, then turned to her lips.

"Now you're going to do the same again," Nanny said, resigned. "I only hope your blessed mother isn't watching from heaven because she'd say it was my fault."

Cressie sat down in front of the dressing table and smiled up at her. "Please won't you do my hair?"

Nanny snatched up a brush. "If I wasn't so fond of you, I'd let you go out there with your hair no better than a bird's nest on fire."

She spent the next thirty minutes lecturing Cressie on the proper comportment of a betrothed young lady. And

Cressie listened silently, and murmured agreement when necessary, and thought hard.

A proper young lady would never invite a gentleman into her bed. She would wait until she was bought and paid for, though of course, that implied a jointure to match the dowry that Cressie didn't have.

In fact, Cressie had nothing.

Almost nothing.

She had one thing that she could give freely, at her own behest. And if she gave it *before* their vows, then it was entirely her choice, and not a gift bestowed on a man in gratitude for marrying her without a dowry.

It would be *her* gift.

"I remember that look of yours," Nanny said, groaning. "You used to be as naughty as Master Valentine. It had slipped my mind."

She had shaped Cressie's hair into a deceptively organized mass of ringlets that had the faintest sense of disorder about it, a touch of sensuality that made Cressie blink and then smile. She stood up and hugged her nanny. "You are wonderful, and so dear to me."

"I suppose I can't stop you from whatever you're planning," Nanny grumbled. Just for a moment, she had a naughty twinkle in her eye.

Cressie ignored that. "My hair looks marvelous."

"Master Elias is getting himself a treasure, and I wouldn't want him to think he's had a bargain," Nanny announced.

Cressie took one more look at herself in the mirror. She didn't look lumpy and round. Swathed in red velvet, her figure curved in all the right places, and her face, topped by a magnificent billow of hair, didn't look ordinary. Not with a rosy lip.

"You'll have them all at their knees," Nanny continued. "I'll see you in the morning, Lady Cressida. I'm too old to act as a lady's maid, at my age. If you need help undressing this evening, you'll be so good as to ring for help from one of the younger maids."

"I shall," Cressie said, wondering whether beauty was a quality that came with lip color. Or with courage.

Or perhaps with love, because it seemed starkly clear that love changed everything.

Chapter Eleven

Cressie had never bothered to make an entrance into any room, not the ballroom nor the breakfast room; she had always been far too busy, a list of things to do echoing in her head and Twist at her elbow, whispering about this or that.

But tonight she walked slowly down the great staircase, hearing the swish of velvet on the floor behind her—for her gown was cunningly designed to be shorter in the front, allowing an alluring glimpse of her delicate heeled slippers, and perhaps even a flash of ankle.

Twist was in the corridor, but he didn't rush toward her with a bevy of complaints and worries. Instead, he bowed, quite as if she were one of her sisters, or another duke's daughter. "Good evening, Lady Cressida."

"Twist," she said, giving him a warm smile. "Is everything all right?"

She didn't want to hear the truth, and perhaps he realized it, for he said, "Of course, Lady Cressida. Lord Valentine has arranged everything to his—to our satisfaction."

Cressida considered that and decided that Elias was right. The Revelry was no longer her responsibility.

Twist said, "If I may be so bold, Lady Cressida, you look particularly lovely tonight." Then he pulled open the doors of the drawing room and announced her in the ringing tones he reserved for—well, for nobility.

Which she was, though she didn't think of herself that way.

A sea of heads turned to greet his announcement. Cressie paused, allowing one side of her mouth to curl up in a smile that she'd seen on many ladies' faces and never imagined on her own.

It was the smile of a woman who is waiting with complete confidence for the gentleman of her choice to come to her side.

Rather to her surprise, four or five gentlemen started towards her. She kept her smile in place, her eyes sliding over them and the rest of the crowd.

He wasn't here yet.

Why had she thought he'd be here waiting for her?

A warm hand wrapped around her elbow and a low voice said in her ear, "Did you know that there is a sprig of mistletoe directly above your head?"

Cressie tilted her head and her smile widened without conscious thought. Elias was wearing a silk coat in a somber violet edged in black. His eyes sparked with desire as they met hers.

"I thought perhaps you hadn't come downstairs yet," she said.

"I've been waiting," he said, an edge of self-mockery in his voice. "Leaning against the wall next to the door like a lovesick swain at fifteen."

"There's a sprig of mistletoe in every doorway," Cressie observed, deciding not to take up the question of lovesick swains. Her heart was racing, and she couldn't stop smiling at him.

"If you smile at me like that, I shall make an exhibition of us," Elias warned.

Gossip had spread throughout the manor, so no one looked surprised as Elias took her around the room, announcing their betrothal with as much pride as if he'd captured the most beautiful lady in all England.

As Cressie smiled and accepted congratulations, she puzzled over it. Elias had decided to marry her, and he wanted to bed her. He said he loved her. Did that account for the barely repressed sense of ownership that clung to him?

True, gentlemen did seem to be responding enthusiastically to the triple threat of her bared bosom, lip color, and cloud of hair. But not to such an extent that Elias had to fix Lord Pendle with a deadly look, forcing him to raise his eyes above Cressie's collarbone.

"It's just as well I'm marrying you," she said lightly to Elias, when he finally lost patience and drew her away from the old lord. "Now that he has me in his sights, as it were."

Elias's brows drew together. "What do you mean?"

"Lord Pendle has an unpleasant habit of finding young women alone and behaving inappropriately. I no longer allow the maids to go anywhere near his chamber; he is served entirely by footmen or his own valet."

His eyes were thunderous. "You must be joking. Why has he an invitation?"

"My father insists. Pendle is influential in Parliament," Cressida said. "He never goes too far with ladies. He might follow them about, accidentally brush his hand against their hips, or ogle at their chests, as he did to me. But he is far worse with maids."

Her explanation made Elias even more angry. His jaw flexed, and he deposited her with one of her nieces, Maeve, saying that he'd be back in a few minutes.

"How did you do it?" Maeve asked. "You know I adore you, Cressie, but I never thought you'd catch a man like—" She waved her hand, leaving in the air Elias's title, his wealth, his attractiveness.

Cressie didn't bother to pretend ignorance. "Neither did I," she agreed. "I feel as if I'm in a fairy tale."

"You look different tonight, quite beautiful," Maeve said, with the frankness of a family member. Something over Cressie's shoulder caught her eye. "Oh my goodness!"

Cressie turned her head and found that Val was escorting Lord Pendle from the room, Elias leading the way.

"He's being thrown out!" Maeve whispered. "Good for Val! Pendle is such a disgusting fellow. He pawed my maid last year. I was so angry, but the next day she led him to believe that she would welcome such a thing again, snatched a pin from her apron, and drove it into his hand."

Cressida gave a little gasp. "He made a terrible fuss about being injured, but I had no idea how it happened."

"I should have told Val," Maeve said. "I can't think why I didn't."

"I suppose because we've come to expect that sort of attention from Pendle," Cressie said.

"He won't be back," Maeve said. "Val is a bit of a rakehell, but not *that* sort of rake, if you know what I mean."

Elias reappeared at Cressie's side and sat down, a satisfied gleam in his eyes. "May I escort you to dinner?" he asked. "Before you ask, yes, Twist already changed the tables so that we are seated together."

"Oh, may I join you too?" Maeve asked eagerly. "I've been having frightfully worthy conversations with Lord Bilbrick."

"I thought you would enjoy him," Cressie said, disconcerted. "You are so clever, Maeve, and so is he."

"Yes, but I don't always want to have clever conversation," Maeve said, dropping a kiss on her cheek. "I'd rather just sit with you." Then she whispered, "It's far more entertaining to watch Elias moon over you as if you had a halo and wings!"

"Hush," Cressie whispered back, her cheeks turning pink.

An elderly acquaintance waved her lorgnette at Elias, demanding his attention, so he rose, bowed, and left. "I fancy I can *see* him making an effort not to look at your bosom," Maeve said with a wicked giggle. "I've never seen Elias show more than token interest in a woman. And I've known him for years! There's not a woman in this room who isn't green with jealousy."

"It's probably just . . ." Cressie's voice trailed off because she didn't know what it was. Or even what it looked like.

"He's head over heels," Maeve said, laughing.

Elias came directly back to them and sat down again. "What are you laughing about, Lady Maeve?" he asked.

"Your downfall," Maeve said, reaching across Cressie and giving him a poke. "You, my lord, are mad as a hatter. In love," she clarified.

"I like that phrase," Elias said, not disputing anything, which made Cressie's blush deepen. "Mad as May butter feels appropriate too."

"I never thought I'd see the day," Maeve marveled.

Cressie bit her lip. Perhaps he *was* mad.

"A March hare?" Elias said in Cressie's ear.

She had to turn her head to meet his eyes. "I'm sorry?"

"Are you mad as a March hare or May butter or the proverbial hatter?" His eyes held just a trace of hope.

Suddenly, it was all right.

"Yes." She smiled at him brilliantly. "Something like that."

Elias registered her smile with a visible start.

She turned to her niece. "Maeve, you will forgive me if I don't eat with you, won't you? I have a frightful headache, and I feel a little dizzy."

Maeve pouted. "You must promise to dine with me tomorrow." They all stood up, and Elias said gravely that he would escort Cressida to the stairs.

But when they reached the stairs, there was no one to be seen, as Twist had all the footmen in the dining room preparing the tables or serving drinks to guests in the drawing room. Cressie tightened her hand around his arm and began to climb the steps.

They walked upstairs silently, except for the clatter that Cressie's heart was making in her ears.

At the door to her room, she dropped Elias's arm and walked inside, turning around with a swish of her velvet skirts. She squared her shoulders—which showed her bosom to its best advantage—and raised an eyebrow.

Without saying a word.

Chapter Twelve

Elias stepped into the bedchamber and closed the door behind him.

Cressie faced him, head high, her eyes seeming even larger than usual. "I'm inviting you to spend the night with me. I have always found the idea that bodies can be bought and sold by a wedding license to be a disreputable business. I would prefer to—to give myself away. You spoke of dishonoring me, but I am making a gift of myself to you."

Elias never knew that joy could fill one's heart and spill over like a fountain. He didn't let himself smile. Instead he bowed, the deep bow of a courtier before his queen. "I would be most honored."

But he didn't move because—to be honest—he wasn't entirely sure how to proceed. If he had his druthers, he'd scoop her up and head for the bed. But she was a virgin, the very first virgin whom he'd ever had the faintest interest in bedding.

If he didn't care so much for Cressie, it wouldn't be a quandary. He would simply kiss her until her cheeks were pink and her eyes were shining and then . . .

Her cheeks *were* pink and her eyes *were* shining.

What's more, she was smiling at him. "I hope we don't have to rely on my experience. Because I haven't any, and no mother to tell me the ins and . . ." Her voice faltered.

"And outs?" Elias supplied, choking back a grin.

She started laughing, and after that it was all quite easy

because he snatched her into his arms and they kissed until Cressie said huskily, "Perhaps you might take off your coat."

Elias nodded, his heart pounding, desire tearing through him. Still, he cleared his throat. "Are you quite certain, Cressie? We haven't known each other for very long, and if you wish to wait until you feel comfortable . . . my father told me that he and my mother didn't consummate their marriage for months."

"If we turn out to be not very good at this, we might wait for months until we do it again," she said gravely. As he watched, she raised her arms—which did amazing things for her bosom—and began plucking pins from her hair. Most of it was already falling down her back like liquid honey.

He cleared his throat. "Hopefully we will manage to do well enough that you won't want to wait for months."

"I don't want to wait until tomorrow morning," she told him.

"Neither do I." His voice seemed to have fallen at least an octave. He wrenched off his evening coat and began unbuttoning his waistcoat. He couldn't stop the way laughter was bubbling up in his chest.

Cressie was watching him, her eyes wide but fascinated, so he glanced down, seeing how the thin fabric of his shirt strained over his muscles. He pulled the shirt free of his breeches. "Off?" he asked, gathering the linen in his fists.

She nodded, looking unnerved but brave.

He felt a throb of raw hunger, and forced it away. Cressie was so beautiful: big curious eyes, flushed cheeks, her bosom, her . . .

His shirt billowed and settled on a chair. Elias had a sudden thought and turned around with one stride and latched the door.

"Nanny already informed me that I have to find my own maid tonight," Cressie said with a gurgle of laughter.

"I can be your maid." Elias turned and walked back, stopping just before her. He never paid much attention to his body, but tonight he sent up silent thanks for the chest and shoulders he'd inherited from his father, because Cressie drew in a swift breath, staring at him.

"You're very muscled," she breathed, raising a hand.

Elias gathered her into his arms because he couldn't stop himself, tracing her lips with his tongue until she opened her mouth, and he surged inside with a rasping groan. She tasted sweet and intoxicating, like raspberries drenched in champagne. They kissed until they were both gasping for air.

"Clothes," Cressie gasped.

Thank God. He wrenched off his shoes and began to pull open the placket on his breeches. Cressie's hand touched his wrist lightly.

"Surely it's my turn?" she asked. Their eyes met and she was smiling at him, amused and wicked all at once, not the smile of a virgin, and yet he knew to his bones that she'd never kissed—really kissed—anyone but him. "I will need you to help."

Elias swallowed hard. "I can do that." He unclothed her far more quickly than he would have predicted, given the way his fingers were trembling. He was acutely aware of his solid bulk moving around her small curvy body, as he removed the layers that hid her from his sight: heavy velvet, structured corset, finally, on her nod: chemise.

At the sight of her naked body, his cock surged toward her like a compass to the true north. She stood quietly, arms at her side, allowing him to look his fill. And he did, drinking in her enticing, shapely curves.

He couldn't hear anything but the pounding of blood in his ears. She was abundant in the best places, and slender in other ones. He wanted to kneel before her and kiss every tempting inch of her.

"Your turn," she said. She didn't sound anxious, but her voice had a thread of uncertainty.

"I'm not as beautiful as you are," he said, hoarsely.

He wrenched down his breeches, kicking them to the side. Then he stood, letting her inspect him, watching her because he couldn't stop: the way she curved out and in, like a piece of art, like something created specifically to convince man that there was a god.

Her eyes had darkened.

She wanted him.

His girl, his Cressie, had chosen him, not for his title, or money, either. In the blink of an eye, he scooped her up and then they were on the bed, and she was exploring his chest, hands flat against his skin, but he couldn't think about that because finally, finally he was touching her breasts.

They were the perfect size, bountiful and soft, spilling out of his hands, making his mouth water. He kissed every curve, dragging his tongue over silky skin, coming closer to cherry-red nipples and drifting away until she was wiggling and complaining, so he gave in and closed his lips over one nipple.

Elias registered every sound Cressie made as the connection between them hummed, as if he were feeling *her* desire when he suckled until she was whimpering, her legs moving restlessly, her hair tangled around the pillow like a cloud.

"All right," she whispered.

He raised his head. She was flushed pink, panting, her skin dewy.

"I'm ready," Cressie told him, straightforwardly.

He shook his head.

"Let's—"

"Think of me as the expert," he whispered. "You let experts do their work, remember?"

From the look on her face, she couldn't remember anything she'd told him.

"I'm going to be the expert in your private grotto," he said, unable to stop himself from grinning, even though he was in the grip of the most ferocious desire of his entire life.

She rolled her eyes.

Elias began to move down her body, lavishing attention on her breasts, loving the tiny sounds she made, moving to the curve of her belly. "I'm going to put a baby here," he said, nipping her.

He looked up to find Cressie staring down at him. "Is that a normal thing to say on a wedding night?"

Elias shrugged. "I've never had a wedding night. Before you ask, I've never had the slightest inclination to do such a thing." He dragged his cheek over her belly and down to the nest of silky yellow hair, as soft as duckling's down. "Being with you is different from any intimacies I've shared in my life." His voice rumbled out of his chest. "I don't want to let you out of this room without my ring on your finger. I want to fill you with my seed and watch you swell with my baby."

That wasn't all he wanted, but he choked off the other thoughts: coming up on his knees, bending her over a chair—

No. Not yet.

"I don't know what you think you're doing down there," Cressie said. She was propped up on her elbows, looking uncertain.

He eased her legs apart. "I'm going to kiss you. Here."

"No!"

"Your mother isn't here to guide you about marital intimacies, remember?" He smiled at her, running his hands up the sweet curve of her thigh, dipping between so his fingers ran up the silky seam between her legs.

She gasped and hissed something, a word that wasn't a

word but an inarticulate cry. He glanced up quickly, but she had slid to her back and had her hands pressed over her eyes.

"Too much?" he asked, his fingers settling into satiny wet skin that made him feel desperate. He needed more.

"Huh," Cressie said, her voice shaking. "I don't think this is appropriate." But she didn't say no.

Elias promptly lowered his head. He had a gift for this particular kind of loving, nurtured and developed because he enjoyed it. He started slow and strategic, nursing his lady's desire until she was twisting and shamelessly crying out, her knees up, open and vulnerable to him. Giving him everything.

When Cressie was wild with need, her hips moving in an unconscious rhythm that was an unmistakable invitation, he took her up and over, his fingers and tongue narrowed to one objective: her pleasure. Her back arched and she came with a raw cry, shaking with waves of pleasure.

Elias rubbed his face on the sheet, then gently eased his body down onto hers, feeling for himself the tremors wracking her limbs. Then he waited, contenting himself with pressing lingering kisses on her forehead and her eyes, even her long eyelashes, curled and mink brown.

His body was tense, longing to pull back—

She looked at him, eyes wide. "That was . . ."

Elias grinned at her.

"Even I know that's not everything," Cressie whispered, her voice rasping.

"Made you hoarse," Elias told her.

She smiled, a lazy, happy smile. "Yes."

"Maybe you'd like to stop there? Take it slowly. There's tomorrow."

She wiggled against him, and an involuntary groan broke from his lips. "I want more of that. More—" She broke off, turning fiery red.

Elias ran a finger over her cheek. "Don't ever be ashamed

to ask me for what you need. We're going to be married. Partners. What you need is my first priority."

He rolled his hips, and she moaned. Her hands had been clinging to his shoulders, but now they slid down his back, leaving lightning streaks behind her.

"Cressie," he whispered, rubbing noses with her.

"Hmmm."

"I love you." The words growled from him, sincerity wrenching them from his chest as if he had only just learned to speak. A man newborn, he thought dimly, knowing that didn't make sense.

Every inch of his body agreed with the words.

Cressie was looking at him, eyes wide.

"You don't have to say anything back to me. I just wanted to say it. That you're . . . Well, that."

Her frown eased into a smile. "I don't think I've ever heard you incoherent."

"I am not incoherent in my head," he told her, the world shaking yet again into a different place. "I know exactly what I mean: that I love you, more than I shall ever love anyone else in this world or the next."

Her hands slid to his rear and then tightened. "Could we converse later?" she whispered, her blush deepening.

His heart sounded thunderous in his ears. He eased off of her and she pulled her knees up as if she knew how they would best fit together.

A moment later, he braced himself and slowly slid home, their eyes fixed on each other.

She shook her head. "It doesn't hurt. Isn't it supposed to hurt?"

"Not if you're lucky," Elias breathed. Every inch of his body was focused on making this last more than—

More than nature would allow.

His cock was rock hard and wanted to end things now. In fact, it was dying to explode in an orgasm so profound that it would—

He gritted his teeth because Cressie looked uncertain; he slipped a hand under one of her knees and watched as she blinked, adjusted until her forehead unpleated and she looked surprised.

"I didn't know," she said a while later. Her hands were on his arms now, clenched, and their faces were so close together that he saw the flecks of green in her pupils, and he breathed in the air that she breathed out, and he smelled something flowery and sweet, the honeysuckle that was essence of Cressie.

Even so, she surprised him.

Her eyes widened and she squeaked, her hands tightened, and then a wave went through her body, pleasure that moved from her to him as if the sea met the shore. Sensation coursed through him so sharply that it was almost painful, and with a groan that could have been heard in the corridor, he dropped his head and thrust forward one more time, everything he had spilling into her, and then again, and again.

In the past, an orgasm had always been a personal experience, whether shared with a woman or not. Pleasure would flood *his* body.

This was different.

He wasn't even sure how it was different except that he *felt* different: he was greedy and starved, but not for the bolt of joy in his body. For something else.

"I love you," Cressie said in his ear. She sounded shy but resolute.

That was it.

Something eased in his heart, and he turned his face against her hair and breathed in happiness.

Chapter Thirteen

The next morning, Cressie woke to find Elias up on one elbow beside her in bed, his eyes hopeful. A smile curled her lips. "Yes," she said.

"Yes, you love me?"

"That's what you want? I thought—" She turned pink.

"That too," he whispered, a hand slipping down her hip and between her legs. "This *and* that. Everything, Cressie. I want all of you. The vicar will meet us in two hours, so we have time for you to tell me you love me, and for me to *show* you how much I love you."

Cressie thought about how long it took to bathe and put on all the various layers of clothing that turned a woman from herself to a member of the nobility. Then she looked at Elias.

"I would have thought that you're too beautiful to marry," she told him.

He frowned.

"I was wrong. It's not important," she said, understanding the point fully, for the first time in her life. "The only thing that matters is you." She turned to her side and flattened her hand over his heart. "I do love you, Elias." Then she ran her hand down his chest and then even farther.

"A lady doesn't—"

Cressie grinned. "Ladies skate." She experimentally tightened her grip and Elias made a growling sound in the back of his throat. "Ladies run the Revelry."

His eyes glazed but he nodded, keeping his eyes on hers. "Only if they want to," he amended.

"Ladies love their husbands in any way they choose."

"Yes," Elias whispered hoarsely. A groan escaped his lips.

"You like this," Cressie mused.

He nodded.

She'd always been good at creative improvisation, so she added a flourish and a twist to her caress and catalogued every sound he made, the way ruddy color rose in his cheeks, the way his breathing became labored.

In the end, Elias married a sadly disheveled bride, at least from the point of view of the vicar. Mr. Maddens was dismayed to see the daughter of a duke standing at the altar with her hair in a twist at her neck, wearing a gown of simple blue silk, the ceremony witnessed by the bride's nanny and the castle butler, Twist.

But later, he thought about the way the bride and groom had smiled at each other, and the way their confident voices had echoed in the empty Greystoke chapel as they said their vows. No matter how solemn the vows, usually a bride and groom put on a performance for their family, for the nobility crowded in the aisles.

Not these two.

These two acted as if their witnesses didn't exist.

"You're more than I ever dreamed of." That's what Lord Darcy de Royleston said to his wife after Mr. Maddens finished the last words of the sermon.

The way his wife looked up at him?

She felt the same way.

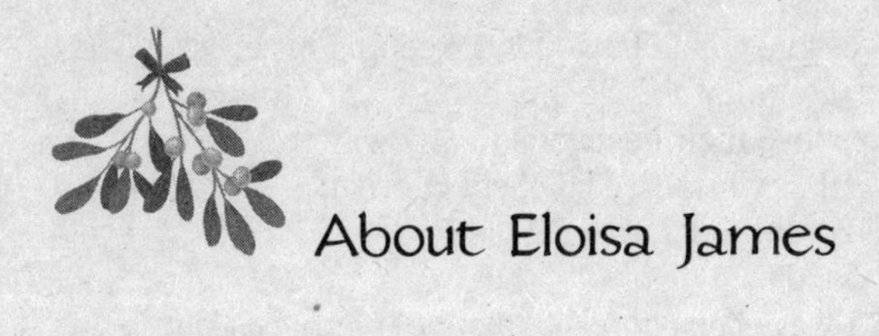

About Eloisa James

Eloisa James is a *USA TODAY* and *New York Times* best-selling author and professor of English literature, who lives with her family in New York, but can sometimes be found in Paris or Italy. She is the mother of two and, in a particularly delicious irony for a romance writer, is married to a genuine Italian knight. Visit her at eloisajames.com.

WISHING UNDER THE MISTLETOE

by Christi Caldwell

Prologue

The Offices of Mr. Cyrus Hill
Gracechurch Street
London, England

December 15, 1805

The whole world, from both Polite Society to impolite, on down to those born outside the peerage, assumed *they* knew what a duke's granddaughter wanted in life.

The only thing a lady of rank could conceivably want was the same elevated title, with a different name attached. And the prestige. And the wealth. There was, of course, the assumption that a lady desired *those*, too.

As it would turn out for Lady Isabelle Wilkshire, her own betrothed shared those erroneous assumptions about her dreams and ambitions.

Which was why she now found herself where no lady should ever be—outside, on a street alone, without the benefit of a chaperone, paying a visit to a man. The world would be scandalized! Even if she intended to spend the rest of her days with that man.

Of course, that future really required . . . well, *marriage.*

And despite an almost-three-year betrothal, Isabelle was decidedly not married. Or, if one wished to be truly precise, anywhere *close* to that state.

An almost-three-year betrothal.

She huddled deeper into her velvet-lined cloak.

Why, she'd lied even to herself.

She knew precisely the length of her betrothal, in years, and days, and minutes: two years, one hundred and fifteen days, and—Isabelle consulted the timepiece affixed to the front of her cloak—forty-six minutes.

Her gaze remained locked on those numbers that marked down each passing moment. From the corner of her eye, she caught a flash of movement and looked up.

She might as well have been invisible to her fiancé. He was far too absorbed in his work to glance out the window.

In a way, invisible was what she'd become. At some point, his smiles had become fewer. His drive had become more. And the connection between the two of them, people who were supposed to marry and live together, had . . . weakened.

I will only ever want you. You are my heart, and I would be lost without you.

A sad smile turned Isabelle's lips.

For, ironically, *lost* was precisely what he'd become. Lost to his work. Lost to growing his fortunes and, in that, lost to her. The frosted windowpane muted the lone figure within those offices, but there could be no disputing the identity of the gentleman hunched over his work. His blond hair, as always, was neatly drawn back but for several strands that protested the work and hours he kept.

Where the mere sight of him had always sent butterflies dancing in her belly, now only knots twisted away at her insides. Not at the fear of discovery, but at the fear of what would come—or *not* come—of this meeting.

But she'd been a coward long enough.

Slipping her hand out from her fur muff, Isabelle lifted the rusted knocker and let it fall once.

There came the scrape of wood along wood as he shoved back his chair, his mutterings muffled.

Despite her anxiousness, she found her first smile.

He had a tendency to speak to himself in an endearingly distracted way.

Cyrus Hill pressed his forehead against the frosted pane. Through the layer of ice coating the glass, Isabelle caught the hard frown on his lips.

Recognition sparked in his eyes.

He disappeared.

A moment later, he yanked open the door.

His eyes fell on Isabelle, and in their depths was joy, so much joy.

Her heart sped up as it always did—and always had—whenever she saw this man. Isabelle pushed her favorite bonnet back further so she might better see him. "Cyrus—"

But then that look, the one that had made her feel as though she was the most important person in the world, was gone, so quickly that she might have merely imagined it.

"What are you doing here?" he asked abruptly, and scanning the empty streets, the cobblestones lightly dusted with snow, he caught her by the arm and drew her inside. He shoved the door shut behind them. "You shouldn't be here, Isabelle."

You shouldn't be here.

To Cyrus, the fear of discovery and the risk of scandal would matter above all else. He'd not always been so concerned with the world's opinions. Somewhere along the way, the teasing gentleman who'd kept her company when her older male kin couldn't be bothered with her had . . . changed.

Her chest tightened. "I daresay I'd expected you'd be a good deal more pleased to see me," she teased in a bid for levity, but she couldn't keep a hurt edge from creeping in.

His frown deepened. "How can you doubt that I'm happy to see you?"

How could she not?

His response came by rote, absent the usual joy that

used to be there when she'd met him at her grandfather's house.

As if he sensed her doubts, Cyrus approached and lightly caressed his palms up and down her arms. "Of course I am."

There was such an earnestness in his gaze and in the tenderness of his touch that she could almost convince herself that she'd merely imagined the gulf that had grown between them. That his affection remained as strong as it had always been.

He released her, and she silently wept inside at the loss of a touch she'd gone so long without. Concern lit his eyes. "Your family," he said. "They are all well?"

"Prodigiously so."

The ghost of a smile softened the sharp planes of his strong features. With his strong nose and even more prominent squared jaw, none would ever consider him a beauty by society's standards, and yet, there was no more magnificent man than he.

"Prodigiously so . . ."

Those two words he echoed harked back, unbidden, to another time, another place. The place where they'd first met once upon a lifetime ago.

Are you enjoying your time here at Somerset?

Prodigiously so.

"You remember that?" she whispered.

A frown chased away the hint of his smile. His gaze moved caressingly over her face. "How could I ever forget that day?" he murmured.

That day, when she, the duke's eight-year-old granddaughter, met Cyrus, the stablemaster's eleven-year-old son. He'd been reading but hadn't turned her away. They'd spoken about books and writing that day. He'd not judged, only listened and asked questions. After that moment, she'd sought a friendship with her cousin Val Snowe, the Viscount Derham, because he was Cyrus's friend, so that she might know Cyrus better.

"You really shouldn't be here, then, Isabelle," Cyrus repeated, and her heart clenched as that link to the past was shattered.

"Yes, you've said as much."

Making no attempt to take her cloak, Cyrus started over to the small hearth in the corner of his immaculate offices.

He'd no intention of allowing her to remain.

Well, that was fine. She had no intention of seeking his permission.

Pushing her bonnet all the way back, she loosened the fastening of her cloak and shrugged out of the heavy, snow-dusted garment.

Grabbing the fireplace poker, he added a log to the roaring fire. The dried wood cracked and hissed, sending sparks flying. "You were to leave this morn for the duke's." It wasn't a question.

She answered anyway. "Yes."

The duke's.

As in, her grandfather's.

As in, the singularly most interesting thing about her, according to Polite Society.

Only, Cyrus was different.

Or, that *had been* the case.

Or mayhap it hadn't. Mayhap she'd been so very enamored of him that she'd been blind to his regard for her familial connections.

"Yesterday morn," she corrected.

Stoking the fire, he glanced up with a question in his eyes.

"My family left yesterday." Isabelle wandered deeper into the room. This place was his palace, the place he preferred above all others. "I chose to stay behind." So that she might have this discussion, so that she might stop hiding from the fears she had and take hold of the future she desired.

With him.

"Whyever would you do that?" he chided. While he attended the fire as if it were the most important thing in the world, Isabelle hung her damp garment over the back of the seat across from him and stripped off her gloves. "You despise London."

She did. But London was where Cyrus and his all-important work were, so even when the rest of Polite Society retreated to their country estates, Isabelle had insisted on remaining . . . just so she might be close to him. "I didn't wish to go to my grandfather's this year."

It was the first time in the whole of her life when she would miss the Revelry, the festive, if peculiar, house party for which the Duke of Greystoke was famous.

"Impossible." Cyrus returned the poker to the small iron rack. "You've always enjoyed the duke's Christmastide Revelry. It's one of the favorite things you do all year."

How very well he knew her. He knew her love of composing plays and music and staging performances, even if the troupe for those performances involved only her younger brother and sister and a handful of servants.

He knew her secret and never judged her. It was one of the reasons she'd fallen so hopelessly and helplessly in love with Cyrus.

Isabelle joined him beside the hearth, staring into the crimson and orange flames he'd stoked.

"It isn't the same without you being there, Cyrus."

He took a step toward her, and her pulse knocked at his closeness. Only . . .

Cyrus continued past her, and drawing out his desk chair, he sat.

Isabelle tensed her mouth. Gentlemen didn't sit while a lady stood. *He* knew that. And though she didn't give a jot if or when or how he sat, his reason for doing so did, however, matter to her. His was a show of defiance . . . a not-so-subtle point he highlighted about her birth versus his.

"I've never been to the Revelry," he spoke with his usual

directness about the ducal Christmastide festivities. "You know as well as I do that invitations are coveted by all Polite Society and more notable people. There's no spare one for the likes of me."

Nay, he hadn't. For as friendly as Cyrus might have been with the duke's family, that close connection meant nothing to His Grace. Rank superseded all. The duke's invitation list was famous. All of the aristocracy held their breath on the day the invitations were delivered; they woke early to scan the paper the next morning when the invitation list was printed to see the fate of their friends and foes.

Shifting her focus from the hearth, Isabelle turned to face him. "Cyrus—" Her well-planned speech died.

He had returned to his work, as engrossed now as he'd been when she'd studied him from outside. He'd forgotten she was there.

She stared at him, unblinking. Of course, she knew what her eyes told her, and yet, that indifference didn't fit with one who *loved* her. With one who had been so very happy to see her. If he was happy anymore.

Isabelle bit at the inside of her lower lip, and in a bid to give her shaking hands purpose, she rubbed at her chilled arms. "Are you *working*?"

He dipped his fountain pen into his crystal inkpot without looking up. "I believe it should be fairly obvious that I am."

She didn't know whether to laugh or cry.

Isabelle took a breath and tried again, this time a different course. "You should be visiting your family, Cyrus. It is the Christmastide season."

A dull flush climbed his cheeks. "I have work."

"That doesn't matter more than being with them." *Or me.*

A muscle rippled along his jaw. "I do not have the luxury of taking part in familial Christmastide festivities," he said tersely.

She shivered.

How easily he'd come to terms with his severed relationship with the man and woman who'd given him life. What did that mean for her? For their future?

She despised not knowing how he was feeling. And worse, being unsure about what was between them. For the first time since she'd waved goodbye to her family, resolved to confront Cyrus, she didn't feel the sting of heartbreak and hurt.

Anger made itself felt instead: a kind of calm fury that steadied her.

Licking the tip of his index finger, Cyrus reached for the puce powder to dry his ink.

The last frayed shred of Isabelle's patience broke.

She slapped a palm onto his just-completed work.

"Isabelle," he exclaimed. "The ink is still wet."

Was it surprise or annoyance that glinted in his eyes?

The inability to decipher what he was thinking fed her anger.

"I don't give a damn about the wet ink or your ruined work," she said in quiet tones that belied the tumult of emotion buffeting her insides. "We have been betrothed for nearly *three years*, Cyrus."

He scoffed. "It's not been three years. It's two years and a few months, less than six."

Any other lady would have taken his calculation as evidence of his devotion, a sign that he, like she, had counted the days since he proposed. But she'd grown up beside Cyrus, first as a friend and then as a young love. He'd always been a master of numbers, so his rapid calculation meant nothing.

His scoffing indifference?

That meant everything.

Cyrus made to turn the page, but Isabelle planted the tips of her fingers onto his tabulations. If he wished to proceed in this battle, he'd rip his page in the process.

"We were to marry in six months," she stated.

Even six months is too long, Isabelle. I want to begin tomorrow with you today.

How pretty that avowal had been, and how easily it had fallen from his lips.

"Opportunities presented themselves," he said. "You know that. We've spoken at length about the possibilities."

Cyrus had become an investor managing monies inherited or earned by his wild friends, including her cousin Val. "You said you meant to manage Val's business, not all these others."

He set down his pen. "You would have us settle for less than what we could have?"

We.

His aspirations and hers had once existed as a *we*. When they'd shared their dreams and hopes and considered their futures. In those talks, their futures had always been joined.

Isabelle took her ink-stained palm away and sank onto the edge of the seat nearest him. "It's not just about what we *have*. It's about our life together. And at the present, we have . . . little together."

A sound of impatience escaped him. "Of course we do."

"Adding 'of course' doesn't make it true, Cyrus," she said softly.

Cyrus gestured toward the ledgers resting on his desk. "I'm doing this for us."

"I only want you."

He went on as if she'd said nothing. "When I proposed, I wouldn't have been able to provide for you or a family."

That was three years ago. "And now?"

His smile was just a twitch of his lips. "I'm still amassing a fortune. Funds to secure us."

"I don't *care* about a fortune." How could he not see that? She caught one of his hands in hers and held firm. "I care only about you and me, Cyrus."

He drew back from her touch in a stinging rebuke.

"You've never been without," he said bluntly. "You don't know what it means to live a commoner's life."

"I know, with you by my side, I'll be happy."

"You've never gone without food. You've never been cold in winters," he said, offering a glimpse of the life he'd never spoken of. "You've never had threadbare boots. You've never been mocked for wearing equally threadbare garments."

Along with an ache in her heart for the struggles he'd known came a sting of shame for how unaware she'd been of what his childhood had been like. "My dowry . . . it can be enough for us."

His eyelid twitched. "I will not have my wife take care of me."

"Why should I not contribute?" she pushed back. "Is there something so very wrong in me contributing, Cyrus?" Isabelle dragged her chair closer. The legs scraped noisily upon the floor.

"Yes," he said uncompromisingly. "I will take care of you. You can save your dowry for our children."

Her gaze locked with his. "Why don't I get to decide what I want?"

A thick, tense silence pulsed between them. Reaching for his pen, Cyrus was the first to break the impasse. "If you've come here worried about whether or not we'll marry, then you needn't worry. It is my intention that we will."

Her heart lifted.

"When the time is right," he added.

Just that simply, with a mere five words, her heart broke.

The rapid scratch of his pen rose into the air as he filled in columns, tabulating the monies of his clients.

"That isn't why I came," Isabelle said, her voice dull.

He paused, glanced up with palpable indifference on his face, and then resumed working. "Oh?"

Look at me.

"You're aware of my friendship with Mary Russell Mitford?"

"I am." He directed that utterance to whatever calculations commanded him. "Is she well?"

In her lap, Isabelle fisted and unfisted her hands. "Prodigiously so," she said.

This time, there was none of the shared tenderness of the earlier phrase. No connection to the moment they'd met. "Mary's family is moving to Grazeley. More specifically, the village of Spencers Wood, just outside of Reading." Before her courage deserted her, before she let herself continue on with this half-life she now lived, Isabelle drew in a deep, steadying breath. "She has invited me to accompany her and her family."

The *scratch-scratch-scratch* of his pen slowed . . . and then stopped altogether.

And yet, Cyrus did not lift his gaze from those so-very-important-to-him numbers.

"You are joining her for the holidays, then."

"Yes." She wet her lips. "And . . . beyond."

That managed to pierce the wall of his icy indifference. Cyrus looked up. "I don't understand," he said flatly.

"Mary, as you know, is a dramatist, and she had the idea that we might collaborate. She invited me to join her. Her family is sponsoring a German dramatist to mentor her." Restless, she came to her feet and spoke on a rush. "I believe I shall go."

"I see." Cyrus carefully returned his pen to the inkpot and sat back in his chair. "Just how long do you intend to remain with Miss Mitford?"

"Indefinitely."

His lips parted the tiniest fraction. She would have missed it had she not been studying him so closely. Desperately awaiting some reaction from him.

"I'm freeing you of our betrothal, Cyrus."

Fire flashed in his eyes. “Have I given you some indication I wish to be free?” he asked, his voice nearly a growl.

“You’ve changed. Only one passion matters to you. I was once that passion. But no longer, Cyrus. Wealth and status are all you care for. There isn’t room for them . . . and me.”

His mouth formed a hard, flat line. “You resent my effort to ensure that we don’t live in poverty? That we live comfortable lives befitting one of your station?”

“I don’t resent you, Cyrus.” Isabelle gathered her cloak. “I love you. That is the difference.”

He remained seated. “You aren’t making any sense.” He clipped out each syllable of that sentence.

“Perhaps someday it will, Cyrus.” Shrugging into her heavy, still-damp garment, she latched it at the throat, picked up her gloves, and started for the door.

Stop me. Please say something. Anything that indicates you in some way care.

She paused to pull gloves over her stained hand, giving him time to compose his thoughts and say something . . . anything.

But he didn’t.

No words were forthcoming, no vows of love, no pleas for her to remain.

With only his silence calling out to her, Isabelle left . . . without saying goodbye to the only man she’d ever loved.

Chapter One

The Offices of Mr. Cyrus Hill
Gracechurch Street
London, England
10 years later

Cyrus despised the holidays.

He despised the incessant good cheer, the festive songs, and the wetter-than-usual—and this year, snowy—English weather.

But more than anything, he despised the fact that his clients took themselves off to their country estates and his business slowed until their return.

Which was why it was so perplexing that his very first client—a close friend and the future Duke of Greystoke—should be in Cyrus's Bond Street offices now, at the beginning of December.

Glancing up at the young servant in the doorway, Cyrus frowned. "Beg pardon?"

Thomas cleared his throat. "The Viscount Derham. I took the liberty of showing him in."

"Turning away your closest friend and longest client?"

Viscount Derham swept past Thomas and into Cyrus's offices with a commanding presence that only a future duke could wield, sending Thomas backing away.

Not bothering to stand, Cyrus grunted. "I'm not turning you away." He grabbed his pen and resumed the calculations he'd been seeing to. "I'm wondering what you're doing here."

Derham scoffed. "You're a miserable bastard, Hill. I expected you'd be a good deal more pleased to see me."

Cyrus froze.

As the other man stripped off his wool cloak, handed it to Thomas, and availed himself of a seat, Cyrus's gaze locked, unseeing, on the numbers before him. A distant memory intruded.

I daresay I'd expected you'd be a good deal more pleased to see me.

How many times she still entered his thoughts all these years later. In the beginning, it had been easier to push thoughts of her away. After all, she'd left. She'd chosen a life without him.

But the memory of her always found a way back to him . . . slipping in at the most unexpected of times.

No doubt, the fact her scapegrace relation sat before him accounted for that unexpected remembrance.

"I come with glad tidings," Val said, his ironic tone making a mockery of the words.

Cyrus snorted. "You're an even more miserable bastard than myself." They were both brooding and cynical, so their friendship had always made sense, even if it was between the stablemaster's son and a future duke. "What glad tidings could you possibly bring?"

Derham rested his arms along the sides of his chair. "The Duke of Greystoke is holding his Christmastide gathering, the Revelry."

Cyrus dipped his pen in the inkpot. "All England knows that. I'll never understand why the bloody invitation list has to be printed in the papers, but even I remember that today is December 1, which means that the evening paper will splay the list on its front page. I'd hardly call that 'glad tidings.'" He gave his head a dismissive shake and finished calculating the last column on his report.

"Didn't you tell me that you were going to rebel and stay away this year?"

"I'm going," Derham said.

What could account for a change of heart in the licentious rogue more interested in spirits and his own pursuits than family parties?

"Because Greystoke promised me Morley House."

Cyrus paused, pen caught above a line of figures.

That would be reason enough to bring cheer to the second-most-miserable bastard in the world—behind Cyrus, of course.

"Indeed."

"Indeed?" Derham chuckled. "I'm the miserable bastard? You're the only one who'd never dare crack your stoic composure at such a revelation."

Derham loved nothing and no one, but he did love that old Scottish property. The irony had never been lost on Cyrus, that Derham stood to inherit a dukedom and fortunes and land, but the unentailed property his father gambled away would be the only one he truly had any interest in.

"There are stipulations."

"Of course there are." Cyrus rested his pen. "Get on with it."

"How is it possible you're even more taciturn than I am?"

"Because I don't have the time or inclination to spend my time chatting when I've fortunes to manage." He raised an eyebrow. "Not excluding yours."

"Very well." At last doffing his tricorne, Derham set it on his knee and leaned forward. "My presence is requested at Greystoke's Revelry."

"Requested."

"Required. My presence is required, and the duke intimated that I will regain Morley House *if* certain conditions are met." A determined glint lit the other man's eyes. "And I am damned well going to do whatever I must to obtain that Scottish treasure."

By the deliberate stare Derham leveled on him, something was expected of Cyrus. "What do you want?" He'd been born blunt, without any patience for dancing around issues, and that directness served him well in his work.

"You to come with me. Along with the others."

There could be no doubting who *the others* were, the duke's circle of dissolute friends. "I cannot."

The other man scoffed. "What do you mean, you cannot? You do not visit your family. You don't have a wife. It is the holidays, when the world ceases to work, and as such there is no activity you can possibly do."

Another might have been insulted by that ruthless catalogue. But Cyrus was wholly unmoved by emotion and appreciated candor. "The world never ceases to work. Not even at Christmastide. I'm waiting for Lord Basil to admit he can no longer hold on to his shares of the Yorkshire mines."

"You're investing my funds. I give you permission to take the Christmas season off."

"I've no interest in taking the season off," Cyrus said coolly, returning to his work. "Nor do I believe you're so sentimental as to want me accompanying you."

The other man laughed. "Of course not. But if I'm going to suffer, I intend to drag along all my friends for company."

"The Duke of Greystoke is quite particular with his list—the same list that will be published in the papers. I doubt he'll welcome extra guests, let alone a former servant's son. He was always a cold bastard, if you'll excuse my bluntness." Life had taught Cyrus that passing years didn't soften a person. Time just added additional layers of cynicism. "Either way"—he closed his client's ledger and reached for another—"I'm too busy to join you in the country for a silly Christmastide party."

Derham leaned farther forward. "My version of the Revelry won't be the same as has been hosted by the duke." He turned his elegant hat in his hands.

"Another might be interested in the information you're

dangling." Cyrus flipped open another client's ledger. "I don't have time for guessing games."

"His Grace is dying. He may not survive through his party. And I'm expected to take part in the festivities and carry on his legacy." He said the word *legacy* with a distaste that revealed his feelings about the affair.

Still, his statement gave Cyrus pause. "You? Take part?"

"As in help organize the affair. As in, examine guest lists, décor, and . . ." The other man waved his spare hand. "*All of it* so that supposedly I can continue to carry on the Revelry next year and thereafter, when he is in the grave."

Cyrus blinked. *"You?"*

Derham nodded.

If Cyrus had been capable of laughter, this moment would have been grounds for mirth. Even as one who disavowed such useless affairs, he was tempted to attend out of morbid curiosity. "The duke is famous for king-making at the oh-so-influential Revelry. Unless His Grace is amenable to your throwing a gathering that will scandalize Polite Society, he'd do well to reconsider the terms of that request."

"The Revelry has never limited itself to Polite Society," Derham said. "As the world well knows, his invitation list includes politicians, opera singers, actors . . . and this year: *you*."

"You jest."

Derham flashed a grin. "Precisely."

"You put me on the list," Cyrus said, and then shrugged. "But there is no conceivable reason for me to attend."

"A sea of potential new clients," Derham pointed out. "Men of money. Some who've recently come into funds. Others born to wealth. All there, Hill. All ripe for your growing coffers."

With that, Derham made the one—and only—point that could have influenced Cyrus. Numbers and investments had always made sense to him. He understood them and excelled at manipulating them, and . . . and they never left him disappointed.

Mary, as you know, is a dramatist, and she had the idea that we might collaborate. She invited me to join her. I believe I shall go.

Cyrus curled his hand sharply around his pen, which quivered, near snapping. He forced himself to loosen his grip.

Nay, there was nothing emotional about money. There was no opening oneself up to the type of hurt that left a heart splayed in two.

Yet she would be there. No relative of the duke's missed the Revelry. For all his threat of rebellion, Cyrus had the idea that Val had attended the party for most of his life.

After ten years, Cyrus's path would cross with Isabelle's.

He flattened his mouth into a line.

What did it matter?

He had his career, and a very lucrative one at that. And she had . . .

What did she have? Was there now a husband? Children? Logic said yes.

Why did that rational conclusion send seething-hot rage searing through him?

"Well?" Derham demanded. "What is it to be?"

What was it to be?

It didn't matter whether Isabelle would be there. Only the clients Cyrus might take on mattered. The business he could secure . . . and grow. The wealth. The power. The stability.

"Very well."

Derham smiled. "Splendid." He came to his feet. "Oh, there is one requirement I forgot to mention."

Cyrus narrowed his eyes. "Forgot or failed?"

"Each guest has to take part in some aspect of the gathering. It's a long-standing tradition at the Revelry, and God knows, my uncle won't let any traditions go."

Warning bells clamored. "Oh?" Cyrus's brows dipped. "What would my role entail?"

The future duke returned his hat to his head. "You will be partly responsible for a theatrical production," he said, his words more an afterthought as he started for the door. "Nothing to worry about. The Revelry runs like clockwork. One of my cousins is in charge."

Cyrus shoved to his feet. "Theatrical?" A pit formed in his gut. A dreaded sense of doom.

Derham paused with his hand on the handle. "You needn't worry. You'll be in capable hands."

Capable hands . . . "Who?" He bit out that syllable between clenched teeth.

"And certainly—"

"Who?" Cyrus repeated more sharply.

"Isabelle."

There it was. Isabelle.

I know, with you by my side, I'll only be happy.

The ghost of her memory was not to stay buried, then. Certainly not this day and not with this task.

His lips curled in a smile born of cynicism. How prettily she'd spoken of wanting him at her side, and then in the next breath, she'd severed their betrothal . . . and everything between them.

Derham frowned. "I trust that won't be a problem? I was under the assumption your end was amicable and mutually agreed upon, a product of each of you wishing to fulfill your own dreams." Those words were uttered as though they were part of a family story that had been passed down.

Cyrus shrugged. He considered himself incapable of strong emotion. The day Isabelle had left, closing the door of his office, all interest in love and feelings and anything weak had gone with her. "I have no feelings with regard to Isabelle at all."

"Splendid. It is settled, then." Val flipped a card onto Cyrus's desk.

Gieves. By appointment to his Royal Highness the Duke of Edinburgh, Naval Tailors & Outfitters. And, scrawled on the card, 3 o'clock.

Cyrus scowled. "I'll be damned if I dress like a peacock."

"Gieves focuses on the Royal Navy, not the fashionable set. You've got too much muscle to wear pink silk. But you'll collect no new clients unless you look the part, Hill. Pay him triple because you need a wardrobe in two weeks, head to toe. You have an appointment for this afternoon. I shall see you in a fortnight." On the heels of that pronouncement, Derham left.

Staring down at the card, Cyrus had half a mind to rip it up. But . . . *Isabelle.*

She was the last person Cyrus should ever be partnered with.

Blast Val to hell. If his friend wasn't as cynical as he, he'd suspect him of trying to emulate the saint he was named for: Valentine. But no. Val's indifferent gaze had indicated that he was paired with Isabelle for expediency and no other motive.

Cyrus returned to his work.

He'd built fortunes for men who'd been on the cusp of ruin. He'd transformed himself, a stablemaster's son, into one of the most revered and feared men in London.

Reuniting with his former betrothed would be child's play in comparison.

Chapter Two

Dearest Isabelle,

You must return on a matter of the greatest urgency, a tragedy. Grandfather is ailing and asks that all members of the family return. He is not expected to survive the Revelry.

Signed,
Your long-lost younger sister,
Maeve

After a very long, very uncomfortable carriage ride to the estate of her grandfather, the Duke of Greystoke, it had taken all of ten minutes after Isabelle's arrival to deduce that she'd been tricked. Twist had told her that His Grace would spend the day working on the Revelry—due to begin in a mere fourteen days—and join the family for the evening meal.

"His Grace is well," she said flatly. Arms folded, she stood over her sister Maeve, who nibbled away at some sugary confection cradled between her fingers as lovingly as the king might cradle his crown.

"For now," their mother, Holly, the Countess of Thorpe, murmured, dabbing at her eyes. "His days are good and bad."

Isabelle's heart squeezed. The duke had never been overly affectionate, and yet, he'd also been the family patriarch and she could not imagine the world without his powerful presence in it.

"Never tell me, you would rather have arrived to find Grandfather at death's door?" Her sister batted her eyes with an innocence that Isabelle didn't believe for one moment.

Isabelle and her mother spoke as one.

"Of course not! That would be terrible."

"Maeve." Mother glanced about the breakfast room, empty but for a neat row of servants stationed throughout the room.

Her sister frowned at Isabelle. "Furthermore, that's hardly a warm welcome for the sister one hasn't seen in three years."

Feeling the heat of her sister's pointed glance, Isabelle tamped down remembrances of that long-ago day she had no place thinking of. Not anymore. "It hasn't been three years."

Her youngest sibling lifted a brow.

Yes, she hadn't come home in some time, but it hadn't been three years. Had it? Isabelle searched her mind. She'd never been one for numbers . . . or dates. That was, but for one date—the day she'd ended her betrothal to Cyrus.

Words, on the other hand? Those came easily to her.

"I'd be remiss if I failed to point out, it's been nearly *four* years since we've seen you." Maeve licked the glazed sugar from the tips of her fingers.

From over the top of her teacup, Mother frowned. "Do not lick your fingers, Maeve. It is uncouth."

"Oh, yes. Licking the remnants of a tasty treat from one's fingers is outrageous, but Isabelle's annoyance at being urged to visit Grandfather after a four-year absence is nothing at all."

"I didn't say that." The countess set down her glass. "Both are unforgivable."

So an absent and unmarried daughter was the equivalent of ill manners. Nothing had changed where their mother was concerned.

"I have come 'round on occasion," she felt inclined to remind her mother and sister.

"For a week here or there," Maeve scoffed. "That hardly counts." Her sister paused to give her a look. "But you are here now," she said softly, her earlier rancor gone.

"Yes! And there is no imminent tragedy," Isabelle said hopefully, returning to the matter at hand, preferring to still believe it had been trickery on her sister's part to draw Isabelle from her work to Grandfather's latest Revelry.

Maeve lifted her perpetually wide, round eyes to Isabelle's. "There might be." She spoke in haunting tones.

"Do stop being so maudlin," their mother said. "I am praying for my father's full recovery. Why, he's made of stern stuff. The whole world knows that." Tears pricked the corner of Mother's eyes, and she brushed them back angrily. "There *is* no tragedy, and there won't be one anytime soon." She said it with force, as if speaking the words would cure an old man's illness.

"Don't speak to me about the lack of tragedies. One"—Maeve lifted a finger—"Isabelle is rumpled. Two, her hair is a tangled mess. And three? I'm fairly confident in saying there's a faint stench of horses hanging about her."

Isabelle sniffed the air. "I don't *smell* like horses."

"Then tragedy four, you've lost your sense of smell," her sister tacked on.

From the corner of her eye, Isabelle caught a pair of footmen stifling matching grins.

"There was a mishap with the carriage, so I continued by mail coach, and then there was a situation with *that* team requiring the passengers to shelter in the stables until . . ."

She caught the teasing glimmer in her sister's eye. Thank goodness, even with everything that had changed, with the passage of time, Maeve had retained her impish spirit, and the levity infused also allowed Isabelle to selfishly pretend, if even for just a few moments more, that it wasn't her Grandfather's impending demise which had resulted in Isabelle's being here. "Either way, my travel accommodations"—*and the smell of me*—"are neither here nor there. What is relevant is the fact that Grandfather is still with us."

"If I might direct us to something less tragic for a moment?" Maeve piped in. "The truth is that Cressie is desperate." Their cousin Cressida now managed all the vast arrangements that turned the Revelry into the most anticipated house party of the year.

There were several beats of silence as her sister's words ever-so-slowly registered. "How can I possibly be of service to her?"

Maeve rolled her eyes.

"Cressie wants me to handle the play?" Isabelle asked, her chest barely moving, as if she was afraid to breathe. It was the dream she'd treasured since she'd been a girl, enduring the painful task of putting on performances alongside the rest of the Duke of Greystoke's guests. Writing plays had long been something Isabelle understood and loved. Acting in them—she repressed a shudder—was altogether different.

"That was what I was trying to tell you." Her sister smiled. "In a roundabout way, of course. Hence my emphasis on Grandfather's illness. But I did give you a hint by calling the matter of urgency a tragedy."

Isabelle stared blankly at her.

"You are a playwright."

"Shh," Mother hissed, staring pointedly at the servants. Isabelle's secret profession was a source of mortification for her family, as her mother had pointed out more than once.

Maeve continued over her. "I was making a play on words." Her sister laughed. "Get it? Play on . . ."

Isabelle and her mother stared silently at the youngest Wilkshire sister.

Maeve wrinkled her nose. "Add missing senses of humor to the ever-growing list of tragedies."

"Why did you not just tell me?" Isabelle said to her mother, ignoring Maeve. "You know—"

"You would have returned to produce a play, but not to see your family?" Maeve asked, picking up a second pastry.

Her words were spoken in dry jest. Bristling, Isabelle opened her mouth to respond but stopped.

Is your sister wrong? a voice needled. *Isn't she telling the truth?* For threaded under her sister's teasing voice, a palpable hurt radiated from Maeve's gaze.

Unable to meet her eyes, Isabelle looked to her mother.

The lady frowned. "The play is a lesser issue."

"Not for Isabelle," Maeve rightly pointed out.

It was the one dream Isabelle carried in her heart: handling the production at her grandfather's grand gathering, the Revelry attended by all the brightest and finest in the kingdom.

Nay, that is not the only dream you carried. There'd been another. Isabelle closed her eyes.

I would follow you to the ends of the earth, Isabelle—ahh.

That memory of Cyrus slipped in, as real and as fresh as if it had been days ago rather than years. She had led a blindfolded Cyrus Hill through her grandfather's forests in a bid to see how much he trusted her.

Pain squeezed at her heart. Not as sharp as it had been. At some point, loss of Cyrus had reduced from a vicious pain to a manageable ache.

"Are you all right?" Her sister's query made Isabelle's eyes fly open.

Maeve was squinting at her with a suspicious look.

"I'm fine." And she was.

In fact, she was *better* than fine. Her betrothal to the man she'd loved hadn't materialized into the marriage she'd yearned for, but she had her work, and her family's support. And like-minded friends. Why, one might argue—*she* would argue—she had far more than any woman in the whole of England.

If she had married, she'd be a wife and possibly a mother.

"You're certain? Because that would mean I am free to tease you once more—"

Isabelle snatched a napkin from the table and tossed the fine linen cloth at her sister, earning a boisterous laugh from the younger woman.

Mother tapped four fingertips upon the table. A thumping fist would be uncouth for the duke's daughter. "Cease."

"You're being entirely too gracious, Mother. Given her prolonged absence, the very *least* Isabelle deserves is—"

"Girls, if you please! This Revelry must be perfect . . . for your grandfather." Their mother's grave utterance brought an immediate surcease to the sisterly bickering. "He rallies occasionally, but he has a dreadful cough and occasionally seems unable to breathe. The doctors despaired only a week ago, but he has vowed to live through the Revelry and I'd have you focus on making it as special as possible for him."

Isabelle's joy at the idea of directing the Christmastide production immediately tempered, she caught the chair on the opposite side of Maeve and dragged the heavy oak seat closer to her mother and sister. It was time she face head-on the truth of Grandfather's condition.

A footman sprang into movement, but she waved him away.

Mother draped a hand over her eyes. "Moving furniture," she murmured in tones that would have suited a funeral.

Ignoring her mother, Isabelle seated herself between Maeve and her mother. "What is the cough?" Perhaps it was nothing more than a cold. Perhaps he was not so very ill, after all. The duke was indomitable. Destined to live forever.

"His Grace is suffering gout," their mother explained. "And there's something else, a problem with his heart. The doctors say that it is not beating as strongly as it ought to."

"He's suffered from the gout for years, but the heart problems are new," Maeve said quietly.

A pang struck that Isabelle had not known as much. It was another reminder of the gap that had grown between her and her family since she'd left all those years ago. Yes, she'd returned on occasion, but only periodically, and she'd not stay long before leaving to attend her work.

"His heart now fails him." Their mother drew in a shaky little breath and caught the exhale with the tips of her fingers. That was the only crack in the regal, immovable woman's demeanor.

"His heart," Isabelle repeated, trying to take it in.

Mother reached for her hands and lightly squeezed her fingertips. "That is why I wished for you to come back."

"Why didn't you tell me?" Isabelle demanded. Surely her mother knew Isabelle would have returned long before this had she known.

"Shh." Ever the duke's daughter, their mother bristled. "Your grandfather refuses to have his illness talked openly about. The Revelry, you see . . ."

Isabelle briefly shut her eyes. "Surely he doesn't think we believe the Revelry is more important than he and his health?"

"He thinks of the Revelry as his legacy," Maeve corrected. "If the news spread about just how badly he is ailing, his last house party would be affected."

It made sense.

Her family had become masters at protecting the Revelry, presenting an aura of infallibility to the world. Bad things didn't happen to them. Or that was what they wanted the world to believe. The Revelry, in particular, was always perfect.

Their mother lowered her voice. "You and Miss Mary are in the midst of . . . important . . . matters."

Work.

Her mother could not bring herself to say that particular word, but that was secondary to the fact that the countess had allowed Isabelle the freedom to pursue her dreams.

Her mother was rigid in some ways, and remarkably supportive in others.

"You still should have summoned me, Mother."

"All that matters is you are here now and that we will all play a part in seeing that this Revelry is the grandest of the affairs ever thrown by the duke. Of everything that matters to His Grace, the Revelry has always mattered most."

Nay, it mattered more than *anything* and *anyone*.

That pronouncement ushered in a pall.

It had nothing to do with a love of cheerful gatherings. His Grace's grand Revelries made the *ton* go 'round. At those events, societal matches were made, deals struck, and politicians deemed worthy . . . or not.

For Isabelle, they'd been so much more than that. Throughout her childhood, they'd meant thrilling music and joyous games. And *theater.* Glorious theater, from the yearly production featuring guests, to the very best theater troupes invited for a night. Her grandfather's Revelry had been the training ground for her theatrical dreams, a nursery for her talent.

And now she was being asked to coordinate the latest production, which would likely be the duke's last.

She had not wanted an honor like this.

"Alter your expression," Mother said curtly.

"What?"

"You appear forlorn and sad."

"I am forlorn and sad," Isabelle returned.

"We still do not show as much. No one at the Revelry must suspect that the duke is dying. Of course, they will find out, but we—his family—must hold the illusion. It's his final request."

"One would expect, as an actress, you'd be far better at dissembling," Maeve noted.

"I'm not an—" She caught the slight glimmer in her sister's eyes.

"I know," Maeve said. "I was teasing."

Maeve had always been the one to add levity to tense family moments, even as a small girl. Even now, with the revelation of their grandfather's impending demise. And yet . . . "Surely this ought to be a time of solemnity," Isabelle said in a low voice. "It is hardly a time for lightness." Or house parties. Or plays.

"We will honor your grandfather's last wishes," her mother stated.

What bizarre world had Isabelle stepped into? Where there was this greatest of role reversals and *she* was talking propriety with the Countess of Thorpe? "It isn't proper. We can't put on the Revelry if Grandfather is dying upstairs."

Picking up her teacup, Maeve spoke from behind the rim. "What accounts for the grand shift in which *you* are lecturing Mother as to what should or should not be done during trying times—or any times?"

The countess again tapped four fingers. "There is no grand shift. Not really. His Grace has stated his wishes." *His final wishes.* Isabelle's heart again tugged. "We shall honor them above any adherence to the rules of Polite Society."

Had Isabelle not been studying her mother so closely, she'd have missed the sheen glossing her eyes. Her grandfather was not an affectionate father, but he had been a pillar in their lives, especially her mother's, after her husband died years ago.

"Now." The countess straightened her shoulders. "Cressie is running the Revelry, of course. And I have it on authority that she fears your grandfather will ask her to share those responsibilities with Derham."

Val, the duke's heir. "Derham?" she echoed.

Also, the lifelong friend of Isabelle's former betrothed.

"Nothing is certain," her mother added, misunderstanding the reason for Isabelle's response. "But you know my father. He is nothing if not unpredictable when it comes to both the Revelry and maintaining order over both the event and people's lives."

Isabelle shook off the memories. She hadn't seen Val in years, but from what she read in the gossip columns, he was unlikely to still be acquainted with his childhood friend. Cyrus was never one to gamble or drink to excess.

"His Grace wishes for the grandest of productions. Naturally Cressie instantly thought of you." Without looking about, Mother raised a finger.

A footman stepped forward and bowed. "Yes, my lady?"

"Inform Cressie that my daughter has agreed to take on the play."

He bowed and left, returning a moment later with a thick book.

Picking up the leather volume, Isabelle skimmed the title. *Cinderella*. She set it down. "I expected a Shakespearean play."

"You don't have much time to prepare the production. A well-known play would be easier as guests will be arriving in a fortnight and you have not much time to work." Color bloomed on the countess's cheeks. "Not 'work,' per se. This is altogether different than *work* work."

"*Work* work?" Maeve mouthed.

For the first time since Isabelle had arrived, she shared a smile with her youngest sister.

"We are certain that, given the circumstances, this is a time for revelry?" Isabelle asked, still uncertain.

"Your grandfather insists upon it." Their mother spoke as if the Oracle of Delphi had issued an edict. Or the king himself.

"I, for one, agree with the idea," Maeve volunteered. "At the end of my life, I wish for there to be laughter and song and witty stories told and shared."

When put that way, there was something to be said for the duke's decision.

Isabelle turned the pages. *Cinderella* was hardly the production she would have chosen.

"Never tell me you think you're too good for *Cinderella*?" her sister asked.

"I didn't say that." In fact . . . "I didn't say anything." She turned another page. This version of the fairy tale involved singing and dancing, hard enough to manage when directing professional actors. But amateur guests?

"Cressie assigned you a partner," her mother said. "I suspect Derham."

Just like that, the one glimmer of joy she'd felt with her role for the house party died. Her dream had never included sharing the work with someone else, even if it was her dear friend and cousin.

Isabelle jerked her head up so quickly that her muscles, stiff from days of travel, twinged. "I don't require a partner." It was bad enough being saddled with *Cinderella*, but on top of that have no creative freedom? Val was a reasonable man. She could explain her position in a way that he'd understand.

"I don't disagree with you, Isabelle," Mother said. "For *obvious* reasons."

"What obvious reasons?" her sister asked, sampling another pastry. "Because of Isabelle's work as a dramatist?"

Mother paused long enough to glare at her youngest daughter.

Unfazed, Maeve carried on. "I think it's snobbish."

Isabelle blinked slowly. Had her sister just said . . . ?

"Snobbish," Maeve repeated, with a firm little nod.

"Me?"

"Mother, too. But in this moment, I'm speaking about you."

Isabelle bristled. "That's hardly fair." She'd long preferred the company of those outside the ranks of nobility, and never cared about fine dresses and fripperies, so this was the first time that particular charge had been leveled at her. "I'm not *snobbish*."

"Why? Because you dress like a poor relation?"

Isabelle glanced down at her floral print dress. Her finest dress.

"And keep company with people outside the peerage?"

Sometime during Isabelle's extended absence, her sister had grown up . . . and honed a razor-sharp intelligence. For the first time in her life, Isabelle found herself looking to the most unexpected person for support.

Mother shook her head. "Maeve will speak her mind, no matter what I say." With a slight lift of her shoulders, the countess resumed sipping her tea.

"You didn't openly bash *Cinderella*, but I'd wager my dowry that you thought it," her sister said with her usual—nay, her even sharper—bluntness. She snorted. "Shakespeare! Do you really believe Grandfather wants some melancholy Dane pacing around moaning about his dead father."

Isabelle narrowed her eyes but held her tongue.

Maeve dusted her palms together, sending sugar remnants falling to her dish. "If the sole reason you believe you're not pompous is because you might mingle with the royals but choose people of another station, then you're more aware of station differences than you've likely acknowledged to yourself."

That confounding logic somehow made sense . . . and stung.

"I would argue that not being aware of those distinctions and divides in rank means one is simply not acknowledging a wrong," Isabelle challenged.

"Fair enough, but that does not change the fact that you are pompous where the theater is concerned." Maeve lifted her nose in the air. *"I must work alone."*

A shockingly good impersonation of Isabelle's own voice.

"I cannot work with someone . . . with anyone," Maeve went on. *"I know theater. I know drama. Other people don't. This is my time to shine. Mine."*

Well. That was quite the set-down by her sister.

Isabelle might have been impressed by her sister's performance if she weren't the recipient of that mimicry. As it was, she felt stung to the bone.

Wonder of wonder, even their reserved mother was hiding a smile. Isabelle looked squarely at the countess. "Are you laughing?"

"Laughing would be gauche, Isabelle," the countess said, with another little shake of her head. "Now, returning to a matter of import . . . as Derham is the future duke, my father has made it clear that we are not one to question whatever involvement he has with the Revelry." She paused. "In fact, we're not one to question him at all."

She rolled her eyes. "This is *Val.* We were friends since . . ." At her Mother's sharp look, Isabelle's words trailed of. "Do not question him," Isabelle muttered to herself. Despite her sister's low opinion of her, Isabelle was well aware that society was unfairly divided by birthright and blood, things wholly out of a person's control.

No, she didn't give a jot about titles or wealth or power.

Unlike Cyrus . . .

She started. Why had she thought of him again? With all the years between them, she'd done a stellar job of schooling herself not to think of him. Until now.

While her mother prattled on with directives as to how her daughters should behave around the duke's heir, Isabelle's mind wandered.

It had to be because she was back in Greystoke Manor, the place where she first met Cyrus. She'd managed to keep his ghost firmly in the past, but it was natural that those memories should erupt now.

There were times when he, and the future they might have known together, refused to stay buried. Times when she wondered what life might have been like if she'd had him to share her triumphs and frustrations and—

Stop.

Her mother recoiled. "Did you just order me to stop speaking?" The countess pressed a hand to her breast in affront.

"No," Isabelle said quickly.

Maeve giggled. "Oh, how I've missed you. Lately, I have been the only one to earn Mother's displeasure."

Isabelle smiled faintly. "I'm very happy to help."

The countess clapped her hands. "Enough. Do behave," she commanded, as if her daughters were girls of three, and not twenty-three and thirty-three years of age. "Cressie asked that I give you this." Reaching into the pocket of her sapphire skirts, she withdrew an official-looking scrap of ivory stamped with her cousin's seal. "The music room has been designated for your use in the next week."

"Splendid," Isabelle said, accepting the note. At least the chamber was suitable for the task assigned to her. Spacious, with glorious acoustics, the duke's music room was grander than most of the formal theaters.

Maeve raised an eyebrow. "Might I suggest that you bathe and change into less dirty and dusty garments?"

The countess gasped. "We do not speak of such matters."

"I do," Maeve said cheerfully.

Isabelle glanced down at her serviceable cambric. "What is wrong with my garments?"

"What isn't wrong with them is the better question," her sister said under her breath.

Hmph. Yes, well, she'd come to develop an appreciation for serviceable garments. And given that she'd be working during The Revelry, she intended to be comfortable doing so.

"Run along, Isabelle. I have matters to discuss with your sister," their mother said.

Maeve turned a desperate gaze Isabelle's way.

"I'm sorry," she mouthed to her younger sibling, before making her exit.

"It seems that we should have a conversation about

common courtesy," the countess was saying to Maeve in grim tones.

As she left her sister to the countess's latest lesson on propriety, Isabelle found herself smiling.

She'd been gone for years, but it seemed little had changed. There was an unexpected comfort to be found in that constancy.

Sometime later, after she'd sent around a request to speak with Derham, Isabelle headed above stairs to quickly bathe and change into new garments, before heading for their meeting. Humming the cheerful tune of "Nos Galan" under her breath, Isabelle made her way down the stairs, focused on the matter at hand—just what she intended to say to her cousin Val. She had to convince him to let her run the production alone.

Determination fueled her steps. She needed to see to this herself. Nay, she *wanted* to. As a woman in her propriety-driven family, she'd never been given the responsibility over a single production during The Revelry. But in the years she'd been gone, Isabelle had dedicated herself to writing original plays and studying all of the most famed ones. As such, she *knew* theater. She knew drama. To Isabelle, the pantomime held at the Revelry wasn't simply a diversion. Surely, she could put in an appeal to Cressie. Her cousin, as a fellow woman, could relate to Isabelle's desire for this control.

"Snobbish," she muttered, cradling the leather volume of *Cinderella* against her chest. She wasn't snobbish.

Why, there wasn't anything wrong with her wishing to oversee the task herself.

Isabelle slowed. Was there? She paused beside a painting in a gilded frame depicting the rolling emerald hills of the duke's estate. Or . . . she hadn't thought there was anything wrong with her wish to single-handedly direct the performance. And she wouldn't have, had it not been for Maeve. Maeve, who'd also correctly pointed out the unforgivable length of time that had lapsed since Isabelle had come 'round to visit her family.

But that was not what this visit was about. That was not what the Revelry, or any of it, was about.

Rather, it was about coming together as the duke wished so that he might enjoy the grand event he so loved. The one he was famous for hosting, that all members of Polite Society clamored for an invitation.

She'd simply been looking at the assignment given her in the incorrect light: her own. Maeve was right. She would accept whatever arrangements Derham had made because this was about her grandfather, not about her.

Springing into movement, Isabelle resumed her march to the duke's music room. This time, a different purpose fueled her steps.

When she at last reached the music room, mentally preparing a neat list on the way, she was feeling excited again. The door hung ajar, and she let herself in.

Derham stood with his back to her at the window, his hands clasped behind him as he stared out.

He was taller than she recalled and broader of shoulder, hardly the boy she'd ofttimes played with during her visits to her grandfather's estate.

"Hello," she called in greeting. "It is so lovely to see you. I confess I felt some trepidation at finding I'd been assigned a partner until I found out it was," Isabelle stopped in her tracks. *"You."*

He turned.

The earth ceased moving, and she was left there, floundering, trying to find unsteady legs through it.

Her mother . . . had been wrong. So very wrong about whom Cressie had paired Isabelle with. It wasn't *him,* as in Val, her cousin. This was an altogether different *him.* A man she'd never expected to see again . . . and never here. Never like this.

She blinked. Perhaps she was merely imagining him.

After all, her journey had been long, and given the difficulty with the team, the snoring passengers aboard the mail coach, and the lack of sleep, exhaustion was surely to blame.

When the sight of him remained, she jammed the heel of one palm against her eyes and rubbed it back and forth hard enough that little flecks danced before her vision.

When her eyes cleared, she looked again at the man across from her.

He was still broad of shoulders and slim of waist, but he looked more muscular, and there were slight streaks of silver at his temples. They didn't age him. They lent him a distinguished air, as if he'd ever needed it.

Yet he had changed. He used to have an eager look in his eyes, and his clothes had been those of a stablemaster's son, not that she cared for such things.

Now?

Even to her eyes, his coat was tailored to perfection.

And the space between them did little to diminish the cynical glint in eyes that had once been filled with warmth.

They were a stranger's eyes.

But then, that was what he was now. Ten years apart would do that. As would a severed betrothal.

For the first time in all the years she'd ever known Cyrus Hill, the unthinkable happened: the laconic man given to careful silences spoke first.

"Lovely to see me, is it, Isabelle?"

Chapter Three

Yellow had always been Isabelle's favorite color. From her parasols to her bonnets, to her day dresses and ball gowns, those articles were often varying shades of that bright hue.

It was an odd detail to recall, particularly given that this was the first time Cyrus had seen his former fiancée since she'd visited his office years ago, and ended his hope for a future with her. Or with any other woman, for that matter.

Mayhap because it was easier to focus on those simple likes than anything deeper.

Or mayhap it was a reminiscence prompted by the somber dress sported by this stranger before him.

Her grey wool skirts were dreary and coarse and different in every way from the vibrant silk gowns she'd once donned. Those most exquisite of garments which had been so very different than the more modest ones, he, a stablemaster's son, had worn.

And yet, her dress did nothing to detract from her graceful beauty. It never could.

Time had changed her. Closer to girl than woman when she'd broken it off, now she had a greater curve to her hip, a fullness to her breasts . . .

And yet, those changes . . . they also marked the passage of time. Years apart.

"Forgive me," Isabelle said quietly. "I thought you were another."

Tension whipped through him as she gave all her attention to the expansive music room.

And he was thankful for it.

I thought you were another.

It was only too likely that she'd given her heart to some other bastard. Likely a gentleman of her rank and class, far more deserving of her than Cyrus ever could have been. A red-hot sentiment dangerously close to jealousy wound through him.

She was quieter than he recalled. More measured with her words. Or was it the shock of seeing him? And here, of all places, this gathering that he'd long been barred from?

But then, that didn't make sense either.

Shock wasn't the same as indifference or apathy. Shock would imply that the lady felt something for him. And the woman who'd walked out of his offices and out of his life almost ten years ago to the date wasn't one who'd carry any sentiments for him.

Watching as she strolled across the room, clearly pretending he wasn't there, he found himself caught in a wave of sadness. They'd been so very close to twining their lives that he would have . . .

Had she not broken it off.

Had she not severed all connections between them.

Had you not put your work first.

He fisted his hands.

He'd done that work for *them*. But that was neither here nor there. He made himself stroll around before her and held her gaze. "Who would imagine we might meet again? And"—he swept his arms wide—"here, of all places." He had so desperately longed to be invited to the Revelry, back when he was a young man. Now he could buy and sell half the men who would walk in the door.

He let his arms fall. "Who was it you planned to meet here, Lady Isabelle?" It was a bold question that a mere man of affairs had no place putting to a duke's granddaughter. She'd never been the pompous lady who thought him undeserving because of his station. It had been just one of the reasons he'd so loved her.

Which brought to mind another thought: "Or is there another name by which I should address you now?"

"No, no," she said, which answered nothing, because she could—*should*—have married a titled man. "I planned to meet Derham here," she continued. "I didn't know you were here. I came here in the hopes of—" She stopped herself midsentence.

A pretty blush blossomed on her cheeks.

Cyrus nodded at the books in her arms. "Securing a different partner?" he supplied for her. Cyrus himself had tried—and failed—to get Derham to agree to a different assignment for him.

She nodded. "Yes." That direct honesty landed like an unexpected fist to the gut. "No," she hastily corrected.

In fairness, when Derham had hurled the task at him and then taken his leave, Cyrus had not wanted it either. It had taken him the journey from London to the Revelry to bring himself around to the idea of working in close quarters with the woman who'd ended their betrothal.

In a bid for feigned nonchalance, Cyrus rested his hip along the side of the pianoforte. "I daresay it can't be both."

She adjusted that burden she cradled. "Actually, it can be. Initially, I sought a modification to my assignment."

Initially.

That particular word gave him pause.

He scoffed internally. *You're making more of that throwaway word than there is.*

Without meeting his eyes, Isabelle looked about the room. Had she been any other, he'd have believed her wandering gaze to be an evasive attempt to avoid contact with him. But he knew her . . . or he had known her. She wasn't one who'd choose the coward's way out of even an awkward exchange.

"I always wanted to be in charge of a production at

the Revelry," she said, a smile quirking her lips. "I can scarcely believe it's happened. I never thought that you . . . that you would be . . ."

Excitement drove her.

An excitement she'd hoped to share with another.

It didn't matter that there was some other man. She'd chosen to leave him, and they'd both gotten on with their lives. And yet, even knowing that as he did, he couldn't keep the question back. "Who were you hoping to find yourself paired with, Isabelle?"

She whipped her attention back to him, a hint that she'd forgotten he was even in the room. It stung as much as her bid to be rid of him and paired with another.

"No one," she answered, shifting her books. "I wanted the freedom to make the decisions in terms of casting and direction and the performance by myself." As she spoke, she transformed back into the animated, vivacious girl who'd ensnared him. Her eyes danced with the same eager excitement that always had been there when she talked of the theater. "You see, I've always wanted the responsibility of overseeing the Revelry performance, always, from the time I was a girl."

So . . . there wasn't another partner whose company she craved. He'd rail at himself later for the giddy feeling in his chest. Now, however, he just let himself feel that buoyant lightness.

"It was a task you always wanted," he murmured, more to himself, the memory pulled easily from a vault of reminiscences. Had she found all the other things she desired? The question was there on his tongue. Was her life she now lived the one she'd set out in search of?

She stayed silent, and they were restored once again to the awkward, stilted pair they'd been upon her arrival in the duke's music room.

Isabelle cleared her throat. "My sister has pointed out the benefits of working with you."

One eyebrow shot up.

"Not *you* you, per se, but the person assigned to the role that you now find yourself in, of course."

"Of course," he echoed.

Another awkward pause fell between them.

As far as he remembered, there'd never been anything awkward between them. There'd only ever been an ease, a remarkable one given their different births.

He found himself . . . mourning that change.

Maudlin. You've become maudlin in your damned age.

"I should go," she murmured.

Yes, she should. He should. Both of them should retreat in opposite directions.

"What benefits did your sister speak of?" he asked as she made to go.

That question brought her back around. "Perspective."

"Perspective?" he echoed. "Mine?"

In *theater*? He didn't have one.

Isabelle nodded. "She didn't say it quite like that." Her cheeks, slightly fuller than they used to be, and even more lovely, pinkened. "And as I said, she didn't speak of you. Of course you have no interest."

Rather to his surprise, he felt a prickle of intrigue. When was the last time he'd been challenged . . . by anything? His work was fascinating, but he understood it. He knew numbers, the way they moved across a balance sheet, better than virtually any man in the kingdom.

But theater?

He knew nothing.

"She pointed out that there was an arrogance to my wishing to work alone, and that a partner might bring an important perspective to the casting and production," Isabelle said, almost under her breath.

Her sister was right—but not when he was the partner in question. Another might provide that perspective.

"Alas, you've found yourself paired with one who'll

make a liar of your sister," he said matter-of-factly. "Now, if the production involved guests performing mathematical computations and the balancing of ledgers? You'd find yourself with a valuable asset."

She laughed. The same exuberant, snorting expression of mirth that had horrified her mother and endlessly captivated him.

This moment proved no exception.

Something moved in his chest. Cyrus had not realized just how very much he'd missed Isabelle's laughter and her smile. Her mirth faded until all that remained were brightly colored cheeks and a small grin. "Yes, well, I do believe you do yourself a disservice."

"I've never been one to search for compliments," he said simply. "I know my strengths, just as I know my weakness."

Her. She'd once been his greatest weakness. It would seem all these years later, with his hungering for her smile and laughter, she still was.

The air crackled and hummed as they gazed at each other.

"I really should go," she murmured for a second time, breaking that impasse.

This time, he'd not stop her.

Even though you want to. Even as you're remembering all too clearly what her smile has done to you . . . and for you. Clasping his hands behind him, Cyrus rocked on his heels. "Certainly."

Except she lingered.

Was it a desire to be with him? The question was so foolish as to give life to his silent musings. And it was promptly quashed by her next words.

"A great deal goes into a production, Cyrus. There are roles to assign, and the decision of whether or not to have some form of setting, and then one must choreograph the movements of each actor."

The list aroused a familiar appreciation for the lady.

When any other nobleman's daughter would have been content to live a pampered existence, Isabelle thrilled at creating words and crafting productions. She wasn't like the rest.

She drew in a deep breath. "I need someone to help me with those details. As such, we'll have to work together . . . and *closely.*" She emphasized that very last word.

Did she seek to deter him from partnering with her? It was an excuse he'd have gladly taken, and had been searching for ever since Derham had revealed Cyrus's expected role in the Revelry. Of course, he wanted nothing to do with the theater. With a production. With a subject of which he knew nothing.

She eyed him warily. "Is this something you are willing to do?" She paused. "That you . . . want to do?" she added.

Even just fifteen minutes ago, his answer would have been an emphatic *no.*

Now he heard himself answer with surprise. "I am willing."

Only because she wished to be rid of him, he thought. Male pride accounted for this sudden desire to work with her. He may not know anything of theater, but surely he could manage actors and stage settings. Sets? He didn't even know what that was. Sons of stablemaster's didn't attend the theater. Even when he'd been living in the high-end of London, there'd always been work . . . and more work. Certainly no time for visits to Covent Garden.

All he knew was, he'd never failed at any task he'd undertaken—other than, of course, to make her love him forever.

He tried to make . . . something out of the indecipherable emotion in her dark brown eyes.

"Very well." There was an almost resigned quality to her agreement. "We'll have to sit down and discuss the details of our assignment." Isabelle held his stare. "Shall we say tomorrow morning at six o'clock?"

Six o'clock. The hour he'd long dedicated to reviewing his clients' ledgers. She knew as much.

The stubborn minx.

He inclined his head. "I would not miss it for the world, my lady."

Her eyebrows crept up the minutest fraction, and it was all he could do to suppress a smile.

Isabelle immediately found her footing. "Six o'clock it is, then. We shall meet here and go over the performance details."

This time, she didn't bother with goodbyes. Her book clutched close, she started for the door.

"Isabelle?"

She slowed her stride and glanced back.

"Your sister? She was wrong. There was nothing arrogant or wrong in your desiring to work alone. You shouldn't feel shame for wishing to have control of something that you are so very good at."

With not so much as an acknowledgment that she'd heard him, Isabelle did what had always come altogether too easily where he was concerned—she left.

Chapter Four

That night, sleep proved a fickle, miserable mistress for Isabelle.

Which, given her long, uncomfortable ride through snow-covered, bumpy terrain, made little sense.

And yet, since she'd climbed into the enormous four-poster bed, her mind had refused to comply with her body's need for rest.

With a sigh, she fell back, and folding her hands, she laid them atop her stomach and stared overhead.

It was Cyrus. Cyrus, whom she'd now be meeting in . . . She stole another look at the clock. Five hours.

Or rather, it was those last words Cyrus had called when she'd been leaving.

There was nothing arrogant or wrong in your desiring to work alone. You shouldn't feel shame for wishing to have control of something you are so very good at.

Nay, it was certainly not him. This broader, slightly graying gentleman. After all, she'd managed to put the painful memories of him, the loss of him, to rest.

It was only this newest, fresh encounter that proved vexing.

She lived in a world where women who wished to work with words were met with resistance from Society. Women weren't expected to dream of anything but marriage and babes. And if they didn't? Well, those women were expected to adopt a false name, a man's name, so that they might have their work taken seriously.

Giving up on sleep, she rolled onto her side and stared at the fire crackling in the hearth.

So . . . why had he said what he had?

Because he always was only supportive of your vision and your dream. When your family was at best indulgent and the rest of the world horrified, Cyrus urged you to do that which brought you joy.

And in a world where men tended to see women only as potential mates and then spouses or mothers, the relationship she'd had with Cyrus had been a gift.

One that you let go.

Letting out a small growl of frustration, she rolled back over and thumped her fist against her pillow.

"I did not let him go," she muttered. He'd found a mistress, one whom he'd loved more and had had an even greater loyalty to—his business. She'd grown fed up with playing second fiddle to that true love.

She'd also gotten tired of waiting for a man who'd grown increasingly distant to settle upon a wedding date.

There'd be no sleep this night.

Giving up on her hope of any real rest, Isabelle tossed off her blankets.

Swinging her legs over the side of the bed, she jumped down.

The cool of the hardwood floor penetrated her feet. Shivering, she hurried to the armoire and drew the painted panel doors open. One of the maids assigned to her had neatly pressed and hung her serviceable dresses. Living away from her family, with her friend and fellow writer, she'd largely seen to the task herself these past years. All tasks, in fact. And having lived with servants always underfoot attempting to anticipate her needs and tidying every aspect of her existence, she'd welcomed every freedom, including that of controlling the placement of her dresses.

She stilled, her fingers lingering on a puffed sleeve.

"You deserve servants."

"I don't care about having servants, Cyrus. We don't require them."

Pacing at the foot of the picnic blanket, he released a sound of frustration. "But you will *care when you don't have those luxuries, Isabelle. As a stablemaster's son, I can promise you that."*

She gave her head a hard shake and dislodged those echoes of their past. She'd wager the successful and purportedly ruthless businessman now employed enough servants to rival most noble families. Yes, by the fine quality of his fine wool garments and lawn shirt with a diamond pin in his cravat, he'd managed to acquire extraordinary wealth.

She would, however, be lying if she said he'd not been a gloriously dashing specimen in the music room, in his impeccable midnight-black jacket and trousers. Those pants had hugged heavily muscled thighs, his long, powerful limbs so very unlike the less-sculpted figures of—

Enough.

Bypassing both day dresses and gowns, she searched through article after article hanging from the pegs. "Waxing on about him and his physique," she said under her breath. She flipped to the next gown, annoyed with herself for noticing, and appreciating, him. And yet, she'd noticed his muscled frame, which hardly fit with the businessman who buried himself away in his offices and devoted himself wholly to his work. She continued turning dress after dress. "Of course, it makes sense that you would notice," she said in the quiet. The hearth crackled and hissed its agreement. He was a handsome figure, and why should she fail to appreciate this more mature version of the younger man he'd been?

Isabelle briefly froze and stared at the collection of garments within the armoire, those articles fluttering softly and then stilling.

For, ultimately, she knew she lied to herself.

This appreciation of Cyrus all these years later was far

more than an afterthought. Rather, her heart had pounded with the same intensity it always had at his nearness.

There'd not been the customary smile on his perfectly formed mouth. The brief grin he had worn had contained only animus and cynicism. Neither of which, however, had detracted from her awareness of him as a man.

Grabbing her ancient and favorite cotton wrapper buried at the far back, she drew the garment on, belting it at the waist.

But it hadn't been only the sight of him that accounted for her inability to think of anything but him—it had been those blasted words. Those encouraging, supportive words he'd used to urge her to feel no shame in wishing for control of the production.

And that realization scared her most of all.

For had she simply had a physical response to his nearness, she could have dismissed it as an irrelevant appreciation.

Collecting her notebook and pencils, she quit her rooms.

Every other gold sconce had been left lit. The tall white candles bathed the hall in a bright light that might have confused one into thinking it was twelve o'clock in the afternoon and not the early-morn hour.

Isabelle wound her way through the long halls and down the even longer staircases to the main level.

In fairness, sleep had never been much of a friend to her. She'd always struggled to keep the words from flowing through her brain.

Cyrus used to tease that all the stories she had to tell rolled through her mind, along with a longing for more time in which to create those plays. When she'd left one life for another, as a dramatist, Cyrus's words had stayed with her.

She'd stopped lamenting her body's inability to find true rest and instead used that time productively. In a way that fed her creative soul, and drove off the frustration, and left her welcoming the quiet when she could write without interruption from the daily world. In those earliest days, after she'd broken it off with Cyrus, her writing had been her greatest escape. A welcome relief. A distraction.

Oh, she'd cried tears, and endlessly. Great, big, ugly tears. The kind that had soaked her pages, and smudged her ink, and made her switch to charcoal pencils.

Only to then smudge that, too.

Until, one day, she'd just . . . stopped. Not because the pain of losing him and the dream she'd carried for them had died, but because she'd learned that it was all right to live with pain and to use it. And in that, she'd found peace.

Until this afternoon, that was.

Until she'd entered the music room and found Cyrus Hill, a ghost from her past fully resurrected and more dashing than he'd been.

Isabelle reached the music room. Balancing her belongings in the crook of her opposite arm, she let herself in.

The well-oiled hinges gave without so much as a squeak, and as she stepped in and pushed the panel shut behind her, the loud hum of the night's quiet served as her only company.

Closing her eyes, she breathed in deep and long.

She was home.

In this grand music room that she'd yearned to transform with a production of her own. And though *Cinderella* was hardly original, and certainly not a play she had created, it would be close enough.

Opening her eyes, Isabelle made to take a step forward—and froze.

She'd been wrong.

The night's quiet wasn't her only company.

Her heart did a funny little jump.

For he really was . . . everywhere.

But then, the nighttime hours had long been a friend to Cyrus, as well.

It was why he'd been such an expert at giving her guidance on embracing her struggle to sleep and make it work for her.

Cyrus, with his head bent and his shoulders forward, had converted the pianoforte into a provisional workstation. Ledgers sat stacked in a neat pile. A silver inkpot with a candlestick in the middle sat at the center of his assembled work.

Through the heavy quiet, her ears picked up the faintest sound that had previously escaped her.

The tip of his pen striking the surface of whatever ledger he worked on had the same musical quality of a composer penning a song.

Clickety-click-clickety-click-click-clickety-click-click.

For a moment, she considered backing silently away, drawing the door open a crack, and slipping out.

But they were required to work together, and that partnership made it so that she had no other choice but to be with him.

So why did it feel as though she fed herself another fib? Why did it feel as though she still *wanted* to be here?

Which was . . . preposterous. She'd not seen him in a lifetime. They were really nothing more than strangers with a shared past. And that past was so very long ago.

In the end, he made the decision for her.

"Unable to sleep?" His quiet query echoed throughout the expansive room.

In fact, with his head still down and writing away as he was, she might have imagined he'd even spoken.

But then he looked up briefly before resuming his task.

Reflexively, she gripped her supplies protectively closer, wanting to shield secrets that he'd always had an uncanny ability to ferret out. "I was planning to work," she offered evasively. Somehow, that acknowledgment felt far safer than the intimate details he'd been privy to long ago.

He didn't say anything.

She should go. With his silence, he gave no outward indication that he wanted her here.

In fact, there were so many reasons she should leave. She had to work. He *was* working.

And the greatest reason of all: should someone come by and discover them alone together—her in her nightclothes and he in his shirtsleeves, no less—that sighting would be ruinous.

So why did she stay, then?

Why did she continue silently forward, getting closer to him? Closer, when the room was enormous and there was space enough for them both? She stopped alongside the magnificent instrument filled with his books. As he worked, she studied him and his things.

Mayhap he'd chosen this room because of the slight connection to her?

As soon as the preposterous thought entered, she shoved it back. Of course it wasn't because of her. For so very long, nothing where Cyrus was concerned had been about Isabelle. It was one of the reasons she'd had to end it. He'd changed. And those changes had impacted the relationship they had shared.

"It is . . . nothing short of a peculiar place for you to have made your nighttime office," she murmured.

He grunted. "Is it, though?"

"Oh, yes. I trust there are any number of places far better suited to lay out your books and keep your numbers."

"It isn't *just* keeping 'my numbers,'" he groused under his breath, very much the endearing young man who'd insisted that the work he did was a fascinating art of its own. "I'm finalizing details of—" He stopped and then resumed writing, scratching several numbers on his page.

Though she'd teased him, she'd long been in awe of his ability to make anything out of those numbers that so confounded her.

Isabelle rested her books alongside one of his piles.

Cyrus stiffened, his shoulders tensing under the stark white lawn shirt he wore.

"Why not the library, Cyrus?" She didn't even bother with formality. They were both grown people tasked with working together. They could certainly use each other's given names. "I trust there are tables aplenty to set yourself up at."

This time, he slowly closed his book and lifted his head, giving her his complete attention. "There were several guests there."

"The duke's office?" she shot back.

He scoffed. "A man doesn't infringe upon another man's offices."

A smile hovered on her lips. "Ah, it is a code of ethics among businessmen, then?"

He bristled. "Is that so very hard to believe?"

"Not at all." It was just a reminder of the many aspects of his life that were foreign to her. Which hadn't always been the case.

Refusing to give in to melancholy, she rested her palms on the smooth mahogany surface of the pianoforte. "One of the many parlors, then?"

"The windows and lighting are far better here," he said, motioning to the floor-to-ceiling crystal panes at his back. As if to help him prove his very point, the clouds outside shifted, and the full moon radiated a bright white light, illuminating the room.

Hmph. Isabelle sank back on her heels. "Never tell me the duke failed to provide a desk and candles in your rooms?"

Cyrus hesitated and then gave his head the slightest shake, nearly imperceptible if she hadn't been watching him so closely. And yet, she was. She'd always been enthralled by him.

"I don't believe in working where I rest," he finally said.

What was there to say to that cogent reasoning?

Picking up his pen, he meticulously dipped the tip in his

inkpot, pinged the excess alongside the glass, and made several notes. He did so several times before stopping and looking up once more.

"You preferred drama without musical elements." He paused. "I believe music is the bane of your existence."

Her chest tightened. Those words, repeated verbatim as she had uttered them a lifetime ago, flowed freely from Cyrus's tongue. He recalled so perfectly the details she'd shared. Why must he speak so freely about those parts he knew of her? Details her own family didn't know. They'd supported her in her dream, but neither had they delved and wished to know about her passion. Not as Cyrus had.

"I've come to appreciate that I was wrong in my initial assessments," she said, her voice husky with emotion. "I learned that it was less that I disliked music and more that I disliked the expectation that I, a duke's granddaughter, be required to play it."

Cyrus slowly stood, giving up his place at the head of that instrument, and she drifted closer, filling the void he'd left.

His gaze worked a path over her face, and she made herself absolutely motionless in the hope that he couldn't see her longing for what might have been. "You learned that in our . . ." *Time apart.* The words hung there, not needing to be spoken. "Your studies?" he finished.

"I did. My mentor insisted I sit at a pianoforte, and he placed music out for me to perform."

He chuckled. "I expect that went . . . as well as your usual concerts."

The disappointment had been keen when Bernd Wilhelm, the great dramatist, novelist, poet, and short-story writer, had insisted that she and Mary spend time working with music.

She laughed with Cyrus. "Worse." The only thing that had made those concerts her mother had insisted she perform alongside her sisters less miserable was Cyrus's presence through them. The beloved stablemaster's equally beloved son had always been in attendance, and she'd found joy just from his being there through those horrid events. "I was this close to leaving." She held her thumb and forefinger close together.

"What made you stay?"

"He ripped up the music."

Cyrus's brow wrinkled. "He . . . ripped it up?"

"Well, several pages of music." She warmed to her telling. "Into hundreds of tiny pieces, and he sprinkled them at the foot of the pianoforte. Then he insisted I do the same."

"Your mother would have been horrified."

She laughed again. "And knowing as much made it all the sweeter. I tore and tore until there was nothing left. Until I couldn't be asked to play from those sheets then or ever again." Isabelle depressed a single key. "Then I learned that was the whole point of Bernd Wilhelm's lesson." She brought her palms into position over the keyboard. "He pointed out that one shouldn't be required to love or even use music in one's performance and should only do so if one feels creatively compelled." Laying claim to the bench he'd vacated, Isabelle stroked the keys, bringing the instrument alive. "And then when I considered music in that way, it made me appreciate it as I hadn't ever before."

"What is it?" There was an ardency to that question as she played.

"'The Beggar's Opera,'" she murmured. The first musical piece she'd come to appreciate. Closing her eyes, she let her fingers fly over the keys.

Can love be controlled by advice?
Can madness and reason agree?
O Dearest, who'd ever be wise
If madness be loving of thee?
Let sages pretend to despise . . .

Isabelle played all the way through the song. When she finished, the strains hovered in the air. Her skin tingled, and she glanced up.

Her mouth went dry.

At some point, Cyrus had drifted closer to her shoulder, hovering beside her. So close that her shoulder brushed his muscled thigh. His was a working man's body, sculpted and powerful and so gloriously masculine.

She came slowly to her feet, expecting he'd retreat. That he'd place some distance that was safe between them.

Only, had there ever been a safe distance where they were concerned?

His heavy, thick, black lashes swept low, hiding those eyes that had long mesmerized her. Ones she had so missed.

And perhaps it was the magic of the witching hour, or the awareness strummed to life by playing that ballad, but she drifted close.

His breath hitched noisily.

Or was that her own?

Everything was confused. Jumbled and twisted.

It was why, as he lowered his head to hers, she leaned up and twined her fingers about his nape, dragging him closer still, and kissed him.

Her body came alive in ways it hadn't in more years than she could remember. Heat, glorious heat, seared her from the inside out as she pressed herself against him.

Cyrus groaned, and she slipped her tongue inside his mouth to tangle with his.

There was a sense of coming home in this embrace.

He still had the deliciously sweet taste of vanilla. It filled Isabelle's senses, driving her wilder still.

His hands were on her. All over. He stroked those long fingers down her waist to the curve of her hip and around, sculpting her buttocks with his palms.

She whimpered as all the energy left her limbs, leaving her weak in his arms.

But he was there to catch her, guiding her down.

Her buttocks collided with the keyboard, sending off a discordant tune that played in perfect harmony to the tumult within her. The coldness of the keys penetrated the thin cotton fabric of her night shift and wrapper.

Cyrus brought his hand up and lightly cupped the side of her neck, angling her head back to better receive his kiss. Their mouths never broke contact.

His lips came down hard over hers. Again and again.

Over and over.

She panted against his mouth. How had she let herself forget this magic? The bliss of his touch and kiss?

Because it had been easier . . .

Not wanting reality and the past and all that was logical to intrude on this brief moment of madness, Isabelle let her legs fall open.

Cyrus stepped between them, rucking up the fabric of her wrapper and shift. His fingers sank into the flesh of her thighs, and she keened his name between each kiss.

A franticness grew between them as their tongues thrust and parried.

Of their own volition, Isabelle's hips began to move, arching in time to that wicked rhythm.

All the while, each movement of their bodies sent up an erotic medley, a bold concert that blended with the steady beat of her pulse in her ears.

And in the end, it wasn't the wild music that brought the moment of madness to a screeching, agonizing end.

Thwack. Thwack-thwack.

Cyrus jumped back as if her kiss had burned in the worst way.

Their chests rose and fell heavily, as in rhythm as they'd been moments ago, through their embrace.

And she was glad, a moment later, when Cyrus bent to retrieve the item that had broken them apart.

Her unblinking gaze caught and held on the pile of ledgers that had toppled onto the parquet floor. The irony didn't escape her in that instant. His work, those important numbers upon his pages, had come between them once more. A frantic, half-mad giggle bubbled in her throat. Those fallen books served as the reminder she needed on the heels of his hot embrace: His love had and would always be . . . his work.

Ignoring the tremble in her legs, Isabelle pushed herself away from the pianoforte and shoved her garments back into place.

Cyrus straightened, holding his books close to him in an endearingly protective manner. A flush suffused his cheeks.

Drat. She bit the inside of her cheek. Must he be so enticing in every way?

"Isabelle . . ."

She waited for him to say something more than her name.

He cleared his throat and tried again. "Isabelle . . ."

Or rather, he failed again.

She found her voice first. "We'll begin tomorrow with the production. And . . . we shouldn't let this be awkward between us, Cyrus. We've work to do, and it was just a kiss."

Liar. It was so much more.

She curled her toes into the hardwood floor.

He inclined his head. "Indeed."

As she grabbed up her things and walked with measured steps from the room, she couldn't tamp down the inexplicable regret she felt because of that lone word he'd uttered.

Chapter Five

It was going to be awkward.

There was nothing else for it.

It was also why he, Cyrus Hill, who'd never been tardy to a meeting, appointment, church service, or any other commitment, found himself late that following morn.

Though, it really was the same morn.

After all, only a handful of hours had passed since Isabelle had entered the music room, and played her song, and embraced him, as eager and as passionate as she'd been as a girl of eighteen.

Lust burned through him.

Where in the past there'd been a timidity to her kiss, now there'd been only a wild abandon, the memory of which had robbed Cyrus of any hope of sleep.

And yet, haunted with hungering as he still was, there came another sentiment. Something darker and more insidious. Jealousy. It roared to life, sinking its vicious claws into logic and reason and sending fire rippling through his veins.

Had that abandon in her kiss come with . . . experience? Was there some other man who'd known her in every way? In a way that Cyrus selfishly and greedily craved to be the only master of knowing?

Stop it.

What did it matter if there had been another man in their

time apart? Or that he and she had kissed? They were adults. She was a mature, strong, capable woman, and he was—

"A liar," Cyrus muttered to his reflection in the bevel mirror. He was a damned liar. And an unconvincing one at that. Why, he couldn't even make himself believe his own falsehoods. Adjusting his already perfectly folded cravat, he made himself leave his rooms and set out in search of his partner.

His partner.

Apt words to describe their relationship, past and present. They'd once been partners.

And he'd imagined a world where they'd live together as just that.

As he descended the stairs toward the music room, Cyrus stopped halfway down at the sight of a woman, dressed in a cloak and bonnet, at the door. Even with her back to him, he knew who she was.

It was the bonnet.

She wore the same one she'd worn as a girl. Even in winter, she'd not been without the article. She'd always selected it to substitute for the hood of her cloak. Oh, the bonnet was ancient and aged, with a tattered feather and faded fabric, and was apparently as loved now as it had been then.

To have been that bonnet . . .

Dressed as she was, she had the look of one who was leaving. And with a large satchel hanging on her arm, mayhap she was. Mayhap she'd decided it was better, safer, if they weren't together. It would be the logical decision, one that he himself should have made. But he'd always been more of a coward, where she'd always been fiercely bold and strong. And the sight of her, as she was, in that bonnet and cloak, set his mind back to the last time he'd seen her in that article that haunted his dreams still—to the day she left.

"You're leaving," he said sharply.

Gasping, Isabelle whipped about. "Cyrus," she greeted, pressing a hand to her breast. "You startled me."

She did not, however, respond to what he'd said.

He started quickly down the steps, taking them two at a time sideways as he went.

Her eyes widened a fraction. At the pace he'd set? Yes, he'd always been measured in everything. "Are you leaving?" he demanded.

"Yes."

Just like that, his heart plummeted to his feet. "Oh."

"Well, we are."

His heart promptly jolted back into its proper place in his chest. "What?" he blurted.

"There is the matter of decorations for the room." Falling to a knee, she fished a heavy leather notebook from within her bag. "I spent the night designing a general set for the pantomime," she explained. Sinking to his haunches, he joined her on the floor. "Pantomime, as you know, is colorful and bright and merry, and as such, the room as it is now is entirely too staid. It must fit with the celebratory spirit of what my grandfather wishes."

"I *don't* know."

She glanced up. "Beg pardon?"

"It is just . . . you assume I've attended a pantomime. I've not." They'd never attended a show together. Why hadn't they? How many other things should they have done together and hadn't? Pushing back those maudlin sentiments, he added, "I fear I'll be of little use to you in any of this." His neck heated as he made that humbling—albeit *true*—admission.

Her eyes softened. "You don't need to be an expert on any of it. I'll explain it to you as we go." With that, she sailed to her feet.

A servant whom Cyrus hadn't detected waiting in the wings came forward with Cyrus's cloak draped over his arm. Another young footman joined them with his hat.

"I took the liberty of having your things called for," Isabelle explained as he shrugged into the heavy wool garment.

He smoothed his cape collars. There was a wifely quality to that act she'd seen to, and once again, regret haunted him.

"You were late," she said as a young maid came bustling over with two wooden baskets in hand. With a word of thanks, Isabelle took one from the girl and handed the other over to Cyrus.

"And . . . you are on time, as always," he murmured, eyeing the basket dangling from his fingers.

"Early."

At his look, she clarified, "I was always early. As were you." To discuss as much invited the past, and the past was something better not talked about. Not if they were to work in close quarters toward the same goal.

In the end, the family butler, Twist, drew the door open, saving Cyrus from having to respond.

A blast of sharp, cold air whipped through the foyer.

Isabelle flashed a smile. "But I see, for everything that's changed, you still despise the cold." With that, she set out through the front door, and he hastened after her.

"You presume much has changed," he pointed out.

Isabelle stole a look up at him. "Yes, you are right there," she said, and there was a sadness to her tone.

He wished he'd shut his damned mouth. Alas, he'd never had the right words. He'd never known what to say or what not to say. That, too, had remained a constant. He searched his mind for some deviation in topic. Something to erase the awkwardness.

"The pantomime," he blurted.

As they walked down the snow-covered path, their soles sinking into the previously untouched snow, Isabelle stole another glance up at him.

"You were mentioning the pantomime."

"Yes. The pantomime is usually a type of musical production. There are songs and slapstick and dancing and gags."

He repressed a shudder. In short, it sounded positively . . . horrifying.

"I saw that," she said, her breath stirring up a little cloud of white in the winter air.

"What?"

She gave him a look. "You winced."

"Hardly," he scoffed. "It was really more of a *shudder*."

Laughter spilled from her lips, fulsome and deep and husky and free of all restraint. He'd first fallen in love with her because of her laugh. Especially when he'd been responsible for it.

They reached the low stone wall surrounding her grandfather's gardens, and Isabelle nudged Cyrus lightly in the side with her elbow. "You are teasing me," she said between her guffaws.

The only thing he was more hopeless at than talking was jesting. But he'd cut off one of his own limbs before he'd admit he'd not been attempting a joke.

As they entered the gardens, Isabelle set her basket down, and Cyrus followed suit. "Luna," she said to the red-cheeked servant who approached, "His Grace leaves the conservatory o-open during his parties. Why d-don't you take shelter from the c-cold in there, and I shall c-call you when I r-require help?"

"Y-yes, m-my lady," the girl stammered between chattering teeth and then rushed off.

The lords and ladies he'd had business dealings with had barely noticed the servants hovering in the wings, waiting for a master or mistress to call out an order. Isabelle, however, always treated them as equals.

Just as she'd treated Cyrus. As the stablemaster's son,

who'd so often been overlooked by his betters, he'd not known what to make of it, and he'd fallen more than a little in love with her for simply seeing him.

That was until he'd discovered just how remarkable and witty and clever and kind she was in every way.

After the maid had gone, Isabelle turned back. "Pantomime is o-often a f-fairy tale," she went on, as if there'd been no break in their previous discussion. "Often, the audience will sing and take p-part, which is wh-why it is perfect for my grandfather's famous Reverly." She sighed, and her breath fanned another small puff of white. "And as you are probably aware, my grandfather has insisted upon *C-Cinderella*."

He'd not been aware of that detail. However, that was secondary to the regretful little glimmer he saw in her eyes. "You don't think much of *Cinderella*," he said, rubbing his hands together in a bid to bring some warmth into his cold digits.

"I—I didn't say that." There was a defensive quality to her protestations.

"Very well. Your tone, however, did suggest you are displeased with that particular aspect of your assignment."

HE'D HEARD DISPLEASURE in her voice with the role she'd been given?

How did he hear that?

How did he know precisely what she was thinking about the assignment her grandfather . . . or cousin, or whomever, had tasked her with?

"There is n-nothing wrong with *C-Cinderella*," she said carefully, her teeth chattering.

"Ah, but the better question would be, is *Cinderella* right?"

He'd always been philosophical. It was why they'd talked until the morning sky gave way to night before realizing all the hours that had passed. She missed that. Even in her time with Mary and the instructors they'd welcomed in, she'd not been challenged in that same way.

"It is the performance my family wishes."

"That isn't an answer, Isabelle."

Wind gusted, tossing the hem of her cloak against his and tugging at her bonnet. The bright ribbons whipped wildly, coming loose. She shot a hand up to keep the beloved article in place.

When the wind had settled, Cyrus reached under her chin and retied those long satin strings. As he did, he said, "Given that you are the one responsible for directing the production, it matters less what your family might want and more what *you* wish." His hands lingered a moment before he let his arms fall to his sides.

"My sister suggested it w-was arrogant to want to do another production."

He scoffed. "Why should your wanting a choice and having an opinion be arrogant?"

Her heart remembered all over again why she'd first fallen in love with him.

Cyrus continued through the tumult. "For years, you dreamed of being entrusted with this role, Isabelle. It would be wrong if you did not have strong feelings about the performance chosen for the pantomime."

"You're making more of it than there i-is," she said. Falling to a knee beside the basket she'd carried, she withdrew pruning shears from inside. "I-it could still be mine," she said, feeling an inherent need to defend herself in the assignment she'd accepted.

Cyrus inclined his head. "Of course," he demurred, ever a gentleman. And yet . . . "But it can also be something that is *truly* yours."

Truly hers?

She opened her mouth to argue her point. Only . . . what was her point? Was he not right? And more, why did he have to be so attuned to whatever she was thinking or feeling? Words she'd not even expressed, he'd guessed. What was more . . . he'd not passed judgment on her.

"You left, Isabelle," he said softly, drifting closer.

"And?" she asked, lifting her chin at a mutinous angle, prepared to debate him on why she'd gone.

Only . . . His gloved palm came up, and he stroked her cheek, and she leaned into the soft leather, wishing the article wasn't there between them so she might feel his touch—again.

"And you did so, so that you could stretch your creative wings," he said solemnly. It would have been vastly easier had his words been accusing rather than tender. "You left so that you could write and create worlds of text. Not so that you could re-create someone else's."

"You're wrong," she said, her voice coming out sharply.

Except . . .

Was he?

"Am I?" he asked, proving their thoughts still moved in harmony.

A bitter taste of regret came to her tongue at his charge that was entirely too accurate, and that was what accounted for the vicious twinge of agony that came with it.

She had gone . . . and she'd grown, but had she? She'd written original stories and plays but ones that had never been performed anywhere. Instead, those dramatic plays existed as nothing more than ink on her notepad.

"What is this?" he murmured.

"N-nothing," she lied. Nor was it the sting of the wind that brought the slight tremble he'd noted. For Cyrus's assertion was everything.

As he stroked her cheek, tenderly, caressingly, as one who sought to refamiliarize oneself with something beloved might do, emotion formed in her throat. How she'd missed him. How she had missed his support and his encouragement to just be herself. In a world where women were expected to conform to the mold Society constructed for them, that had been a gift.

Their gazes caught before he dipped his stare lower . . . to her mouth.

Isabelle's stomach fluttered, and she ceased to feel cold. Everything inside and outside centered upon one truth: *he is going to kiss me again.*

Isabelle angled her head to receive him.

Another gust of wind whipped through the gardens, sending her bonnet sliding forward and between them, and the moment was lost.

Cyrus dropped his arm to his side, and as she pushed her bonnet back into place, she wanted to call his touch back.

"The decorations."

She looked at him.

Cyrus again rubbed his gloved palms together. "You said we have to collect some things for the pantomime."

"I did?" she asked, still dazed. Her eyes widened on the previously forgotten shears in her hand. "I—I did!"

The details of the performance and the decor she sought to collect were altogether safer and more comfortable than deep thoughts about what she truly wanted—for this show and for her life. "I thought to weave traditional holiday flowers and sprigs into the performance as they relate to the characters or s-story. H-holly being one of the plants we require." Lifting her hem, she hurried through the grounds, her boots sinking into the snow as she marched to the plant she sought. Cyrus followed closely.

She brought them to a stop beside a bush. "Are you familiar with *Cinderella*?"

"I'm not."

"It goes back to a French story about a girl named Cendrillon, which became Cinderella. She has a devoted father who dies, and she finds herself left w-with a stepmother and two stepsisters. The stepsisters are vain and selfish."

He grimaced. "Wouldn't a more suitable choice for the Christmastide season include a devoted, loving family?"

"Hush." She softened that with a smile. "You're not wrong, though." The wheels of her mind spun rapidly as his question spurred the idea of an altogether different story. One with loving stepsisters who helped the struggling—

"You're rewriting it, aren't you?"

"I . . . might be." She most definitely *was.*

"You are."

Unable to acknowledge yet again the unerring accuracy of his read on her thoughts, she returned to her telling. "As I was saying, I—I thought to incorporate flowers and plants typically associated with the holiday season into the production. Christians have long associated holly leaves with the crown of thorns worn by Jesus, and as such, they evoke thoughts of evil," her words rolled together quickly as she spoke. "But those crimson berries *also* evoke thoughts of salvation and God's love. Therefore, that more loving meaning can be conveyed and represented in a necklace of sorts for those who play the stepsisters."

He rocked back on his heels. "That is . . . brilliant."

Emboldened, and as excited as she'd not been in longer than she remembered, she gestured wildly as she spoke. "The Druids, however, believed holly branches provided one with protection against evil spirits."

"Ahh, as such, Cinderella should also be adorned with some holly of her own."

"Precisely," she exclaimed, pointing at him and coming entirely too close to his chest with her scissors.

Cyrus ducked back.

Isabelle gasped. "My apologies."

"It is quite fine. You were saying?"

"I imagined us making a crown of sorts to mark Cinderella as the lead and also to represent a loving bond with her stepsisters." At some point, her frayed ribbons had come loose. The wind battered them against her face.

"Here," he murmured, his melodic voice like music washing over her as he carefully tied them once more under her chin. "Sh-shall we, then?"

She and Cyrus working side by side, snipping branches of holly and tucking them into their respective baskets, had the feel of a lifetime ago, when they'd been partners and friends in life.

When they finished a short while later and started for the conservatory doors in a companionable silence, she could not stifle her regrets about what they'd lost . . .

Chapter Six

Cyrus had always known he'd never do his father's work.

He'd watched his father toil at the backbreaking work of a stablemaster, his body suffering, and Cyrus vowed to never follow in those steps. He'd wanted a different life and future for himself.

It hadn't been that he'd not respected his father's trade. It had simply been that Cyrus had wanted more.

He'd resolved to use his mind and had absorbed himself in whatever books he could find. Those books had been given to him by his boyhood friend, Isabelle's cousin, Val Snowe. Val's late father, the Viscount Derham at the time, had even been the one to offer schooling to Cyrus, a gift he'd resolved to never squander.

As such, there'd never been a time in his life for silliness or frivolity. Rather, he'd looked with disdain upon those pastimes and pleasures . . . until he'd met Val's cousin Isabelle. Through her, he'd looked upon the world in an all-new way. Between reading books, there'd been games of hide-and-seek and also acting out plays she'd written.

When she broke off their betrothal years later, those moments of gaiety and any playfulness on his part had gone with her.

Or mayhap they'd gone even before she left.

On the fringe of the room, with his arms folded at his chest, Cyrus stared on, a silent observer through the revelry unfolding within the duke's parlor. Never, however, had he felt more awkward amidst joy than he did at that very moment. At some point, the servants had dragged the furniture from the room, leaving the space open for the guests to take part in one of the night's *games*—blind man's buff.

The laughter and joyous cries mingled with his maudlin musings about yesteryear.

He saw his life in two parts: before Isabelle and after Isabelle.

And yet, reflecting on the period of their betrothal, he saw that he'd thrown himself even more into growing his fortunes so that he would be completely worthy of her. Money had mattered more, and the opportunities for fun . . . had come less.

"I've got you," a young woman cried as she grabbed one of the gentlemen.

Laughing uproariously together, the pair untied her blindfold, the captured became the seeker, and another game commenced.

Cyrus sneaked a glance at the tall case clock that had been spared when the furniture was moved out.

Five minutes past nine o'clock.

These bloody games were infernal. How long did they go on for?

From across the room, a laughing Derham caught his eye. "Come," he mouthed, gesturing with his arm.

Cyrus waved him off.

"Come," the other man repeated.

"No," he repeated.

Blessedly, the other man relented and went back to joining in the fun.

Fun. Cyrus resisted the urge to squirm from the discomfort that came from simply watching the lords and ladies as they pranced about the room. To think he'd once longed to be part of this . . . this notorious, celebratory affair, thrown annually by the duke back then.

Why had he come to join in the evening's games?

To see her.

He gave his head a frustrated shake, but didn't even bother to try lying to himself. Yes, the hope of seeing Isabelle was the only reason he'd suffered as long as he had through the joviality.

Because where else would she be but in the midst of the jubilant fun?

Only, that was who she had been. And that served as yet another reminder that they were no longer the same people.

Well, he was. Miserable and uncomfortable amongst people and crowds. Better suited for his books than casual discourse.

The masked lady at the middle of the room squealed loudly and lunged, but the gentleman nearest her reach evaded that desperate grab.

He again grimaced. Yes, he'd do well to escape this hell.

When Isabelle had left him years before, any merriment had stopped altogether.

Another round of laughter went up throughout the parlor.

He winced. It was time to quit this, after all. Cyrus turned to leave.

"You are very serious, good sir."

He stiffened as those words were spoken on his other side, and he was transported briefly back to a long-ago day, when he'd been a boy, and a little girl had come upon him.

"I'm not a sir," he said, his response pulled from another time. "I'm just a stablemaster's son."

"You remember." Her face brightened as he turned toward her. Or mayhap that was his own reflection in the clear of her eyes.

"I remember," he murmured. Remembering her was remarkably easy. Forgetting her had proven impossible.

"You were leaving." It was an accusation.

"I've ledgers to see to." There was always work. "Several notes were delivered this morn pertaining to some of my clients' business that cannot wait . . ." At the sad little glimmer in her gaze, he let those words trail off. "*You* aren't taking part. In the games."

"No. I was making notes for our assignment."

"I should have joined you." *I would have rather joined you.*

"And have you miss out on this?" Isabelle glanced out at the revelry. "You always wished to be part of the duke's gathering. I'd not dare take you away."

"I now work with a number of the duke's guests," he said, and her head tipped ever so slightly at the change in topic. "Your cousin Derham. Lord Stephen. De Royleston. And a very many others. Men whose finances I am responsible for and whom I deal with quite regularly, and yet . . ." Cyrus looked out. "Knowing them even as I do, I find myself . . . at sea here." Such an admission should have left him exposed and discomfited, but there was a freeness in being raw in his honesty about just how out of place he felt here. "I've never much understood fun."

"You *did*," she insisted.

"Because of you," he allowed. He'd lost that along the way. "I don't know how to take part . . . in . . . in . . ." He discreetly motioned at the other guests prancing and sprinting about the room. "This."

"You just . . . *do*, Cyrus," she said gently. "Even if it feels uncomfortable. Happiness depends upon ourselves."

"Aristotle?" His eyebrows lifted. "You despised Greek."

"My mentor," she muttered.

"Ah." Of course an old theater figure would insist on studying the Greek plays.

"Though in the spirit of absolute honesty, I only just tolerated it," she said on an outrageously loud whisper.

Cyrus found himself doing something he'd not done in more years than he could remember—really, since she'd been gone—he laughed. His body shook, and how very good it felt.

She joined in.

When their amusement faded, they resumed watching the latest partygoer don the blind man's buff mask. "You've always been more than you credited. Your father, too."

It took a moment for him to register those words. He pulled his stare back from the game in progress. "I know what my father was," he said matter-of-factly. "I'm not ashamed of him."

"I didn't say you were," she said gently.

"Mr. Hill?"

They both turned at the unexpected intrusion.

A servant held out a folded note. "This arrived for you a short while ago."

Accepting the missive with a word of thanks, Cyrus opened the page and read.

I've finally convinced my employer to release his majority shares of the coal mine. He wasn't, as you know, easily convinced, and I'd rather we seal the transaction as quickly as possible, before Marley gets it into his head to keep the investment.

At last! The sale had come through. It had been hard-won. He felt the same thrilling rush that came with success.

His skin prickled under the feel of a gaze on him. He looked up.

Isabelle stared sadly back. "Wonderful business?"

"The . . . most."

Yet again, they borrowed phrases of the past. Isabelle turned to go and then stopped. "You, however, were always the one working to shape yourself into something different." She looked as though she wished to say more . . . but with just that, she slipped off.

Frowning, he refolded the note and stuffed it inside his jacket pocket.

Leave she would.

That was what she'd always done.

Timing his exit while also following her escape, Cyrus started after her.

When he reached her, he called out, "Something more." He quickened his pace after her. "It wasn't about being something different, but something more."

"Is there a difference?"

That gave him pause. For . . . was there? He'd been so busy attempting to build a new life, but had he really just been trying desperately to erase pieces of his past . . . of his family? The same family he hardly made time to see?

As they turned the corner, Isabelle trailed her fingers over a strip of garland that ran the length of the wall. "And who is to say what is more, Cyrus?"

"Society," he said flatly, clasping his hands behind him. "It is Society who decides it."

Isabelle paused and glanced back. "And you think Society should be the arbiter of those decisions?"

"That is just the way, Isabelle." He joined her beside a portrait of some bewigged Greystoke duke of long ago. "You don't know, though," he said, without anger. "You have a view of people and the world that is favorable. But"—he motioned to that ancient painting of her relative—"as the granddaughter of a duke? Your view is a skewed one."

A frown puckered the place between her eyes. "*Because* I'm a duke's granddaughter?"

"You don't know what it is to be cold in the winter, or hungry because there's not quite enough food to leave you sated after a meal. If you wished to write a play or read a book, there wasn't work that you had to see to completing before you could attend those endeavors."

CYRUS'S WORDS WERE an echo of those words he'd spoken to her ten years ago.

And yet, that day she'd been so very fixed on the end

of their relationship, and the end of a dream she'd carried for them, that she'd not properly allowed herself to think enough about what exactly he'd shared in terms of his life-experiences and his fears.

Her sister hadn't been far off in that opinion, though. When Maeve had tossed the words, they'd been accusatory. When Cyrus spoke them, they had an unvarnished quality to them.

One that gave her greater pause.

All these years, she'd resented him. But . . . what if it was simply that she'd not fully understood him? Or the life he'd lived?

She'd thought she knew him. She'd thought she knew everything there was to know *about* him.

Only, she'd not properly considered the fact he'd been hungry or cold. Which, loving him as she had . . . she *should* have known about his struggles. Instead, self-absorbed and privileged, when he'd come—his arms full of books—and joined her for games, she'd focused solely on being with him. She hadn't thought about what he'd done when they were apart or what had made him different.

How wrong she'd been. About so much. She had been naive in thinking she knew him.

The struggles he spoke of were not ones she'd ever experienced. Or even really ones he'd spoken to her about.

"I never thought of it that way," she said quietly, and shame made it a physical struggle to face him. Nay . . . not *it*. He deserved more than the overgeneralizing way in which she'd just thought that. Isabelle forced her gaze up to Cyrus's. "I never thought of *you* . . . struggling or suffering." She bit the inside of her lower lip, hating herself for the truth of that admission.

He stuffed his hands inside his pockets. "I didn't *want* you to think of me in that light." Cyrus directed his focus to a portrait of a previous duke from years ago. "Perhaps

we would have been better served had I shared with you," he murmured.

Because then she would have known. Because then his drive and passion for his work would have made sense. Mayhap their parting had been inevitable, but there would have been a greater understanding of . . . why they could never be.

Isabelle shook her head, refusing to allow him the blame that was hers alone. She moved, her skirts *whooshing* noisily about her ankles as she placed herself in front of him. "You shouldn't have had to tell m-me." Her voice caught. "Loving you as I . . ." *Do.* She'd always loved him. She'd never stopped. Nor had she thought to try to convince herself she didn't. She had, however, gone out of her way to not think about him.

His eyes sharpened on her face, and she stumbled around for the rest of her response. "I should have known about how you lived and what you feared and why you feared it." Because then everything would have made sense.

"You couldn't have known what I was unwilling to share. What I was too ashamed to share." A sad smile curved his lips. "I was too proud," he said, his voice more distant, as if he spoke to himself.

His answer, however, was no absolution. It couldn't be. The failure to know him fully rested with Isabelle herself. She released a long, shaky sigh. "How blithe I was." *Worse* . . . "How ignorant." *What if I hadn't been?* An image slipped in of the two of them, with a child, joining in the evening's fun . . . together. Her legs trembled from the wave of longing that slapped at her.

Cyrus briefly palmed her cheek, and he angled her face toward his.

Isabelle's heart danced under that tender touch. "If you'd known, it would have changed *nothing*," he said, a note of sadness threaded through that profession. "Not then." He released her.

"Both of us would have benefited from communicating with one another." Instead, he'd become lost in his work, and she'd pined, but never told him how she felt.

"I was always rubbish with words. We were therefore likely doomed for that alone."

Voices and footfalls spilled into the corridor, indicating the assembly had concluded and the guests were retiring to their rooms, or . . . what other pleasures they intended to seek out.

"I should go," she murmured.

"Yes."

Isabelle tried to make her feet move . . . but could not. What she and Cyrus had shared had returned them, if only briefly, to the couple they'd once been. And she was loath for it to end.

The voices grew increasingly closer, and that managed to break the spell. "Good night, Cyrus."

He lowered his head. "Isabelle."

Making off in the opposite direction of the approaching guests, she headed for the servants' staircase that led to the rooms above stairs. Halfway down the corridor, she stopped, compelled to steal another glance back.

Cyrus stood where she'd left him, still studying that portrait they'd stood beside. The candle's glow played off the faint silver that streaked his temples. She wanted to say more, but she was unable to find anything that would make any of this right. Not when they'd already lost so much. She wanted to go back and erase that final meeting, and try in ways they should have tried to save their relationship and their love.

Unable to resist one last look, she found Cyrus's gaze on her this time.

It was too much.

Drawing the door to the stairs shut, Isabelle took the steps quickly, tripping and stumbling over them as she went, the effort to draw breath increasingly difficult. And that had nothing to do with the frenzied pace she'd set.

When she reached the landing that led to the guest quarters, she stopped and sank onto the top step.

Isabelle dropped her head into hands that trembled.

Her sister was right. In having left home, and living with her friend, and writing as she had, Isabelle had deluded herself into thinking she was somehow different than a usual duke's granddaughter. Nay, worse, she'd prided herself on being aware, on being in touch with those who were not part of the nobility.

But having been friends with—and in Cyrus's case, being *in love with*—a man born outside those ranks didn't make their experience hers. It remained a life she didn't know anything of. Not truly. As Cyrus had pointed out, she'd only ever known a comfortable life as a nobleman's daughter. There'd been no strife. No struggle. There'd simply been a desire to write plays and pantomimes when Society told women they could not do those things. And because of that, she'd thought herself wise in some ways. And perhaps she had been, but she'd not been wise in the ways that mattered most.

The door opened, and Isabelle jerked her head up.

A startled maid stood framed at the entrance. "Forgive me, my lady. Is everything all right?"

"Fine," she said, coming to her feet. As fine as one could be when presented with her own self-absorption. With all the dignity she could muster, she rose.

That night, after she'd changed her garments and lay under her covers, sleep remained elusive. One statement Cyrus had uttered—nay, particularly, *two words*—lingered in her mind. *If you had known, it would have changed* nothing . . . *not then.*

"Not then," she mouthed into the silent room.

What had he meant by that?

The words as he'd spoken them suggested that things now might be changed.

You're being silly. He'd given no indication he wished to resume a life with . . .

I've ledgers to see to. Several notes were delivered this morn pertaining to some of my clients' business that cannot wait . . .

Why, by his own admission his work remained his everything. This very evening, when she'd come upon him in the parlor in the midst of the evening's games, he'd spoken of the importance of his work with the same intensity he had the day she'd walked out of his office. Those parts of him that made his work first and everything else a distant second couldn't be changed. Not truly.

Could they?

Isabelle touched her fingers to her mouth.

Yes, there'd been the kiss, but passion was easy. It was mindless and born of just feeling. When passion went away, reality remained, and with it the same divides that had always been between them.

And would always be between them.

Chapter Seven

Cyrus should have left.

The moment the servant came forward with the note from Marley wanting to divest those properties, he should have headed to Yorkshire, signed and sealed the papers, and closed the transaction.

That's what he always did.

And this time . . . did not.

Over the course of the week, Cyrus had worked alongside Isabelle. Together, they'd assigned roles for the pantomime. She'd written lines tailored to the Christmastide production. And Cyrus had rearranged the music room according to the detailed outline Isabelle had drawn for him.

And through it, there was no tension, no bitterness, no regrets. They simply lived in the moment, working toward a shared goal with the same ease they'd shared as children in the countryside.

In fact, Cyrus could almost convince himself there'd been no lapse in time. That they were still the same carefree pair they'd once been. Nay, not even that. That they were a couple now who worked so very well together and laughed, and . . . he could almost imagine a life forever with her.

Why could they not have a chance at a new beginning?

A lightness filled him. Unlike anything he'd known or felt since Isabelle had walked out of his office, and continued walking all the way out of his life. Unlike anything he'd thought to ever again know.

Now he stared at her bent head as she scribbled away frantically in her book. "I have made some improvements to the dialogue," she was saying, wholly oblivious to the imaginings that played out in his mind.

"Have you?"

"Mmm."

No answer, however, was required on his part.

Isabelle continued to let her pen fly over the page. With time melting away, Cyrus sat back in the French fauteuils she'd had brought in earlier in the week, and he just watched her. And he found he loved her all the more, this grown-up, engrossed, more mature version of the young girl who'd once toiled over each word before hesitantly writing them down.

Her lips moved as she wrote, as if she were speaking aloud the lines as they came to her mind and filled her page.

She had a confidence as she worked that hadn't been there before. No matter how many times he'd told her how magnificent she was with words, she'd still doubted and been tentative with her craft.

A blond curl fell across the middle of her brow, and engrossed as she was, Isabelle didn't so much as pause in her efforts to brush the tress back.

His fingers itched, and he almost gave in to their desiring . . . to his desiring.

"I've just the idea," she said, the excitement lacing her tone as captivating as the eager way in which she threw all of herself into her work. "We transform the entire space." She picked her head up from her notes, and her gaze collided with his. "We . . ." She dampened her mouth. "What is it?"

"You."

Her cheeks pinkened. "Me?"

"I admire how you work. You have both passion and purpose."

Briefly setting her pencil on the curved kingwood desk she worked upon, Isabelle rolled her shoulders. "My mentor called my process painstaking."

"Painstaking is a good thing."

"Not if it suppresses one's creative urgings," she said, as if delivering that lesson from her old mentor verbatim. "Then, it only distorts the message and intent of one's writing. Bernd urged me to just . . . write."

In his youth, Cyrus might have been resentful that she'd somehow listened to the words from another that Cyrus himself had given her countless times. As a man nearing his thirty-sixth year, he appreciated that lessons in one's discipline were oftentimes heeded when given by those who understood one's world. And her former mentor had understood Isabelle's world in ways Cyrus simply couldn't.

"May I see it?" he asked when she lowered her head to return to her writing.

Her eyes went round. "Y-yes. O-of course."

As a young man, had he ever truly attended her? Or had his attention been more half-hearted? He was ashamed to admit to himself that it was very much the latter.

Isabelle handed her notes over to him, and Cyrus scanned the pages written in her meticulous hand.

"There are so many versions of the story," she said as Cyrus read. "The Chinese have the tale of *Ye Xian*."

"And you are familiar with it?" he asked, turning a page.

"Oh, yes. My—"

"Mentor?" He paused and looked up.

Isabelle nodded vigorously. "Bernd worked closely with Jacob Ludwig Karl and Wilhelm Carl."

"I . . . ?" Cyrus shook his head.

"They are the Brothers Grimm."

"I'm afraid I've never heard of them." They'd never read those titles together, and then after she'd gone, all he'd bothered with were finance-based books and ones connected to his clients and their investments. He'd never thought there was anything wrong in that single-minded focus that had consumed him since her leaving . . . until this moment. Now he saw how empty his life had been. How cold.

Drawing her legs up, Isabelle settled into her telling. "The two brothers have collected European and German tales."

"Which *Cinderella* is?"

"Exactly!" She nodded. "Bernd provided an entire lecture on them, and *Cinderella* is one of the most-told tales." She let her legs drop to the floor. "And then it occurred to me," she said, her eyes lit.

He moved his gaze over her face, wanting to imprint this moment of her . . . and them . . . in his mind forevermore. "What?"

"You were right."

He was . . . ? Cyrus puzzled his brow. "I am afraid I do not follow."

Isabelle dragged her chair closer, the wooden legs scraping along the marble floor. She stopped when their knees practically touched. "My sister called me selfish for wanting to direct some different performance. You, however, made me see that there is no shame in wanting the freedom to choose the pantomime." Isabelle removed the book from his fingers and set it on her lap. "You helped me see that," she said softly. Taking his hands in her own, she squeezed them.

Warmth passed between their palms, and he stared down at their fingers, linked in perfection.

"And then it occurred to me," she said.

"What was that?" he asked hoarsely. How was her voice so calm? How was she so unmoved at the feel of their flesh kissing?

"There is no reason I shouldn't create something that is my own, while still honoring my dying grandfather's wish." Disentangling their fingers, she gestured excitedly to the book on her lap. That stubborn curl fell over her eye once more, and she left the strand to its recalcitrance.

Cyrus redirected his attention to the pages that contained the story she was so very proud of, and he picked them up, the need to share in her joy even greater than the greed to hold her hands once more. Cyrus resumed reading. Occasionally, he'd laugh at the clever repartee she'd crafted.

Cyrus continued reading until he'd finished.

Isabelle sat stiffly erect, her hands clasped primly on her lap. Nervousness was stamped in her features. "Well?" she asked, that question proof that his opinion mattered to her. "I've used general elements, but I've also made the story my own. It is mine. Just as you encouraged. I—"

Cyrus touched a finger to her lips. "It is"—*she* was—"magnificent." Everything about her was.

"Truly?" Joy wreathed her face. "I was going to distribute everyone's assignments for the production tomorrow. You aren't just saying that?"

She glowed, so very breathtaking in her happiness.

She always had been.

And with her cheeks flushed with the excitement of her telling, she was even more so.

The right corner of his mouth quirked up wryly. "Isabelle, you better than anyone should know I'm wholly incapable of anything but blunt directness."

She laughed softly. "Yes, this is true." Isabelle covered his hand with one of her own. "And I'd not change you for it."

Something shifted.

The air . . . it sizzled.

At last, Cyrus gave in to the urge. He captured the lone curl that obscured her vision, and he made to tuck it behind her ear. Except . . . he froze. Nay, they both froze. The moment, however, was confused in his mind as he found himself absorbed by the silken texture of the strands. He'd never thought to again feel them sliding against his palm, slipping through his fingers.

"Cyrus." His name emerged as a faintly breathless whisper.

"Yes?" He knew what she was asking, what she sought. And yet, even trying to make himself release her, he could not.

Her eyes slid closed, and then, leaning into one another, their bodies moving in unison, they kissed.

Chapter Eight

It was as though Cyrus came alive under the shocked charge of their lips meeting.

Nay, they'd both come alive.

There was nothing tentative or searching or unsure in their embrace. It was born from the flames of passion and stoked all the higher by their years of separation.

She kissed him, laying bold claim to his mouth and then giving herself over completely to his exploration. It was the most glorious of surrenders . . . Isabelle would have given any part of herself if he so sought it.

Needing to be closer, she climbed onto his lap. Cyrus hiked her skirts and chemise up, and as he kissed her, he worked his hands over the heated flesh he'd exposed. Isabelle's head fell back, and she thrust against him. Her core pulsed and ached, longing to be filled by him.

"You are splendid," he panted against her mouth. Filling his hands with her buttocks, he guided her closer.

She bit her lower lip to keep from crying out and undulated, pressing herself into the hard muscles of his flat belly. Cyrus sank his hands into her hips and urged her on as she ground herself against him. "It isn't enough," she keened plaintively.

"It will never be," he rasped sharply, and lowering the bodice of her gown, he brought one of those orbs to his lips. To worship.

He licked and suckled at her, and the sound of his mouth on her added a feverish pitch to her need and movements.

Reaching between them, he slipped a finger inside her channel, alleviating some of her suffering.

Briefly.

"More, Cyrus," she demanded, her breath coming in sharp, painful bursts.

And yet . . . his touch eased.

"Please," she implored. She'd proudly beg him in this moment, for this. Then, as she'd always loved, he pressed his four fingers into her mound, working that sensitive place over and over. The narrowness of the seat, however, restricted her movements. Shoving his jacket off of him, she tangled her fingers in his shirt, and never breaking contact with his mouth, Isabelle came unsteadily to her feet.

And he followed.

She backed up until her buttocks collided with the pianoforte, setting the keys a'jingle.

All the while, Cyrus stroked his hands up and down her thighs. "I have dreamed of this," he said between kisses. "Is this a dream?"

"Then our dreams are moving in harmony, because it is mine, too."

The passion in his gaze deepened and darkened, and as his thick black lashes swept down, hiding that emotion there, he slammed his mouth over hers. There was nothing tender to his kiss. It was rough and violent, and it was glorious bliss for it.

As they tangled their tongues, she lashed her flesh against his.

His shaft pressed hard against her belly, and as she'd done so many times before, she released him from the confines of his breeches.

Cyrus's head fell back. But she'd not let him do that. She

needed him more. Needed his kiss. Needed all of him. He groaned.

His gaze, his mouth . . . Her entire body bespoke the desire she felt for him still.

They strained toward each other, their bodies arching over the keyboard.

The discordant tinkling of the keys lent a frenetic quality to the moment, playing as an afterthought in Isabelle's mind, a desperate and gloriously beautiful melody as they rediscovered each other all over again.

Cyrus dragged up her skirts once more, exposing her legs to his touch.

She moaned and brought one of her calves up. She looped that limb about his waist and pressed herself against him.

The heavy rasp of each breath he drew was swallowed by her mouth. With his spare hand, Cyrus slid a palm between her legs. Easing through the slit of her drawers, he slipped his fingers inside again.

Isabelle cried out his name. "Cyrus!"

HE'D MISSED HER . . . in every way.

He'd missed her laughter and wit and spirit.

And he'd missed having her in his arms.

She keened over and over.

Or was that his own incoherent sound of desire?

As Cyrus palmed her moist curls, Isabelle let her legs fall open. That slight shifting of her body allowed him full access to the place he so ached to touch again.

He slipped one digit inside her channel. Heat. She was all wet heat that slicked the way for his touch.

"Cyrus," Isabelle cried softly against his mouth. Nothing more than his name, pulled from her in desire, and it sent another bolt of lust through him.

His shaft rose higher and he swelled all the more, and as he slipped another finger inside, and another, and began to stroke her, he arched against her hip.

"I've missed you," he whispered, his voice ragged.

Her eyes squeezed shut, Isabelle bit her lower lip and thrust into his touch. "A-and I've m-missed youuuu." That last word stretched out into an endless syllable as he toyed with her nub.

"I've missed this," he added, his breath coming in little puffs, his chest rising and falling in the same rhythm as hers. She was the last woman he'd known and had thought to never again know the feel of her in his arms. This meeting was a coming home.

His shaft sprang achingly toward her, and she wrapped her fingers around his length, stroking him in that slow up-and-down he'd loved.

He *still* loved.

Groaning, Cyrus squeezed his eyes shut and rested his forehead against hers.

"Are you certain, y-you want thisss?" His question dissolved into a hiss as she gripped him tighter.

Isabelle answered by seating herself upon the keyboard and guiding him between her legs.

And he went.

Burying his head in the place where her shoulder met her neck, Cyrus thrust home.

He caught her soft scream, swallowing the sound of his name. Wet, tight heat surrounded him. Her channel squeezed him. Cyrus withdrew and pushed inside again. Thrusting and retreating. Thrust and retreat. And she met every single glide of him inside her.

Isabelle bit at his shoulder. "Cyrusss," she pleaded, her movements as violent and desperate as his own.

He lunged deeper, their thrusting bodies sending that frantic, wordless, nameless song upon the keys. That discordant noise added a dangerous layer that threatened discovery, and he couldn't care. He couldn't care about earning the wrath of this family. He knew only that he wanted this. That he needed her, Isabelle. And he'd sell his soul to the devil in this moment to take all of what she offered.

Her body stiffened under his. A soft, little intake of breath spilled from her lips, and she exploded in his arms.

Cyrus continued pumping. Sweat soaked his brow and dripped down his face as he thrust and withdrew.

Then, as she went limp on one final gasp, he groaned long and low. Cyrus spilled his seed in a shuddery rivulet over the side of the pianoforte and onto the floor. He collapsed over her.

Cyrus struggled to get air into his lungs. "Isabelle," he whispered, placing a kiss against her temple.

Isabelle folded her arms about Cyrus and clung to him.

Chapter Nine

After years of missing Cyrus, and searching for peace . . . contentment . . . happiness: she was home.

Moments of bliss, however, always proved entirely too short-lived.

Cyrus stiffened and then straightened.

She winced. The sharp dig of the piano keys against her back had been previously transmuted by the glory of his touch.

Reality was a constant, cold bitch who never failed to rear her head.

Rummaging through the garments cast about, Cyrus removed a kerchief. Returning to Isabelle, he gently cleaned any remnants of himself from her person in an act so intimate and tender that tears sprang to her eyes. She blinked them back. No words were needed in this moment.

After he'd finished, he more quickly cleaned himself and the remnants of his seed on the floor. As he did, Isabelle adjusted her skirts. Together, silently, they righted their clothing. She stole a sideways peek at him while he dressed. Fetching his shirt, Cyrus pulled it on, stealing her view of his muscled chest and abdomen. Her heart jumped. He'd always been beautiful. But how much more so he'd become with the passage of time.

As each piece of clothing was returned to its proper place or order, the beautiful moment they'd just shared seemed to become a more and more distant memory.

"Isabelle," he began.

What had she done? What had they done? "This shouldn't have happened," she said at the same time. Ten years earlier, her heart had almost not recovered. It wouldn't from another break at this man's hands. Except, there had always been an explosive passion between her and Cyrus Hill. One that she'd been hopeless to resist or deny, no matter how much pain her bond with this man might bring.

"And why not?" he asked solemnly.

"Because of you," she said impatiently.

His frown deepened. "Because of *me*?"

"Because we aren't happy together, Cyrus," she said on a furious whisper. "We couldn't make us make sense," she said quietly, unable to keep sadness from creeping in.

Cyrus scoffed. "Of course we could." He briefly presented his back as he adjusted himself. That glimpse of his devotion to propriety even after lovemaking drew a little smile before he continued in terse tones, recalling her back to the tension that would always be between them. "We've known one another since we were children. We always worked . . . until we didn't." He leveled her with a hard stare. "Until you left."

Until . . . ? Her eyes shot up. "What? Until *I* left?" That was truly what he believed? "I think you'll find, if you look close enough, that you left me long before I did you." Her gaze slid away. No, that wasn't altogether true. What he'd shared in the corridor of her grandfather's home had opened her eyes to the truth. Not just one of them was to blame. They, and their mistakes and decisions, both played a part in their breakup. "We quit each other."

"It doesn't have to be this way."

"What are you saying?" she asked, running her eyes over his face.

"I'm saying . . . Mayhap we might . . . begin again?" The question, tacked on at the very end, contained a vulnerability that she'd never heard from this man.

Her breath caught.

Or was that his?

Her heart lifted and soared at the prospect of a future with this man. "You . . . ?" Her legs weakened, and Isabelle sank onto the pianoforte bench.

Cyrus raised a palm. The hand that had moments ago strummed her body so beautifully now trembled. "I—"

Footfalls sounded in the hall.

Their gazes whipped to the door.

"Oh, bloody hell," she whispered, frantically stuffing the loose curls hanging about her face back behind her ears.

"Here," Cyrus murmured with his usual calm. Holding the still-tidy parts of her chignon in place, he removed her butterfly pins and rearranged them.

Knock-knock-knock.

"Do I look presentable?"

"You look perfect," he murmured, his gaze moving over her face.

"E-enter," she called out, her voice tremulous. She took a hasty step away from Cyrus and folded her hands before her.

A servant entered with a silver tray clutched between his gloved hands. "This arrived a short while ago, Mr. Hill."

Cyrus accepted the note and slipped a finger under the seal.

She stared on while Cyrus read, his gaze making quick work of the page, and her heart twisted.

She'd been wrong. The keys under her back hadn't been reality's intrusion. This moment was. Cyrus's business. How many moments before had been just like this one? With them together and then some grand business coming between them, commanding his attention, and taking him away, both physically and, worse, emotionally.

"Is there anything else you require?" the servant asked when Cyrus had concluded reading and refolded the ivory vellum.

Cyrus hesitated. "Not at this time."

At which time, then? she silently screamed. Not in this very instant? Not tomorrow? Not ever?

Nay, not *not ever*. He'd see to his affairs, secure his—and others'—fortunes.

"You're leaving," she said softly, not knowing where she found the calm in those words.

"I . . . There are affairs I need to see in order. Ones I've been remiss in attending."

"You'll not even stay for our performance?" she whispered, hating the wounded quality to her voice. God, she'd been a fool to believe he might somehow put this—nay, *them*—before his work.

His expression was pained. "I . . . I would like to. It's less than a day's ride."

"There is snow, Cyrus." And she hated herself for pleading all over again. Hated herself for not being enough for him, still. And hated herself for having allowed herself the illusion of moments ago that matters between them could be different.

Chapter Ten

Cyrus stared on hopelessly as Isabelle organized the materials she'd been working on . . . *They'd* been working on, rather.

Wanting desperately to go back to how they'd been just moments ago, before the servant had appeared and Isabelle had withdrawn.

He dragged a hand through his hair. "I'm not planning to miss our performance."

"You said as much."

He was intending to leave for only a short while.

And she would make it as though this was somehow like the past. It wasn't. Then, he wouldn't have even taken part in the details of the pantomime.

He was making a blunder of this—of them—all over again, and what was worse, he was as helpless to fix whatever this was now as he had been then. "I'm not the same man, Isabelle." Silently, he tried to will her to look at him.

She paused only briefly in her tidying. "Are you trying to convince me, Cyrus?" she asked quietly. "Or yourself?"

Cyrus flexed his jaw.

Sighing, Isabelle finally put her things down and gave him her full attention. "These past days? They have been wonderful. I remembered things I didn't let myself remember about how very good it feels just being in your company."

A buoyant lightness filled his chest. "I feel the same way."

But she didn't appear to be hearing him. Isabelle went

on as if he'd not uttered those words. "It is foolish to expect that we can have a relationship now when we couldn't then."

"Why can't we? Why?" A plaintive quality wound its way through that last word.

"Because we're still the same people," she cried, displaying the first crack in her control. "Your first love will always be your work."

He blanched. "Is that what you believe?" he whispered.

"How could I n-not?" Her voice broke. "How could I not?" she repeated, lifting tear-filled eyes to his.

At the sight of her suffering, he felt his heart crack and break and bleed, just as it had when she'd left.

Cyrus took her cheeks in his hands, framing her beloved face. "I loved you endlessly. I still do. Everything I did was for us. For *us*."

Her lower lip quivered. "It wasn't for me, because I didn't want it, Cyrus." *You did.*

She didn't need to speak those two words aloud for them to be heard in the silence.

And he wanted to fight her on them. He wanted to rail and call them out as a lie. Only . . . he couldn't. All these years, he'd been committed to increasing his wealth and power and status, and he'd come to believe that quest had begun because of her. But if he was finally being truthful with himself, he'd acknowledge it had come long before her.

For just as she'd charged, that quest went back to his views of his father and his family.

His hands fell to his sides. She was right . . . about so much. His heart pounded under that revelation. He sucked in a shuddering breath and stepped away. "I loved you the best I knew how." It hadn't been enough. Nor had it been as she'd deserved.

"You are driven, Cyrus, and I love that so very much about you. But this?" She gestured to the note he'd accepted from the servant. "Will always come before everything. Just as then, when I wasn't willing to be second to your first mistress, I cannot do it now."

She was being unreasonable. He presented her his back and stared blankly out at the ballroom.

And yet, was she? What else had she been correct about?

How many times before had he put his work first?

He snapped his jaw so sharply that pain radiated up his cheeks.

Cyrus tried again. "I have to go."

"Then go," she said calmly.

He turned to leave . . . and then stopped.

From a place deep inside, he knew that if he left, even for just a half day's time to see to the closure of the deal, he'd acquire that mine, but he'd lose her.

I am making the same mistakes. He felt it. He was losing her all over again. Losing the hope he'd had of a new future with her.

Knock-knock-knock.

"Bloody hell, what now? Enter," he boomed.

Footsteps sounded outside the room, and a moment later, the doors were drawn open. "Presenting Mr. Bernd Wilhelm."

Isabelle froze and then lit up in ways Cyrus had not seen in so long: her eyes glowing, her round cheeks filled with happy red color. She sprinted across the room as the girl she'd once been. To a man Cyrus had heard only mention of.

That same man flung his arms wide and caught Isabelle.

Cyrus stood off to the side, forgotten, a silent spectator to the happy exchange. In all the times Isabelle had mentioned her mentor, Cyrus had imagined an old, eccentric German with wild hair, cracked spectacles, and mismatched garments.

Never had he expected, or allowed himself to think, that the man who'd served as her mentor was in fact . . . *this.*

This tall, wiry bloke, with perfectly tousled blond hair

and the thinnest of mustaches, was debonair and dashing and wearing a smile.

Cyrus despised him with every fiber of his being. Jealousy sluiced through him, red and hot, born of hatred so deep it scorched the blood running through his veins.

For *this* was Mr. Bernd Wilhelm, Isabelle's mentor.

It was too much.

Cyrus started for the door. He made it no further than three paces.

"You're leaving?"

He forced himself back around to face her and her mentor. "I . . . have business to see to."

"Of course," she murmured.

Cyrus merely imagined the regret in her tone.

He felt the German's probing stare on him and turned a frosty look on the bloody bastard. This same bloody bastard who'd imparted guidance on topics so important to Isabelle.

The ghost of a smile grazed the other man's slightly narrow lips. "Good day," he said in slightly guttural tones.

Go to hell. Cyrus suppressed the words he really wished to hurl at the German and inclined his head. "Good day."

With that, he stalked off.

There appeared to be a reason after all that Cyrus and Isabelle couldn't simply be together.

ISABELLE HAD BELIEVED Wilhelm headed for Germany and hadn't anticipated seeing him for another year. The last place she'd ever expected to see him was here, at her grandfather's estate.

"What are you doing here?" she managed.

"Some viscount interfered in my plans to travel."

"Derham?"

"The same. A stubborn man who'd not take no for my answering. Insisted that I come here and . . . be a part."

Her mouth slipped open. "When did he do *that*?"

"Notes. He's been asking me. Week. And week." Weeks and weeks. "I ignored his missive. I don't have time to indulge some English person's fancy." He paused. "No offenses taken, Bella."

She chuckled. "No offense taken."

"But the latest?" Wilhelm whipped out a sheet and waved it about. "This one I could not ignore. No matter how much I liked to." He added that part under his breath. Her mentor folded the note and placed it back inside the front of his jacket.

She eyed him quizzically. "He offered you funds for your theater."

"It is not my theater. Not yet. What I can say?" Wilhelm stretched his arms wide. "I am a peasant to my craft."

"Slave," she said dryly.

Her loyal teacher jabbed a finger at the air. "That one."

Given all that, what Wilhelm stood to earn, and just his presence alone, should have filled her only with joy. He should be the one commanding all her attention.

And yet, she had to stop her gaze from sliding to the front of the room where Cyrus had just stood, unable to keep the tears from springing to her eyes once more.

Bloody hell.

She dashed the back of her hand over her eyes.

Her mentor rested an elbow on the pianoforte. "The love?"

The problem with having a mentor who'd schooled one for nearly ten years was it was nigh impossible to keep a secret from him. He'd urged her to share her greatest heartbreak and use that in her craft. When she had, however, she'd never envisioned her first and only love coming face-to-face with her teacher. Now she wished she'd not been so candid.

"The love," she muttered.

"Ah." Wilhelm inclined his head. "He is more handsome than I expected. I expected a thin . . ." He brought his hands together so his palms almost touched. "Pale . . ." Wilhelm gestured to his face. "A short fellow. He is not those things. He is not those things at all."

Her lips twitched in her first smile since the servant had come in with his letter of business for Cyrus. It was the closest the other man would ever come to a compliment about an Englishman. "Whyever would you imagine that?"

"He is English," he said, as if that explained it all.

"No, he was never those things. He's always been handsome and tall and clever and . . ." Her lower lip trembled. "And he is leaving." It physically hurt to even utter those words.

"For good?"

"Hmm?" She stared at him. "No. No," she said. "There's a transaction he must complete."

He puzzled his high, heavy brow. "And so you do not like this transaction?"

"No. It's not that."

"Would he expect you to put your work aside?"

"I'm not asking him to . . ." Except, hadn't she? She found her footing. "You don't understand." She began to pace. "He's always loved his work more."

Her mentor folded his arms before him. "You've always loved your writing. I'd not have worked with you had you not."

"It is different." It was. Wasn't it?

"I don't see how."

Wilhelm's pronouncement might as well have been an echo of her thoughts.

"Is it me who doesn't understand?" he asked. "Or you who doesn't see?" He wagged his enormously thick blond eyebrows. "It is . . . How do you English say it? Nourishing?"

Nourishing? Isabelle searched her mind before landing on his intended meaning. "Healthy?"

"That!" Wilhelm circled a finger at the air. "Should he not see to his work?"

"Of course he should."

"You do not trust that he can balance his love for you with his love for his . . ." Wilhelm's lips pulled. "Numbers." He said that with the loathing only a man who dealt in words could.

"He never could." That wasn't altogether true. She touched a hand to her breast. "I told you before . . . he did love me, wholly, and then he stopped seeing me, stopped sharing my life."

"And is that how he's been during this . . . reunion?"

"N-no." She stumbled over that word.

Her mentor gave her a gentling look. "Isabelle? A person? A person should have more passion than just love for one person, and mayhap with time he's learned how to . . ." He lifted his palms, as if weighing them. "Measure them?"

"Balance them," she whispered. She felt knocked off-kilter. She'd been so stuck on seeing Cyrus of the past. But these past few days, Cyrus had worked steadily at her side. He'd taken part in every aspect of the preparation for the pantomime. Unlike that time of their betrothal, he'd shared her writing. He'd even gone and collected plants and brush and seen to decorations with her.

This week, he'd proven himself . . . *changed.* He'd not disappeared to attend his ledgers. He'd not locked himself away to do his work. Had it been her fear of being hurt again that had made her reject his plea for a new beginning? She came to an abrupt stop.

"Ten years changes a person, *nein*?"

"You're right," she whispered.

"I'm German. I usually am."

Ten years had changed them both.

She didn't want Cyrus to go.

She wanted him. All of him.

She wanted the brilliant man he was, who loved his work with the same intensity she loved hers. She wanted his gruffness and his tenderness. She wanted the man who pushed her and encouraged her in ways that she'd never pushed herself.

And by God, she was determined to have him.

Chapter Eleven

"My God, have a care! Whatever did your garments do to deserve such rough handling?"

Cyrus ignored Derham's jesting and hurled another garment into his trunk. It didn't make Cyrus feel better. He added another. And another. The articles formed a growing mound. "Don't you have somewhere else to be?"

From where he stood at the front of the room, his back lounged against the door and the bottom of his left boot pressed along the panel, Derham watched him. "What would make you say that? The fact that I'm the heir? The fact that my uncle is bedridden?"

"That is it, exactly," he muttered, yanking out two more jackets and tossing them into his trunk. The mound of garments crested the top of the trunk, and Cyrus eyed it for a moment. He stepped inside and stomped his boot, making further space.

"You know, I *do* have servants who can help with that," Derham drawled. "There's a whole houseful of them."

"I don't need a damned servant to pack my things," he snarled. Yes, he had a valet, but he could see to his own needs.

The irony, however, wasn't lost on him. Cyrus had once envied the other man for his lifestyle. He had dreamed of it for himself. But what had he really been wishing for? He now had more money than Croesus and servants to boot . . . and what had that brought him? Only *she* made him smile.

Alas, another had been making her smile all these years.

Growling, Cyrus ripped the remaining garments free of their pegs and hurled them into the trunk.

"My, you are in a very festive holiday mood, are you not? The spirit of the season and all that."

Cyrus made a crude gesture with his finger, and the other man laughed.

At least one of them could laugh.

And of course it should be the one responsible for all the good cheer.

"Well, I've good news for you. There's a performance to do."

"The pantomime isn't until tomorrow," he said, finally stopping his frantic packing. "She wouldn't move it up."

"She didn't. She has, however, added a performance for the evening. For this evening."

"She and the German."

"The German?"

At Derham's puzzled expression, Cyrus gnashed his teeth.

Understanding dawned in his friend's eyes. "Wilhelm."

As if there were another German present. Nay, there was just one. A handsome, deucedly charming one who made Isabelle smile. He growled, stomping over to the armoire, and grabbed up three pairs of boots.

"Nice fellow," Derham, his now-former friend, traitorously offered. "Though a bit stubborn. You do know what they say about the Germans."

"I don't," he gritted out, carrying his things over to the second nearly filled trunk.

"The fellow put up quite the resistance to coming to the Revelry, but I managed to sway him."

All the shoes slipped from Cyrus's grip, raining down with staccato, noisy thumps, one after the other, upon the floor.

"Only cost me a small fortune," Derham added.

Cyrus seethed. "You invited him."

"Oh, yes."

Cyrus waited for his friend to say something more.

Which he didn't. That was it. *Oh, yes*?

He'd never punched Derham. He'd never punched anyone, to be precise. But in this moment, Cyrus very much wanted to.

"So it promises to be a festive evening, and you could use some cheer and—"

"I'm not staying." She'd been clear that there wasn't a future between them. And he was selfish enough to admit that he couldn't be around her and not have her in his life in every way.

Derham finally shoved himself away from the door and strolled over. "So I gathered when I saw you packing your things, but I assumed now that you know about the production"—*and who is behind it*—"you would wish to remain."

"I don't," he said coolly. "I want to head to Yorkshire . . ." Cyrus slammed one lid shut. "And finalize this deal . . . your deal . . ." When the top of the trunk resisted the contents within, he shoved the heel of his boot atop it several times. "And make you your damned *money*," he thundered. His ears immediately went hot at that display.

Good God, what had happened to him? He was never without control. "Forgive me," he said tightly.

Any other employer would have sacked him for that insolence. And mayhap had Derham not been a lifelong friend, he would have.

Derham merely waved his hand. "You don't sound much like one eager to journey to Marley's."

"Of course I am," he said tiredly. "I—"

Derham lifted his palms. "You needn't worry about convincing me. I will let you to your business." The other man paused. "Or should I say *my* business?"

"Thank—"

"However, as your employer, I will insist that you first attend the impromptu performance presented by my cousin this night."

Bloody hell on all fifty-two Sundays. Derham never played the employer card. "Derham," he tried.

"I insist," the other man said. "The performance begins in ten minutes. Don't be late." He started for the door. "When it is over, you can go about your quest to make me even more obscenely wealthy," he promised without looking back.

A moment later, the other man was gone, and Cyrus . . . was alone.

All the life and energy went out of him. Sinking to the floor, he rested his back against the trunk nearest him and buried his head in his hands.

He was in hell.

There was nothing else for it.

Cyrus slowly picked his head up and stared at the window, its curtains open. Snow swirled amidst the ink black of the night sky.

Nay, mayhap this wasn't hell.

Perhaps it was more that he was being made to atone for his sins. For having neglected to have a relationship with the parents who'd worked so hard. Or for having failed to properly ask after his elder brother. Yes, he'd sent money, but he'd not been a son or brother to any of them.

Isabelle had helped him see that.

The same Isabelle with whom he'd now be forced to sit in the same room, while she joined another man whom Cyrus wished he could be. But he should be there. Because it was her production, and it wasn't about him.

That was why, with one minute and thirty seconds to spare before Isabelle's performance, Cyrus found his way to the crowded music room. Gilded chairs had been arranged throughout the room, with a small dais set up at the center.

Cyrus headed for the last row.

From the front of the room transformed into a makeshift theater, Derham stood and motioned him over.

"I'm quite fine." *In the last row.*

"I insist," the other man boomed. Which was viscount for *I order you to sit your arse where I tell you.*

His cheeks going hot under the stares thrown his way by the other guests, Cyrus made his way to the required seating. "Is that better?" he muttered, plopping into the end seat his *friend* had saved.

"Eminently," the other man said. "Given as how I did ask you to sit there."

"Oh, was it realllly asking me?" he said from the side of his mouth.

"What was that?" Derham asked distractedly as he angled his head, his gaze scouring the room.

"Nothing. Nothing at all."

Derham's eyes registered someone he recognized. Coming to his feet, the viscount raised his arm, signaling for that someone to join them.

Cyrus followed the other man's stare and went absolutely motionless as his gaze landed on the approaching pair.

"Oh, hell," he whispered.

"Some advice, if I may." Derham discreetly lifted a hand to his mouth and concealed his lips. "Proper greetings and less cursing when they arrive."

Just then, the *they* in question reached them, and Cyrus gave thanks for the small reprieve as Derham greeted Isabelle's mother and sister.

A couple of ladies who would have been, if life had worked out differently, his family by marriage. A pair he'd known so very well, but hadn't seen since Isabelle had broken their betrothal.

"I trust you remember Mr. Hill?" Derham was saying, bringing both women's attention to Cyrus.

Cyrus sketched a bow. "Countess Thorpe, Lady Maeve," he greeted. It had been years. When last he'd seen Lady Maeve, she'd been a small girl joining him and Isabelle for trips to their grandfather's lake for a picnic and fishing.

"My goodness, it has been years," Maeve exclaimed. "But surely we are family enough that you'd still call me Maeve! It has been years. Has it now, Mother?"

"Years," the countess agreed, with an emphatic nod.

With the loquacious pair chattering on about favorite memories they shared, he felt like perhaps he'd stepped into a pantomime in which he didn't have the benefit of knowing his lyrics or verses. Because they weren't supposed to greet him so . . . warmly. That wasn't how families treated the betrothed who'd been discarded. Or . . . that wasn't how he thought it went. Bitterness. Antipathy, even. But not . . . this warm friendliness.

"We simply must have Cyrus to visit," Maeve decided.

Too polite to point out all the reasons that wouldn't be wise or proper, he bowed his head. "Perhaps one day in the future."

Maeve scrunched up her nose. "That doesn't sound very committal. Does it, Mother?"

The countess shook her head wildly, her round ringlets bouncing. "It does not."

Then mother and daughter launched into a discussion that apparently required no input from Cyrus or Derham.

Cyrus looked helplessly over the heads of the chattering pair to his friend.

The other man shuddered. "It is a bit too much," he mouthed.

"What was that?" Maeve piped in. Isabelle's sister and mother leveled identical frowns on the always unflappable, more-often-than-not-frosty viscount.

And the girl . . . nay, the young woman managed the seemingly impossible. She elicited a blush from the viscount. "Uh . . ." His gaze landed on the corner of the room. "It is about to begin," he wisely said.

Isabelle's family immediately found their seats, along with the other guests, and as the players took their places, Cyrus's gaze bypassed the wiry German at a desk that had been set out and found the woman who hovered at the edge of the makeshift stage.

His heart beat a double-time rhythm, as it always did whenever he saw her.

She was attired in that bonnet she loved and—

His nape prickled.

That entire apparel was familiar. The cloak she wore was different than the one she'd donned for their jaunt outside earlier in the week, and yet, the sapphire article was embedded in his memory.

Isabelle wrung her hands, and periodically she went on tiptoe and stared through what seemed to be an imagined window at the gentleman, who had his back to her. Then Isabelle's voice cut through the quiet of the music room.

"It has been two years." Upon the stage, Isabelle huddled deeper into her velvet-lined cloak, and Cyrus sat absolutely motionless. Unable to move. Unable to breathe. "You lie, even to yourself. It has not been two years," she murmured. "It has been two years, one hundred and fifteen days, forty-six minutes, and"—she consulted the timepiece affixed to the front of her cloak—"a handful of seconds."

Oh, God.

He sat, stone-cold.

"This does not *feel* as though it is a pantomime," Maeve whispered loudly. "It seems quite . . . serious."

"Shh," the countess said on an outrageously loud whisper of her own.

Isabelle took a step forward and reached for . . .

A door handle.

But she didn't open the door. She'd knock—

Isabelle removed her hand from within her fur muff and let her fist fall upon an imagined surface at the very moment she stamped her left foot.

Knock-knock-knock.

There came the scrape of wood along wood as her mentor shoved back his chair and muttered.

Only, he wasn't her mentor. Not really. Rather, Cyrus was on that stage, represented by the other man.

Cyrus had been engrossed in his work, some business or other. He couldn't even recall what it had been or who it had been for. All he recalled was his annoyance at the interruption.

Isabelle's lips curved in a smile.

A pit formed in his belly, because he knew how the rest of this played out.

Why . . . why was she doing this?

And what manner of friend would force him to sit through it?

Cyrus started to rise, but Derham put a hand on his arm and scowled him back to his seat.

Mayhap this was some family form of punishment for all the ways in which he'd failed Isabelle all those years ago.

Her mentor pressed his forehead against the pretend windowpane that Isabelle herself had been peeking through moments before.

I frowned at her? I . . .

And then . . .

Recognition sparked in the gentleman's eyes. A moment later, the door was yanked open.

Mr. Wilhelm's gaze fell upon Isabelle, and in his eyes there was so much joy that it reached across the music room and hit Cyrus squarely in the heart.

"Silas—"

"What are you doing here?" he asked gruffly, and sticking his head out the imagined door, he scanned the streets.

Taking her by the arm, he drew Isabelle forward and inside. "You shouldn't be here, Bella."

How much time Cyrus had spent worrying about scandal. Why had he cared? What had it mattered? It hadn't always been that way, though. Somewhere along the way, he'd become lost in his business. Fearing what the world might think.

"I daresay I'd expected you'd be a good deal more pleased to see me," she teased.

I am. I am.

Cyrus sat rooted to his narrow chair, silently screaming those words he should have given her. How had he not heard the hurt quality to her words that day? How?

The gentleman's frown deepened. "How can you doubt I'm happy to see you?"

Only, the annoyed tone, at odds with that question, sent a rumble of laughter through the crowd.

The levity immediately died.

Isabelle's mentor lightly caressed his palms up and down her arms, and Cyrus couldn't even hate the other man in that moment, because the other man . . . was him. He embodied Cyrus in the darkest, most regretful moment of his almost forty years. "Of course I am happy to see you, Bella." The other man let his arms fall. "Your family," he said swiftly. "They are all well?"

"Prodigiously so."

A smile formed on the other man's face. "Prodigiously so . . ."

And Cyrus's eyes slid closed as those words he echoed harked back to another time, another place. The place where they'd first met once upon a lifetime ago.

Are you enjoying your time here in Somerset?

Prodigiously so.

"You remember that?" she whispered.

I do. I always did. I never forgot. I'm sorry that I let you believe I'd forgotten.

A frown formed in place of the mentor's smile. His gaze moved caressingly over her face. "How could I ever forget that day?" he murmured. That question and the tone of it were both at odds with the expression the man now wore.

That day, when she, the duke's eight-year-old granddaughter, had come upon him, the stablemaster's son. Cyrus had been reading, while his friends had been in the midst of a game of hide-and-seek, when she had stumbled upon him. He'd forsaken that book and his friends that day, all to remain in the shelter of the copse, asking her about her writings. He'd been fascinated by her, this little girl who loved words. Their friendship had been born in that moment.

"You really shouldn't be here, then," the stuffy version of Cyrus's younger self repeated.

Why shouldn't she? Why did it matter? She was the only one you wanted near. Celebrate her being with you.

"Yes, you've said as much."

Making no attempt to take her cloak, his younger self started over to some imagined place in that room, and he stretched out his hands and rubbed them together. The hearth.

Isabelle removed her cloak and draped it over the only other chair upon the stage.

Grabbing a pretend fireplace poker, he added a log to the pretend fire. "You were to leave this morn for the duke's."

"Yes. Yesterday morn," she clarified.

Still stoking the fire, he glanced up with a question in his eyes.

"My family left yesterday." Isabelle wandered deeper into the room. "I chose to stay behind."

With him.

She'd chosen to be . . . with him.

Cyrus's throat moved painfully, and he had to look away from the action unfolding.

"Whyever would you do that?" the actor chastised. All

the while, he attended that fire as if it were the most important thing in the world . . . when it hadn't been. When she had been. "You hate London."

She did. When he'd established his business, he'd not even taken that into consideration. It had been a foregone conclusion that his offices would be in London.

"I didn't wish to go to my grandfather's this year," Isabelle was saying.

That would have been the first and only time in the whole of her life that she'd not wanted to take part in the notorious house party.

"Impossible." The man playing Cyrus returned the poker to its rack. "You've always enjoyed visiting during the duke's Christmastide festivities. Your family's annual holiday production is one of the favorite things you do all year."

Isabelle joined him beside the hearth, staring into the pretend crimson and orange flames he'd stoked.

How much damned time had he spent on the fire? So much time, when he should have been only attending her.

"It isn't the same without you being there, Silas," Isabelle said softly.

He . . . the actor . . . took a step toward her.

In the moment, all of this was . . . confusing as Cyrus played silent observer to his younger self and his greatest mistake.

Young Cyrus continued past her, and drawing out his desk chair, he sat. "I've never been there," the other man said with such a complete lack of emotion that Cyrus winced. "To the ducal Christmastide festivities."

Nay, he hadn't. For as friendly as Cyrus might have been with the duke's nephew, that close connection meant little to His Grace.

Shifting her focus from the pretend hearth, she turned and faced the actor. "Silas—"

He'd returned to his work, as engrossed now as he'd been when she'd studied him from outside.

She stared on, unblinking. Her hands shook, and she rubbed at her arms. As if to give them purpose. As if to hide their trembling. "Are you *working*?"

He dipped his pen into his crystal inkpot. "I believe it should be fairly obvious that I am."

Licking the tip of his index finger, the young Cyrus reached for the pounce powder to dry his page.

Isabelle slapped her palm down on his just-completed work.

"Bella," he exclaimed. "The ink is still wet."

His heart hammered with a slow, sickening dread. He knew where this went. How it ended. And all over again, he wanted to flee. Cyrus eyed the door behind him, and in doing so, his gaze found the guests riveted, their eyes fixed on the performance that was his life.

"I don't give a damn about the wet ink or your ruined work," Isabelle said in quiet tones. "We've been betrothed for nearly three years, Silas."

He scoffed. "It's not been three years. It's two years and not even six months."

You bloody pompous bastard with your understanding of numbers and not much more.

Again, the young Cyrus made to turn the page, but Isabelle planted the tips of her fingers onto those tabulations so that if he wished to proceed in this battle, he'd rip his work in the process.

"We were to marry in six months," she said.

Even six months is too long, Isabelle. I want to begin tomorrow with you, today.

His mouth moved with that avowal he'd made.

"Opportunities presented themselves," he said. "You know that. We've spoken at length about the possibilities."

His eyes slid shut once more, and he sat in his cowardice, just listening, unable to watch. Not seeing, however, did little to dull the throbbing ache in his chest.

"It was only to be the viscount's business you saw to."

The gentleman set his pen down. "And you would have us settle for less than what we could have."

"It's not just about what we *have*. It's the life we have together. And at the present, we have . . . little together."

A sound of impatience escaped him. "Of course we do."

"Adding 'of course' doesn't make it true, Silas," she said softly, as he was wont to do when trying to hammer home a point.

The young Cyrus swept his arms over the ledgers resting on his desk. "I'm doing this for us."

"I just want you. I don't *care* about a fortune." She gathered his hands and held firm. "I care only about you and me, Silas. I want a future with you."

Cyrus's mind stalled. That wasn't what had played out. He searched through his memory for pebbles of what they'd said that day. He'd hurled her origins in her face.

"I don't know what your struggles have been," Isabelle murmured. "I don't know what fear compels you. I only know that I want you to let me in so that we can face each challenge together."

Cyrus's eyes flew open, and his throat constricted. At some point, Isabelle had quit the side of the actor playing him and had wandered to the very edge of the dais. She stood there, staring out at the audience. Nay, not at the other spectators. At him.

"I don't understand."

Had he spoken aloud? He couldn't hear anything over the hammering of his heart.

She stepped down from the dais, and the crowd gasped as she drifted closer to Cyrus. "We stopped speaking to one another. Stopped listening. I was jealous of your work and could not find the words to tell you what I wanted . . . what I needed for us."

Before he knew what he did, he quit his chair. The crowd gasped as he walked toward Isabelle, meeting her halfway.

He and Isabelle faced each other, all the guests forgotten. "You shouldn't have had to," he said quietly.

"But I should have," she said with a quiet insistence. "I know that now. Because that is what couples who love one another do, Cyrus. They communicate, even when it's about the ugly topics that hurt the most." Isabelle tipped her head back and met his gaze. A sheen of tears glossed the surfaces of her eyes. "I don't want you to give up on your dreams, just as you didn't demand I give up on mine. I just want to be a part of them. I love you," Isabelle whispered.

His shaking hand came up to touch her cheek. "What are you saying?" he asked hoarsely.

And then the silken softness of her flesh was gone from his palm as she sank to a knee. "Marry me, Cyrus."

Another round of gasps went up, so loud they drowned out the pounding of his heart.

"Spend forever with me."

And when he remained absolutely motionless, silent, Isabelle lifted her gaze to his. The uncertainty there cleaved him in two. "Please."

Please.

With a groan, he swept her into his arms. "Yes, Isabelle," he rasped between kisses, half laughing, half crying. "Yes, I will spend forever with you."

"Is this real?" Maeve whispered loudly in the crowd. "I cannot tell if this is the performance."

"I . . . I . . . do not know," the countess mused, looking to Derham, and then Isabelle's mother and cousin winked at one another.

Holding Isabelle close, Cyrus stared briefly over the top of her head to Derham. His friend, her cousin, winked again. This time . . . at Cyrus.

And then it hit him. The invitation, the pairing with Isabelle for the pantomime. The German mentor. Cyrus looked down at Isabelle. "He coordinated all this. Derham," he clarified. "He was . . . playing matchmaker . . . and by your mother's look and smile, she was also part of it."

Isabelle's puzzled gaze followed Cyrus's to Val. Uncertainty flared in her eyes, and when she spoke, her words emerged haltingly. "And . . . do you have any regrets at their interference?"

"Yes," he said automatically, and Isabelle's face fell. Cyrus lightly caught her chin, bringing her eyes up to his. "I regret they didn't interfere sooner."

Her lips parted, and then a watery smile formed on her lips, and Cyrus kissed the shock from her mouth.

"I love you, Isabelle. I always have. I want to spend forever with you," he said, his voice hoarsened with emotion.

Isabelle lovingly stroked her palms along the lapels of his jacket. "Tell me, Cyrus Hill, are you saying yes to my proposal?"

He grinned. "I am."

And with the guests cheering wildly and clapping and crying behind them, Cyrus kissed her once more.

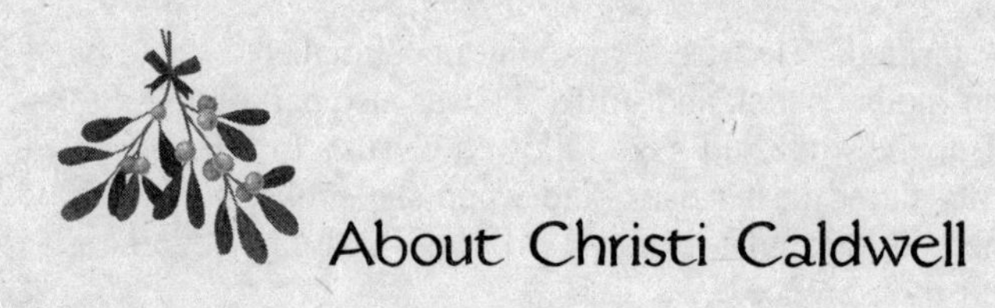

About Christi Caldwell

USA TODAY bestselling, RITA-nominated author **Christi Caldwell** blames Julie Garwood and Judith McNaught for luring her into the world of historical romance. While sitting in her graduate school apartment at the University of Connecticut, Christi decided to set aside her notes and pick up her laptop to try her hand at romance. She believes the most perfect heroes and heroines have imperfections, and she rather enjoys torturing them before crafting them a well-deserved happily ever after! Christi makes her home in southern Connecticut where she spends her time writing her own enchanting historical romances and caring for her three spirited children!

COMPROMISE UNDER THE MISTLETOE

by Janna MacGregor

Chapter One

Old Halig Inn
Cheshire
December 1815, the happiest of seasons . . . at least for some

Caroline Whitmore tightened her stomach for the all-out brawl that was in her future. A familiar, deep voice wished the innkeeper a Happy Christmas. The dark, rich vibrance in his greeting reminded her of a perfectly aged brandy. The slight pounding of boots and the slap of a hat against a thigh provided further proof that Lord Stephen Whitmore had finally arrived.

She glanced at the clock on the fireplace mantel. He was early, as was his custom. Yet this time he was only five minutes ahead of schedule instead of his normal ten. Perhaps he'd changed his habits since she'd last seen him. After all, it had been exactly one year to the day since she'd left him.

"M'lady?" The friendly innkeeper, Mr. Bertram, called out as he knocked on the private sitting room door. "Your husband is 'ere to fetch you for the duke's Revelry party."

As Caroline forced her gaze to her husband's, the quill she held between her fingers cracked under protest. Damn him for looking so fine.

That was a lie. He was better than fine. The sharp angles

of his cheekbones framed his face just as she remembered. His eyes were still huge, with the same bold blue color. They'd always had the ability to steal her breath.

But not today.

Caroline threw back her shoulders in defiance. She would not allow herself to moon over him.

His nostrils flared, and one side of his mouth quirked upward. It made little difference whether it was in anger for her disappearance or because she was under the same roof as he. She'd not allow herself to feel any guilt for her decision to leave him last Christmas. It was his favorite holiday, but she'd had no other choice. She would have lost her sense of worth if she'd stayed any longer.

Enough of such thoughts. There were more important things to attend to.

Namely, business.

And that business would take place at the Duke of Greystoke's Revelry party: an annual gathering during the holidays and one of the most highly sought-after invitations in all the kingdom. Of course, it helped that her uncle *was* the Duke of Greystoke, and her cousin Cressie issued the invitations. Though the duke selfishly took all the glory for the event, her cousin had shared her involvement with Caroline. It was Cressie's work that made the event spectacular.

She stood slowly as Stephen came to her side. As she tilted her chin and pasted on a slight smile, his rich scent surrounded her, marking her, reminding her of all the times they'd made love. Their compatibility in bed had never been an issue.

A sudden rush of heat marched across her cheeks. It always occurred when she thought of him pleasuring her—putting her above everything else in his life. That had only happened when they were in the bedroom. All other times, she had been nothing more than a piece of furniture gathering dust.

"Caro, how lovely to see you again." His voice dropped an octave, making her blood thicken. With a surprise attack, he took her hand and brought it to his lips. Though the kiss was perfunctory, her heart fluttered in approval.

One would think after a year, she'd be immune to him and his charms.

"Do either of you wish for tea or something a little more celebratory?" Mr. Bertram waggled his eyebrows. "Ah, Christmastide is always a favorite of me and my missus. A little mulled wine or spiced grog for the occasion?"

Caroline smiled politely. "No, thank you—"

"Mr. Bertram, I've already prepared a tray. Never you mind, my lady. 'Tis no problem at all," Mrs. Bertram called out as she entered the room, then set out the mugs of mulled wine and a plate of shortbread.

The aroma of mulling spices filled the air. Perhaps it wasn't such a bad idea to have a drink for fortitude. At least it would keep Caroline's mind off Stephen's tantalizing fragrance of evergreens. Mixed with his own unique masculine scent, the combination was deadly.

At least to her self-control.

Her husband gifted the innkeeper's wife with a generous smile. "Thank you, madame. I'm sure Lady Stephen will enjoy it immensely. I'm certain I will."

Mr. Bertram's good wife blushed at Stephen's kindness, then curtseyed before leaving. Her husband waited at the door. Without warning, Mr. Bertram caught his wife around the waist and pointed above.

Like a wedge of geese following the lead goose's directions, they all—at the same time—looked above the door. Mrs. Bertram giggled like a young girl of fifteen at the sight of the mistletoe before the innkeeper kissed her soundly on the lips with a loud smack.

"Merry Christmas," they called out in unison as they shut the door behind them, the happiness in their glad tidings echoing through the room.

Quickly, the joyfulness evaporated, leaving Caroline alone with her husband.

Without a word, Stephen walked to the opposite side of the small table. The fire blazed in welcome, and he waved a hand for her to sit.

She was the granddaughter of the previous Duke of Greystoke and the niece of the current duke. That fact alone meant she knew manners, and it was still her duty to serve her guest. She'd been the one to initiate their rendezvous. After sitting on the edge of the wooden chair, she straightened her skirts and reached for a plate to serve him.

Before she could do so, Stephen sat across from her and picked up a plate where he piled several pieces of shortbread. Caroline had expected him to set it in front of himself. Her eyes widened slightly when he handed the plate to her.

Caroline took a sip of the delicious wine and forced herself to relax. At least, they were being civil to one another. She cleared her throat, determined to be pleasant. "I believe that's the first time you've ever waited on me."

"If you'd have stayed with me during the last year, maybe it wouldn't have been the first time." The devilment that flashed in his eyes pinned her in place.

Why was she surprised that anger roiled under the surface of his calm demeanor? "Stephen, don't."

He didn't acknowledge her plea, nor did he continue to badger her. With a natural nonchalance, he leaned against his chair and took a swig of wine as he studied her.

Carefully, she set her mug down. "I'm sure you have questions."

Before she could continue, he shook his head. "Actually, I only have one."

She cocked her head. For him to go along with her plans without asking about every detail was a shock. He was the most diligent man she'd ever met when it came to work. Unfortunately, he never considered her as important.

"Why?" he demanded.

"Why what?" she countered.

He leaned forward, halving the distance between them. His eyes weren't flashing anymore but blazing in smoldering anger. "Why did you leave me?"

"I told you." She nibbled on the inside of her cheek. It was a burdensome habit, but it kept her somewhat calm.

"Because of Betsey?" The incredulity in his voice shot through the room.

"It wasn't Betsey." She kept her voice even.

"That's not what you wrote in this note." He pulled a piece of her stationery, torn and well-read, from his coat pocket. He opened it, flipped it onto the table, then pointed at a paragraph as if daring her to read it.

Though Caroline had every word memorized, she dipped her gaze to the letter.

> *Furthermore, if you remember, Betsey destroyed my flower garden, the one I spent months creating. You said it wasn't her. However, the evidence suggested otherwise. Rose petals fell out of her mouth as she stood in my garden chewing her cud. I can't live where a meandering, vagabond ruminant is believed over me.*

"I stand by what I wrote," she said calmly.

With a smirk, Stephen slid her a side-eyed glance. "In defense of the old girl, that week her milk had a divine floral essence to it. I thought you enjoyed it."

He would not ruffle her, though the fifteen thousand butterflies in her stomach were threatening to fly off and take her with them. "This isn't about Betsey and her gastric adventures. I've tried to talk with you about our marriage dozens of times. We didn't *have* a marriage, because you were never around. Except at night in our bedroom, I never crossed your mind. You never told me when an emergency arose at the Heartfeld Hall estate that needed your assistance. You'd be gone for hours doing estate work without me knowing what you were doing. What about when you had to travel to London for a week? I found out that you'd left from a servant."

"Caro," he said softly. "I was completely devoted to you, and you were aware I had responsibilities that demanded my attention. That's my work. Every new marriage is an adjustment."

"No." She shook her head curtly. "Being considerate isn't an *adjustment*. Let me make it easier for you. I wanted . . . no, I *needed* to be important to you, and you never allowed me that opportunity."

He stared at the table as if trying to divine the proper response before addressing her. "You're my wife. Of course you're important to me."

"Not as important as the rest of them." She waved a hand in the air. "For instance, practically everyone on the estate, not to mention Betsey, follows you as if you're a gift from heaven."

"I must be imagining this," he mumbled. "My wife is jealous of a cow."

"I'm not jealous of Betsey." He was deliberately twisting her words. The fierce urge to pace the room made Caroline itch. Instead, she lightly tapped one half-boot under her skirts. "She's not just a cow, and you're well aware of that fact."

"You make it sound like something tawdry." Stephen raised an infuriating eyebrow. "I suppose I can see where the jealousy comes from. I admit we are close. I did raise her from birth. She's always seen me as someone special." He leaned a little closer, never taking his eyes off hers, and lowered his voice. "You did once, too."

She felt that familiar pull, the one that neither of them could resist. It would be so easy to close the inches between them and press her lips against his. The fullness of his bottom lip always intrigued her. She never could deny herself the opportunity to nibble on that tender flesh. The blue of his eyes sparkled like a dark, rushing river. Betsey the cow probably thought his eyes resembled sapphires, but they were deeper in color. They reminded Caroline of cobalt, and like a magnet, she was drawn to them.

"Don't twist this into something as simple as Betsey. It's the whole herd, your tenants, the community, the entire estate, and everything and everyone else. You have your priorities, and I have mine. You're an intelligent man. I thought you'd have understood." She forced herself to lean back, breaking the spell between them.

"Perhaps I get a little too focused on a task when I'm working and can't be distracted." He appraised her with a stare designed to tear down her defenses. "You want more attention? Is that fair to say?"

"Seriously, Stephen. It's more than that—"

"I'm at a loss. What is it then?" He thrummed his fingers on the table. "Would children be the answer?"

"Children?" she asked in disbelief. She pressed the serviette to her mouth to smother the urge to scream. After a few seconds, she felt it safe to continue without lashing out.

"It might help," he offered guardedly.

"Another thing to add to your daily to-do list, have children?" Were all men this obtuse or just her husband? "Unbelievable," she muttered. "You still don't understand. If we did have children, you would just ignore them."

"I don't understand why you feel that way." He crossed his arms over his chest. "You have my utmost esteem. And our children would too." A slight hesitation lurked in his hawklike eyes. "If you wanted a dog instead, it would hold my esteem also."

Fighting to stay composed, she rested her head in her hand.

"You want to be my partner?" he asked.

"Yes." Perhaps he was beginning to understand.

"I don't need one of those. What I need is a wife."

She released a stilted breath. Why had she allowed herself to hope he'd changed?

"Caro." Her name sounded like a plea. "Tell me what to do."

"Help me convince my uncle that we're happily married. Only until he releases my money." The disquiet between them vibrated until she couldn't take it any longer. She made the mistake of glancing at his lips, the very ones that had tasted every inch of her.

She could not let herself be swept away by him or his perfect lips. It had to be the Christmastide enchantment that made her mouth water when she looked at him. She shook her head once to remind herself why they were together again.

Twenty thousand pounds.

That's what this whole visit was about. Pretending she and Stephen were a happy couple, so her uncle, the Duke of Greystoke, would give her the money from her trust. Caroline would soon turn twenty-four, and the trust ended when she turned twenty-five. Only the duke had the power to give her those funds early. When she made the request weeks ago, he had demanded she attend the party with Stephen.

With a quick, efficient movement, she pulled her chair closer to the table. "I've drawn up a plan that should make the entire holiday pleasant and agreeable for us both."

"A plan? I'm agog with curiosity. Feigning to be a happy couple during the Revelry should be easy for you. You were always an excellent actress, as can be attested by your acting abilities when you played the happy wife." He lifted his mug and took another sip of wine, then pressed his lips into a straight line. "Or at least, I thought you were happy. But I digress. Pray tell me your thoughts."

Her left eye twitched at his sarcasm. "May I remind you that I'm willing to split the amount with you? Ten thousand pounds is something to take notice of." She slid her eyes over his body, then back up as if evaluating him. "Even for you."

"You wound me, wife." He ran a hand through his raven-black hair, the length too long to be considered fashionable by the dandies around town. It suited him perfectly, softening his sharp, masculine features. "That amount *would* come in handy." He exhaled ever so slightly and leaned against the back of his chair while straightening his legs. "The mill suffered some damage recently, and it needs repair. I would be forced to dip into Heartfeld Hall's reserves, but with this money, I wouldn't have to."

His eyes creased in worry.

She'd seen the expression once before, and it had unsettled her. One of his tenant farmers had been in an accident that resulted in a crushed leg. Stephen had been consumed with guilt, because the farmer was helping with the estate harvest. Her husband had made it his mission to find the best medical treatment. He'd paid for the cost and had taken care of the man's family.

Things had to be dire at the mill if he was actually considering taking money from the estate's reserves. To Stephen, those coffers were untouchable.

He truly cared for the people who worked on his estate.

If only he had cared about her with the same ferocity.

Now, she was being maudlin. He'd always taken care of her financially. He'd been generous in his allowance. His generosity had allowed her to reside in London for the past year.

Caroline tucked her chin and examined the paper on the table. Slowly, she slid it across. "I think this will come in handy if we're caught by surprise or question how we should act around one another. All we have to do is follow the plan I created."

Stephen reached into his morning coat and pulled out a pair of spectacles.

Caroline stilled at the sight. They were the ones she had given him during their first year of marriage for his birthday. She didn't even think he had appreciated the gift. He'd simply murmured his thanks, then tucked them away in his desk, never to be seen again.

Completely unaware of the turmoil running amok through her thoughts, Stephen's eyes raced over the page. He slipped the spectacles from his face and put them away without a sound. He pressed one fist against his mouth as if he battled for control over his emotions.

She'd shocked him with her demands—obviously.

Yet, something wasn't right. She leaned closer to examine the page that had caused him such irrefutable anguish. Everything she'd written had been straightforward and clearly laid out as to the expected behavior between the two of them, both privately and publicly. That's when she noticed that his shoulders were slightly shaking.

The cad. He was laughing at her document.

He was laughing at her.

STEPHEN'S OLDER BROTHER by a year, the Marquess of Rancourt, would have punched him in the shoulder if he were here. "Never anger a lady" had always been the family's mantra, and Stephen tried to follow that creed, but some of Caro's terms were absurd.

He peeked across the table and saw that her cheeks were flushed. Her brown eyes shot sparks of raw anger in his direction, which made her that much more beautiful. Her chestnut hair was neatly arranged around her heart-shaped face, but the moue of displeasure around her mouth gave him pause.

How long had it been since he'd last tasted those delightful, full lips that always reminded him of the brilliant pink of spring's blossoms? Too long.

Exactly a year and three hours.

It didn't escape his notice that today marked the anniversary of her leaving him without a goodbye, other than the letter he always carried on his person, a reminder that his wife had chosen London over him.

He shouldn't have teased her about Betsey, another bad decision on his part.

"Caro, don't be angry with me." He smoothed the corners of the document before him. "You must admit, the idea of dictating that we share a pot of chocolate when we break our fast is a little controlling."

"I wouldn't say controlling. I'd say prepared. We must plan for every contingency." She pursed her lips. "If my uncle is well enough to come downstairs, he eats later than everyone else. I thought it best that we break our fast and are gone from the dining room before he arrives. I'm willing to change the chocolate to tea. The important thing is that everyone else see us together so that word travels back to my uncle that we're husband and wife." This time, she was the one to thrum her fingers against the table.

"We *are* husband and wife and will always be so." He clenched his teeth so tightly that, for an instant, he thought he might have broken his jaw. "You're willing to forgo the chocolate and will consider tea? When shall we partake in that, and how shall I drink it? With sugar and cream or just cream? What if I want coffee? What impact will that have on our appearance as a happy couple? I know you despise the brew."

She studied her clasped hands. "Don't mock me."

"I'm not. I'm making a point about how ludicrous this is. It's Christmastide, a time for people to celebrate and enjoy one another's company. It's my favorite time of year, and I'll be damned . . ." He let the words trail to nothing, then blew out a breath. "I've been devoted to only one woman in my life. You and *only* you." How in God's name was he supposed to address the real issue that bothered him? Oh, to hell with it. Best to lance the wound, as they say. "This proviso that we share a bedroom, but I'm relegated to a cot in the dressing room?" He sliced the air with his hand. "No."

Her eyes widened. "What do you mean 'no'? If we're not together, then my uncle will know we're pretending."

"The servants tidying our rooms will know we're not sleeping together. Word will reach the duke within minutes, I expect."

Caroline leaned forward, and a slight smile tugged at her lips. "I've thought of that. You can make the bed every morning before they arrive."

He smirked at the suggestion. "No."

She stared at the ceiling for a moment. "All right. I'll sleep on the cot and make the bed."

"No," he repeated. "If you want my cooperation, then we sleep in the same bed every night."

"I can't allow that," she answered while waving a hand in dismissal. "We'll climb into bed, then things will happen."

"Tell me what things you imagine happening."

"That comment is beneath you," she murmured.

"As I recall, you like to be beneath me except for that time in the library. Remember?" He lowered his voice. "What about the kitchen when we both wanted food? We ended up eating something else."

"Stephen."

The hesitation in her voice encouraged him to continue. "The last time was a little over a year ago when I bent you over the chair in my study, then I whisked you upstairs. Then I was the one beneath you, remember?"

Her slight nod was as clear as if she shouted her answer from the window.

Her mouth softened, and desire smoldered in her eyes. It always reminded him of a banked fire that threatened to blaze instantly. Blood roared through his veins as his own desire threatened to incinerate him from within. One long, lonely year of sleeping without his wife was about to come to an end if he had his way.

"Whatever problems we had with our marriage didn't move into our marriage bed." He leaned closer until a mere inch separated them. Her sweet fragrance surrounded him, and her breath, that familiar peppermint scent, caressed his cheek. It would be so easy to close the distance and kiss her as he longed to do. Instead, he caressed his finger up and down the soft skin of her cheek.

She closed her eyes in response. Abruptly, she leaned away as if awakening from a bad dream. "All right. We'll sleep in the same bed, but that is all. We sleep and nothing else."

It was a slight victory on his part, but it wasn't enough. "We make love at least once. I will choose the occasion." He reached for the well-worn goodbye letter she had written him and carefully put it back in his pocket. "Otherwise, I'm going home and spending the rest of the Christmas holiday with my brother's family. The decision is yours. Shall I have both carriages readied or just one?"

Chapter Two

Caroline had little doubt she resembled a mouth-gaping-open trout caught by a fisherman's hook. How in the world was she supposed to respond to Stephen's demand that they share the marriage bed and its pleasures?

It would be easy to say yes. When she had recalled all their torrid lovemaking sessions, her pulse had pounded at the base of her neck. Stephen had seen it, too. The way his nostrils had flared when he'd studied her had made her feel naked.

The truth was she always ached for his touch, and he the same for her. Every time, she'd enjoyed their lovemaking. After her favorite maid had explained what to expect from the marital act in bed, Caroline quickly learned that a significant amount of detail had been skipped over. She had been more than surprised and, frankly, thrilled when Stephen had filled in all that missing information.

However, his prowess between the bedsheets and in the other rooms he'd mentioned did not negate the fact that he'd left her alone the rest of their time together.

In essence, he was married to his estate and not her.

She would not and could not forget it. She'd made a promise to herself. She would not be treated like a piece of artwork hidden behind a screen, only to be noticed when it was time to dust.

An apt analogy if she did say so herself.

As a young girl, she'd spent her time roaming the portrait gallery of her home. It was her favorite place. One day, she'd found a discarded self-portrait of her great-aunt Agatha in the attic and had become enchanted with it. She'd immediately hung it in the portrait gallery. Forsaken by her mother while her father barely registered her presence, Caroline had taken a vow in front of her great-aunt Agatha's self-portrait that she would never allow herself to be ignored by family again.

Stephen was her closest family, and he only paid her attention when it suited him to do so—at night, in bed.

She slowly rose from the table. Stephen stood after her, nodded his farewell, then walked toward the door.

Caroline swallowed her immediate outrage and forced herself to think. She'd always prided herself for the ability to ferret out the logics of a matter. But with him, it was a difficult task at best. She made the mistake of looking across the room where he stood with his legs apart. The stance emphasized his broad chest and narrow waist. Yet, it was the determined gleam in his eyes that made him breathtaking.

"Caro, it's not that difficult of a proposal." He depressed the latch of the door and pulled the door open as if to leave.

"Stop, I beg of you." She rushed forward.

He slowly closed the door, never taking his gaze from hers.

If he helped her with this, it would be worth it. Besides, why shouldn't she enjoy a night of lovemaking? "I agree."

One side of his mouth quirked upward in a roguish smile. Now he wasn't playing fair. She had seen that same smile a hundred times before, and it never had failed to charm her.

For the love of heaven, she was in trouble. Whatever argumentative abilities she possessed, she needed to guard them with her life. The situation before her called for diplomacy and friendly persuasion—not her strong suits.

She couldn't allow him to control the situation any longer. For one thing, he might well threaten to leave again.

"On one condition," she volleyed.

"And that is?" Stephen's entire body tensed at the words.

Good. She still had the ability to get a reaction from him.

"I will sleep with you every night in bed, and I will make love to you one night of *my* choosing, not yours."

"I choose the night," he corrected.

"No." She straightened her shoulders and narrowed her eyes for effect. "The only way I agree is if I choose the night."

"That settles it," he said. "I'll take my leave now. Merry Christmastide."

Bother. "Wait. I agree only if you promise not to leave the house party nor will you threaten me with leaving again. After my uncle sees we're a happy couple, then by all means, go on your merry way."

Silence met her demand. Caroline held her breath until she was certain her lungs were on fire.

"Done."

That one word broke the silence, and Caroline gasped for air. It was finished, and she couldn't help but smile in triumph.

But then, a wicked grin spread across his lips. "Congratulations, dear wife. But I must share a little something."

His words melted the smile from her face. Warily, she regarded him. "What is it?"

"The truth is . . . I was never going to leave you. Leaving is your forte, as you demonstrated a year ago. It's not mine." With that, he walked out of the room. His demeanor turned immediately jovial as he called for his carriage.

She stood frozen as her mind whirled.

He hadn't cared enough to find her in London when she'd gone there.

For days, she had expected him to come to her after he realized how much he missed her. Heartfeld Hall was only an hour from London. As the months drifted by, he never deemed her important enough to come see her. He wrote a few curt words every month when he sent the monthly allowance.

She'd answered immediately for the first two months, but when he never answered her *answer*, she'd realized it was a wasted effort. At some point in the last year, she had actually tried to figure out whether her husband said more to her in those notes than he had on an average day when they lived together, but the task was too depressing.

He didn't care to visit her, nor did he try to persuade her to come home.

The truth was that her husband didn't really give a damn where she was, though obviously, he'd prefer that she was in his bed. Even now, his only request had to do with bedding—not with conversation, or dancing, or . . . or anything that distinguished a wife from a mistress, to be blunt.

Caroline folded her papers and slipped them into her reticule. Her time would best be spent working on how to convince her uncle they were a happy couple.

She marched out of the room and found Stephen enjoying a conversation with the innkeeper and his wife.

"Darling, there you are," Stephen announced with a smile, holding out his hand as if nothing unsettling had occurred in the moments before. "The carriage is here. We mustn't keep the horses waiting. Mr. and Mrs. Bertram were kind enough to place several hot bricks in the coach for our comfort."

"How thoughtful," she cooed. "Thank you."

When she reached Stephen's side, he took her hand in his and raised it to his mouth. At his warm touch, she blinked twice. She'd forgotten how long his fingers were and how big his hand was.

"I can't wait until we're alone together, my love," he whispered.

At Stephen's murmurings, Mrs. Bertram sighed.

Caroline wanted to roll her eyes.

Well, who knew her husband could play the besotted lover? Two could play at his game.

Caroline beamed at him. "Oh, darling, you mustn't say such things." She turned to Mrs. Bertram. "I've always considered a good husband resembles a well-trained hunting dog. Don't you?" She didn't wait for a response. "All you have to do is feed them regularly, scratch their belly every once in a while, perhaps give them a treat or two, and they're devoted to you for life."

Mr. and Mrs. Bertram's eyes widened.

"Charming analogy, darling." Stephen chuckled, but the sound held little humor. He turned to the couple, and they quickly exchanged Yuletide greetings before he escorted Caroline out into the cold.

As everyone in the courtyard examined them walking together, she hooked her arm around his.

After nodding to a couple who were entering the inn, he leaned near. The warmth of his breath tickled her ear. "What do you think happens when you kick that same dog out into the cold? I wonder if he's still as devoted."

"I think the proof is whether the dog still begs to sleep in the bed." She squeezed his forearm, then regarded him with a sweet smile. "You weren't kicked out. I left." By then, they'd reached his carriage. "I want to take my vehicle. Where is it?"

Stephen shook his head slightly as if shaking off a physical blow. "I told the coachman to return it to London."

Once again, he was making a unilateral decision for both of them. "You had no right. My trunks were in the other carriage."

"I had the groomsman move your things here." He smiled slightly. "Besides, mine is bigger. If the duke discovers your carriage is here, he'll know we're not really back together. This way, it appears we've traveled together and stayed at the inn before the party to spend time together."

"How thoughtful of you," she said sweetly. Without waiting for him to respond, Caroline took the footman's hand, then stepped into the carriage as if she owned it.

Stephen followed with a slightly stunned look on his face.

Caroline sat in the forward-facing seat and adjusted her cloak about her as she rested her feet on the warming bricks. She took a breath and collected herself. "How will I travel home after the house party?"

"I'll make certain you arrive home safe and sound afterward." He crossed his heart with his forefinger. "On my honor."

She leaned back against the squab, watching Stephen as the carriage jerked into motion. "I wish my uncle wasn't making me do this."

"Perhaps this is his way to ensure you would come."

Caroline shook her head. "I'd already accepted Cressie's invitation to attend before her father sent the letter demanding both of us join the party, or I wouldn't receive my money."

His mouth thinned into an angry line; the displeasure written all over his face. "You were planning to attend the most celebrated Yuletide festivities without a single thought of me. The most popular event in all of England where men and women seduce each other, marriages are destroyed—"

"Marriages are made there, too," she countered, then glanced down and pretended to study her clasped hands. Guilt consumed her that she hadn't considered his displeasure at being left alone at the holidays. "I'm not really fond of large gatherings." Her confession would show how alone she was in the world. But he deserved the truth. "But I had nowhere else to go for Christmastide. I thought you'd go to your brother's house to celebrate. No one else invited me, because they think I'm married . . ."

She let the words trail to nothing. All her friends were

visiting their relatives in the countryside, and no one had thought to include her except her cousin.

Stephen leaned forward and placed his hand over her clasped ones and squeezed gently. "Did the thought ever occur to you to come home for Christmas?" he asked softly. "To come home to me?"

A DULL ACHE rattled around Stephen's chest as his anger evaporated. The look of forlornness on his wife's face practically brought him to his knees. Caroline had always been strong and confident, but this reaction meant her wounds were deep. She kept silent and focused on the snowy landscape racing by as they made their way to the Duke of Greystoke's winter estate.

He ran a gloved hand down his face, hoping to find something he could say to ease the gulf between them. "You're always welcome home."

She shook her head slightly but still kept her gaze trained on the view outside the window. "I'm aware you would allow me to live at Heartfeld Hall, but it's not home." She finally turned her attention to him. "Home is where you're appreciated, and a part of something greater than yourself. I'm trying to create that in London."

He tamped down the urge to argue about her not being appreciated. "Tell me what you're doing in London."

The brightness in her eyes was reminiscent of a perfect sunrise, ready to rule the world. He'd always thought her pretty, but now she stole his breath.

"I plan to buy the building I've been living in. I'd like to open an art gallery for women. There are apartments for studios on the main floor, along with two large rooms that would be perfect to display their work. So many wonderful artists are women and never get a chance to show their talent. I plan to change that."

Interesting. In two years of marriage, he'd never heard her speak about her love for art. Perhaps she was right—he hadn't made time for conversation. He wished he had. "Will you paint also?"

Her cheeks flushed a perfect shade of pink. "No. I have no talent, but at my father's country estate, I roamed the portrait gallery and studied every piece. They were so lifelike and seemed to come alive." She stopped suddenly and bent her head. "You'll think this silly, but when I was a girl, I would sit in front of my great-aunt Agatha's portrait and just stare at it."

"Why would I think that silly?"

She met his gaze and tilted her chin in that defiant pose he'd remembered during their year together. She always did it when she was unsure of herself.

"Sometimes I'd talk to her. She painted it herself, you see. She was so present in that self-portrait, as if she was standing before me."

He didn't respond immediately, understanding falling into place. Caro had been lonely growing up with no siblings after her mother had abandoned her father. And her daughter.

She would have told him this years ago, if he'd taken the time to ask.

Caroline straightened her shoulders as if daring him to say something insulting.

"Darling, I would only think it silly if your great-aunt Agatha had answered you."

When her eyes filled with a fierce sparkling light, he knew he'd said the right thing.

"After my mother left, there wasn't anyone who took an interest in me. I really didn't have anyone to chat with except for the servants. But they all had tasks and duties to perform so"—she smiled and wrinkled her nose adorably—"I made my great-aunt's portrait a sounding board, a friend. When I got older, I filled my time with the biographies of the masters and learned everything I could about the business of representing artists."

Her life had been so different from his. Stephen had grown up in a large, loving family. But their father had instilled a strong work ethic in all his children including that one's responsibilities to the estate and the people who worked the land came before pleasure.

Perhaps he might have taken that responsibility a little too far. "I wish I'd known this before."

The fragile peace between them shattered when she shot him a chilly stare. "You never asked. Why, would it have changed anything?"

"Of course, it would. You're my wife."

"So you say, after I've been gone a year," Caro said. "I don't want to argue. Forget I said anything."

Her unhappiness lingered in the air. Stephen struggled to find a way to keep her talking. The sound of her voice, even if she was angry at him, filled the emptiness that had haunted him for the last year. "Would you continue to live in the building?"

She nodded briskly. "There's a large apartment on the top floor. I plan to hold receptions and salons there." She smiled. "I already held several, inviting artists and patrons."

He narrowed his eyes. He didn't like the idea of her never coming home. She'd made a life without him. For a moment, he thought of her mother running off with her lover to the Americas, but Caro was entirely different from her poor excuse for a parent.

The urge to bring her home had been fierce. He hadn't wanted to force Caro to return to Heartfeld Hall. That would have been a recipe for disaster. He wanted her to make the choice to be with him for herself.

As with many couples, theirs had been an arranged marriage. Their fathers had been lifelong friends and thought their children should marry. Both Stephen and Caro had been young when they'd said their vows. He was only a month older than her. But in their year of separation, he felt as if he'd aged a decade.

If only he could have their first months again. He'd fallen in love with her and had foolishly believed that she had fallen in love with him.

The carriage turned off the main road onto a drive lined with stately elm trees. In the distance, the large estate of the Duke of Greystoke reigned over all it surveyed.

Fittingly, the stone used to build the hall was gray. It would have been stark and ugly except for the merry boughs of evergreens and holly that decorated the windows, doors, and even the massive staircase that led to the front door. The festive atmosphere seemed to glisten before them.

"We're here," Caroline said softly. "Remember to follow my plan."

Stephen would follow *his* plan. He intended to use this holiday to woo his wife. He should have done so when they were first betrothed. It would be the toughest challenge he ever faced, but he believed in Christmas miracles.

"Don't worry, Caro." He knocked on the carriage door and a footman in the duke's livery instantly pulled open the door. "I know exactly what needs to be done."

Chapter Three

As Caroline and Stephen entered Greystoke Manor, her trepidation grew with every step, until she felt as if the wisest decision for both of them would be to return to the inn and skip Christmas altogether.

She chided herself for such a thought. Where was her backbone? She had promised herself she would see this through, and so she would. She just had to remember that every day she spent at her uncle's party, the Revelry, brought her closer to securing her future along with providing opportunities for women artists.

Besides, she relished the opportunity to see her cousin, Cressie. Too much time had passed since they'd last been in each other's company.

When she and Stephen reached the top steps, the butler, Twist, greeted them with a deep bow. "Lord and Lady Stephen, welcome to the Revelry at Greystoke."

The opulence of Greystoke was always awe-inspiring, but decorated for the Revelry, it took her breath away. Her gaze darted from the evergreens arranged in beautiful vases to the garlands spread throughout the room. The scent reminded her of a forest. The ceiling held branches of mistletoe and kissing boughs suspended from hooks. It looked as if they had entered a magical Christmas fairyland.

Twist nodded to a footman, who stepped forward to take their coats and wraps. Stephen helped her with her cloak then gave it to the footman.

"Caro, you're finally here!" Cressie came running down the steps with a reassuring, incandescent smile.

Though such an action might be looked down upon by the most proper dames of society, no one chastised Cressie. She was the Duke of Greystoke's daughter.

"It's been ages." Cressie pressed a kiss to each of Caroline's cheeks and followed up with a tight embrace.

Caroline did the same. "I know, but I'm here now. We have much to discuss."

Cressie turned to Stephen. "Welcome, my lord. My father and I are delighted you're here to celebrate with us."

He executed a perfect bow and raised Cressie's hand to his lips. It was irritating to watch him turn the simple greeting into something significant. Anyone receiving his attentions felt as if they were somehow special and privy to his deepest thoughts.

Why, why couldn't he have bothered to do that with her?

Perhaps she had expected too much. He had a tremendous amount of responsibility for running his estate, taking care of his tenants, and managing the hundreds of acres of land and forest that surrounded their house.

No, it was his house.

Not hers.

To think anything different would negate all the tears she'd wept, and the sacrifices she'd made over the last year.

Cressie announced, "This year all guests are given a task in the preparations for Christmas. There are two remaining items on the list appropriate for couples." She pulled a piece of paper from her skirt pocket and quickly perused it. "You can find the yule log, or you may take responsibility for the children's Christmas carol performance."

The only choice was the yule log. She and Stephen could pick out a log, tag it with a ribbon for the footmen to bring to the house, then be back in front of a fire within an hour. The children's choir would require hours of practice time, which meant they'd be forced to spend hours in each other's company. "The yule log," Caroline stated.

"The children's choir," Stephen answered at the same time.

Stephen took her hand and brought it to the middle of his chest. "Darling, your wish is my command. The yule log it is. I always wanted to see the duke's estate."

If there was one thing Caroline detested, it was tromping over frozen land in the cold. An hour to secure the log was her limit. "If you have your heart set on seeing the estate, I'm sure Cressie could arrange a tour of the barns and stables."

"The list of gentlemen's activities includes just such an event," Cressie reassured them.

"I'd rather you joined me," Stephen said to Caroline with a sinful smile. "If it's cold, I'll keep you warm. Besides, you appreciate my fascination with animal husbandry, particularly cattle." He raised an eyebrow.

She never should have allowed him to bring Betsey into her reasons for leaving. The word *no* was on the tip of her tongue, but then she thought better of it. Best to give in and prevent an argument that the other guests might overhear.

"We'll have to see what other events are planned. But to spend time with you and the cows? It's almost as if we're at Heartfeld Hall for Christmastide." Caroline clasped her hands together, then turned to Cressie and nodded with a forced smile. "We'd be delighted to find the yule log."

"It's settled then," Cressie announced.

Twist begged for Stephen's attention to discuss the duke's preferences for the perfect yule log, and Cressie took Caroline's arm and led her a slight distance away.

"Do look at this stained glass Christmas panel; it has been in the family since the first Duke of Greystoke," Cressie said. Discreetly, she stole a glance at Stephen, who was listening to Twist. "Is everything all right between the two of you?"

Caroline nodded. "Yes."

Cressie smiled hesitantly. "I'm happy to hear it. Mrs. Peters is in charge of the bedchambers, and I suggested she put you in the green bedroom. It's one of the biggest. I thought you'd be more comfortable there, away from the others. I chose the decorations with you in mind."

"It sounds perfect. I can't thank you enough for inviting me," Caroline said.

"You are family and always welcome. I'm sorry you missed last year, but don't thank me yet. Father instructed me to inform him the minute you arrived. He wants you and your husband to meet his solicitor in the ducal study. Unfortunately, my father won't attend. He hasn't left his bed in several weeks."

"I'm sorry, Cressie," Caroline said. She wasn't fond of her uncle, and she didn't like the way he turned her cousin into something of a superior servant, but she was still sad that he was dying.

"His Grace is determined to live through the Revelry," Cressie said, an unreadable expression on her face. "He will be glad that you both arrived safely."

"Before we see the solicitor, may we change out of our traveling garments first?" Caroline hadn't expected to be thrown into the lion's den so quickly.

Cressie's smile turned sympathetic. "You know how he is. When my father wants something, he wants it right now. Sometimes he reminds me of an adolescent, and even more so now that he is ill."

Just then, a group of guests came down the stairs, demanding Cressie's attention. "I must go. We'll talk soon." With that, she squeezed Caroline's hands once more and walked away.

As Caroline waited patiently for Stephen to finish talking with Twist, three more couples arrived. Luggage and servants crowded into the entry that grew loud, with a frantic energy, like a cacophony of chaos. The duke's dogs barked in excitement. Children squealed in glee over boiled sweets in bowls placed strategically around the room. Above it all, the din of female laughter echoed around her while male voices guffawing over some story joined in the chorus.

It was overwhelming after living quietly on her own. When she turned away from the clatter, Stephen was staring straight at her as if he would devour her. Her heart somersaulted in her chest.

Of course, it was all part of their act. He was expressing desire, not love. She had to remember that critical part and not let her heart lead her brain down the wrong path.

In two strides, he stood before her and took her hand in his. "What's wrong?"

She inhaled and shook her head slightly. "It's nothing."

"You look as if you'd rather be anywhere else but here." He bent ever so slightly and whispered in her ear. "If it's any comfort, I agree with you. Perhaps we could visit the duke's cowshed."

"You're incorrigible," she answered.

"If it brings a smile to your lips, then I don't care."

She dipped her head to hide how much Stephen could affect her. When he brought her hand to his lips, she tried to pull away.

He tightened his grip slightly. "Don't, Caro. People are watching," he murmured.

She released a shaky breath and nodded. Unfortunately, such false shows of affection were necessary over the next fortnight.

"Look, Doretha," a haughty voice said behind them. "There's nothing more romantic than a couple mending their differences."

"Lady Riverton," Stephen whispered. "She's directly behind you."

"I'm not certain she understands the word *mending*," Caroline said with a syrupy smile. She tamped down the urge to turn around and stare. Instead, she batted her eyes at Stephen in a show of modesty. "When she used to visit my mother, they would embroider together. Lady Riverton never could stitch a sampler, let alone actually mend a garment."

Stephen tilted his head back and laughed. Really laughed, one of those jovial sounds that stopped all conversation around them.

Ignoring the rest of the guests, he bent down and brushed his lips against the sensitive skin below her ear, then whispered, "I can't attest to your mending abilities being any better than hers. I never saw you with a needle."

She leaned back in feigned outrage. "I'll have you know I can sew a straight line with my eyes closed."

Still chuckling, he shook his head. "Well then, darling. I can't wait to see how you'll mend our differences."

She blinked at him. Did he think that was even a possibility? She'd never entertained the thought.

With a wink, he continued, "I have every confidence that, between the two of us, we'll become excellent tailors before this holiday is over."

"What does that mean?" she asked, frowning at him.

"Let's investigate the possibility later." He linked her arm around his. "Twist mentioned that your uncle's illness delays our greeting him, but the duke's solicitor is ready for us." Then he said the words that only she could hear. "It's time to break a leg. The real performance is about to begin."

THE FOOTMAN WHO had escorted them through the endless maze of intersecting halls knocked once on a massive door. On the other side, another footman in matching livery swept it open.

Bile rushed up her throat. Caroline placed her hand on her stomach in an effort to control her nervousness. To show any hint of weakness would end their visit early.

As if aware of her unease, Stephen squeezed her hand. "I'm right beside you."

Indeed, he was, and it was comfort. With a contrived calmness that was at direct odds with her disquiet, she stepped into the duke's study.

It was empty but for the duke's elderly solicitor, Mr. Beakens. The massive desk where her uncle would normally have sat was vacant.

"Lord and Lady Stephen, welcome," Mr. Beakens called out, coming creakily to his feet. With a wave of his ink-stained hand, he motioned both of them inside.

Without taking her gaze from the solicitor, Caroline walked to the table at the far end of the duke's study where the solicitor had set up his portable desk. "Good afternoon, Mr. Beakens."

The solicitor nodded in greeting.

"How is my uncle? My cousin mentioned that he is bedridden. I'd like to greet him."

The solicitor shook his head. "The poor man. He isn't receiving visitors today except for his immediate family."

"Is he so ill that my husband and I cannot see him? I'm his niece," she pressed. "Aren't we family?"

The solicitor lifted one corner of his mouth in a vestige of a smile. "Perhaps tomorrow. The duke requested that I handle the matter of your trust. Please be seated."

"Thank you." Caroline's voice wobbled slightly. Apparently, she was a "matter" and not a part of the immediate family.

Once she and Stephen were comfortably seated before the elderly solicitor, he picked up a piece of foolscap and peered at it. "The duke wished me to inform you that the last time he saw you, you looked more and more like your mother." He looked up from the papers he was reading and added, with an apologetic air, "He also said that it wasn't a compliment. 'Her mother was a pretty woman but had as much good sense as the goose we'll eat tomorrow.' His words, not mine."

"I will not tolerate incivilities toward my wife." Stephen's voice was even but with an unmistakable menace underlying it.

Caroline swallowed. It would be lovely if he actually cared enough to defend her as his wife, rather than merely as part of a performance.

The solicitor bowed his head. "My lord, I'm aware this is uncomfortable, but the duke demands I say his piece." He sighed. "I'm to report to him about the status of your marriage. Every day."

Mr. Beakens's gruff admission launched a thousand goose bumps across Caroline's arms as if she'd suffered a sudden chill.

"You can assure the duke that Caro and I are together as husband and wife," Stephen answered curtly, insulted rather than afraid.

If only she could be more like him.

The solicitor held a silver monocle to one eye, magnifying it. Under his intense stare, Caroline held still, never looking away. He turned his attention to Stephen. After a tense moment or so, he dropped the eyepiece and looked back at his papers.

"Lord Stephen." The solicitor looked to Caroline. "Lady Stephen. I'm merely doing my work as the duke directs. He doesn't want either of you to waste his time."

That told Caroline precisely how important she was to her uncle. She swallowed hard but reminded herself that she knew that already.

Stephen reached out and took her hand in his. The warmth of his palm against her own was a balm to her rattled nerves.

"I have it on good authority that you two met at the Halig Inn this morning." Mr. Beakens leaned forward in his chair. "You arrived in two separate carriages. If you'll forgive the presumption, that fact does not suggest you have healed your differences. I'll have to inform the duke, and he has strong views about marriage, as you know."

"Appearances can be deceiving, Mr. Beakens," Stephen answered with a sly smile. "We're here, aren't we? I guarantee you that nothing would keep me from attending the Revelry with"—he turned to Caroline and smiled—"my wife."

Her heart pounded against her ribs as if trying to break free. Whether it was to escape the solicitor's scrutiny or fly into Stephen's arms wasn't a question Caroline wanted to examine too carefully.

Yet, one thing was certain. Her husband's smile should have been declared a lethal weapon. A woman could definitely become lost in a romantic labyrinth with such a look. She definitely had before.

She could not allow it to happen again, or her heart would lay in shambles just as it had when she left him a year ago.

Still, it was comforting to have him by her side, facing the duke's solicitor.

"Here is the duke's final word." The solicitor cleared his throat as he pulled a document from the corner of the duke's desk. "His Grace has generously agreed that Lady Stephen will receive the sum of twenty thousand pounds"—he wrinkled the bridge of his skinny nose—"only if he's fully and completely satisfied you are living as husband and wife."

Caroline didn't move a muscle, but her stomach was performing an endless loop of somersaults. "How will we prove it to him if we can't see him? Only we know our true regard for one another." Caroline directed her gaze to the solicitor. If they obtained a clearer definition of the duke's requirements, the task might not be as burdensome as she once thought.

"That's for the duke to know and you to prove." The solicitor smiled faintly. "His Grace possesses a wry sense of humor, you know." When neither of them responded, the solicitor blinked. "Now, where was I? Oh, yes, right here." He pointed midway down the paper before him. "If you're truly together, it will be apparent for all to see."

No one uttered a word.

Mr. Beakens grimaced slightly, as if embarrassed, then gazed out the window. After a moment, he looked back. "The duke is dying. He wanted me to tell you that . . . before he meets his maker, he wants to do right by you." He nodded to Caroline. "He said it was the least he could do for his dearly departed brother, since you were his only child."

She wanted to hiss at the comment "dearly departed brother." If her uncle had truly cared for her father, then the selfish man would have visited them at least once to see how her father fared after her mother had abandoned them. Perhaps, the duke could have helped.

After Caroline's mother left for the Americas with her much younger lover, her father faded, and when the news came of her death, he crumbled like a piece of decayed wood. As Caroline grew from a child to a young woman, her vibrant father, who had once been a joy to be around, had turned into someone she didn't recognize. He became a shell of a person, ready to wither away. Caroline had no doubt that the desperate sadness her father suffered caused his early death.

She bit her tongue to keep from challenging the duke's words. He'd never cared for her father or for her.

Stephen lifted one perfectly arched brow. "I was unaware that His Grace had been close to Caro's father. I never heard any mention of it." Though his tone was even, he leaned back in his chair, the challenge in his body there for all to see.

"The duke cares for your wife. That's where you come

in," the solicitor declared. "The duke is concerned that if she receives those funds now, you'll lose her forever. He doesn't want his niece turning into a flighty piece of baggage like her mother, who only thought of her own happiness. He believes the move to London—by herself—doesn't bode well for her future."

"That's not true." Caroline tilted her chin in defiance. "I am nothing like my mother."

"Beakens, enough." Stephen's rebuke was clear to all. "Caro will never be like her mother."

The solicitor winced. "Pardon my frankness, sir, but how would you know? Lady Stephen has been living in London this past year. Everyone knows it. Society is talking about it. Prove to the duke that you're both happy with each other. If he believes it, then she'll have the money. The duke won't attend many, if any, of the events that Lady Cressida has planned, but he will have eyes and ears everywhere. He'll know if you're trying to fool him." Mr. Beakens smiled slightly. "For your sake, please don't. The duke will see through it. If he feels you're attempting to gammon him, he'll make access to the trust even harder." The old man relaxed against the back of his chair. "But never fear. His Grace is a fair man. Whatever tales come his way, I'm certain he'll make his own judgment."

She wanted to roll her eyes but managed to keep her expression impassive.

The solicitor examined his paper again, then glanced at them. "I forgot one thing. The duke demands to see you both at the pantomime. If he is able to attend anything, it will be the pantomime. *Cinderella,* this year."

"What are you talking about?" Stephen's voice was so low it sounded like a growl.

"The pantomime is an annual custom. Lord Stephen, I understand this is your first time at the Revelry. The duke expects everyone to attend." Mr. Beakens tidied up his papers. "It's mandatory for you both. If you'll excuse me, I have other business."

Stephen stiffened beside her, then murmured for her ears only. "Why do I feel like we're two puppets, and the duke is pulling all the strings."

A footman stepped forward to usher Caroline and Stephen into the hallway. Once there, the liveried servant, who closely resembled an automaton, bowed then returned to the study leaving them alone.

"Stephen," she said softly, hoping to calm the anger that flashed in his eyes.

"We should depart now, Caro. I don't care for how your uncle treats you. The duke can't order you about like that." The stiffness in his body practically screamed fury. "He doesn't deserve your company."

She placed her hand on his arm. "You promised you'd stay here . . . with me."

He studied her hand as his nostrils flared.

She'd never seen him this angry before. Was this how he'd reacted when she left him?

Her common sense answered: No.

If he'd cared half as much about her departure as he did her uncle ordering them to attend a pantomime, he would have come after her.

Chapter Four

Stephen scanned the corridor and then drew his wife into a diagonal hallway before one of the duke's ever-present footmen could appear. He walked another fifty yards before he stopped and turned to face her.

"Your uncle is barbaric." His words were sharp and cold much like ice chips. "This whole event is a waste of time." He had little doubt the veins next to his temples were pulsing in time with the angry beat of his heart.

He could tell from her eyes that he'd startled her. She looked almost heartbroken.

A stab of guilt pierced his gut.

"It's *Cinderella*." Caro blew a stray lock out of her face. "All we have to do is attend. You don't have to participate." She peeked up at him and smiled. "It might even be fun."

"I *won't* participate. Your uncle is outlandish, puerile, not to mention controlling." He huffed out a breath hoping it would tame his frustration. "Nor will I attend."

"But what about my uncle?" Caroline worried her lower lip between her teeth.

Instantly, he stilled like a wolf with a rabbit in its sight. Whenever she did that in front of him, he wanted to devour her. Right there. Up against the wall.

Again, she nibbled her lip. "He'll guess the truth if I attend by myself, and you heard Mr. Beakens, he doesn't want me to visit his bedchamber."

The next two weeks were going to be torture. He should have just said no to this whole interlude, but his wife still intrigued him. She would always intrigue him, even when they were both in their eighties.

A movement caught his attention at the end of the hall: a flash of someone in ducal livery. Spying on them.

Caroline rested her hands on her hips, much like a governess scolding a recalcitrant boy. "You mustn't—"

Stephen leaned forward and pressed his mouth against hers, then swept her into his arms. Their teeth clashed. It was the most inelegant kiss he'd ever given his wife, but he didn't want anyone overhearing their argument.

At first, Caro pushed against him as if she wanted him to let her go.

He turned slightly so his back was to whomever was behind him, shielding Caro from spying eyes. "Someone is watching," he whispered as he caressed her mouth with his. "Make it look real."

Her eyes widened for a moment before they fluttered closed. She reached up and placed her arms around his neck and gently caressed him. When she pressed her body against his, Stephen wanted to roar in approval.

He groaned when she flicked her tongue against his lips. My God, how he'd missed holding her in his arms. Her mouth was like a feast spread before a starving man. He'd never have enough of her.

With one hand resting on the small of her back, Stephen pulled her sharply against the hard angles of his body. "Caro," he whispered, long denied desire rumbling in his voice.

At the sound of her name, she moaned softly and then pressed her open mouth to his. Their tongues tangled in a sensuous dance that threatened to incinerate them both. He was already hard, but now he felt an ache that only she could soothe. His rigid cock strained against his breeches as if begging for attention.

Caro's lips softened under his, and he brought her even closer. But it wasn't enough. He'd been denied tasting her for a year, and he'd not let her go until he had his fill.

She was such a wee thing, yet she fit perfectly in his arms.

God, he could take her right now. *Here.* In the corridor.

As that thought crossed his mind, Caro broke the kiss. By the dazed look in her eyes, she wanted him, too. Panting slightly, she was clearly out of breath. She had that faraway look he'd come to recognize in their married life. It was a haze of desire that the two of them could conjure up in the spur of the moment. It had always been that way between them.

He bent and pressed a kiss on the perfect indentation at the base of her neck. The tremble of her pulse against his mouth made him feel protective, and he suddenly remembered the prying eyes of the footmen set to watch them.

"Aha!" a voice called out, as if in answer to his thought.

Instinctively, he tightened his arms around her before he turned his head to see the intruder.

Twist, the butler, regarded them, one eyebrow raised. "I see you have found the mistletoe I directed to be hung here. I didn't think anyone would venture into this corridor, but just in case"—he clasped his hands behind his back, clearly pleased with himself—"better to be overprepared, I say."

"Mistletoe?" Caroline whispered. But loud enough that Twist heard.

"Indeed, my lady. Just look." He pointed above them.

They tilted their heads back at the same time. Fifteen feet above them, dripping with festive red and white ribbons, was the largest kissing bough of mistletoe that Stephen had ever seen.

"Don't mind me." Twist turned back the way he came with a military precision that would have made any soldier in the British army proud. "Nothing more romantic than mistletoe kisses." His voice faded as his footsteps retreated.

Caroline blinked twice as if trying to clear the passion that swirled in the air. "Good thinking," she whispered.

"What do you mean?" Stephen rasped.

"To find a mistletoe kissing bough." Caro ran her hands lightly down his chest, smoothing his coat. He still had his arms around her, and when she dropped her hands, he felt empty as if something rare and precious had been stolen from him.

To keep from taking her in another kiss, he stepped back and cleared his throat. Too much too soon would ruin his chance to woo her. He had to make her see that they belonged together.

Not just in bed, but at all times.

"I think it's time we changed from our traveling clothing," she said.

"Perhaps we should scout for other mistletoe kissing boughs scattered through the house?" With the sincerest expression Stephen could muster, he captured Caroline's gaze. "You never know when we might have need of one again."

Her brow furrowed into delicate lines as her desire melted into wariness. "Perhaps our time would best be spent joining the others and not arguing," she said. Though she clearly intended to be stern, the effect was ruined by her swollen pink lips. "We'll discuss the pantomime later."

As they walked back to the main hall, Stephen was careful to hide the smile that lingered on his lips. This might be the best Christmas of his life.

With Caro by his side, he could sit through the pantomime while daydreaming about sharing kisses with his lovely wife under every single kissing bough they could find.

CAROLINE AND STEPHEN parted when they entered the main hall, as several acquaintances demanded Stephen's company. New guests were milling about, partaking in seasonal treats such as mince pies, fresh oranges, and mulled wine. The scent of cloves and cinnamon filled the air.

Caroline closed her eyes and breathed deeply. Her lips tingled from Stephen's kisses. For a moment, she felt as though she were back at Heartfeld Hall, where they'd shared such intimacies before.

There was no denying that her husband was an expert at kisses.

It wasn't enough, she reminded herself. He hadn't abandoned her, the way her mother had, but he was still absent from her life, even when they lived together. He was completely uninterested in her as a person.

Perhaps it was his nature, and she would never change it.

Or perhaps she was just not the sort of person who could inspire that devotion. Her own mother's departure proved that point.

It was beyond foolish to wish for something she could never have—a real marriage between two people who loved each other more than they loved anything else in the world.

It was best to focus on creating a community of her own in London while helping women with a passion for art find a place to belong. She could give back to her childhood friend and confidante, her great-aunt Agatha, a marvelous artist whose talent had been completely ignored by her family and the world.

"Caro, is that you?"

She turned to the familiar voice and immediately smiled. It was one of her friends from finishing school, Miss Diana Holden, now Lady Fordcastle, after she'd married the Earl of Fordcastle last year. Diana was one of the few true friends Caroline had made during her years at the institution. It wasn't just because Diana never gossiped about Caroline's scandalous mother. Diana had a truly kind soul.

"My lady." Caroline dipped a curtsey.

"Stop. I'll always be Diana to you." Her friend gave her a hug. "I'm so happy you're attending the Revelry this year."

"Congratulations on your marriage." Caroline examined her friend, who positively glowed. "I'd say it agrees with you."

"Indeed. I'm very much in love," Diana answered, then sought her husband's gaze. "And so is my husband."

The earl gave his wife a blinding smile.

Caroline's heart squeezed at the sight, and she had to blink away a sudden rush of tears. She received heated glances from her husband—but never a smile like that.

Now she was feeling sorry for herself. Just because she wanted that and hadn't found it in her own marriage didn't mean she should begrudge others.

Diana tilted her head toward Caroline and held her fan to cover her mouth so others couldn't hear. "If you find yourself alone at the party, you can always join John and me."

Before she could respond, Stephen left the group of men he was chatting with and stood at Caroline's shoulder. "I plan to keep this beauty by my side."

Diana's eyes widened slightly, but with her usual grace, she recovered her composure quickly. "Lord Stephen, I didn't know you were attending the Revelry. How pleasant for you both."

"Indeed," he replied as he gazed into Caroline's eyes. "I'm the most fortunate man on earth."

When she searched his face for the teasing she expected to find there, her heart tripped a beat. For in his dark blue eyes, he seemed to be pleading with her to believe him.

She hesitated, unsure what was real and what was pretend. Before she could respond, the Earl of Fordcastle slid to his wife's side. "I beg to differ with you, Lord Stephen. *I* am the most fortunate man. I received that distinction the day my wife agreed to marry me."

Diana blushed again, and the earl wrapped his arm around his wife's shoulders and pulled her tight against his side.

Caroline couldn't imagine what such devotion would feel like. She'd never seen it in her parents' marriage, nor did she have it with Stephen. His behavior this fortnight wouldn't change anything . . . even though her heart begged her to believe him.

What made matters more complicated? It was *she* who had made the list of rules that he was following so carefully. *She* had dictated that he had to behave in a loving manner in front of others.

Caroline released a pent-up sigh. She was in danger of falling for the story that *she* had created to fool her uncle. And she didn't need more heartache. Truthfully, the party and all of its events were proving to be a challenge she hadn't expected.

After Diana and Fordcastle took their leave, Caroline waited a few moments before addressing Stephen. "You're trying too hard."

"Meaning?" One corner of his mouth tugged into a half smile as if they were sharing something between them and locking out the rest of the world.

She reminded herself that none of his behavior would continue once they each left the event ten thousand pounds richer. "The compliments such as 'beauty' and 'most fortunate man on earth.' It's not necessary," she whispered.

The befuddlement on Stephen's face would have been endearing if she wasn't trying to protect her heart from trusting romantic drivel. If he hadn't felt this way about her back when they'd been together, he certainly hadn't fallen in love with her after she was gone.

"You're exaggerating," she pointed out. "All we have to do is be seen together."

"I'm telling the truth. I do think I'm fortunate, and I definitely think you're beautiful." Stephen reached out and, with the lightest of touches, ran the back of one finger down her cheek. "Your lips are still swollen. It makes me want to kiss you again."

"You're caught up in the Revelry," she protested, taking a step back. Indeed, her lips were still tender, and like him, she wanted to kiss him again. Because that was what they did best together.

It wasn't enough. She wanted their hearts to connect, not just their bodies.

"Oho," the Earl of Fordcastle called out. "Lord Stephen, look where you're standing. Directly under one of Twist's mistletoe creations."

Everyone's attention turned toward Caroline and Stephen.

"Good eyesight, my lord," Twist called out. "Nothing like a good mistletoe bough to liven our merriments."

"You must kiss her," someone cried out. "It's a Christmas rule. Besides, she's your wife."

"By George, if he won't do it, I will," another man chortled.

"She should kiss him," a female called, then laughed.

Heat marched up her cheeks, while the crowd's expectation for a kiss hung in the air like a thick London fog. She lowered her gaze slowly until she met Stephen's. For an eternity, they stared at each other. Neither made a move.

"I don't know what to do," she whispered.

"I do," he murmured without hesitation.

Then, with an infinite slowness, he leaned toward her. He didn't take her in his arms as he had earlier that afternoon. Instead, he cupped her cheeks as if in his regard he found her precious. He stared at her, and in those depths, she saw something she'd never seen before. Uncertainty, embarrassment, or perhaps it was uneasiness that shone deep in his eyes. Whatever it was only magnified her own fragility.

Was he waiting for her to do something?

She carefully rose on the tip of her toes until only an inch separated their lips from one another. "May I kiss you this time?" Her voice so soft she didn't know if he had heard her.

He let out a shuddered breath, then a ghost of a smile broke across his lips. "I would like that very much."

When she pressed her lips to his, the rest of the world

fell away, and it was just the two of them. He didn't make a move to deepen the kiss as she might have expected. Instead, he allowed her to do as she pleased.

It pleased her to make this an expression of tenderness, the kind that she had dreamed of in her marriage, but never experienced.

The moment of their kiss was a heady feeling, and she reveled in it. She didn't turn the kiss to a passionate, burning display. Instead, she slowly swept her mouth against his, then whispered his name against his lips as if saying a solemn prayer.

In answer, he brushed his thumbs across her cheeks.

They ignored the din of the jubilant cheers around them. He pulled her tightly into his embrace as if he'd never let her go, while she buried her head against his chest to soak up his warmth.

For the first time since she could remember, she felt cherished for who she was.

But she fully recognized what peril lay before her. With that kiss, she might have fallen in love with her husband all over again. Whereas he was playing for the crowd and following her rules.

When she drew away, their gazes locked once again. His hooded eyes had widened. His earlier wariness was gone, and affection seemed to have taken its place. If only she could see through to his heart. Then, she might know the truth.

It couldn't be real; it wasn't real. Doggedly, a small voice pointed out that he hadn't even written her a letter asking her to return.

And yet her heart yearned to believe him. To risk being hurt all over again.

God, what had she done?

Chapter Five

Stephen rested one shoulder against the window frame in the billiards room, where most of the men had congregated after dinner. Port and brandy were in no short supply. After he had escorted Caro to their bedroom, he'd made the excuse that he needed fresh air. He wanted to give her time alone.

He had little doubt she needed a respite. After their very public kiss, Caro had retired to their bedchamber to bathe and change, while Stephen talked to Cyrus Hill and Elias, Lord Darcy de Royleston, two of his friends. Then when she came down to the drawing room, he went to their bedchamber and summoned his valet.

At dinner, they'd been seated away from each other. The Revelry was famous for seating people at separate tables, and never allowing a husband and wife in close proximity. That was a good thing, as Stephen didn't know if he would have been capable of forming a sentence, let alone a complete thought, if Caro was within kissing distance.

Thankfully, Lady Eloise Bennett had been seated beside him and had proven adept at the art of conversing, nattering on about an opera singer, her husband, and the health benefits of blackberry wine. Every once in a while, Stephen had offered a noncommittal answer, but that was the extent of his titillating contributions to their conversation.

All he could think about was the sweetness in Caro's kiss.

For a second or two, he'd believed she would refuse to kiss him in front of the crowd of guests. Never in his entire married life, all two years of it, had they shared anything as intimate as that kiss.

Granted they'd made love a multitude of times, but they had never revealed themselves in a way that every barrier between them had been stripped . . . at least for that moment.

He had no clue what to do when it came time for them to retire. To sleep in the same bedchamber—nay, in the same *bed*?

How could he give her what she wanted? He'd given her attention, boundless passion in bed, not to mention, fiery kisses that threatened to consume them both.

It hadn't been enough, obviously. She wanted more than his body. She wanted him to share more. She wanted to be his partner. How was he going to accomplish that?

Currently, Caro was upstairs, perhaps nestled in bed, while he was down here in the billiards room staring at revelers.

He ought to retire upstairs with his wife. Yet he didn't think he could bear it if she didn't want to have anything to do with him outside of their pretend relationship. He took a sip of port and inhaled the scent of fresh greenery that adorned the room.

There was only one way to find out where he stood with his wife, and that was to talk to her.

If she wanted nothing to do with him, he could always lick his wounds in his valet Percy's room. But Percy was likely below stairs with the other servants. The man loved Christmastide almost as much as Stephen did.

Stephen had loved the festive season even more when he had a wife. A true wife. A home.

"May I join you?" The Earl of Fordcastle stood next to Stephen, a glass of brandy in his hand.

"Of course. I'd enjoy the company," Stephen answered politely, though he really wasn't in the mood for conversation.

"That kiss you and your wife shared became quite a conversation piece at my dinner table. Several gentlemen around me felt it was tame and staid. More like a kiss from a couple who had been married for twenty years, instead of only two." The earl twirled his glass gently. "A year ago, I might have agreed with their assessment. But you and I are both aware that kiss was nothing of the sort."

"Hmm." Stephen didn't want to share his personal feelings with Fordcastle. The earl wasn't someone Stephen would call a friend. More along the lines of an acquaintance.

The man's reputation as a rake had been cultivated over the years. Many women had compared him to a perfect male: attractive with golden blond hair, fit, healthy, and exceedingly rich. Somewhat surprisingly, Fordcastle had made an obvious effort to transform himself into a loving and devoted partner since he'd exchanged vows with his countess.

The earl continued, "The reason I know that kiss was something special is because my wife and I shared one very similar. May I tell you a story?"

Stephen nodded.

"I was at my most vulnerable, and she kissed me with a frank sweetness that practically undid me. Made me believe she cared, even when all my faults and sins were laid before her. She never looked away but held my gaze until I believed there was something bigger than myself to care about." The earl's voice cracked with emotion, and he exhaled with a whoosh of breath.

Stephen swallowed. Even he was affected by the flickers of gratitude, wonder, and love that shone bright in the earl's eyes.

"In that moment, I became a man with a purpose and not some whirling dervish trying to shock everyone I met. Her kindness and deep regard transformed me." Fordcastle took a sip and glanced at the other men in the room. "They have no clue. Poor chaps." He held up his glass in salute to Stephen. "But you and I know those type of kisses are remarkable. I saw it on your face. It was exactly the way I felt when Diana and I shared ours."

Stephen took a sip of port before answering. It gave him a moment to collect his thoughts. "You're aware that my wife left me, and we've . . . we are . . ."

"Trying to find your way back to each other?" The earl smiled with a wisdom beyond his years. "Trust me. I experienced the same thing with Diana."

"Truly?" Stephen asked. Who would have thought that a former rake might give him, a failure as a husband, advice. "How did you find your way back?"

"I took her to bed," the earl replied.

Stephen raised a brow. "I don't think that would work for Caro and me."

"Ah, it's not what you think, my good man." The earl nodded. "I took her to bed and held her while she talked, and I listened. That was all." Fordcastle looked outside at the dreary darkness that had descended, but he smiled. "I won't say it resolved all our differences, but I'll never forget that night. It led the way to true happiness." He bent his head and studied the glass in his hand. "I sound like a besotted fool." The earl lifted his gaze to Stephen's. "I don't care."

"No, you sound like a man in love," Stephen said flatly.

"Let me ask you a question." The earl put his glass down on the table, then crossed his arms across his chest with the attitude of a judge. "Would you care if I thought of you as a besotted fool?"

"No," Stephen answered honestly. "I would think of myself as a very fortunate man." He slid his empty glass onto the side table and nodded his farewell. "I'll see you in the morning, perhaps."

WITH THE HELP of an upstairs maid, Caroline had made quick work of undressing and completing her nightly ablutions. To keep her mind off the eventual arrival of her husband, she concentrated on the lovely room that Cressie and Mrs. Peters had assigned to them.

The name, the green bedroom, fit the décor nicely. Lush green velvet bed-curtains surrounded the massive four-poster bed. When she'd visited over the years, she'd first been assigned to the nursery when she was a young girl, and as a young adult, she'd been assigned one of the spare bedrooms in the family quarters. But this room, located in a completely separate wing of the estate, could be fit for a king. It was easily the finest bedroom she'd ever stayed in.

Sitting upright against the headboard, she slid her fingers over the luxurious brocade bedcover in a dark greenish blue that resembled the colors of a peacock's tail. Cressie had decorated the room with evergreens accented with pinecones and peacock feathers. It was simple, stylish and elegant—as was her cousin's style.

Cressie never bothered with her own appearance overmuch, but Caroline knew that she was secretly the guiding hand behind the exquisite Revelry that all of England admired.

But the room's beauty could not keep Caroline from worrying about how she'd survive a night with her husband lying beside her. She flopped on her back and stared at the canopy above her. Stephen's kisses . . . were dangerous.

At least to her heart.

When they'd shared that last public kiss, her heartbeat had thumped in a joyous raucous dance she was certain Stephen had heard. That warm smile of his had instantly appeared. Like a coward, she'd buried her head against his chest in an effort to hide his effect on her.

She could not allow herself to be carried away in these romantic fantasies. The festive atmosphere didn't help matters. She now understood how treacherous Christmas could be. It made you want to open your heart to others and start anew, and that was a disaster that had to be avoided at all costs.

Soon, it would be over. January with its blistery, frigid air would extinguish all those warm romantic notions that things might actually change between her and Stephen. Once he received his half of the money, he'd return posthaste to his one true passion—his work. She'd never see him again.

To his tenants, he was the much-beloved Lord Stephen, but to her? He was the man who forgot her birthday and the anniversary of their marriage. The man who failed to greet her when she walked into the breakfast room after he'd just finished making passionate love to her. Who forgot to come to dinner and forgot to tell her when he was going to London.

Who didn't give a damn about her outside of the bedchamber.

Why, oh why, had she agreed to let him in her bed? Nothing good would come from it except the possibility her heart would be shattered into a million pieces again when they eventually parted.

A soft knock on the dressing room door sounded before it opened. Stephen peeked in. "Caro, are you awake?"

"Yes." Incapable of uttering anything else because her throat had cinched tight, she moved up until she leaned against the headboard again.

He stepped into the room with two mugs, then turned and pushed the door closed with his foot.

Every muscle within her quivered like a rabbit ready to flee from danger.

Stephen wore an exquisite satin and silk bayan. When he turned to face her, her breath caught. Sans evening coat and waistcoat, he still wore his white lawn shirt and evening breeches. He toed off his evening slippers, then strolled to the empty side of the bed. Without a word, he rested the two mugs on the bedside table. He sat on the edge of the mattress and stripped the stockings from his legs. With ease, he swung around, resting one bent, practically naked leg on the brocade covering.

The lines of his calf muscles were gracefully defined in a way that would make an experienced artist salivate to sketch them. It gave her a tiny thrill that she was the sole recipient of the spectacular view. She slowly dragged her gaze from his legs to his midsection. The fine lawn of his shirt stretched across his chest until it split at the neck.

Her body tingled in awareness that little stood between them, nothing more than several garments and a few feet of distance. She swallowed the swirling disquiet that had settled around her and forced her gaze to his. She let out a breath, trying to shake her unease.

No seductive or coy smiles tugged at his mouth. Instead, curiosity and warmth radiated around him.

"How should we sleep together?" Not making a move toward her, he rested his hand on his bent knee. "Shall I rest atop the covers?"

She glanced at the window. Even with a robust fire in the room's fireplace, the windows were frosted with ice from the inside.

"I don't want you to be uncomfortable with my presence here," he said.

"Won't you be cold?" She glanced at her fingers where she was fiddling with the hem of the cover. "I don't want you to be uncomfortable either."

Such a silly response. Now it sounded like she wanted him in bed with her.

Everything was off kilter. Her brain was screaming "whoa," while pulling the reins of the runaway organ that lay in the center of her chest. Or at least slowing it to a cautionary trot. When she'd agreed to make love to him earlier, she'd wanted Stephen. In all candor, she still did.

"I thought perhaps we could chat for a while. We don't have to decide immediately." He leaned forward until he was eye level with her. "Would that be acceptable?"

"Of course." Her voice had dropped so low she sounded like a virgin on her wedding night. She had to snap out of this befuddlement. The best way to do that was to change the subject. "What do you have there?"

"I almost forgot." He twisted his torso and reached for the two mugs. "Chocolate. One of your terms was that we should share some at breakfast." As Stephen handed her a mug, a grin tugged at his lips, one that reminded her of his attitude on their wedding day—full of good cheer and laughter. "But I thought we might need the practice." He held the mug up in a toast. "To sharing."

"To sharing." She took the mug he offered her. The first sip was somewhat tepid, but she didn't care. He had thought of her, and her recalcitrant heart picked up speed again. "I had a lovely conversation with Percy earlier."

"Indeed?" Stephen took a sip and scrunched his face as if it tasted bad.

"Don't you like it?"

"No. I mean yes." He shook his head as if trying to get things in order. "It's a little different from my accustomed drink of whisky. So, what did my valet have to say?"

"He was on his way down to the servants' area for dancing." Caroline fiddled with the cup in her hands. "Out of the clear blue, he told me you were a good master and always brought him along wherever you celebrated Christmastide since he had no family of his own."

Stephen held up his hands in surrender. "I never asked him to intervene on my behalf. I promise."

Caroline laughed and shook her head at the same time. "I wasn't challenging you or him. I didn't know he had no one."

"Percy's been with the family for over sixty years." Stephen shrugged his shoulders. "When he first came to work for my grandfather, he was a young boy in the stables, who'd just lost his mother and father. An only child with no other relatives, he worked his way up until he became my valet. When I moved to Heartfeld Hall, he came with me. He loves to take care of my things."

He looked around the room before continuing, as if what he was about to impart was secret, then whispered, "But he loves Christmas more. Almost as much as me. He gladly accompanies me when I travel to my brother's house. It's as if he's created his own family with my brother's servants."

"Oh," she murmured. "I hope I didn't ruin his Christmas by asking you to join me here."

"As long as he can celebrate, he's happy. And the Revelry is famous. Who wouldn't want to see its magnificence? I promised we'd go to my brother's house when we leave here."

Her heartbeat faltered at the news. They had never discussed what would happen once they left the duke's house. Naturally, they'd go their separate ways. That's what she wanted. "How lovely that you're going to your brother's house for Percy's sake."

"I'm not that altruistic. It's for me also. I love my brother and his family." He reclined on the bed next to her, holding the mug and staring at the fire. "I like spending the Yuletide with them. I wanted to take you there last year."

"Hmm," she said vaguely. "I haven't seen your brother or his family since we married. Give them my regards, will you?" Tears from nowhere threatened. She would not cry. All her tears for what she lost had come in her first weeks in the city.

Stephen sat still and stared at her, then asked softly, "Would you tell me more about London?"

"What would you like to know?" She glanced at him over the mug's rim. A hint of cinnamon added a nice touch. Anything to keep her mind off those terribly lonely first two months.

"Anything. Everything." He shrugged slightly. "Let's start with how you found the building."

"When I arrived in London, I had nowhere to stay, so I paid a call to my friend Diana. It's her family's building. They offered to rent it to me at an extraordinarily reasonable price." She shifted so she faced him. "It was difficult at first, but I adapted." That was an understatement. In the first week, she'd almost returned home from pure loneliness and sorrow.

She corrected herself. She'd almost returned to *Stephen*, not home.

His face remained impassive, but his grip on the mug tightened until his knuckles turned white. "It drives me mad to think you went alone into the city without any place to stay or anyone to look after you."

"I had acquaintances and friends. Like Diana, but she wasn't married when I arrived. There was no cause for worry, Stephen. I wouldn't have jeopardized my safety."

His grip relaxed. "I know you wouldn't. But I can't help but react to your description. You're my wife."

"I knew you would fret. That's why I sent word where I was."

He leaned a little closer as if sharing a secret with her. "You always had a good head on your shoulders. It's one of the things I immediately recognized about you. But go on. I want to hear more."

He straightened and immediately she wanted to protest the distance between them. This intimate moment was something she would have never imagined. Countless times, she'd tried to initiate such conversations to no avail. Now, he was talking to her, curious about her life.

"The building was already furnished, and Diana's family introduced me to friends with whom they thought I'd have interests in common. Her family is well-established in society and knew of artists, all women, with no place to exhibit their work. When I first moved there, I gave a few lectures about art, and what to consider when starting a collection. It was successful." She gave him a shy smile. "Soon, I had artists and art enthusiasts asking me for advice. My art gallery was a logical next step."

"How many are you working with?"

"I have five at the moment, but three more artists have asked to join. I have to look at their work and see if it fits within our group. I also ask the other artists for their opinions." Caroline bent her head, but she could feel the heat of his gaze on her. "I've sold three paintings in the last month. I think I have a talent for it."

When she lifted her gaze to his, the admiration on his face stole her breath.

"I'm not surprised." He placed his warm hand over hers. "Anything you set your mind to will always be a success."

"Thank you," she said softly. "I'll use my portion of the trust fund to buy the building. I will continue to sell their work. Within a couple of months, I can stop taking the allowance you give me and pay you back."

"No. I don't want that. It's your money. I want to give it to you." He rubbed the back of his neck as he stared into the fire. "I know you think me heartless"—he turned back to her—"but you're still my wife, and I do care for you. Always."

She feared she'd drown in the depth of emotion in his eyes. "I've never thought you heartless. I was just insignificant in your world." She shook her head. "It's water under the bridge. You care for the estate, its tenants, and the servants. Let's just leave it there."

Silence stretched between them until he murmured, "I'm sorry for that." He stroked her cheek with the back of his forefinger. "Don't hold it against me for always wanting to take care of the people whom I'm responsible for. I'm accountable for you also, even if you can take care of yourself. It's a weakness of mine." His gaze caught hers, and she couldn't turn away. "You'll always be a weakness of mine."

Caught off guard at the vibrancy in his dark-as-sin voice, Caroline stilled. All her defenses against him seemed to crumble.

She waited for him to lean closer and kiss her, but instead he resumed his position, resting against the massive headboard behind them. "Let's see if we can get some sleep. We have a busy day tomorrow."

She had one sip left of her chocolate.

It did not wash away the taste of her disappointment.

Chapter Six

"I need to clean my teeth," Caro mumbled. Stephen felt the slight shift of her weight as she rose from the bed.

He folded his arms across his midsection as he watched her go into the dressing room where their toiletries sat side by side next to an exquisite china bowl and pitcher.

Just as their toiletries once had at Heartfeld Hall.

Their bedroom hadn't been as grand as this one, but it was still a large and comfortable room, big enough they could enjoy each other's company.

He was making himself sick with such comparisons.

From the excited blush that dusted her cheeks to her silence when he made the declaration that he would always care for her, he was certain that he'd pushed too hard and too fast. Caro had looked ready to bolt from the bedroom.

He wished he had more experience wooing women other than Betsey. He ran a hand down his face. Now he was comparing his wife to a *cow*.

Perhaps he'd chased Caro away. Why had he ever let her go in the first place? Pride. It had to be his foolish pride.

But if he hadn't let her go, he knew deep down inside he would have lost her for good.

He was thinking too pessimistically. When had he ever shied away from a fierce struggle? When the estate's crops had been in danger of not being harvested in time before the first frost, he'd worked side by side with his tenants to ensure every bushel of grain available was harvested.

But the hardest struggle he had ever faced was letting his wife go and not racing after her. He had every right as a husband to bring her back home, but that would have been a coward's way of handling the situation. If there was any hope of them finding their way back together, she had to make the decision to try.

The struggle to not take her into his arms and make love to her until she agreed to come home was even tougher. She was absolutely stunning in that nightgown. The way it framed her neck and face was an invitation for him to explore every delectable inch of her.

He had to find a way to prove to her that she mattered to him.

He needed her to realize she was the most important person in his world. But he hadn't a clue how to go about it.

From the shadows, Caroline silently crossed the room until she stood next to the bed.

"Stephen?" Her dulcet voice could teach mortal men how angels sounded.

"Yes, darling," he answered, not hiding the affection in his voice.

"I think you should get under the covers. It's going to be cold tonight."

"I don't—" His voice broke midsentence.

The glow from the fireplace was the only light in the room, but it was enough that he could see the uncertainty in her eyes. Damn it all. Not for the world would he hurt her again. Not if he could help it.

"I don't think that's a bad idea. It is a bit chilly in here." Rather than move over, or make his way under the covers, he swung his feet over the bed then stood before her. With an ease that came from knowing her as his wife, he pulled her gently to him.

In return, she placed her arms around his neck and stared wordlessly at him. They were playing some kind of chess game, and she was waiting for him to make the next move. Her familiar rose scent twined around him, bringing forth memories of nights they had shared together. He breathed the scent deep into his lungs, allowing it to seep into every inch of him.

She was as vital to him as air.

Without a word, he pressed his lips against her forehead and held them there as he hugged her tight. He wanted her to know she was the most precious being he had in his life. If only he could go back a year, and tell her how he saw her, appreciated her, and needed her.

Starting tonight, he would. He pulled away and studied her face. Caro's eyes had always reminded him of a weatherglass. You could guess her mood from the expression in her chestnut eyes. But not tonight. He'd have to find his path without any help.

"Come, let me see you to bed." He took her hand in his and brought her around to the other side. He unfolded the covers.

She sat on the edge and swung her legs in. A show of skin at her ankles was the only intimate glimpse of her body, but it was enough that his blood heated.

Once she settled into a comfortable place, he pulled up the covers.

"Aren't you joining me?" Her brow had crinkled adorably in confusion.

"I am, but I will sleep on the other side." He pressed his mouth to hers. The temptation to take her in his arms grew as he tasted the sweetness of her lips.

But he had made a promise that he wouldn't break tonight. Their marriage was more than just physical pleasure. They hadn't learned the joy of being together, but they could. They would. At last, he broke away, then went to his side and climbed in. By that time, Caroline had moved until she lay in the middle.

Better to see her, he turned and rested his face on his bent arm. She had already done the same. Then she slid even closer until there were perhaps three inches between them, although it felt like a mile. He smiled at her and, astonishingly, she breached the distance between them until she was in his arms.

He wanted to shout to the heavens that she chose to be close to him. Hopefully, it meant she was beginning to trust him again. From now on, every step she took toward him, he'd take two steps toward her.

He only hoped it was enough.

Every tense muscle in his body relaxed. Since she'd left him, he'd never slept well. Most nights he'd wake in the darkness and reach for her. Her side of the bed was always cold, then he'd remember. She was gone. He'd lay awake wondering if she was safe, worrying about her. But now, he could hold her all night and relish the feel of her warm body next to his.

"Caro, I've missed you so," Stephen whispered. "More than you can imagine. I think for the first time in a year, I'll actually be able to sleep all night."

She nestled closer, and he tightened his arms around her in acknowledgment.

"How did you sleep in London?" Without waiting for a reply, he continued, "Did you have trouble like me?"

She answered with a gentle even breath. She was asleep. It was little wonder since they'd had a long day from arriving at the inn, meeting with the solicitor, and then the delectable mistletoe and kissing boughs they'd managed to find.

He pressed a light kiss to her cheek. In protest, she nuzzled a little closer.

"I like to think that perhaps you'll sleep better with me beside you, too," he whispered. "At least, that's what I'll dream about."

THE NEXT MORNING, Caroline woke to an empty bed. She snuggled a little longer under the covers as the room had chilled during the night. But when she peeked over the bedcovers, a blazing fire was warming the cold room. The maids must have stolen into the room early in the morning, perhaps after Stephen had dressed or had gone downstairs.

Downstairs.

He'd gone to breakfast without her.

How could he? That was in her rules.

The bedroom door suddenly opened. Expecting a maid, Caroline sat up.

"My slug-a-bed is finally awake." Stephen stood at the doorway with a tray balanced on one hand.

Caroline's heart pounded at the mischievous smile on his face.

"I have a fresh pot of chocolate for you." He waggled his eyebrows. "And coffee for me."

"You didn't have to do that. I could have asked a maid to bring me a tray. Or we could have met in the breakfast room, as planned."

Stephen walked in and carefully placed the tray in the middle of the bed. "It's still early. I didn't want to bother the maids, so I sweet-talked the cook into preparing this little feast just for us."

Caroline glanced at the tray. Two small pots with cups sat at the center surrounded by an assortment of all her favorite treats along with plates and napkins. Of course, it'd been written in her notes. Still, it was a lovely gesture. She adored eating in her room and lounging around in the morning.

Quickly dismissing the thought, Caroline focused on the tray before her. She hadn't realized she was hungry. Fresh toast with berry jam, apple tarts, shortbread, and gingerbread just begged to be eaten. "It looks delightful."

She glanced his way to discover him rocking back on his heels, his hands clasped behind his back, with a huge smile on his face. "You approve?"

"Most definitely. Would you care to join me?" Before she could serve him a cup of coffee, he made himself comfortable on the bed and served her the chocolate.

This morning's cup tasted significantly better than the chocolate he had brought to her the night before. He was being extremely attentive, even when no one could see them, which was odd and completely out of character.

Stephen leaned back against the headboard and took a bite of gingerbread. "Hmm, it's still warm." He offered her the piece he held in his hand. "Take a bite."

She shook her head, then studied him. "No, thank you. Why are you doing this?"

"I thought you might like some fresh gingerbread. I wish you would've been in the kitchens with me. It smells divine, and the dishes the cook is preparing for tonight's feast—"

She narrowed her eyes.

"What?" He cocked his head as if confused by her manner.

"This." She scooted closer, then waved her hand toward the tray. "Why are you bringing me this? Why are you acting so kind and attentive?"

He rested one of his hands on his flat stomach. The pose was intended to be relaxed, but the slight tick of his right eye betrayed his irritation. "Is it so unusual for a husband to perform an act of kindness for his wife?"

"For you? Yes. There's no need for you to be romantic in private. No one can see your behavior except me." She took another sip of chocolate in a show she wasn't affected by his actions.

"The duke will know of my little sojourn to the kitchens by midmorning, I expect."

And there it was.

His real reason.

Stephen was playing his part in a performance she directed. For all he knew, any apparent interest on her part was also an act. She should be relieved, but something deep inside of her crumbled at his words. She looked at the window to keep him from seeing her disappointment.

"But more importantly, I wanted to." His words were so low that at first, she didn't think she had heard him correctly.

"Why?" she asked without turning from her study of the sky, which had started to lighten in greeting of the new day.

"Caro." He waited until she turned her attention back to him. "From the moment we arrived at the Revelry, I hoped we could start anew."

"For what purpose?" She tried to make her voice light. Perhaps things had turned worse on the estate than she'd thought. "I suppose ten thousand pounds gives you ten thousand ideas. If I return to Heartfeld Hall, then those ten thousand ideas might turn into twenty thousand." Her smile faded when she saw his expression shutter.

His voice was even and courteous. "You think that I am trying to gain the whole sum, rather than the ten thousand that you promised me?" His eyes were colder than the frost on the windows. "Why are you so suspicious of my motives?" He studied her much like a hawk before it dove for its prey.

Though it was only natural to want to hide, she did the opposite. She met his gaze while lifting her chin an inch in challenge. "I lived with you and your *motives* for a year, remember? I know how you think and how you act. This isn't you. All you care about is the farm." She slid to the side of the bed, stood, and pulled on her dressing gown.

"You decided that I'm desperate for money, so desperate that I would try to lure you home."

"No." His mocking smile infuriated her but Caroline kept her voice even. "I know you don't care whether I come home or not."

In a flash, Stephen rolled from the bed and faced her. Flipping the sides of his black woolen morning coat away, he rested his hands on his powerful hips.

The stance reminded Caroline of a painting she had once seen of a king about to sentence a traitor.

"I can't believe you would think such a thing of me," he bit out. "You are deliberately misconstruing my actions."

"No, I'm not. You, sir, have already shown me what marriage is like. These gestures are outside your normal conduct and I refuse to be fooled by them, even if your motive is not an extra ten thousand pounds."

"You're purposely pushing me away," he countered, then grunted to himself. "After last night, you're scared."

Caroline rolled her eyes. "Of what?"

"Of what we could have together." He turned toward the door in such a rush that the tails of his coat flew up as if hastening to follow him. He came to a stop, then slowly turned back to face her. "Some of the men are going shooting this morning. I'm of the mind to join them." There was a definite chill in his voice. "That will give us time to reflect on this conversation."

"I don't need time," she snapped.

"Perhaps I do," Stephen answered before he left, shutting the door quietly after him.

As the echo of his words faded, Caroline collapsed on a chair and studied the fire.

Her heart slogged through its beat, hurting in a way it never had. Mayhap, Stephen was correct. She had never considered his side of things. His acts of kindness showed his consideration of her. What if he suffered the same loneliness as her? And she'd just insulted him.

She had a sinking feeling she had just lost something very valuable.

Chapter Seven

Every shot Stephen had taken that morning had missed by a mile.

He wasn't surprised. He was still livid over Caro's insinuations. He wasn't angry at her but himself. His lack of action over the year resulted in her believing she didn't matter to him.

After an hour, he'd given up and left the other gentlemen to ride alone around the duke's estate. Perhaps a little fresh air would exorcise the demons that frolicked in his thoughts.

He rode the bay stallion hard through snowy fields, then brought it to a trot as they came to a peak that reigned over a scenic valley below. A frozen creek meandered through the field where timber dotted the landscape. It would make an excellent stop when he and Caro looked for the yule log.

If they could tolerate each other long enough to accomplish the task.

A dull thudding sounded from behind him, the gallop of a horse. Stephen whirled his horse around to see a man coming toward him, the capes of his greatcoat whipping behind him. As the man came nearer, Stephen could finally make him out.

Stephen's annoyance fled as he waited for the Earl of Fordcastle to come to his side. After the earl had given him advice yesterday, Stephen was of the opinion the man had changed for the better because of his wife.

The earl brought his mount to a stop and pulled off his hat to wipe his brow. "Morning, Lord Stephen."

"Lord Fordcastle," he said in return. "What brings you out this way? I was surprised you didn't join the others in shooting this morning."

"No. I needed the exercise. It allows me to work off some of my worry."

"What do you have to be worried about?" Stephen asked. The Earl of Fordcastle seemed to have a perfect life.

"My wife."

Stephen nodded. "The bane of every man's existence."

The earl shook his head. "No. Not in my case. Diana is carrying a babe. It's still early, but she's ill in the mornings. She vomits and vomits, and sometimes she hardly holds down a cup of tea. The midwife says the nausea will end, but I go mad seeing her suffer. She's asked me to leave her alone until noon. By the afternoons, she's fine." The earl gave a rueful smile as he looked over the valley. "I ride to keep from worrying."

"Congratulations," Stephen offered, and settled his horse with a couple of pats on the neck. Apparently, the bay didn't care for the newcomer's mount. "It sounds hellish. If Caro was ever that ill . . ." He didn't finish the thought, so Fordcastle did.

"You'd never leave her side?" The earl raised a brow, then laughed. "Believe me, I thought the same thing, but Diana had different ideas. In both of our best interests, I decided to follow her wishes." When the earl adjusted his seat, the saddle's leather creaked. "So, speaking of wives, how is your fair wife this morning?"

"I have no clue," Stephen answered abruptly.

The earl's laugh reverberated down the valley. The echoes that returned seemed to mock Stephen.

"I'm glad you find some amusement in my predicament." He delivered his best disdainful look.

The earl straightened in the saddle. "I apologize, but you

sounded so much like me in the early days of my marriage to Diana. I was as miserable then as you are now."

"I'm married to a woman who doesn't want a thing to do with me," Stephen spat out.

"As was I to Diana."

"Yours was an arranged marriage as well?" Stephen patted his horse again.

Fordcastle shook his head. "We were forced to marry after we were discovered together in Lord Lyon's library. Neither of us wanted to attend the event, and we found the same hiding place. It was just my luck that we were caught. I developed a sudden interest in protecting Diana's reputation after I ruined her." The earl's gaze turned steely. "I didn't ruin her on purpose, but I'm glad that I did. That changed my life in more ways than you could imagine."

"I know," Stephen agreed.

"The right woman can do that."

Stephen grunted in response.

"And she tells me that I changed her life for the better, too. If I were you—"

"Which you aren't," Stephen pointed out a little too sharply.

"You're right." The earl had the good sense to wince. "However, I was in a similar situation. I didn't know how to win the regard of the woman who was already my wife." The earl allowed his horse to step closer to Stephen's mount. "How did last night go?"

"Fine." Stephen expertly handled his nervous bay who promptly sidestepped away from the earl's horse. "Actually, better than fine. I don't think I've ever felt so close to her before."

"What happened?" The curiosity on the earl's face encouraged Stephen to share more.

He shrugged in frustration, then turned slightly in the saddle toward Fordcastle. "Honestly? I have no idea. We just talked, as you suggested. I thought it was a good conversation. Then this morning, when I brought up a breakfast tray, she first accused me of pretending to care for her in order to steal her inheritance, then she accused me of being the same man I always was."

The earl nodded as if in deep thought. "Sounds like you were quite successful last night then."

"No," Stephen answered wryly before his frustration took over. "Are you daft? Did you hear what I said?"

Fordcastle nodded enthusiastically. "Indeed." He lifted a hand when Stephen was about to argue again. "Hear me out. Think about this logically. Your wife is confused by what she sees, what she feels, and what she thinks she knows of you. It's like an illusion. She doesn't know what's real and what isn't." The earl rested his hands on the pommel of his saddle.

"My wife is the most levelheaded and astute person I know. I take offense at the thought that she's delusional. I can't fix what's wrong in one night. It's going to take time to prove I've changed. I'm not sure I have enough."

"No, no, no. You're not seeing the point. Think of it this way. Her heart wants to move forward, but her mind is vehemently disagreeing." Pleased with himself, Fordcastle leaned back in the saddle. "That's what you're seeing, my friend."

Stephen managed not to roll his eyes. "I suppose you have advice readily at hand?"

"Don't change course. Keep a steady pace. Give her as much attention as you think she can stand." The earl adjusted his seat, and his horse stepped in tandem. "Listen to her. Talk to her. She'll trust you again. She wants to."

Stephen's horse had to be soothed once again. "What do you mean, give her as much attention as I think she can stand?"

"It means you don't want to ignore her, or she'll think you weren't sincere in your earlier actions," the earl said. "But at the same time, you don't want to drown her in cloying devotion either. Don't lavish her with a false display of regard. Allow her to see the real you."

Stephen wanted to reply, *What if the real me isn't good enough?*

"If I were you, I'd go back to the house party. Make yourself available." The earl's conviction rang through the air. "Do as I suggest, and you'll reap the rewards. I must return as well. I need to see my wife." A charming look slid across Fordcastle's face. "If she'll allow it." With a nod, the earl wheeled his horse, then set off at a full gallop, leaving Stephen behind.

The sun grew a little brighter, blanketing the valley in a golden glow. He would take it as a sign of encouragement. For the first time since he left the bedroom he shared with Caro, he smiled. He decided to ignore the clouds gathering in the sky.

CAROLINE WAS RELIEVED to find the dining hall empty. Thankfully, the servants hadn't taken away the remnants of luncheon, so there were a few tarts and pieces of fruitcake left. It would make a fine midafternoon snack.

"Good afternoon, Lady Stephen." Mr. Beakens's voice broke Caroline's solitude.

Startled, she placed her hand on her chest.

At the far end of the room, a chair with its back to Caroline overlooked a pretty courtyard with iron urns decorated with evergreens, birch twigs, holly, and pinecones. Mr. Beakens peeked around the chair back and waved.

"Would you keep me company?" Mr. Beakens stood and motioned her forward with a wave of his hand, then pointed to an empty chair.

"Of course." Though she wanted no further conversation with him, she couldn't refuse, so she joined him. He was the intermediary between her and her uncle.

"Have you eaten, Lady Stephen?"

"Yes, I have," she answered.

He waited for her to continue, but she didn't budge, blink, or try to fill the air with small talk.

Finally, he nodded. "I've heard it from good authority that you and your husband shared a kiss, perhaps two, yesterday."

Heat crept into her cheeks, but she refused to look away. "Now I know who the duke's informant is. Twist was present for the kisses."

"Perhaps." The solicitor shrugged. "I can't say."

Mr. Beakens took a long look out the window before turning his attention back to Caroline. "The informant said it was a pretend kiss. All a setup so you could fool the duke."

"No, it wasn't."

"So, there was only one?" The solicitor's questions were starting to feel like an inquisition.

She shook her head. "There were two. Pretend kisses," she said, allowing disdain to drip through her tone. "How can a kiss be pretend? Whoever the duke's eyes and ears are, they're not doing their job."

Ignoring her answer, Beakens changed the subject. "Your husband left with a party of gentlemen this morning. If you're trying to convince others that you're happily married, then he should have stayed by your side."

Caroline straightened her back. "I find your line of questioning impertinent, Mr. Beakens. This is a house party with events planned for the guests' enjoyment. Is my husband not allowed to partake in the Revelry?" She smoothed her hands down her ivory velvet morning dress, upending the nap.

He showed no reaction to her insult. "Did you two have an argument? Is that why he left you?"

Caroline narrowed her eyes. Mr. Beakens was questioning her as if she were a kitchen maid caught stealing the family silver. Fury swept through every part of her.

Just as she opened her mouth to eviscerate the objectionable lout, Stephen's whisky-dark voice sounded behind her. "There you are, darling."

She turned around and found her husband striding into the room.

"Beakens," Stephen said, his face the perfect vision of an offended aristocrat.

The solicitor stood and bowed. Stephen responded with a slight nod.

Then he turned to Caroline, clearly dismissing the solicitor as beneath his notice, and lifted her hand to his mouth. The feel of his cool lips against her skin caused a shiver to snake up her back. Not from the cold but the heat of his gaze. Instead of releasing her hand, he drew her to her feet in a clear show of affection for the solicitor's observation.

"There is a chill in the air," he said, to her alone. "If I was a betting man, I'd say snow was coming."

A sudden commotion erupted in the hallway. Feminine and masculine laughter combined to fill the air with merriment. Caroline turned to the door at the same time as Stephen. A small crowd outside of the breakfast room had gathered with everyone's attention focused on a kissing bough held above a young couple.

Caroline had not met either the woman or man. At the cheering of the guests, the man took the woman in his arms and sealed his lips against hers in a passionate kiss. The crowd's roar grew louder at the display.

After what seemed like a scandalous amount of time, the couple broke apart, clearly stunned.

Caroline had attended the Revelry several times, but somehow this year seemed to be more raucous than previous years. Perhaps it was because her uncle was so ill, and his heir was attending. Valentine Snowe, Viscount Derham, had the reputation of a rakehell with no interest in marriage.

Caroline caught Stephen's gaze when he squeezed her hand. Something passed between them, a recognition of some sort that they'd shared a similar kiss yesterday. It was unfortunate the duke hadn't heard of *that* display of affection between them. He would have been convinced of their true regard for each other, and would have believed their marriage was sound.

Of course, whatever they had shared yesterday had been destroyed when she had argued with him this morning.

"See that?" the solicitor asked.

Reluctantly, she returned her attention back to Mr. Beakens, who was standing.

"That's what the duke wants from you. He wants to know your marriage is real." The man almost seemed to be begging. He peeked around them, but the group was gone, the party continuing elsewhere. "He wants to know that if he gives you the money, it will be put to good use. Specifically, that you won't use it to live in London on your own. The duke wants you to live with your husband."

"I'm not learned in the law, but if the duke gives Caroline the money, it won't be his," Stephen pointed out.

"You're right. At least, about one thing." Mr. Beakens turned suddenly serious. "You're not learned in the law."

Caroline bristled. She'd had enough. Her uncle, through his solicitor, could cajole and threaten her all he wanted, but Mr. Beakens had no right to attack Stephen. Then and there, she would put an end to it, no matter if it meant she'd forgo the monies promised.

"I'd ask that you be civil to my husband," she said, giving Beakens a furious glare. "He doesn't deserve any of your rancor. Save it for when you bring the duke's insults to me, or when the duke compares me to my mother."

"I meant no harm, Lady Stephen." The solicitor had the good sense to sound contrite. "Even if you convince your uncle you're happily married, he can have me write so many contingencies around the dissolution of your trust that you will never see it in your lifetime. I have to follow the duke's directives. He will evaluate the two of you at the pantomime tomorrow."

Stephen stiffened at the mention of the pantomime.

"If you'll both excuse me? I have an appointment." The solicitor bowed, then took his leave.

"I'm sorry you had to witness that unpleasant behavior." Caroline turned to the window. Snow was beginning to drift down in lazy spirals; she leaned against the cool glass in hopes it would douse her temper. "What a sour, unkind man my uncle has turned out to be."

"Don't worry about me." Stephen stepped next to her, but rather than looking at the snow, he looked down at her. "What did Mr. Beakens say before I arrived?"

Caroline blew out a breath, making a piece of her hair fly up in the air. "My uncle heard about our kisses, and sent Mr. Beakens to poke and pry, trying to find out if we were pretending. I asked how a kiss could be a pretend one."

Stephen smiled down at her as he brushed away the lock of hair that had fallen in her face, then tucked it behind her ear.

Her insides jangled in response to his touch. How keenly she'd longed for moments like these in the first months of their marriage.

"Did you think our kisses were pretend?" His whisper made the moment between them even more intimate, but it was the tenderness in his expression that terrified her.

She felt the truth in her bones.

Her feelings for him were intensifying, and she hadn't a clue as to how to protect herself from heartache.

"Answer me, darling." Stephen came closer until the heat from his body wrapped around her, warming her instantly.

"No, of course not." To keep from revealing too much of herself, Caroline studied the subtle pattern of twining leaves and vines on his green silk waistcoat until she recognized that the florals were actually holly and ivy. Lightly, she traced a bundle of red berries across his chest.

In answer, he captured her hand against the place where

his heart beat strong and true. Immediately, her heart matched the rhythm of his.

The traitorous organ.

When Stephen leaned closer and pressed a kiss to her cheek, Caroline closed her eyes and allowed herself to concentrate on the feel of his bristles sliding across her skin, while his scent of evergreen teased her senses.

He brought his mouth to her ear. "If you want to know what I think . . ." He bit down gently on her earlobe.

"Yes," she begged in a voice that sounded a little too breathless.

She could feel him smile against her skin.

"I didn't think they were pretend." He kissed the tender spot below her ear, then licked it, sending a throbbing heat through her that settled low in her belly. "But the only way to be certain is to repeat our performance."

"Ahem, excuse me."

Stephen growled under his breath, clearly unhappy with the interloper. Frankly, she felt the same way. Yet, the longer they continued this conversation, the more completely she would fall under her husband's spell.

"I forgot something," the intruder dared to utter.

They both turned around, together. Stephen pulled away, which gave Caroline an unfettered view of the person.

Mr. Beakens was walking toward them. "I forgot the cloth I use to clean my spectacles." Without a hint that he had interrupted something between the two of them, he pushed his spectacles up the bridge of his nose. "You are blocking the chair."

Caroline stood aside and managed to murmur, "Pardon us."

The solicitor observed them for a minute before a smile erupted, causing his reddened cheeks to round. "Bully for you, there's no mistletoe around," he commented. Then grabbed a scrap of cloth from the chair and headed out of the room. Just before he reached the door, he said over his shoulder, "The duke will be pleased. Merry Christmas, indeed."

"It's a Christmas miracle. I think we might have secured your money, darling." Stephen's soft laughter melted into a smile.

She gloried briefly in their shared moment, the moment when they were a united front, standing together to combat whatever hardship they faced. That's what she had always wanted with her husband. With Stephen.

For the first time in months, she dared to wonder if they might be able to achieve that dream.

"According to my itinerary, I am supposed to join the ladies' tour of the hothouses this afternoon. What are your plans for the rest of the day?" Caroline asked, hoping they could spend some time together before the children's singing performance and the evening meal.

Stephen narrowed his eyes, and his brow furrowed into neat lines. He always did that when he was tackling the bookkeeping for the estate. But today, that focus was on her. "The duke has arranged for his land steward to give all the gentlemen a tour of the estate. I thought I might go . . . unless you need me."

She shook her head, trying not to let her disappointment show. "I know how you wanted to see the outbuildings and pastures."

"If you want me to spend the day with you, Caro, all you have to do is ask. You could come with me to see the estate."

"Thank you, but"—Caroline glanced down the hall where ladies flitted in and out of the drawing room—"I'm planning to meet Diana. We have so much to catch up on. Later, Cressie is taking us to see the grotto. It's always a delightful treat. This year the theme is King Arthur and Queen Guinevere's castle."

"The grotto. Of course." A flash of disappointment crossed his face. But in usual Stephen fashion, he brushed it aside immediately. "Then allow me to escort you." He offered her his arm.

Caroline hesitated a moment, considering whether to ask him to stay with her. She even considered spending the day outside with him plodding through the snowy fields and battling the winter wind just to see a couple of cows and grain storage bins. She shivered slightly.

She was being nonsensical to want his company. It would only be harder to leave him at the end of the party as the foolish attachment she felt for him strengthened. Instead, she wrapped her hand around his arm. "Thank you for joining me with the solicitor. The conversation was unbearable."

"And rude," Stephen added.

She focused on his arm where her hand rested as she struggled to find the right words. "I'm sorry I was argumentative in our room earlier. It was a kind and generous thing you did, bringing me food and chocolate. I should have thanked you, instead of questioning your motives."

She forced her gaze to his. His smile had faded, and he studied her with a keen awareness. Never had she felt her faults so exposed before him. She'd usually considered herself to be in the right. Well, she usually *was* right.

But in all honesty, she rarely considered his side.

"That's the first time I've ever recalled you apologizing for anything," he said.

She forced herself to accept that. She would not defend her actions, as that would divide them once again. "I am truly sorry. Since the inn, we've reached an accord and a semblance of understanding. I don't want to lose that."

"Nor I," he agreed. "I accept your apology."

Without another word passing between them, a new peace settled between them as they proceeded down the hall. Stephen left her after greeting the ladies who were entering the drawing room. Caroline soon discovered that the day's activities included making decorations for the salon where the children's concert would take place.

She kept the smile on her face throughout the day, acting as if she enjoyed the women's company. Diana never joined them; word spread that she was in a delicate way and unfortunately, she was resting this afternoon.

Though Caroline missed Diana's company, she spent her time touring the hothouses, trimming the salon, then bundling up and walking through the snow to the grotto. It truly was a magnificent structure. Her cousin Cressie excelled at making whimsical creations from ice and snow, or rather, in directing artisans to make the structures for her.

As they toured King Arthur's castle, she halfheartedly listened to the latest gossip and nodded when she had to. Though mistletoe and kissing boughs were everywhere, naughty giggles exploded when they came across a fainting couch crafted from ice, draped in a fur robe. An active argument broke out about whether it would be the perfect place for a liaison—further evidence that the Revelry, this year, had taken on a more dissolute tone than previous years.

Caroline didn't care. She couldn't see how anyone would want to make love on a block of ice. She'd rather be somewhere warm.

Specifically, somewhere warm in the company of her husband.

All day she wondered what Stephen was doing, and if he was thinking of her as much as she thought of him. His company was definitely preferable to that of anyone else attending the party.

As the hours dragged by, she realized she didn't care if she did appear smitten with her husband.

She should have spent the day with him.

Even if she risked being introduced to several stinky cows.

Chapter Eight

The next day, Stephen awoke on his side, with his arm around Caroline's waist while she was snuggled against him. As was usual when he held his wife with her lovely derriere nestled against his groin, he found himself with a hard and ready cock.

It had always been that way, and he'd missed her like this, warm and sleepy. This morning, it was torture. Last night, after spending the day outdoors, he'd found excuse after excuse to delay coming to bed. They'd sat together at the children's concert, and Caroline had seemed genuinely pleased with his company. But he knew that if he accompanied her to bed, he'd want to make love to her.

It was too soon.

If she wasn't ready, then pushing Caroline to make love—to come home—would ruin the new rapport building between them.

She moaned slightly in her sleep, a sound like a siren's song. Unable to resist, he pushed his erection against her, and she moaned again. Then, the luscious vixen snuggled closer, so he pulled her tighter against him.

The morning straddled the horizon of the old night and the new day. It was his favorite time of morning, and hers too.

Or at least, it used to be.

He used to count the day already a success if he strode into breakfast, his entire body filled with energy and happiness from having made love to his wife. They would begin the day in such harmony that they wouldn't even have to speak over the breakfast dishes, and he would stride off to work feeling . . . happy.

"Stephen?" Caro murmured.

He rubbed his nose against the fragrant mane of her hair and inhaled deeply. Her scent brought back all the memories of gently waking, leisurely making love, his body and soul happy to be one with his wife.

"Hmm," he answered, allowing the sweetness of those recollections to tempt him.

"How long have you been awake?" Caroline stretched, the movement rubbing her soft breasts against the arm he had wrapped around her.

The innocent contact made the fire in his groin burn hotter. His initial reaction was to cup her breast and kiss her neck. She loved to be woken by a thumb stroking one nipple.

But he didn't caress her. He was determined to control himself.

"Same as you," he whispered as he kissed her temple.

"I waited up for you last night," she said with a yawn and another stretch. "What time did you come to bed?"

He never wanted to let her go, even if her every movement resulted in blissful agony.

"Late," he answered.

"Stephen," she whispered, her voice a husky invitation. She took his hand in a languid movement and placed it over her breast. Her nipple was hard, and the heat of her flesh seared him. His hand curled around her as if it was the old days, when they greeted the sun almost every day with shared pleasure.

When she moaned in answer to his caress, he closed his eyes, praying for control.

"Are we going to make love?" she asked, her voice a mere thread of sound.

"Do you want to?" *Dear heaven, let her say yes.*

"Hmm," she murmured in answer. She slid his hand away from her breast.

Damnation.

Then a miracle occurred. Caro guided his hand lower. His wife had always known what she wanted: the same thing he wanted. As her hand pushed his against the silkiness of her nightgown, Stephen counted the ribs his fingers traced before pressing gently against the soft curve of her stomach.

But Caro didn't stop. She brought his hand farther until heaven waited for *her* and *him*, a finger touch away.

She made a faint sound in the back of her throat, a whimper of invitation. "Stephen . . ."

"Is this what you want?" He licked the soft skin of her throat, his hand curving and tightening, blood heating as he felt her body stir.

Before she could answer, a gentle knock sounded against the door.

He lifted his head, eyes kindling. Whoever it was, he would send them away, hopefully to the farthest corners of the earth so they wouldn't interrupt Caro and him again.

"Lord Stephen?" Percy asked behind the closed door.

What the devil? His valet knew better than to interrupt them in the morning. The man never entered until Stephen rang for him.

Caro scooted out of his arms and pulled the cover up to her chin.

Stephen flipped on his back and laid his arm over his eyes, curses filling his head.

Another knock sounded on the door. "Lord Stephen?" Percy had the good sense to clear his throat. "Sir, I hate to bother you, but Twist has informed me the duke prefers that you and Lady Stephen find the yule log immediately."

When they remained silent, Percy added, "Twist says pick out a good one, sir. Apparently, the duke's health is failing, and his mood is—ahem—irritable. He says that you will understand if I tell you that the duke is making rash decisions because he is in pain."

So was his cock. Blast Percy and his damnable timing, when heaven had been so close to Stephen's fingertips.

The mattress depressed slightly as Caro rose to dress. "Please wait until I'm in the dressing room before you bid Percy to enter."

He nodded, not lifting his arm from his eyes, listening to the sound of her footsteps pad away from the bed.

"Stephen?" Caro called.

He lifted his head, unable to speak. Her gown was transparent in the dawn light with every curve on display. He hadn't seen Caro naked for a year, since the last morning when they made love—and he came home to an empty house.

She had grown even more exquisite, the lush curve of her breasts just the right size for his large hands. Her waist curved in before swelling to hips that he loved to grip, bending her over a chair, or supporting her as she poised in the air above him, taking her pleasure with her head thrown back . . .

He managed to mumble, "Yes?"

"I liked waking up with you. That way." She dipped her head as a smile tugged at her lips. Then his proud, brave wife lifted her eyes to his. "You used to, as well."

"I did." His voice cracked a little.

A little more insistently, Percy knocked on the door again.

"I could send Percy away." His voice came out in a growl.

She shook her head slightly, and the soft waves of her hair skated across her shoulders as if in agreement. "We shouldn't disappoint the duke."

He slid from the bed and stood before her naked. He didn't dare touch her. "Caro, we don't need this money. I have enough. I can support you. Why don't we tell your uncle and his ugly little game to go to hell?"

Her eyes grew large. *"We can't."*

Instantly, Stephen remembered not to pressure her.

A blush rose in Caro's cheeks. "Besides, I'm looking forward to spending the day with you."

The dawn that flooded the room suddenly matched the lightness in Stephen's heart. He reached out and touched the curve of her cheek, afraid that if he even took her hands he would sweep her into bed. "And I look forward to spending it with you, dearest."

"Then you'd better hurry and have your valet dress you," Caroline announced, turning toward the dressing room. She called out over her shoulder, "The first one downstairs gets to pick the log. Ask Percy to summon a maid, will you please?"

As she shut the door behind her, Stephen stood still for a moment, getting control of his body before he pulled on a robe.

He needed to win her challenge and make certain they were front row center for the late afternoon pantomime so she could secure her money. Though if he had his druthers, they would search all day for the perfect yule log and miss that damnable pantomime. He didn't care if the duke became apoplectic when they never appeared.

The only thing Stephen cared about was spending every second of the day in his wife's company.

CAROLINE STOMPED ON the frozen, hard ground to ensure her feet were still attached to her ankles. Her warmest half-boots did little to protect her from the cold that crept up her legs.

Stephen had beaten her downstairs by a good quarter hour, which meant he was allowed to choose the log they'd bring back for the duke's celebration. Well, actually, they weren't carrying the log themselves; Twist had given them a scarlet ribbon to tie to the winning log so that the ducal grooms could haul the monstrous thing home.

She huffed a breath of silver steam through the air.

They'd had a nice time driving the cart around the fields, but now she was cold and tired and wanted to find a warm fire.

They had been tromping around the duke's formidable estate for the last several hours, and by each increasing minute, she grew more and more miserable. She stole a peek at Anise, the carthorse. The poor creature was as miserable as Caroline was. The mare's head hung low, and she stomped her feet the same as Caroline.

To make matters worse, it was snowing. The horse was covered in a blanket of snow. The flakes had started as the fluffy sort that drifted through the air and lent a lovely atmosphere to the holiday.

In the last few minutes, it had started to blow sideways and was pelting her face with ice crystals. Enough was enough. She went to find Stephen, who had disappeared in a copse of oak trees.

"Stephen," Caroline called, against a wind that howled louder than a tweaked banshee.

"Steph—" *Swoosh.* Her feet flew out from underneath her, and she landed on a sheet of ice. Pain shot through every limb of her body as she struggled to regain her breath.

Caroline stared at the sky for a moment, or rather, she stared at the sheet of snow that separated her gaze from the sky.

Damn him for wanting to find the *perfect* yule log.

She struggled to rise, finally rolling over onto her hands and knees and pushing herself up. Snow went over the tops of her boots and soaked her stockings; she could feel her garters begin to give way. By the time she got to her feet, she couldn't feel her feet and her teeth were chattering. She took two careful steps forward.

Stephen suddenly appeared like a specter out of the swirling flakes. "Oho, Caro! You're covered in snow." He laughed with the unfettered glee of a child. "Have you been making snow angels? You should have called me to join in the fun."

"Stephen, we need to leave. The horse—" Without warning, he encircled her in his arms and swung her in the air.

"Merry Christmas, Caro." He smacked one cheek with his lips before putting her down. "You aren't still disappointed that I beat you downstairs?" His cheeks were as red as the cherries in the breakfast tarts.

Truly, he was a handsome man, but she was too frozen to admit it. Her chattering had increased, and her entire body was shivering.

"Come, I want to show you what I found. There are some sturdy oak branches we should mark for the grooms although they'd better get out here soon if they want to escape the snow. I thought we could instruct them to chisel holes wide enough to hold some candles and then decorate it with holly."

She couldn't hide her misery any longer. Tears muddled her vision. The only thing she could see was the bright red scarf tied around his neck. One rebel tear fell after another.

He grabbed her hand and began to escort her back into the treasure trove he had found in this godforsaken tundra.

She dug in her heels and pulled her hand away. "N-no," she uttered through her chattering teeth.

He turned around.

"Would you prefer to make the candlesticks from the ash branches we collected? I think the birch is also an excellent choice." He moved closer. "Caro, are those tears?"

Tears pooled in her eyes, and her throat felt numb from breathing in the cold.

"Darling? What's wrong?" Stephen framed her cheeks with his cold gloves, and she pulled away. Recognizing his error, he tore off his gloves with his teeth. Tenderly, he placed his warm hands on her skin and cradled her cheeks.

"We've been outside for hours. I can't feel my face." The

warmth from his hands gave Caroline a reprieve from the cold and, in those seconds, all those old stirrings of being neglected crept to the surface, begging to be voiced. "I'm tired, hungry, thirsty, and most importantly, I'm frozen."

His gaze inventoried her body before his eyes came to rest on her face. "Didn't you dress warmly enough?"

"No lady can dress warmly enough for a blizzard," she growled. "People aren't designed to be out in this type of cold." She pointed to the horse. "And neither is our horse. She and I are both miserable."

"Don't you want to pick out the yule log?" The confusion on his face proved he still had no idea what she was talking about.

"I don't care about a log now. I care about a warm fire and a warm drink. The horse wants a bag of oats and a warm stable." Before he put in a word in defense, she continued, "We've spent our time looking at birch, oak, ash, along with every other possible wood that resides in this countryside. You could have picked one out an hour ago."

The wind swirled snow around them, wrapping their feet in drifts. She was at wit's end and would be returning to the house . . . with or without him.

"I'm not standing in the cold and waiting for the snow to reach my ears." She turned to the cart. "Stephen, we should go."

"Wait," Stephen said behind her. "I thought you chose this task over the choir because you wanted to impress your uncle with the biggest log we could find."

"I should have told you earlier. You can't divine what I'm thinking." Caroline planted one foot in front of the other. On the third step, her boot caught on the uneven ground. With her arms flailing like a windmill, she tripped and went flying through the air. She broke most of her fall with her hands, but her left cheek collided with the cold, hard ground. A thousand shards of pain pricked her injured cheek.

The next moment, Stephen had her in his arms, carrying her to the cart.

Feeling his strong arms around her, Caroline did the thing that she swore that she would never do.

She wept, leaning her cheek against his icy greatcoat and sobbing—because she was cold, because she was bruised, but even more, she should have told him how miserable she was out in the snowstorm. She had the notion that he was genuinely trying to heal their marriage.

So many missed opportunities to talk to him. There's nothing like nearly freezing to make that fact clear.

It was the first time she'd ever cried in front of him and she couldn't seem to stop, hiccupping into his coat.

"Caro," he softly crooned.

Hearing her name said in such a caring manner just made her cry harder. He'd never talked to her like that before.

But then she remembered about every tree and every bush they'd stopped at along the way. He'd ask for her opinion of its suitability for the festive yule log, and when she'd say it would be perfect, he'd announce that they had to continue roaming the fields.

"I shouldn't have kept you out here so long." As he settled her into the seat, he declared, "We're heading back now. They'll just have to do without a yule log."

Then he did something that made her cry even harder.

With the gentlest of touches, he pressed his lips against her scraped cheek. After a quick pat to the horse, he stepped into the driver's box. In a jerk, they were on their way.

To where, who knew? The path they'd followed was completely gone, covered by drifts of snow.

After Stephen loosened the reins and allowed the horse her head, he reached under the box and retrieved a blanket. Caroline silently took the blanket from his hands and spread it over both of them.

"Come here," he commanded, wrapping his arm around her waist and bringing her flush against him.

The warmth of his body helped a little. She was still shivering, but at least her teeth weren't chattering anymore.

"Where are we going?" she managed, swallowing back tears.

"Back to the estate." Stephen pulled her even closer. "I'll get you there as fast as I can. But this damn snow is making it difficult."

"Is that why we're going in circles? This makes the second time we've passed that holly bush that looks like a bear."

Chapter Nine

Stephen pulled the cart to a stop. He saw the holly bush she pointed to, but he had no idea if they'd passed it before. It appeared that the horse had no sense of direction, and the storm didn't help matters.

Caro sat beside him, shivering. He felt a flash of rage at himself. What an idiotic idea to find the perfect yule log in order to spend time with her. "Why don't you sit on my lap, and I'll wrap my coat around you. It'll be warmer."

At her nod, he unbuttoned his greatcoat, picked her up, and settled her on his lap. She leaned against his chest, and he pulled his coat closed around her. The wet snow on her cloak melted, sending a chill through his chest. But that wasn't what concerned him.

His wife was still shivering, so much so that he feared she would fall off his lap.

"Can we make it to Cressie's grotto?" Caroline's words were garbled from the shakes that racked her body. "I think it's that way." She tried to point to the west.

Instinctively, he held her against him with one arm around her waist. He bent his head to answer. "I don't like the way the storm is intensifying. Anise will never make it, and I don't want you to suffer any more." He didn't add that he didn't want to see her endangered any further either. "If I have my directions right, there's a hunting lodge not too far from here."

When she nodded, the movement rubbed the back of

her head against his chest. Melted snow trickled down his shirt. "Cressie mentioned that all the hunting lodges have been supplied with food, drink, and wood for the Revelry. We can wait out the storm there."

Stephen guided the horse through an open field, then followed the tree line that bordered the north side of the field. A quarter of an hour had passed since the snow intensified, and the driving wind wasn't lessening. If anything, it had increased.

A stream of curses went through his head. A fine way to court his wife: by nearly freezing her to death.

Fear that they wouldn't find the lodge in time chilled his body worse than the wet snow and the wind slapping his cheeks. If he caused Caro any harm from their outing, he'd never forgive himself. Nightmare scenarios whirled around him faster than the swirl of snow.

"Look. Over there." Burrowed in his greatcoat, Caro pointed one finger in the direction to the right.

"Excellent," Stephen exclaimed and pulled her tighter against him in celebration. No more than fifty yards away, a small hunting lodge lay sheltered by a copse of trees. As they came closer, Stephen let out a breath of relief. The small cottage even had a one-stall lean-to that would protect their horse from the elements.

"Whoa," he called at the same time he pulled to a stop in front of the cottage. He looked down at Caro. "Stay here and let me look inside first."

Caro turned her head to face him. Her face was tearstained, but she managed a crooked smile. Proving once again that his wife was stouthearted and perfect.

Stephen tied the reins, then jumped to the ground. He shook out the snow-covered blanket. Thankfully, the door to the lodge was unlocked. He returned to Caro's side and lifted her into his arms. In seconds, he had her in the small sitting room, resting in a chair placed strategically in front of the cold fireplace. A fresh blanket, softer than the one he'd found under the driver's box, was neatly folded on a small sofa next to Caroline's chair. He quickly wrapped it around her, then went to the fireplace.

Stacked wood lay in the fire grate, and a new tinderbox sat on the mantel. Within minutes, Stephen had made quick work of lighting a fire. Finally, the room was cast in a warm glow.

He bent down on his haunches until he and Caroline were eye to eye. "Better?" At her nod, he said softly, "I'll be right back." He headed again into the storm to make certain the horse was sheltered from the wind, with a nice armful of hay and a few handfuls of oats. A placid animal, she flicked her ears at him, then lowered her head and started eating.

"You're a brave girl," he told her, patting her withers. "I know you'd rather be in the stables."

That was his fault as well. What in the bloody hell had he been thinking?

He knew the answer.

He hadn't.

He was so happy to simply be with Caro that he lost track of time and didn't even really notice the weather. Once again, he wished he didn't possess such single-mindedness. He could have escorted Caro out of the elements sooner. Thinking of regrets, he should have gone to London immediately after she left and begged her to come home. Instead, he'd found solace in his work.

When he returned to the lodge, Caro's shivering had stopped. She was leaning back against the chair. "I'm better."

He drew closer and inspected the scrape on her reddened skin. Three small scratches covered in dried blood marred her cheekbone. He pressed a kiss to her still-chilled cheek. "You need to take these wet things off."

"Take my clothing off?" She tilted her head adorably in confusion. "Certainly not. I'll freeze."

"Indulge me," he countered. Without waiting for her to answer, he untied her half-boots.

"Thank you," she said softly. "I did want those off, but my fingers wouldn't cooperate. Leave my stockings for now, please. They're dry."

He grimaced as he pulled her half-boots off. How could he possibly tell her how sorry he was for putting her through the misery of the day?

WARMER THAN FROZEN, but colder than chilled, Caroline couldn't make herself move. She really should force herself up from the chair and put away her cloak and lay her shoes neatly on the fireplace hearth. But it was so lovely to sit here in front of the fire.

As Stephen eased her cloak from her shoulders, she noticed his boots. "They're ruined," she said, nodding.

"They're an old pair." Picking up two warm blankets, he piled them on top of her until only her eyes were visible—and then he took a third blanket and wound it over her head.

"I can hardly see," Caro protested. Yet, she was starting to feel warm.

He shrugged one shoulder, then with a sucking sound, he pulled the wet boots off his feet. "When I left Anise, she was happily munching on oats. The staff must have thought of everything for an event like this. The lean-to held a bucket of oats, water that hadn't frozen yet, and fresh hay. She's safely out of the elements."

He pulled off his wet stockings, and then made his way over to stand before her. "Hungry? Thirsty?"

"Yes to both." She made to stand, but he stayed her by bending close, hands braced against the back of her chair.

Her breath caught instinctively. Was he looking at her lips? There was just a flash of something in his eyes . . .

It was gone. He straightened. "Let me see what I can find." He walked to a cupboard next to the fireplace and opened the doors, then tossed over his shoulder, "You, my lady, will be dining in style."

"How so?" she asked, enjoying this playful side of him.

Stephen waved a hand at the open door. "There's wine, bread, cheese." He peered inside. "A couple of pieces of ham. Apples." He turned with a frown. "Unfortunately, no chocolate makings, darling. But there is port."

"Shall I help you prepare the food?" Caro asked, hoping she didn't have to move.

"No, stay there," Stephen called out, pulling things out of the cupboard.

She was thankful for his refusal. She was just beginning to get the feeling back in her toes. Her feet were another matter. If she had stood, Caroline was confident her face would have met the floor.

Stephen returned with a tray ladened with food, and the all-important port.

"Drink this." He held out a glass of dark crimson liquid. He went to the hearth and hooked a pot of water onto the rod suspended in the fireplace.

The potent wine slid down Caro's throat like a promise, warming her instantly. She took another sip and sighed.

"You better have something to eat with that." Stephen handed her a plate, then took a deep swallow of his own port.

They ate and drank in peaceable silence, only the wind battering the cottage and the crackle of the fire breaking the quiet between them. As Stephen took the pot of boiling water from the fireplace, Caroline placed her empty plate on a small side table next to her, then finished her port.

He poured a bit of water in a cup and set it on the side table.

"How are you?" Stephen dropped to his knees before her.

"I'm fine. No, I'm better than fine. That was a feast." She lifted her hand and swept aside a lock of wet hair that fell across his cheek.

He took her hand in his and pressed a kiss against her palm. "Will you forgive me for getting carried away with the outdoors and keeping you outside too long?"

Never taking her gaze from his, she nodded.

She meant it too.

She even managed a wavering smile.

Stephen dipped a clean serviette in the cooling water, then held it up. "May I tend to your scrape?"

"Careful," she warned. "It still hurts."

"I'm sure it does." Gently, he pressed the cloth to her skin.

She pulled away. "Ouch."

"I'm sorry, darling," he whispered, brushing the cloth against her wound. "It's all clean now."

He was so close that his scent filled her with longing, a yearning to be back with him at Heartfeld Hall.

"Thank you." Her words were barely above a whisper. His eyes smoldered in the dimly lit room. She swallowed, trying vainly to think of a subject of conversation that would counteract the tension that was building between them.

"I was selfish," he stated. He was kneeling before her, his clear eyes looking into hers. Stephen gently touched her uninjured cheek. "I should have been more observant to your needs." He pressed his forehead to hers and lowered his voice, but his turmoil was easily heard. "My God, Caroline. What if you had truly hurt yourself? What if we hadn't found this place? What if you come down with a lung infection? If I lost you . . ."

His words trailed to nothing, and neither of them said a word.

It was completely illogical, but she shivered at the feel of his warm palm and long fingers against her skin.

"If I lived in a world without you, knowing you were gone forever, I wouldn't want to exist." When Caroline started to protest, he rubbed his thumb across her lips, and she lapsed into silence. "I didn't ignore you in the snow because I didn't care. I was too joyful to be with you again, to have you to myself for a whole afternoon. Just as I never ignored you over the breakfast table, as you said in your farewell note. I simply didn't know what you wanted. You see, my parents never spent time together in the morning. It was my mother's preference. I thought all ladies wanted quiet mornings, so I was trying to be accommodating. Truly, I thought I was being the best husband I knew how to be. Now, I recognize that I wasn't." He took her hand and squeezed. "But know this, Caro. After we made love in the mornings . . . I always felt as if I talked to you without words."

He studied her, his eyes fierce with emotion, and a slender thread of understanding began to grow between them. Could she truly believe him? It would be so easy to put her heart on the line and believe something special could be created between them. The urge to take the first step grew fierce.

"Caro, I will always hope and pray that someday—"

She didn't let him finish. Instead, she pressed her lips against his, igniting the desire that always simmered between them.

"Caro," he groaned against her mouth.

She took it as an invitation to deepen the kiss and slipped her tongue inside his mouth, welcoming the sweet taste of port. He pulled her into a close embrace when Caroline wrapped her arms around his neck, pressing her body to his hard chest.

Her breasts ached and felt heavy against him, and her nipples tightened. She rubbed against him like a cat who'd been too long without any attention. As their tongues mated, it felt as if they were finally conversing with each other—sharing themselves in a way they'd never done before, all by way of kisses.

He brought his hand down to her waist and froze for a moment. Then he broke away, and she moaned in protest. Dazed by the storm they'd created inside the cottage, Caroline blinked, trying to focus on what he was doing.

"Your dress is soaked, and your feet feel like ice," he said harshly. He had grabbed her feet and was rubbing them.

Her heartbeat raced as he devoured her with his eyes.

She'd seen that look a thousand times, and it never failed to send her senses reeling. Her body softened and grew wet in anticipation of what was to come.

They were both breathing heavily as he slipped his hands under the blankets keeping her warm and pushed her skirts up toward her waist. When his slow caress reached her thigh, he untied one garter, the movement so slow she couldn't breathe.

With a jerky movement, she pushed off the blanket so she could see what he was doing. She had gone from cold to burning, and his large hands against her thighs were a sight she'd remember forever. She tilted her pelvis, enticing him.

Stephen grinned at her, a wicked spark in his eyes, but she'd been without him so long that she didn't care if she was begging. He'd soon be the one pleading with her.

"Let me enjoy the unveiling of your skin," he said huskily. "It reminds me of the finest silk." He pressed a kiss against her mouth, then deepened it. Just as she met her tongue with his, he drew back. Watching her closely, he slowly rolled down one stocking until her foot was uncovered. He placed it against his warm thigh. "Leave it here."

He wouldn't have to ask twice. His warmth surrounded her, and she pressed the ball of her foot against him. The hard muscles were a testament to the estate work he so enjoyed. He was pure male, and the feel of him made her feel drunk yet more alive than she had been in the last year.

Slowly, she slid her foot upward as he unrolled her other stocking. His gaze caught hers, and she smiled. She'd found what she wanted. Rubbing the ball of her foot against his hard length, she heard his quick intake of breath.

He caught her ankle, stopping her teasing caress. Instead of pushing her away as she thought he might, he held her firmly against him. "Do you feel that?" His hoarse voice made her pulse pound. "That's what you do to me."

"Unbutton your falls," she commanded.

Never taking his eyes from hers, he did as she asked. Caroline slowly allowed her gaze to fall down the breadth and length of his chest to his hands. He held his straining cock in one hand. The light from the fire glowed, casting a light around the glistening crown. She licked her lips at the sight, and he groaned her name.

Without another word, he started to undress her. Acting as her lady's maid, he coaxed her to stand and made quick work of unbuttoning the back of her gown. The sodden mess fell to the floor in a heap.

"There's a bed." Stephen nodded toward a corner.

Caroline shook her head. "It's warmer by the fire. Let's stay here."

"Whatever my wife desires."

"I desire you."

"And I you," he answered softly.

He made quick work of loosening her stays. In an instant, they were discarded, leaving her clad only in her chemise. As he reached to lift it over her head, Caroline stepped away. "You first."

A smile tugged at his lips. In seconds, he'd discarded his coat, waistcoat, and shirt. Her knees weakened at the sight, and she gasped for air. He could have been the model for the Adonis statue that stood in the entry of Heartfeld Hall. Each muscle was perfectly defined. The breadth of his body reminded her that he carried a tremendous amount of responsibility on his shoulders. For the love of heaven, he was gorgeous, and he was hers.

If only for the night.

His muscles twitched at her examination. Slowly, she reached out and trailed a hand down the center of his chest where a smattering of black hair curled. He placed his hand over hers. She felt as if she were swimming in a warm pool, and he was beside her, coaxing her.

The truth was she had never wanted to leave this oasis they'd created for each other.

"Now you," he rasped.

She slipped the chemise over her head. His gaze locked with hers before it slowly slid down her neck, then lower to her breasts.

"Caro, you've grown even more beautiful in the past year," he whispered.

Before she could respond that she could say the same for him, he walked in all his rugged, naked grandeur to the bed where he stripped off the covers.

He quickly arranged the blanket and linens into a makeshift bed in front of the fire and held out his hand to her in invitation. With an unsteady breath, Caroline took his hand in hers.

As sure as the dawn would welcome them tomorrow, whatever happened tonight, there would be no going back. She knew that, but she was ready to take the risk.

Unaware of her tumultuous thoughts, Stephen settled on the floor in front of the fire, then joined her, covering her body with his own. Immediately, his heat warmed her, and the feel of his naked skin against hers rekindled the need to have him inside her.

As he took her in another kiss, he cupped one of her breasts, making Caroline cry out, the sensation exquisite. She pressed upward, offering more. He broke the kiss, then trailed his lips downward, tonguing the indentation at the base of her neck where her pulse fluttered frantically. Every place he touched, her heart seemed to try to follow, its beat wild and frenzied.

"Please," she begged.

In response, he pushed his cock against her lower belly. He took her in another kiss, then turned his attention to her breasts. He sucked and laved one nipple until she thought she would break apart. She whimpered as he turned his attention to the other one.

Neediness rushed through her veins, and she pushed her hips against his once more.

Continuing to attend to her swollen, achy breasts, he traced a path down her ribs with his hand, then lower down to her hip. As Caro held her breath, he combed through her curls until he found her sensitive nub and slowly circled it. Gasping, she bucked into his hand, her legs moving restlessly. The longing for him—for intimacy—was all-consuming.

She latched her fingers into his dark hair and pulled him until he was face-to-face with her. "Don't make me wait. Now," she demanded.

He pushed one finger into her, testing her readiness. "You're so wet," he breathed against her lips. He added another, and she bucked even harder.

"Please," she cried, the word echoing in the small room.

With a heady kiss, Stephen positioned himself at her entrance and slowly entered her, inch by inch until he was firmly seated.

Finally, Caroline felt as if her world had achieved some sort of equilibrium. This, *this*, was where they had always been happiest. Where she had been happiest.

He pulled out slowly, then entered her again, keeping up a steady, but toe-curling, pace until she thought she couldn't take it anymore. Her body was spiraling. Each push, move, and withdrawal took her to a new place. As Stephen's rhythm increased, what little control she had evaporated. She wrapped her legs tighter around his waist and squeezed.

"Come for me, Caro," he whispered.

"I—" she cried, then she was lost.

As filaments of heat slid through every part of her,

he tucked her head close to his chest, murmuring sweet words, coaxing her to feel. And she felt everything—their hearts beating only for each other.

With one last thrust, Stephen moaned her name and collapsed against her. She held him close and trailed her fingers lightly back and forth over his sweaty back as their breathing slowed.

Eventually, he pulled up, resting his weight on his elbows. She brushed kisses on his chin in the languid moments of the aftermath of their lovemaking, loving how firelight danced across his face.

"Damn it, Caro, I almost lost control." Stephen leaned down and swept his lips against hers. "That doesn't happen to me. *This* . . . this never happened to me. Before you."

He was saying something important; she let the words sink into her heart. She continued to stroke him while basking in the tenderness of his gaze. Even if she didn't receive her trust money, this would always be a treasured Christmas.

Stephen looked back steadily. "I love you," he stated. "I fell in love with you shortly after our marriage. I want you to know that." The warmth of his gaze peeled away layers of her carefully crafted defenses, the very ones she'd built between them.

The emotion and warmth in his gaze undid her. "I love you too," she whispered.

"That means everything to me," he said.

All she could do was nod.

Stephen settled on his side, curled his body around hers, then held her. Their legs tangled as if locking themselves together. In the first year of their marriage, they had always slept this way.

The tempo of his breath grew even as he surrendered to sleep.

But Caroline lay awake, staring at the sparks flying up

the chimney. She clasped her husband tightly in a desperate attempt to keep all the lovely feelings close and never let them escape.

She kept swallowing against an unexpected thickness in her throat. As a young woman, she'd dreamed of this moment, when she and her husband would say those three words to each other.

Foolishly, she had thought it meant they would have a happy life. But she knew better now.

Over these days they shared, Caroline came to a startling conclusion. She'd loved Stephen from shortly after they married. Irretrievably, head-over-heels in love with the man.

Yet, love didn't always mean happiness and contentment. Still, love was why she had held the last strings of hope by inches, refusing to let them go on the chance he'd change. Notice her. *See* her.

How could she trust if he really had? More importantly, had she changed?

Chapter Ten

Daylight streamed through the windows. Stephen had woken a few times in the night to replenish the fire. It was still blazing when he opened his eyes, but it was the warmth he held in his arms that drew his interest.

"Is it still snowing?" Caro stirred beside him but didn't move to sit up.

"I don't believe so." He turned on his side to face her. "Good morning, love."

"Good morning," she echoed, but fiddled with the cover thrown over their bodies, not meeting his eyes.

His cock stirred at the mere sight of her, suggesting he would never get his fill of this woman. After last night, he should be bone-tired. After the first time, he'd taken Caro twice more, every time he woke to throw a log on the fire, each time more intense and needy than the previous. He had tasted every last inch of her, and she was still as divine as he'd recalled.

After three bouts of lovemaking, she must know that they had to live together. He'd always dreamed his marriage would be one built on love and companionship. Whatever arguments she might have against coming home, surely she had changed her mind.

"Caro." He pulled her close. "I think we should discuss where we go from here."

"Your meaning?" She flipped on her back and studied the ceiling.

"I think you should come home with me. We can travel to my brother's estate after we convince your uncle that you deserve the funds in your trust. If we go home together, he'll have no argument. He cannot fear that you will turn into your mother."

She pulled away and caught a spare blanket to her chest, shielding her body from his gaze. "I don't know, Stephen." She studied the fire, not looking at him.

His body stiffened, but he kept his voice even. "We don't have to go to my brother's house. If you'd prefer, we can go home to Heartfeld Hall and spend the rest of our holiday there." He stroked the back of his fingers across her cheek. "May I have a look at your injury?"

She turned slightly to give him a better view.

"You have a small mark, but it'll be gone in a day or two." That's when he saw the single tear that drifted down her cheek.

His heart stumbled in his chest, and he fisted one hand by his side. "Tell me." An icy fear stabbed him in the gut when he saw the miserable look in her eyes.

Caro glanced at the fire again before she looked him in the face. "I can't come home with you."

"Caroline, last night was . . . wonderful. I love you and shared my love last night." He caught her gaze. "You told me you loved me. It was the happiest moment in my life."

"Stephen, of course, I love you. I will always love you." Caro's voice was so low he could barely hear it. "You have to understand that sometimes love just isn't enough."

"I don't understand." Sometimes he didn't think they spoke the same language. Yet his heart swelled in his chest because she would always love him. "I'm honored that you love me, and I promise to honor that gift every day."

She scowled at him so he must have said something wrong.

Again.

"Let me be blunt." Caro straightened the blanket that

she still clutched to her chest before her gaze captured his. "I need to know that I'm the most important person in your life, just as you are mine."

"You are," he said instantly.

She shook her head, then took a deep breath and released it. "I'm not trying to be obscure, but if I shared examples with you, perhaps you'll understand."

"All right," he said. "That would be helpful." Whatever offending behavior he'd displayed, it would be his first priority to change.

"You truly don't know anything about me, except what you learned when we were in bed together. When we were living together, you gave a potted palm more attention than me."

"Do we even have a potted palm?" The moment her face fell, he felt lower than a bottom step. "Darling, I know we have one. I was trying to get you to smile."

She raised the corners of her mouth obediently, but there was no real humor in her face. "When you would return from your work on the estate, I'd sit beside you at dinner, desperately trying to start a conversation, and you'd answer my every comment with a grunt. I wanted to help you." Her voice broke on the word *you*. "I wanted to be a part of your world too."

"Heartfeld Hall was never profitable, but I was determined to make it so," he said, stumbling into speech. "The last couple of years it just began to make money. I think it will continue to be profitable. I didn't want you to worry. I thought you would become bored, but sometimes it was all I could think of."

"You acted as if I was the boring one. You always held me at arm's length." Caro twisted her fingers together over and over, a sure tell she was miserable. "When I tried to tell you about my day, you nodded at all the right breaks in conversation, but Stephen, I *knew* you weren't listening to me."

He rubbed his chin, trying to find a way to defend himself, but she was right. He hadn't given her the attention she deserved.

"Do you even know when my birthday is?" Caro's voice wasn't sharp, but miserable. "Do you know that not a single person since my mother left has remembered my birthday? No one. Not even my father." Her eyes glistened with tears. "For a little girl of eight not to hear some recognition of her birthday, it's devastating. As a woman, I found it unsurprising, but it wasn't what I dreamed of in marriage. I want more, Stephen. I deserve more."

"Caro, I'm sorry." His voice had dropped an octave, hoarse with self-loathing.

"I'm feeling sorry for myself." She waved a hand in the air in dismissal. "Cressie writes to send birthday wishes."

She bit her lip and turned to the fire. "My mother didn't care and neither did my father. I just wanted some acknowledgment I was important enough to remember. I'd always hoped when I had married, my husband would remember me. And I prayed that person would be you."

He replayed the year they lived together in his mind. He hadn't remembered her birthday, but she'd remembered his. All of his favorites were prepared for his birthday dinner, and she'd given him a new quill set for his desk and his favorite spectacles.

A brisk knock echoed through the room. "Lord Stephen? Lady Stephen? Are you there?"

They sat frozen, staring at each other.

This was horrible timing for an interruption. He had to make this right for her.

"Caro, forgive me. I didn't understand, proving I'm a fool. Please, let me make it up to you."

Another knock sounded more insistent. "My lord, are you in there?"

"You'd better dress." Stephen stood and threw his shirt

over his head and pulled on his breeches before he answered the door.

"Good morning, Lord Stephen." One of the duke's grooms, clad in a bright red greatcoat, tipped his hat.

Stephen wanted to curse at him but he stopped himself. The man was only doing his job.

"I can't tell you how relieved I am to have found you."

"Thank you," Stephen muttered.

"At first you weren't missed, but when you didn't join us for the pantomime, everyone in the household began to worry," the man continued, in a relentlessly chatty fashion. "Are you and your lady wife well?"

Stephen nodded.

The groom motioned to a small carriage waiting on a narrowed shoveled road. Another footman was tying Anise to the back. "We caught sight of the smoke from your chimney at dawn, but it took hours to shovel the snow so we can take you back to the manor."

"Allow me and my wife to dress, then we'll be ready for your escort." Stephen shut the door, not waiting for the footman to answer.

Caro stood beside the fire clutching her dress to her chest. They dressed in silence. Finally, he looked at her, wanting to say so much, but this wasn't the time.

His wife made it to the door first. When she reached for the handle, he gently took her elbow. "Caro, we aren't finished with this discussion."

She nodded, then raised her hand and cupped his cheek. On tiptoes, she brushed a kiss as light as a feather.

Her brown eyes seemed to glisten with an emotion he couldn't define. This time he was the one to bring her close. He pressed a kiss to her mouth. Hard and rough, it was a kiss designed to show her how much he needed her.

Truly, he did see her, although obviously he hadn't made that clear. She was a treasure, and he was so fortunate to have married her. He just had to find a way to show her, and he would. He'd not lose her again.

She whispered his name against his mouth, the sound tender and dear to him.

It took every piece of resolve he possessed but, somehow, he broke away from her.

The bemused expression on her face didn't surprise him. Her lips were wet and swollen. Anyone within fifteen yards of them would know she'd been thoroughly kissed.

"What was that for?" Caroline asked in a low voice.

Good, he'd surprised her. "To remind you that you are the most important person in my life." When she started to protest, he pressed his thumb against her lips. "Let me prove it to you."

He wanted nothing more than to pull her back into his arms. But he had things to do at the duke's house. He threw open the door, and a blast of cold air slapped them in the face. "Shall we? Your destiny awaits. I understand the duke is quite worried about you."

"Oh no," she said lightly. "Not my uncle. I expect that Cressie is worried, though, and Diana as well."

She accepted her uncle's lack of interest.

Accepted it.

At that moment, then and there, in the snow, Stephen added a silent vow to those he made at the altar. Whatever he did in life, he would make certain that this woman, his beloved, knew how precious she was—to him and to the world.

Stephen had a plan. It was his last chance.

And it had to work.

THE COACHMAN DROVE slowly back to the ducal estate, the groom hanging on the rear, carefully staying to the shoveled road. Inside the coach, Caroline sat hip to hip with Stephen. Even though they were physically touching, a chasm a million miles wide lay between them.

She stole a side glance.

His shoulders were straight, and he sat tall, but a coil of reckless energy seemed ready to spring from him. When the carriage hit a rut and she jostled against him, he came awake.

"Shall I give you more room?" His smooth voice didn't reveal a hint of what he was thinking.

She shook her head. "I prefer to sit next to you."

He gave her a slight smile and turned away to stare out the window, lost in his thoughts.

Caro did the same. She'd revealed so much of herself to him because she had wanted him to understand why she left. She wanted love, but only if it came with someone valuing her for who she was—*all* of her, and not just the skills she'd learned from Stephen in the bedroom.

Bedding wasn't enough. She knew that after creating a life for herself in London. The women she worked with respected her, and in turn, she valued them.

However, the mistletoe kisses and the lovemaking at the lodge that they'd shared were signs of their love and fidelity to one another. It symbolized their deep commitment. She knew that now.

As the carriage cut through the snowy landscape, she closed her eyes. The chilly beauty didn't hold her attention. The only thing she wanted was her husband.

No matter what, she would always love him and stay true to him. Without any doubt, she was fortunate to have shared so much with him.

Mayhap she was self-centered to want more. She fisted her hands. What was selfish about wanting to be visible and to matter to her husband? Yet, perhaps she was part of the problem also. A marriage takes work from both sides. In the past, she should have been more forceful in encouraging Stephen to share his worries with her. That might have been the path for each of them to open their hearts and share their mutual concerns and dreams.

Greystoke Manor loomed through the carriage window.

She longed for a bath, clean clothing, and a hot pot of chocolate—in that order. The carriage pulled to a stop in the circular drive where another groom waited for them.

Before he could open the door, Stephen did the honors. He jumped down, then held out his hand. As he helped her descend the steps, he gently squeezed her fingers, the touch endearing. She smiled and squeezed in turn. Whatever kindness he offered, she would answer with one of her own.

"Lord and Lady Stephen, the duke has requested that you visit Mr. Beakens at your earliest convenience." A footman had advanced down the manor steps to greet them. He bowed and turned his attention to the groom who had escorted them back.

When they arrived in the entry, Twist was beside himself at the sight of them. He immediately called for a hot bath to be delivered to their room.

"Darling, you go to our chamber and bathe." Stephen pressed a kiss to her uninjured cheek. "I have a few things to attend to, and we'll see the solicitor together."

Caroline nodded, then walked up the stairs. Unable to resist, she glanced back at Stephen. Her husband stood in the center of the atrium, staring after her. Caroline lifted her hand in farewell, then ascended the stairs with the heat of her husband's intense gaze upon her back until she was out of sight.

Not long after she reached her chamber, a maid joined her, taking a fresh gown from her wardrobe. A hot bath had been prepared in the dressing room. The maid went back and forth, taking her wet clothing to the laundry, returning with a breakfast tray. An hour later, Caroline sat by the fire, sipping her chocolate. Normally, the drink instantly lifted her spirits, but today, nothing helped the dreary miasma that had enveloped her.

"Ma'am?" The maid interrupted Caroline's thoughts. "Mr. Beakens asked that I inform you he is waiting for you downstairs in the duke's study."

"How is His Grace this morning?" Caroline asked.

The maid pressed her lips together. "The same, I understand."

Caroline nodded. "Do you know where my husband is? He's expected to meet with Mr. Beakens also. I thought he would come up to bathe and change his clothing."

"I thought you knew, m'lady." A momentary look of discomfort flitted across the young maid's face. "He rode to the Halig Inn. I don't know when he will return."

Caroline released a shallow breath.

Could Stephen be preparing her transportation back to London? He might not even want to stay at the duke's estate any longer after what she said this morning.

The emptiness in her chest grew sharper until it almost became unbearable. She refused to sit here in a melancholy state. She had to see Mr. Beakens.

After she thanked the maid, Caroline descended the stairs and made her way to the duke's study. The normal hustle and bustle of the house during the holiday festivities was absent this morning.

She knocked on the door. A muffled "enter" greeted her. With a deep breath for fortitude, Caroline swept into the duke's study.

In his usual place at the large table in front of the row of windows overlooking the estate, the solicitor stood and bowed. "Come in, Lady Stephen."

"Good morning, Mr. Beakens." Caroline walked across the room and took a seat adjacent to the solicitor. "I don't believe my husband will join us. Unfortunately, he's been called away on an errand."

The solicitor nodded. "I understand he went to the inn." He pulled out a sheaf of papers from a leather pouch and glanced at them briefly. "Lady Stephen, the duke has decided not to grant your request to distribute the funds from your trust."

"What?" She gasped. Suddenly, a roaring din sounded

in her ears. It couldn't be. How could the duke refuse her request?

"The duke will not give you the money." The solicitor had the decency to look abashed "My lady, I tried to persuade him, but he was adamant. The duke had demanded you attend the pantomime as a couple, and you weren't there."

"We were stranded in a snowstorm." She stood, unable to keep sitting as she argued the decision. "How could we possibly attend?"

"I do understand, my lady. But your uncle's word is law."

She would lose the building if she didn't have that money, which meant that the women artists who had come to depend upon her would lose a place to develop and showcase their art. They wouldn't have anywhere to go.

"I want to see my uncle and try to convince him otherwise." She'd asked before and been refused. This time she demanded. "You can't keep me from seeing him. This decision cannot stand."

Mr. Beakens shook his head slowly. "I'm sorry, Lady Stephen. You're just going to have to wait for the money. The trust provides you will receive it when you turn twenty-five. That's only a little over a year."

"But my husband and I did everything the duke wanted us to do. Everything he demanded, except the pantomime, and that was hardly our fault." Caroline glared as she waved a hand around her at the magnificent furnishings. "The Revelry likely costs more than that sum every year."

"Aye, my lady, so it does. I hope you understand." The solicitor stood, collected his papers, and efficiently placed them in a portfolio before tucking it under his arm. "If you'll excuse me, I have other matters to attend to."

In seconds, he was gone, leaving her alone in the room.

Alone and with nothing left to look forward to, especially since she'd driven her husband away.

Chapter Eleven

Stephen gave his coat, hat, and gloves to a footman, nodding at Twist, who met him at the door. "Where's Lady—"

"She just left the duke's study, where she met with Mr. Beakens." Twist took him by the arm and escorted him quickly to the hallway that led to the duke's inner sanctum.

"She didn't wait for me." A twinge of worry took a bite out of Stephen's gut.

Twist shook his head. "I'm sorry, sir. The solicitor couldn't wait. The duke has had him in and out of his bedchamber all day, changing his will, as I understand." The butler motioned down the hallway. "Her ladyship is seated on a bench."

"Is everything ready as I'd asked?"

"Yes, sir." Twist stopped several feet into the hallway. "Good luck, your lordship."

Stephen walked on, calling thanks to the butler over his shoulder. It was doubtful Twist heard it since Stephen was practically sprinting to reach Caroline. He rounded a corner, then slowed to a stop not more than two feet in front of her.

She sat on a bench with her head bent, staring at her hands. She seemed surrounded by a sense of hopelessness much as she had appeared when she'd told him he hadn't remembered her birthday.

"Caro, what happened?" He slid on the bench next to her and took her hands in his.

"The duke has decided not to give me the money from my trust." She swallowed and wiped below one eye. "He apparently said that because we didn't attend the pantomime, I didn't meet his expectations."

"That was my fault, Caro," Stephen said, his voice deepening with anger. "We would have made it back for the pantomime if I hadn't gotten carried away outside." He bent toward her and lifted her chin with his hand. "I shall see him and explain what happened. I promise this trip won't be for naught."

"Don't waste your time," she murmured. "He's always been an unkind man, and I think impending death has only made him more spiteful." She leaned her head back against the wall and stared at the ceiling. "I have to return to London and try to find a way out of this mess. The women, the artists, they depend on me."

Still holding her hand, Stephen leaned back against the wall next to Caroline.

"Would you wait for me?" she asked, turning to him. "I need to help my artists find another avenue for their work. After that, I could come home to you if you'll have me? I'd like to try again."

He couldn't believe what he was hearing. Earlier, he was convinced that he'd lost her, and the Revelry had been his last chance to win her back. "I'll wait forever for you." His voice came out in a low, fervent growl. He cupped her cheek with his hand.

Caro placed her palm against his hand, holding it in place. "I've learned so much these past couple days. The fault for our troubles wasn't just yours. I'm to blame also. If you're willing, I want us to be husband and wife again."

He rested his forehead against hers. This was everything he wanted for Christmas. It was a miracle. "We could compromise."

"What do you mean?" she asked.

"We could spend half our time in London and the other

half at our country home." Before she could say no, he continued, "Just hear me out. My brother could lend me one of his land stewards to help when we're in London."

"Stephen, I couldn't ask you to do that." She shook her head, but a sad smile tugged at her lips. "But it's lovely that you thought of it."

"Please let me show you something else before you make up your mind one way or another." Stephen helped her stand, then tugged on her hand to follow him.

"Where are we going?"

"You'll see," he answered.

He led her down yet another hallway before stopping before the door to a small sitting room. Cressie had told him that the chamber was one of Caro's favorites.

"What is this?" A hint of a true smile brightened her face.

"You'll see." He brought her into his embrace and kissed her. "Merry Christmas, darling." He threw the door open with a dashing display of swagger, if he did say so himself.

Garlands of evergreen covered every table in the room. Nestled in their fragrant branches were hundreds of lit candles casting a warm, soft glow. It looked as if the stars had descended from the heavens just for Caro's pleasure.

The children who had performed in the choir earlier in the week stood in front of the room like little angels. One of the musicians hired for the Revelry stood in front of them and nodded.

Instantly, the children started to hum.

"Oh heavens," Caroline said. Her gaze drifted from the decorations to the children before it finally landed on Stephen. "What have you done?"

"It's something I want to give you." He took her elbow and led her down the room. "Come, let's sit down."

As soon as they were seated, the musician raised both hands and, instantly, the children started to sing "God Rest You Merry, Gentlemen," his wife's favorite song to hum in December.

Caro's eyes widened as their sweet voices combined into an enchanting rendition of the song.

At the end, they left the room quietly. The last performer was a little girl who had something behind her back. When she reached Caroline's side, she pulled out a beautiful bouquet of red roses, white lilies, and sprigs of green holly with bright red berries.

"Thank you," Caroline said.

The girl smiled, then skipped happily out of the room, closing the door behind her.

Finally alone, Stephen turned to Caroline. Tears again filled her eyes, but it wasn't from sadness. He could tell it was joy. For the first time that week, he had real hope in his heart that he'd done the right thing.

"How did you know?" she whispered.

"How did I know that 'God Rest You Merry, Gentlemen' is your favorite? Because last December before you left Heartfeld Hall, you hummed it constantly." One tear fell down her cheek, and he gently brushed it away. "The bouquet is an improvisation, but I know that you bathe in rose water. The lilies?" He shrugged. "The duke's hothouse didn't have any lily of the valley this time of year, and I know that's your favorite flower. I thought the lilies looked lovely with the red roses. I do remember that you like to pick them in the summertime."

"Oh, Stephen." Tears trailed down her cheeks.

"Darling, I do know what is important to you." He cupped her face, tilting it gently so she would meet his gaze. "I know your birthday is February fourteenth, and if you give me a chance, I plan to make this year and each thereafter extraordinary." He pressed his lips to hers. "I have a plan. That's why I went to Halig Inn to post a letter; I didn't want to wait for the duke's grooms to post it for me. I've asked my banker to enquire about purchasing your building."

Her eyes grew wide. "But you'd have to pull the funds from your reserve account."

"I want you to have this, Caro." He studied her face, determined to remember this moment for all his days. "Do you know why I never came to London for you?"

The brief glimpse of pain on her face nearly brought him to his knees. She shook her head.

But he had to say it. Confess it. "I was hurt and prideful." He hung his head grappling for the right words. "I started for London three times to bring you home. But I knew it wasn't the solution. You had to make the decision."

"What decision?" she asked softly.

"You want me as much as I want you."

"Oh, Stephen." The sound of his name on her lips was far sweeter than any honey he'd ever tasted. "I will always, always want you. Just as I will always need you."

He pressed a reverent kiss to her lips. "I'll always need you also. You can live in London if you choose, but I'm praying you agree with my compromise. I want you to come home to me. Then I want to go to London with you. I want us to start our marriage over again. That's all I want for Christmas—a chance to make this right for you."

Her hands flew to her mouth, as the biggest, brightest Christmas miracle of all came to fruition. Caroline wrapped her arms around him, then gave him a kiss that sent his heart reeling.

"Yes. A thousand times yes." She pressed her lips against his again. "You've given me the most wonderful Christmas gift I've ever received." Her voice trembled. "You've given me *you*."

"I beg to differ, my love. You've always had me." He kissed his wife again.

"Let's leave now for Heartfeld Hall." She ran her fingers through his hair and smiled. "Just for a few days, then go see your brother and his family before we travel to London. I'd like to see Betsey."

"Really?" he asked, completely astounded. "I thought you didn't care for her."

"I now appreciate what a delightful cow she is." Caroline glanced at her flowers. "Betsey would adore these roses. I think she deserves them as a Christmas present."

"Why?" He laughed.

"In her own way, I think she tried to help us when she trampled through my rose garden." Caroline smiled. "She wanted us to talk and learn to compromise, don't you think?"

The joy on his wife's face brightened the entire room. "I've always thought she was a special girl." Stephen stole another kiss. "But you, my love, are an extraordinary woman. I agree. Let's go home."

A hearty laugh sounded from the hallway.

They both looked to the doorway where Twist and Beakens stood together, their hands clasped behind their backs, chortling.

Beakens pointed to the ceiling above their heads.

"I think I know what we're going to find there," Stephen whispered.

"Indeed," Caroline agreed, laughing into his chest.

But they both allowed their gazes to drift upward where a bunch of fresh mistletoe hung in a beautiful arrangement.

"Do you know what we have here, my lord?" Twist called out.

Stephen stole another kiss from his bride, then whispered for her ears only, "A compromise under the mistletoe."

"And the best Christmas ever," Caro answered.

Epilogue

London
The following February

"Darling, you have a post," Stephen announced, then stole a kiss from Caroline. "Happy birthday."

"That's the tenth time you've said that this morning."

"Prepare for at least ten more before noon," he told her.

Caroline set down her cup of chocolate that her husband so thoughtfully brought to her in bed. After a lengthy "good morning" kiss followed by an eye-opening bout of lovemaking, Caroline was ready to start her day.

Caroline's first major exhibition for women artists would be in two months' time, and invitations would be sent next week. Stephen's brother and his wife would be attending, along with Diana and Fordcastle, Caroline and Stephen's cousins and friends, and, of course, Valentine Snowe, Viscount Derham. They even planned to send one to the duke.

And it was all because of her husband. He'd done more than anyone to turn the exhibit into a success.

The fact was that Stephen could make any endeavor into a success.

The land steward his brother had sent him had proven his weight in gold, but the truth was that he was building on Stephen's successes. The hardworking young Scotsman religiously wrote Stephen weekly to keep him informed about his estate.

At the end of April, they would go home for the spring planting, see Betsey and her calf, then return to London at least once during the summer to check on Caroline's art gallery and studios.

If everything went as planned, they would return to the city when the Season was in full swing. That's when Caroline had the most success in selling the paintings.

All in all, it had been a grand and glorious compromise.

Stephen stretched on the bed beside her. "I would dearly love to have your assistance in hanging the new portraits. But I would also"—he leaned in to nip her ear with his teeth—"like to wish you happy birthday again."

"All right," Caroline whispered, then propped herself up against the headboard. With a mischievous smile, she caught her husband's gaze. "Do you think we'll ever tire of bed?"

Stephen waggled his eyebrows. "Not if I have anything to do with it."

"You're boasting," she playfully scolded, then sighed. "You were pretty glorious this morning."

"You were the definition of magnificent yourself," he crooned as he pulled her into his arms and rearranged them so that his back was to the headboard, with her on his lap. His hands slowly slid down her legs.

Her eyes grew dreamy.

"Read your letter, darling."

She broke the seal and unfolded the foolscap. "It's from Mr. Beakens." Her eyes widened, and she brought a hand to her mouth. "The duke dissolved my trust. He's released the money."

"In truth?" Stephen sat up and took the letter she gave him. As he scanned the contents, he said, "Why?"

"Perhaps Beakens and Twist told the duke what you gave me after I first learned he wouldn't dissolve the trust."

"The choir and the flowers." A lopsided grin, the kind she never could resist, tugged at one corner of his mouth.

"Don't forget the building." She ran her fingers down his ridged abdominals and was rewarded when Stephen pressed a blazing kiss to her lips. "Now I can repay you for the reserve money you used to help me purchase it." When he started to protest, she raised her hand. "Please. This is what I want for my birthday. I had planned to repay you all along. It's *our* money, darling."

Stephen had a stubborn gleam in his eyes.

"My love, allow me to share with you. Please."

Finally, Stephen nodded, but reluctantly. He took her in his arms, then gently flipped her on the bed. "I love you, darling. Forever."

"I love you." She searched his eyes, and the tenderness and love that shone bright made her heart beat faster. "This is my best birthday ever."

"I think it'll be better than best," he whispered. "With Mr. Beakens's help, I persuaded the duke to secure the self-portrait of Great-aunt Agatha and send it to you."

Her heartbeat tripled, and a few tears threatened to fall. "You did?"

"I did." He brushed his nose against hers in an endearing show of affection.

"Thank you," she said softly, then kissed him on the lips. "You are everything I ever dreamed of."

"I should thank you for agreeing to the compromise under the mistletoe," Stephen said with a tender smile. "You are all I ever wanted." His mouth claimed hers in a smoldering kiss before he spoke in a hushed voice against her ear. "I feel the urge to give you another birthday present. Because . . . it *is* your birthday."

"I know," Caro said, laughing.

Her husband shook his head. "You need another present. And I know just what will make you happy."

He lowered his mouth to hers and almost, but not quite, smothered the happy laughter that filled the room.

About Janna MacGregor

Janna MacGregor was born and raised in the bootheel of Missouri. She credits her darling mom for introducing her to the happily-ever-after world of romance novels. Janna writes stories where compelling and powerful heroines meet and fall in love with their equally matched heroes. She is the mother of triplets and lives in Kansas City with her very own dashing rogue, and two smug, but not surprisingly, perfect pugs. She loves to hear from readers.

MISCHIEF & MISTLETOE

by Erica Ridley

Chapter One

December 20, 1815

No matter how hard she concentrated on the snow-dusted fields rolling past the carriage window, Miss Louisa Harcourt could not drown out the sound of her mother's well-meaning attempts to solve all of the problems in her daughter's life.

Louisa was two-and-twenty.

Nearly decrepit, or at least unmarriageable, which was much the same thing, according to Lady Harcourt. One's aim was to sufficiently stand out from the pastel debutantes in order to snatch a marquess or a duke from under their pert little noses.

That was what Louisa wanted, wasn't it? *Wasn't it?*

"Yes, Mother," she murmured dutifully.

It was the only thing she ever said, and the only way she ever said it.

The truth was: it didn't matter what Louisa wished. What if she wanted to be Queen of England? Or a bawdy Vauxhall soprano? Or a rainbow-haired unicorn? If there was one thing all women of any class could agree upon, it was that what they *wanted* was not as practical a concern as making the best out of whatever they were burdened with.

Louisa's mother was a baroness. This made her Lady Harcourt.

Louisa was the daughter of a baroness. This made her . . . Louisa.

Not "lady" anything. An untenable, unacceptable situation, which Lady Harcourt had been attempting to resolve since the moment of Louisa's birth.

Had there been a stray marquess nearby with whom to form a childhood betrothal contract, Louisa would have been married off years ago, without her social awkwardness getting in the way.

"Next Season is your final Season," the baroness continued.

"Yes, Mother," Louisa murmured.

This was old ground. Next Season was Louisa's final Season not because of her impending advanced age of *three*-and-twenty, but because her mother insisted Louisa find a titled husband by the following summer.

Louisa didn't care about any of that. As long as her future home included a cozy writing nook in which she might curl up with—

"I don't think you should wait," her mother announced.

Louisa turned from the carriage window in alarm. "What?"

"I heard a rumor that the Duke of Greystoke is unwell. This may be the last Christmastide Revelry." Mother's eyes glittered. "You may have failed during the ordinary Season, but His Grace prides himself on the betrothals forged during his party. Before the fortnight concludes, you must attract the suit of a well-heeled guest."

"But you said that I have until next summer," Louisa stammered.

This was not at all how she'd planned to spend the festive period. She'd even brought fresh pencils, and a new notebook. She'd hoped for quiet moments to work on her poetry, not angling to become some titled bachelor's timid bride.

"July," she managed, her heart pounding. "What happened to July? I promised. *You* promised. We—"

"The only promise that matters is the one you and your future husband will make in front of the altar." Mother gave Louisa's hand a comforting pat. "You'll see. Once the marriage contract is signed, we'll both be able to sleep soundly."

Louisa doubted this outcome very much.

She also loved her mother, and knew the baroness was simply doing everything in her power to ensure the best future for her only child. As soon as she'd recovered from the loss of her husband eight years earlier, Lady Harcourt had thrown herself into being everything Louisa could need: mother, father, chaperone, sponsor, champion.

A good marriage wasn't just the conventional outcome parents traditionally desired for their children. It was proof that the baroness was a good mother. Proof that all of Lady Harcourt's effort, all the sacrifice, had been worth it. Louisa could then start her own family, secure knowing her children would want for nothing.

Louisa wanted that, too. She just hadn't planned on having it *yet*.

The coach-and-four swept them up a long, sweeping path, curving past wide swaths of snow-dusted gardens that would bloom with landscaped precision at the first hint of spring. The carriage drew to a stop.

"Here we are." Excitement vibrated in her mother's voice as she handed Louisa her bonnet. "Ready for battle?"

No. Not even a tiny bit.

Louisa tied the silk ribbons beneath her chin. "Yes, Mother."

Greystoke Manor was at once imposing and welcoming, with its three stories of sharp, gray stone decorated with countless festive wreaths, and candles at every window.

The front door swung open. Out spilled half a dozen

handsome footmen, with matching height and impeccable livery, moving quickly to ensure the new arrivals needn't spend a single moment more than necessary exposed to the cold wind.

Before Louisa could take a breath, she was whisked inside an elegant entranceway, divested of her winter outerwear, assured her trunk would be sent to a charming bedchamber, and lured into a large parlor with the promise of tea cakes and chocolate.

Lady Cressida, the duke's youngest daughter, came to greet them at once.

"Everything is gorgeous, as always," Louisa gushed. She hated to imagine the amount of effort that went into planning the Duke of Greystoke's annual fortnight-long Christmastide Revelry. "You've outdone yourself once more."

Lady Cressida smiled. "You're among the first to arrive. Please, come and join the others."

Mother lifted a delicate painted fan she carried about expressly for the purpose of murmuring things to Louisa that she wished her mother would never say.

"Among the first to arrive," she whispered. Her eyes shone with satisfaction above the painted trim of her ivory fan. "No one else has paired up yet, which gives you the pick of the litter."

"Not now, Mother," Louisa whispered back.

She did not carry decorative fans about in wintertime, in grand part because it gave her an excuse not to indulge her mother's machinations in public.

As she often did when forced to mingle with large groups, Louisa disappeared into her head and allowed her Automaton Alternate to take over.

The best part about performing the endless play of Perfect Social Interactions was that it did not require conscious thought—or much in the way of consciousness at all. One made one's greetings in a specific order, said certain things to certain people, placed one's hands like this and one's knees like that, exclaimed over the quality of the tea and food and china, made the required amount of banal observations about the weather, and then sat in silence unless spoken to.

Having an Automaton Alternate took all the guesswork away. It was *easy*.

The worst part was how much it made her nose itch.

Every time Louisa accepted a kiss to the back of her fingers, despite the kisser prattling on about tobacco blends or hunting foxes, her nose gave a little twitch. Every time she said *Lovely to see you again* instead of *I saw you pinch that chambermaid*, her skin began to crawl. Every time she exclaimed in delight over discovering a profusion of raisins in her biscuit, despite her firm belief that any baked good thus defiled ought to have a large sign to warn the innocent before it was too late—

"Lovely biscuits, are they not?" Mother murmured.

Louisa's nose itched. "Delicious."

Squidgy little blobs that never failed to get stuck on her teeth were not the enemy. She'd guzzle raisins by the handful for the next five decades rather than hurry along the future.

Was it foolish to want to . . . *want* her future husband? To like him because *he* was likable, not because his title outranked another, or because of the large size of his . . . country estate.

Yes, yes, she would hold out for an aristocrat of means, not out of deference but because her mother was right—Louisa wanted to provide as best she could for her future children.

She just wished that finding a husband felt less like losing herself. Once she became a countess or some-such, her Automaton Alternate wouldn't be the alternate anymore. That would be New Louisa: a full-time automaton.

Old Louisa would become a memory that faded a little more every day.

It made her nose itch like the devil.

A maid hurried into the room. Whatever she said to Lady Cressida had her darting from the parlor without a word of explanation.

"Likely my uncle," said Val Snowe, Viscount Derham, nephew to the Duke of Greystoke. All of Society knew that Derham held his uncle in disdain and saw him only on express command during the Revelry. "He's found fault with the food or the flowers or the shape of the clouds in the sky overhead. Or, even more likely, with Cressie herself."

His companions, with their fashionable neckcloths and merry disregard for daytime sobriety, lifted their glasses of brandy in salute. "A Happy Christmas to all."

By the raucous sound of their laughter, this was a reference to a witticism the heir had made earlier, prior to Louisa stepping into the parlor.

She wished she never had to be in the same room with them, much less smile and simper and hope one of them offered for her hand. Her nose twitched.

"I've increased your dowry," Mother murmured behind her fan. "I'll throw in our Bainbridge land. Perhaps the right gentleman will take notice."

The Bainbridge land abutted the Greystoke property, which was not only how the two families had met, but also why Louisa and her mother were always among the first to arrive.

The Bainbridge property was also their *only* property. It had belonged to the maternal side of the family for generations. They rented rooms in Town during the Season, and then returned home to Cheshire the rest of the year. If Mother relinquished it . . .

"Where would *you* live?" Louisa hissed, hating that she'd been drawn into a public whispering match against her will.

Mother's brow furrowed. "With you, of course. I'm certain our cottage will be trifling compared to the elegant dowager quarters your future husband will arrange for me."

There. If making a match that ensured the best advantages for herself and her children was insufficient pressure, her mother's expectations as a future dependent increased the stakes nicely.

"It won't work," Louisa whispered. "No one knows about the new dowry because no one is interested enough to wonder—and money is too crass a topic to discuss."

"Too crass for *us* to discuss," Mother corrected. "I sent an anonymous note to that scandal paper."

"You *what*?" Louisa's muscles shook with fury. "Those scandal columns ruined my life!"

Mother smiled. "And now they'll mend it."

As disheartening as it was that men must be bribed to show interest in her, Louisa wasn't certain even an eye-popping dowry would be enough to attract a lord.

Louisa sent a dubious glance toward the heir and his cronies.

For years, the harder she'd tried to be perfect, the farther she seemed to fall. No effort was ever enough. Even when she performed every curtsey and measured every word with Society-mandated precision, the petty scribes of the scandal columns referred to her as "freckled and forgettable" and "wealthy, but awkward."

As if she were not a woman of flesh and blood, but a spotted influenza dressed in the latest French fashion.

In the past, the Revelry had been a respite from the desperate rivalry of the Marriage Mart. Her mother had flocked with her friends to enjoy the activities Cressida planned every day, leaving Louisa to join the younger crowd—or secretly retire to the library.

It seemed the past two-and-twenty years had been her respite. The real trial was yet to come. Her mother was desperate enough to give up her home to ensure her daughter's best chance.

Louisa could not be churlish in response.

Besides, Mother would be happy once her shy daughter landed a titled aristocrat.

Perhaps Louisa would be happy, too.

Her friends would be impressed. Her future, secured. The scandalmongers would find some other befreckled bore to gossip about. She would become Lady Louisa. Important in her own right. A matron with a voice.

"Very well," she whispered from behind a biscuit. Perhaps she *ought* to carry a fan in the wintertime. Once this raisin biscuit ceased being usable as a shield, Louisa was going to have to eat the blasted thing. "I will spend Christmas throwing myself at every unwed lord beneath this roof."

No matter how badly her nose itched.

"Inelegant, but accurate." Mother surveyed the room. "If the dancing includes waltzes, make certain one of yours is with one of Derham's set. Start with Lord Paxborough. I heard that his father has issued an edict: he must marry within the year."

Louisa tried not to send a disappointed look in the man's direction. He was a viscount, like Derham, but that was where the resemblance ended.

Paxborough was clearly in a merry pin at three o'clock in the afternoon. Were there worse traits a man could have? Yes. And Paxborough had quite a few of them. Smirking, self-centered, entitled, prone to flitting carelessly from one conquest to another.

Perhaps the latter was a blessing, not a curse. A lord such as Paxborough could be counted upon to spend more time in the arms of a lover than at home with his wife. Wealth, property, prestige, an absentee husband . . . An arrangement like that would yield considerably more freedom than Louisa could achieve as a spinster.

If her newly fattened dowry failed to bring Paxborough up to scratch, well, there was his flock of followers. They fawned over the viscount as if he laid a golden egg every time someone told him how clever and handsome and witty he was.

Fools. Paxborough wasn't going to marry *them.*

Her mother murmured from behind her fan, "Are you thinking what I'm thinking?"

Louisa doubted it.

"What are you thinking?" she whispered in trepidation.

Mother's eyes sparkled. "That Lord Paxborough is a witless, feckless child driven primarily by lust and gluttony."

Louisa's mouth fell open in shock. They *were* thinking the same thing!

"Very much," she stammered in relief, unused to being Real Louisa openly. "He is as obvious as he is odious."

"Which is why," Mother continued with growing excitement, "the most direct way to his heart is to pretend your romantic interest lies with one of his friends. Charm both Derham and Paxborough. They'll fight each other to win your hand. Derham is the better catch, of course, but if you must settle for Paxborough . . . I'll allow it."

No. Louisa's shoulders deflated. They were *not* thinking the same thing.

She sent a defeated glance over the possibilities in the room. Wilkinson, who was laughing harder than Paxborough's wit merited. Meekings, who nodded enthusiastically without pause. The newest sycophant, Mr. Ewan Reid, whose chiseled jaw tightened almost imperceptibly every time Paxborough made yet another thoughtless, self-absorbed observation.

Wait. *What?*

Louisa snatched the ivory fan from her mother's fingers and flapped it before her own face to hide her stare. Tall, wide-shouldered, an air of casual languor. And yes, a tic at his temple whenever Paxborough said something abhorrent.

Perhaps Mr. Reid wasn't like Viscount Paxborough's other social-climbing companions. Mr. Reid might be willing to play the game, but he didn't always like it. He could be *pretending.*

Just like Louisa.

"Has Lady Cressida ever said anything about Mr. Reid?" she whispered urgently. Why, oh why, had she allowed her Automaton Alternate to doze through the introductions?

"Poet." Mother's voice dripped with scorn. "Thinks himself the next best thing to Byron, or at least Derham claims as much."

Good God. Louisa started fluttering the fan in earnest.

She had never met a fellow poet.

Her heart pounded in equal parts excitement and terror. Would he be pleased to make the acquaintance of someone else driven by the same creative passions? Or would he dismiss a "poetess" out of hand, shrugging off a lifetime of inspiration and hard work because she was a woman?

She did not dare find out, she realized with a sinking sensation. Any friend of Derham's was not to be trusted. Even if Mr. Reid did not laugh at her outright, he might mention her secret passion to the others, who would declare her quaint and unmarriageable. No amount of competitiveness could compel Paxborough—or Derham, for that matter—to take a wife with *thoughts* in her head.

"Is he the one?" Mother snatched the painted fan back. "The distraction you'll pretend has piqued your interest, so that the heir snatches you up for himself?"

"No." The word barely escaped Louisa's parched throat.

The more she looked at Mr. Reid, the more she noticed. Long, lean body. Clothes no longer in the first stare of fashion, but well-made, showing off his musculature to best advantage. Dark, thick lashes, stern jaw. The brooding air, and mysterious half smile playing at the edges of his lips.

The wisest course of action—the safest, *only* path to take—was to stay far, far away from Ewan Reid. Her mother would never give her daughter to a man of low birth. But this was a house party. For the next fortnight, guests would dine together, dance together . . . Louisa swallowed hard. She definitely would not be dancing with Ewan Reid. Or conversing with him. Or—

"I know!" Mother's ivory fan concealed her triumphant expression from the others. "Trap him with an 'accidental' compromise."

Mother's words merged with Louisa's thoughts and for a brief, mad moment, she thought her mother was suggesting Louisa throw herself at a poet.

"Paxborough loves his drink." Mother's eyes shone. "You can lure him with a glass of brandy and he'll follow you into a private room like a dog after a bone. Just think," the baroness whispered, giddy with excitement. "You'd be a *marchioness* one day."

"Not like that!" Louisa recoiled, aghast. "Swear to me we'll employ no underhanded tactics."

"Perhaps I won't need to. An entire fortnight, trapped beneath the same roof . . ." Mother gave a conspiratorial wink. "Anything might happen."

Chapter Two

The following afternoon, after all of the guests had arrived, Mr. Ewan Reid was first to present himself in the yellow parlor. Whilst he was alone, Ewan drew a sharpened pencil and a small composition notebook from his jacket pocket, and gazed soulfully about the sumptuous silk wall hangings.

He knew he was gazing soulfully because he had practiced this particular gaze at great length before his looking glass. He was not a *rakish* poet, jotting scandalous couplets about this liaison or that conquest. Nor was he an *angry* poet, forever casting dark scowls at the cruel and heartless world before lowering his fiery glare to line after line of rhyming angst.

Soulful. Present and observant. Inscrutable.

From his vantage point near the window, Ewan was in the perfect position to witness action unfold. As each guest entered the parlor, he jotted short phrases in his notebook, annotating previous profile sketches with who spoke to whom, or blushed, or flirted, or flounced, or smirked, or narrowed eyes in thoughtful consideration.

Not every detail would find its way into a published piece, but keen observation was a writer's second-most important skill.

The *first*-most important was the ability to be in places where interesting things might occur.

For Ewan, it meant staying visible-but-invisible. Invited,

but inessential. A part of everything, without actually ever risking any part of himself in the process.

The problem was that he had grown tired of staying in the shadows. Once he was finally at the helm of the family business—

A familiar kick of shame twisted in his gut at the wonderful, terrible thought.

He *would* inherit, but only when Grandfather died. The grandfather who'd raised Ewan after they'd suffered the worst losses of their lives. The grandfather who had taught him to read, to write, to dream. The grandfather whom Ewan loved more than anything. His last remaining relative. No inheritance on earth would be worth such a loss.

Ewan gripped his pencil tighter. He couldn't let the old man down; not now. Nothing could distract him.

New movement in the parlor doorway caused him to lift his gaze from his notebook. He forgot about his notes and his pencil. He might have also forgot to breathe.

Miss Louisa Harcourt stood at the threshold, draped in a gauzy, fluttery gown the color of warm sunshine. The bodice was neither high-necked nor shockingly low, the sprigged muslin neither cheap nor ostentatious. Her soft brown hair was arranged in painstaking curls, yet devoid of a tiara or ostrich feathers. She was neither looking down her nose nor smiling engagingly.

The effect should have been off-putting at best. An unremarkable entrance in an unremarkable gown by an ordinary chit wearing an unremarkable expression should have made for an unremarkable *woman*.

And yet Miss Harcourt was the furthest thing from unmemorable. Since catching her watching him the day before, Ewan had thought of little else. What had she been thinking? What was she thinking now?

Miss Harcourt's mother appeared at her elbow. Sharp nose, sharp mouth, sharp tongue—Lady Harcourt was infamous for delivering a cutting look, or letting fly with a "teasing" comment blunt enough to send its recipient fleeing in tears.

Her daughter's expression was anything but cowed, however. At the sight of her mother, Miss Harcourt's bright gaze had softened, as if there was no other person she'd rather enter a room with.

No one had ever looked at Ewan like that. He could not stifle a short pang of longing at wanting to know how that might feel.

Oh, plenty of women *looked* at him, to be sure. What could be more carefree and romantic than a torrid affair with a poet? But it was not his arm they longed to cling to when entering parlors as fine as these. That honor belonged to lords like Derham, whose wealth and title made up for any lack of charm.

Ewan's lip curled. The heir's relative lay in his sickbed just overhead, and the viscount could not be bothered to pay him more than a perfunctory visit. If it had been *Ewan's* grandfather, he—

Miss Harcourt was coming closer.

Reflexively, Ewan unfocused his gaze and assumed his broodingest expression, as if luxurious ducal residences and lively Christmastide gatherings held no distraction for a soulful poet caught in the throes of an emotional, internal verse.

A distant, wistful sigh indicated his long-practiced pose had not gone unnoticed by at least one female member of the party flocking in through the door after the Harcourts. Sometimes this was accompanied by a whispered *Don't interrupt him; he's composing poetry before our eyes.* A strong jaw and a faraway gaze were usually all that was required to keep his social shield firmly intact.

Miss Harcourt did not slow.

Although Ewan kept his face averted toward the window, he could still *feel*, rather than hear, each dainty, slippered footfall coming relentlessly closer.

His heart picked up speed. He hoped she did not speak to him. Wealthy, pretty, unwed after several Seasons—the facts could only add up to one thing. Miss Harcourt was praying the rumor that the Duke of Greystoke's annual Yuletide party was a better Marriage Mart than Almack's was true.

But why was she heading toward *Ewan*? She was the sort of lady who married gentlemen with money and old titles.

Ewan had a family secret and old debts to pay. He tried to appear unmoved. Maybe she wasn't coming this way to speak to him. Maybe he'd oversold his brooding sulk out of the frost-covered window, and she was curious to see what the devil he was looking at with such poetic angst.

He wished the window reflected Miss Harcourt. It was exceedingly difficult to gauge someone else's intent whilst pretending to be riveted by an endless white landscape.

Yet he would not turn to face her. His success—and livelihood—depended on no one learning anything more about him than what he chose to reveal.

"Reid!" A masculine hand clapped down on Ewan's shoulder. "Did Derham inform you of my hunting expedition? He can't be bothered, so I'm leading the group myself."

Paxborough.

Ewan hadn't noticed the viscount's arrival. Possibly because Ewan had been staring out of the window hard enough to melt glass.

"He did." Ewan turned around. "I am sure you will find it diverting."

Miss Harcourt had frozen in place, two paces behind Paxborough. As if she hadn't noticed the viscount either, until almost crashing into him on her way toward Ewan. Judging by her startled expression, she was now more likely to flee than to speak to either of them.

To his consternation, Ewan wished Paxborough would leave, and Miss Harcourt would stay. Ewan could not risk being open with others, but that did not stifle his irrational desire to know *her* a little better. He wondered what she had wanted to say.

"Oh, that's right." Paxborough let out a hearty, overloud laugh. "You never do accept my little hunting invitations. Not poetic, mmm?"

"Slaughter for sport can be violently poetic," Miss Harcourt said quietly. "That doesn't mean he has to like it."

Paxborough wheeled and stared at her.

So did Ewan. What an appallingly *interesting* thing to say. How was he meant to ignore her now?

"What would *you* know about poetry, dear?" Paxborough gave an indulgent shake of his head.

Miss Harcourt swiped at her nose as if blocking a sneeze.

"I daresay her left shoe knows more about poetry than you do, Paxborough," Ewan said blandly. "As I recall, your attendance during literature lectures was rather disrupted by—"

"A gentleman never tells tales!" Paxborough placed a hand to his chest in faux shock, then gave Miss Harcourt an exaggerated wink. "Don't believe anything this wretched scribe says about me."

She arched a brow. "Because he tells falsehoods?"

"Because he does *not*." Paxborough grinned. "And I want you to say yes when I ask you to dance later. We shall leave Mr. Reid to his little scribbles."

Ewan schooled his features into a mask of ennui. Being left to his scribbles was exactly what he wanted. It was the plan. The *mission*. He should not be fantasizing about planting his fist in Paxborough's smug face.

Even if it *would* add drama and flair to Ewan's "passionate poet" reputation.

"Then I shall see you on the dance floor." Miss Harcourt rubbed her nose as though the thought gave her the ague.

Paxborough raised his brows at Ewan.

Ewan pretended not to see, and jotted a hurried line in his

notebook instead, as if he cared more for the muse in his head than the man standing before him.

Nothing infuriated Paxborough more.

It had always been this way between them. Paxborough had everything Ewan was *supposed* to want. Wealth, power, and the connections that came with it. Ewan had a penny journal and a poet's mystique. The viscount loved to sweep in and prove himself the better catch whenever Ewan attracted too much female attention.

Fortunately for them both, Ewan was not in search of a bride. Paxborough could keep his conquests. Ewan would play the role he always had, and then return to his real world.

Far away from pretty Miss Harcourt and her itchy nose.

Chapter Three

Now look what she'd done! Louisa's heart fluttered in dismay. Her ardent desire to meet another poet had attracted the attention of the person she least wished to spend time with.

Lord Paxborough was staring at her as if he'd only just noticed her. Perhaps it was true, despite both of them having spent every Christmastide under this roof since leaving their respective schoolrooms.

Her mother would be so proud.

The irony was, if she had heeded Society's dictates, and comported herself like a lady, she might have blissfully carried on another fortnight without Paxborough's gaze ever once flicking in her direction.

"I say, you're dashed pretty." The viscount cocked an eyebrow at Louisa. "I don't suppose you'd skip the tour and join me on my . . . hunt?"

The invitation was inappropriate, and therefore most likely meant to nettle Mr. Reid. Louisa's indifference toward Paxborough inched closer to distaste.

"No." She spoke softly, but enunciated every syllable. "I would not."

"Pity." His amused laugh rankled. "I'll settle for a dance with you this evening. The first waltz."

Derham walked over. "Twist has the grooms assembled for your hunt, Paxborough." He turned. "Miss Harcourt, what a pleasure."

Paxborough arched his brows at him. "She's dancing the first waltz with me tonight."

"The second with me," Derham said.

Louisa thought she saw a mocking gleam in his eyes. As if he knew that Paxborough was motivated only by rivalry and had chosen to encourage it for his own amusement.

In any case, her mother would be pleased. Without any effort, Louisa had managed to catch the attention of both viscounts. Nothing could be more foreboding.

A moment later, the ladies joined Lady Cressida on a tour of the greenhouses, and shortly thereafter, Lord Paxborough and his friends vanished to the stables.

Louisa stayed where she was, gazing out at the frosty landscape.

As did Mr. Reid.

Being alone in a vacant parlor with Mr. Reid was infinitely more dangerous than conversing with him at a window before two dozen chaperones. Yet Louisa had made no attempt to leave the room.

Neither had he.

His gaze had increased in intensity. His jaw was tight, his head cocked, one hand toying absently with his lapel. But there was nothing distracted about him.

He was looking at her as though she were a puzzle he was trying to figure out.

Mother would be affronted.

Young ladies weren't puzzles. They were to be exact replicas of each other, obedient daughters with perfect reputations and ordinary thoughts. The only reason she wasn't dragging Louisa to the next room by her elbow was because she had followed the tour, happily believing Louisa to be in Lord Paxborough's company, not Mr. Reid's.

Louisa felt a pang of guilt. If she had accepted Paxborough's invitation to join the hunt—the only young lady to do so!—there would have been no reason to fake a compromise. Louisa's freedom would likely have been over, just like that.

They would be paired, in Society's eyes.

Mr. Reid pinned her with his penetrating gaze. "Was there something you wished to say to me, Miss Harcourt?"

Yes. A thousand things. His poetry wasn't something he hid, but rather his most iconic feature. He was invited places because of it, swooned over, talked about, admired. Envied. What had she hoped would happen when she joined him at the window? A dome of invisibility would settle around them, and Mr. Reid would treat her like a fellow artist?

"I just want a few days of Christmastide," she said, though he wouldn't understand.

His brows lifted. "I have learned to expect twelve days of Christmas every year."

He was teasing her. Yet enjoying the full twelve days of Christmas before giving up on her dreams and marrying someone like Paxborough sounded divine.

On the last day of the party, she would do exactly what Mother wished. Louisa was a good daughter, had always been dutiful, would make exactly the sort of wife any lord could be proud of.

Paxborough had been told to marry, and Louisa had sparked his interest.

But she wouldn't give in yet. For the next fortnight, she wouldn't define herself by what she was to others: daughter, wife. She would let herself be Louisa. If only in stolen moments.

"When you were looking outside," she said shyly, "were you thinking of a poem?"

There it was again. That look, as if she were the mysterious one. "I was not."

She blinked in surprise. "I assumed . . ."

"Most people do." He tilted his head. "You're the first to ask."

Louisa wished she hadn't. She didn't know how to talk to other poets. Heat rose up her neck and would soon stain her cheeks.

His tone was wry. "Does everyone compose poetry every time they look out of a window?"

"No." She forced herself to meet his eyes. "But some do."

Why hadn't she added, *Like me*? This was her chance to show him it was all right, that he could be himself with her; she would not judge him. But perhaps he needed no such assurances.

Mr. Reid was a draw to any party, a coup for any hostess. His tendency to be more engrossed in his omnipresent poetry book than interested in the world around him only made ladies swoon all the more. Especially when he lifted those dark-lashed eyes from the page and pinned some breathless young miss in his passionate gaze.

It was a wonder he could walk without tripping over all the dainty perfumed handkerchiefs tossed in his path.

Was that what he thought Louisa wanted? A dalliance? A flirtation?

Her knees did not weaken in the presence of dark, brooding talent. She was able to glance at his form without noting the coiled muscle beneath the superfine, or the determination in his strong jaw. She did not fill with longing at the thought of kissing the hard planes of his lips, or yearn for his heat to banish the cold with a night of torrid—

Blast.

Perhaps she wasn't immune.

She turned away from him, as though she craved neither his proximity nor his beauty, and strode purposefully toward a different window, one facing north.

As the Harcourt coach-and-four had approached Greystoke Manor, the snow-covered pines reminded her of jutting incisors, the gilt-encrusted gate a wide-open maw swallowing her into the bowels of Yuletide expectations and Mother's lofty dreams.

Into an unhappy marriage.

Ewan Reid wouldn't see it that way. For him, this would be a romantic holiday. The gate would be beautiful, the estate grand, the trees . . . Well, who knew? She had never read his poetry. Perhaps the trees were forest nymphs bringing winter cheer, or the sharp pine scent a warm reminder of friends roasting chestnuts in a crackling fire.

She sensed him joining her at the window. "What do you see out there?"

"Snow?" He was not looking at the garden. He was staring at her as though she were far more interesting than any creature that could be found in the woods.

She pointed a trembling finger at the trees. "What do those look like to you?"

His brow furrowed, as though he had just realized her question was serious.

She braced herself for ridicule.

Mr. Reid turned to look out of the window. He looked at the snow. He looked at the trees. And then he turned to look at Louisa. "What do *you* see?"

No one ever asked what she saw. Mother said Louisa should be glad. No lord wanted a wife with *flights of fancy*. The sort of woman who thought trees looked like teeth.

"Spears," she blurted out, and immediately regretted it. Evergreens didn't look like spears but rather spear *tips*, which at all events was a more violent image than if she'd said "teeth" and refused to explain it.

"Are they protecting or threatening us?"

She squinted at him.

Mr. Reid's gaze held no mockery. His dark eyes were simply curious, as if this were a perfectly ordinary conversation to have.

Louisa took another look at the trees. A few minutes ago, she would have said *threatening* without hesitation. Now she wasn't as sure. The endless field of snow-capped fangs marked the barrier between this moment here with Mr. Reid and the world she'd be forced to return to when the party was over.

A *new* world. One with even more expectations to meet.

The trees were protection, but only temporary. The threat did not come from them. They were just a reminder that fighting the future was like fighting the weather. It came whether one liked it or not.

"A warning," she said at last.

Mr. Reid nodded. "I feel the same way."

A warmth spread in Louisa's chest. He had not thought her strange. He had found her *similar.* After years of cursing her inability to be just like everyone else, she'd managed to have something in common with Ewan Reid without even trying.

She wondered if he, too, sometimes felt like an actor in the wrong play. If perhaps the reason he'd been staring out of the window in poetic despondence was because he knew whenever anyone else looked at the forest, all they could see were trees.

"Actually . . ." Louisa's voice was so soft, she wasn't certain he could even hear her. "I think the trees look like teeth. A giant maw, swallowing the manor whole, with us inside."

He nodded, as if that were a perfectly reasonable thing for a young lady to say.

Her chest fluttered. They weren't colleagues, much less friends. But perhaps they *could* be . . . if only for the length of the party.

"Do you think," she began, her voice trembling, "just until Twelfth Night—"

"*There* you are." Louisa's mother stalked into the parlor, her blue eyes glittering. Giving Mr. Reid a curt nod, Mother's thin fingers curled around Louisa's wrist like talons. "Come at once."

Louisa went.

Her stomach churned with acid. She didn't care about chasing Paxborough, but she cared very, very much about not being a disappointment to her mother. Lady Harcourt's life had been a string of misfortunes. The last thing Louisa wanted was to be one more source of pain.

"We were just . . . talking." Louisa stumbled to keep pace.

"Talking to a *poet*." Said in the same tone as *rat* or *spider*. "What in heaven's name were you thinking?"

That he might like the parts of me everyone else wants me to hide.

"I'm sorry," she said instead. And she was. But she didn't promise not to do it again. Louisa had already vowed to be wed by the end of the party. She would not surrender a moment sooner. She brushed her scratchy nose.

"Darling, listen to me." Mother pulled her into a shadowed corner and placed her palm to Louisa's cheek.

The fingers were drier now, more papery, with the first hint of age spots, but the touch was as soft and loving as it had always been.

Mother's tone was earnest. "I want the best for you, darling. The *very* best. You might not think you deserve it, but I *know* you do. I'm your mother. I know what a treasure you are. If you would just stop trying to sabotage—"

"I wasn't trying—"

"We're close, Louisa. *You're* close. I've arranged a private audience with the duke, and I need you on your best behavior. *I* know you weren't flirting with that poet, but try to think. What if someone had seen you? You must be pragmatic. Romance is for fools, and Harcourts aren't fools. We use strategy."

"Then why are we bothering the duke?" Louisa's maid had intimated His Grace was on his deathbed. Surely, he didn't wish to spend his last Christmas hosting the Harcourts at his sickbed.

"Because." Mother lowered her hand and pulled Louisa down the next corridor. "We want his *heir*. Everyone says that he is only entertaining visits from family, but of course we are virtually family, living next to him as we do."

Louisa sneezed.

"Stop that," Mother hissed. "Roll back your shoulders. Look like a future duchess."

"None of this is necessary. Paxborough has already begged a dance tonight, all on his own. And then Derham did as well."

"Good. Be sure to inform His Grace about his heir's request. We're here." Mother pulled up short and raked her gaze over Louisa before nodding. "Come on, then."

Louisa was so stunned at meeting her mother's approval, she followed her into the strange room without question.

The Duke of Greystoke lay in an enormous bed, his thin frame propped on all sides by pillows.

Mother's eyes softened. "You're looking much improved, Greystoke."

"Hester. Always a"—he gave a rasping, rattling cough—"dreadful liar."

Louisa curtseyed uncomfortably. "Good afternoon, Your Grace. Thank you for another wonderful Revelry."

He narrowed his eyes. "Haven't got a man up to scratch yet?"

"Your heir has begged her to save a dance this evening," Mother said smoothly, ignoring Louisa's pointed stare. "I hope you wouldn't object to seeing more of us."

The duke's white eyebrows shot upward. "Wouldn't object to Derham settling down." *Cough, rattle.* "Could do a fair sight worse than Louisa," he finished with a rasp. "She's a good lass."

Wait . . . had he just given his *blessing*? Her eyes widened in surprise. Oh, dear God. If Mother had been relentless before, now she would be impossible. Louisa's flesh ran cold. Would she even *have* all twelve days of

Christmas to be herself before she had to become someone else?

"She'll make you proud," Mother promised the duke, then turned to beam at Louisa. "You'll make us all proud."

Louisa did her best to smile back. She certainly couldn't trust herself to speak.

The trees foretold danger after all.

Chapter Four

Ewan looked up from his poetry book. He and Viscount Derham had been lounging in one of many private parlors when a footman had come with an urgent message.

"Damn." Derham turned away from his footman before the door had fully closed. "The duke orders me about like a green lad in short pants."

He's a duke, and your uncle, and the host of this party. You're his heir. Of course he orders you about.

But Ewan couldn't say any of those things. Or grab Derham by the well-tailored shoulders and shake some sense into him. Not if Ewan wanted to remain a welcome guest of both the current and future duke.

Did Ewan want such an honor? Had he ever?

"Sickbeds can be . . ." Ewan's throat dried before he could form any other words. Unwelcome memories filled his chest, making it difficult to breathe. Of course Derham wouldn't wish to see his uncle wasting away a little more each day. But duty and family came first. "I'll go with you, if you like."

"I do not require a nursemaid," Derham snapped. He refilled his sherry. "You're free to be a hanger-on if you choose. Perhaps you can write a poem about your feelings. I won't go upstairs until after the dancing."

"You wouldn't want to miss the musicians," Ewan murmured. He didn't understand why the man didn't seem to care about his uncle's imminent death. Perhaps a violin to the cranium was exactly what Derham needed.

The viscount sighed. "My uncle is trying to force me to host this damn party for the next decade."

That was interesting. Ewan's fingers tapped his notebook.

This was why he was here, was it not? To be a barnacle? Grandfather would be over the moon to think Ewan had been in the same room during a private conversation with the duke and his heir.

Ewan . . . mostly felt empty.

"I'm going to dance with your Miss Harcourt," Derham announced, a speculative gleam in his eye.

Ewan shrugged. "She's not mine."

"You're not interested?"

"I didn't come for her."

"Who did you come for?" Derham leaned forward with interest. "Not Cressie!"

Ewan gave him a brooding look rather than respond. Brooding looks were safe. People read into them what they wished.

No, he didn't want the duke's daughter, Lady Cressida.

"It *is* Miss Harcourt." Derham straightened with satisfaction. "You didn't come for her, but now that you're both here . . ."

The brooding look was not working on Derham. The man was far more perceptive than Ewan expected.

Ewan opened his notebook and idly skimmed its contents. It had been purchased specifically for this holiday. The sight of all those blank pages usually churned his stomach. Filling each sheet with words until there was no room left, then beginning all over again.

Sometimes Ewan felt like all he ever did was begin anew, with nothing ever changing. He *could* change, that was the maddening part. He could stop at any time. Fling his notebook in the fire, sprint through the spears of evergreens, and never look back.

But he wouldn't.

He shoved the notebook back into his inner pocket and picked up one of the discarded broadsheets from the mahogany table.

Normally he wouldn't display any interest in newspapers in front of witnesses, but Derham had known him since before that rule was in place, and besides, the viscount's attention was on refilling his glass.

Ewan smoothed out the broadsheet.

Unseasonably cold weather? He scowled at the large type. Fog was not breaking news. This was *England.* At Christmastide. He turned the page.

Lord Byron had written a poem about a beautiful unnamed woman. No one had read it yet, but it was to be published the following year, and was already certain to be a success. Humph. Ewan wasn't jealous of Byron's fame and success. Byron was the reason Ewan had any place in Society at all. The poet was only one man. When hostesses couldn't obtain the original, Ewan was there to take his place.

Ewan could not help but imagine replacing these articles with his own. Trim this, add more detail to that, livelier opening lines, more illustrations, and most importantly: real news, not gossip.

He closed the paper in disgust. How he hated the scandal columns! Why should identifying Byron's muse hold more public interest than the changing political landscape on the Continent? Why should gossip about one's neighbors be more interesting than the latest East India Company Act, ending the company's commercial monopoly and asserting the Crown's sovereignty? Or the new Apothecaries Act prohibiting unlicensed medical practitioners? If Ewan owned a proper newspaper, he'd—

But he didn't, did he? Not yet.

He wrote what he was told to write, not what he wished to. There were no brimming coffers to live on, no entailed property to live in. There was a cottage, and a grandfather, and a printing press, and a small, but lucrative audience. And what that audience wanted was gossip.

Derham was muttering under his breath about vintners and vintages. "Perhaps I'll spend the afternoon right here."

Ewan didn't mark that down in his notebook. It was so quotidian, so *boring*. Yet when Grandfather's scandal column had run a vague reference to whether any lady would be attracted to Lord D—'s sardonic profile, the letters had flooded in. That line had been more popular than the Sir Francis Burdett riots and the division of the Order of the Bath combined.

Ewan had never written about Derham again.

It was one of the few times he'd denied a request from his beloved grandfather. Ewan had argued that gossiping about the person whose association was the primary reason Ewan was invited anywhere would be both reckless and dangerous.

The real reason was that it got harder every year to write about people he actually knew, regardless of his opinion of their character.

It also got harder every year to stop.

Grandfather counted on him. Had given him everything. And now it was Ewan's turn. Every time he returned home, Grandfather was a little frailer than before. His hands and legs more unsteady. His hearing and eyesight less acute. He could no longer look after his grandson, as he'd done when Ewan was a child. Someday soon, he might not be able to look after himself.

What his grandfather wanted most was to see Ewan's future secured. Now they lived simply, in order to allow their nest egg to grow. When it reached a certain sum, Grandfather would no longer need to worry. The cottage would be secured. Ewan would be fine. The newspaper . . . Well, at that point, the newspaper could be whatever they wanted, because they wouldn't need scandal columns anymore.

More importantly, reaching the magic number would mean Ewan had fulfilled his duty. Granted his grandfather's only wish. So what if he had spent his adolescence and all the following decade brooding thoughtfully in Society's shadows in pursuit of fodder for a popular column he despised? It was almost over.

Ewan was *close*. Another year, two at the most, and the Reid men would have savings to rely on rather than scandal broth. Grandfather could retire. He needn't *die* for Ewan to inherit the paper.

As long as Ewan followed the plan until then.

Perhaps if he gathered enough intelligence during the Christmas party, he could dribble it out for several weeks and finally have a much-longed-for period of rest to spend with his grandfather. Ewan would never forgive himself if something awful happened whilst he was out sipping port with the beau monde in search of gossip.

He pushed to his feet and slipped from the parlor without disturbing Derham. Where were the other guests? Surely there were cutting insults or secret liaisons or irresponsible card games afoot. From now until the end of the Revelry, he'd resume his role of omnipresent poet, brooding emphatically between bouts of scribbles on paper.

But when he rounded the corner, he found Miss Harcourt.

Not the same corner, blessedly. At the opposite end of the corridor. She was coming his way, and he was heading hers. Or would be, had they both not frozen in place like duelers in Hyde Park, armed with pencils instead of pistols.

He frowned. She *was* carrying a pencil. And a journal. It wasn't *his*, was it? No, a quick tap to his chest assured him he still had his book. It also indicated his heart was racing uncommonly fast and Ewan had gone utterly barmy. Of course he had his book. He'd been leafing through it moments before. That Miss Harcourt also had a book did not signify.

The supper gong would ring in an hour. She had already changed into her evening clothes. Blood rushed in his veins.

Gone was the buttery, billowy gauze of her yellow dress. A stunning gown of aquamarine French satin clung to her bosom before flowing gracefully to the floor.

His chest gave a strange lurch. The vast corridor seemed to press in from all sides, depriving his lungs of air and forcing him to walk ever closer to Miss Harcourt.

Observe, but do not engage, he repeated to himself frantically as she moved in his direction. Every sway of her hips carved itself permanently into his brain. He willed himself not to look.

Her eyelashes fluttered in his direction. She smiled.

He smiled back before he could mask it.

Every muscle tightened. Her hair looked impossibly soft, her rosy lips plump and inviting. He'd start by placing a kiss at each corner, then sliding his tongue between them to taste—

He didn't belong here, he reminded himself firmly. Never mind what his damp palms and dry throat seemed to think. Miss Harcourt was an esteemed guest. Ewan was a hanger-on. She was here to select a title. He was here to jot it all down for the later enjoyment of those who only dreamt of such a life.

He did not envy her hunt.

Marrying for love was considered foolish in the *ton*'s rarefied circles. Much better to have gold, or properties, or status. His lip curled at the thought. Once Ewan finished with the scandal columns and his own duplicity, once he became the man he longed to be, with the newspaper he yearned to run, he would be free to fall in love, to behave foolishly and passionately in matters of the heart.

Today was not that day. Miss Harcourt was not that woman. And Ewan had a task to do.

"Miss Harcourt," he said congenially, as he passed her on the left.

Or meant to.

Miss Harcourt stepped into his path before Ewan could check his forward momentum.

He swung one arm about her midsection to catch her and flung the other hand to the wallpaper to break their fall.

In the space of a heartbeat, they both were spinning, breathless, and then Miss Harcourt's back was to the wainscoting, with Ewan's arm trapped behind the curve of her spine. He had her pinned against the wall. If his heart banged any louder, she would feel it pulsing against her bosom.

The entire corridor tilted out-of-balance.

"Good evening, Mr. Reid." She smiled up at him as if this were the way her chance encounters in hallways tended to go.

"Good evening," he repeated inanely.

She was still pinned to the wall. He was pinned to *her.* Neither of them moved.

Their mouths were close enough to intermingle breath. Hers smelled like lemon and ginger. It would add a delightful zing to the taste of her tongue if he kissed her. Which he definitely was not going to do. His tightening body seemed to have other ideas.

Why couldn't they trip and sprawl onto the floorboards like normal people?

She angled her head. "Your eyes aren't golden brown. They're brown with flecks of gold."

"Your hair smells like lavender," he countered, and would have immediately buried his face in his hands, were his arm not trapped behind the delectable curve of her spine.

She nodded. "I just came from my bath."

That was it. Ewan was extricating himself from this ridiculous situation before his dreams were haunted with images of Miss Harcourt bathing in clear water strewn with flower petals.

He was too late.

His arm would not budge, but if he wished to, he could stroke the curve of her waist with the tips of his fingers. The satin of her gown was soft and slippery, just like other parts of her might be. Her skin was warm between the layers. He longed to know what it felt like without expensive satin in the way.

This would not do at all.

"If you'll . . ." He tried to adjust himself. "Perhaps lean away from the wall . . ."

"How? My body is already touching yours," she pointed out politely.

Yes. Ewan had noticed. Only the fingers of his free hand splayed against the wall above her head had stopped him from being plastered fully against her in the fall. Now their bodies merely grazed against each other. Bodice to chest. Thighs to thighs.

They were going to have to get closer in order to break away.

Ewan hauled her soft curves flush against him, spun them both away from the wall and back to the center of the corridor, then immediately forced himself to let go.

"My apologies," he said gruffly.

Her gaze didn't waver from his. Her eyes were a deep coffee brown, with nary a gold fleck. They were the prettiest eyes he'd ever seen.

"I'm not sorry." Her words were almost too soft to hear. "I liked it."

"Well, yes, so did—" What were they *talking* about? He had to put a stop to it at once. "I didn't mean to waylay you, Miss Harcourt. Please carry on."

Her brow smoothed. "I was looking for *you*."

"What on earth for?" He raked his fingers through his hair in desperation for something to do with his hands other than reach for her.

"I . . ." She took a deep breath and exhaled slowly. "I don't wish to be mocked by the others."

An unsettling wave of protectiveness washed over him. "Who has been mocking you?"

"Nobody. I won't let them. They don't know me well enough to wound me." She bit her lip, then said in a rush, "I thought it would be nice to make friends with another poet."

He stared at her.

She stared back.

He cleared his throat. "Yes. Of course. I am happy to be your friend."

"Not . . . just friends." She peered up at him from beneath her lashes.

His pulse jumped. "Miss Harcourt, I hardly think—"

"Colleagues. Fellows, if you will." Her gaze was earnest. "Just for this fortnight. Then you will go your way, and I will go mine. But for one Christmas, at least, it would be lovely to have someone who understands me. Who understands *poetry*."

Ewan could barely conceal his horror.

He would be unable to hide his absolute ignorance about anything and everything poetry-related if forced to speak on the subject for more than two or three seconds. He brooded for a *reason*. People didn't interrupt broods. They also didn't interrupt scowls or sulks or intensely unfocused eyes gazing off over the horizon, or any number of other signature looks Ewan had developed out of necessity over the years.

He could *not* be Miss Harcourt's colleague, or confidant, or fellow. *Especially* if she had any knowledge of poetry.

"I see." Her lip wobbled. "It was a long shot. I could not hope to be of your caliber. Of course I am not worth your time. Please forget that I . . ."

She turned away.

"Wait." The word scratched from his throat despite his better judgment.

She glanced over her shoulder, a gut-wrenching mix of hurt and hope in her eyes.

"It's not you," he said hoarsely.

It was all he dared to say. He could not risk losing his cover, but nor did her bravery deserve to be rewarded with rejection. She had trusted him. Even though she shouldn't.

"It's me. I'm—" *An idiot. A devoted grandson. Not who you think I am.* "—better alone. I don't share my work, and I never talk about my process. I'm sorry to disappoint you."

She gave him a tight smile that did not reach her eyes and hurried back down the corridor with her head held high.

Ewan slumped against the wall. Never before had he wished he *was* a proper poet. Or at least had read some poetry. It would have been marvelous to have shared a meaningful conversation.

His chest tightened with the familiar longing. He completely understood why Miss Harcourt would risk sharing her secret with a virtual stranger.

Sometimes having no one who understood you was impossible to bear.

Chapter Five

The Revelry was famous for the elaborate seating schemes that might well place a duke next to a commoner, but Ewan was seated far from Miss Harcourt during the evening meal. There was no risk of meeting eyes, much less being forced to make small talk with one another.

That was good.

That was excellent.

He meant to avoid her for the rest of the party, and would not have to worry about stilted five-course candlelit meals.

He *did* have to worry about the mistletoe.

Bunches of the dratted stuff were hanging all over Greystoke Manor, and hung strategically from far too many surfaces. The Revelry was a minefield. He escaped to the men's withdrawing room as soon as he could, but it did not last forever.

Slowly, the other gentlemen left for the ballroom where musicians would play tonight, because apparently the music room would be used for the pantomime in a few days. Likely, they were already playing; perhaps dancing had begun. Derham had left, followed by Paxborough.

Was Derham dancing with Miss Harcourt right this moment, whilst Ewan was brooding unobtrusively into fleur-de-lis wall coverings in order to overhear highly embellished braggadocio?

He could not stop thinking about his conversation with Miss Harcourt.

A "conversation" that primarily consisted of Ewan pinning her against the nearest wall, pressing her soft curves tight against him, and then running away when she'd accused him of being the very thing he pretended to be: a poet.

But what if he *had* been a poet? What would he have done then? Kissed her? Rhymed to her? Compared the sizes of their notebooks?

He wanted to read *her* poems. Anyone who felt all this splendor was comparable to being swallowed by monstrous jaws must write intriguing poetry indeed. She fascinated him against his will, damn her.

Ewan glared at innocent fleur-de-lis wallpaper that probably looked to Miss Harcourt like . . . oh, who knew what was inside that imaginative brain of hers?

He'd run because she'd trusted him, and she shouldn't. Because she'd confided shyly, *I don't wish to be mocked by the others*, and Ewan was personally responsible for that very thing happening.

Her name had appeared in his grandfather's popular scandal columns not once, not twice, but thrice. And who had put it there?

Ewan, that's who. What crime had the dark-haired beauty committed? What horrific scandal worthy of national public interest?

Ordinariness. Shyness. A tendency to be overlooked.

Rumor had it, she was as insipid as Almack's lemonade. Rumor had it, only fortune hunters were desperate enough to ask her for a dance.

Rumor had it, because Ewan overheard the gossip and then printed it.

He scowled at the pristine wall covering, grateful it wasn't a looking glass, or he would have been tempted to put his fist through his reflection. He couldn't believe anyone had ever thought her plain or ordinary. No matter what the papers had said.

Would she have had more offers to dance if Grandfather's newspaper hadn't spread the rumor that nobody wanted her? Would her lip have trembled in fear of rejection today, had those bloody scandal columns not reinforced the public's belief that Miss Harcourt was somehow lacking?

He hadn't meant to ruin her prospects. It hadn't been personal at all. Just one line, out of many. Grandfather's scandal columns had printed hundreds of names over the years. Some of which . . . neither sought nor deserved the attention.

New rule: No more casual gossip about debutantes and ingénues. He yanked his notebook from its hidden pocket and blacked out names on several pages. He felt only marginally better. What else?

Stay away from Miss Harcourt.

He'd caused more than enough damage, had he not? Life was challenging enough just with trying not to let Grandfather down. Ewan had no room for anyone else.

One more year, he reminded himself firmly. Two at the most. He would no longer have to pretend, to lie. He could live his life on his own terms. Have conversations as his true self. Give up brooding for good.

Fall in love.

Deserve love.

Until then . . . Ewan shoved his book back into its secret pocket and glanced about the men's parlor.

Empty. *Empty.*

Had the others noticed him, brooding against the wallpaper, flipping through his poetry book and dramatically striking lines from its contents?

If so, it worked in his favor. Such stunts made him legendary. *Lost in his head, attacking his own poems like a madman* was exactly the behavior people expected from volatile, emotional poets. They found it sigh-worthy and romantic. He'd probably have five more invitations to soirees on the morrow.

And it was all hogwash. Miss Harcourt wrote poetry, and he had not caught her sulking conspicuously at the walls. Right this second, she was probably . . .

In Derham's arms.

Ewan stalked from the parlor and followed the music to the ballroom. He found an unobtrusive corner with a good vantage point to settle in and glower poetically.

There was Miss Harcourt. Had she already danced with Derham? Ewan hoped he'd missed it. To be safe, he'd avoid looking in her direction altogether. Semi-avoid. The harder he tried, the harder it was to do.

He pulled out his journal to distract himself, and turned to a blank page. He would not look at her, but he could write about her. What would he say if he really were a poet? The stub of pencil grew slick in his hand, despite his viselike grip. He had no idea what a poet would say. This was a ridiculous exercise.

Very well, what would *Ewan* say about her?

The pencil started to move. *Imaginative* was the first word. Then *clever.* Then *lovely eyes.* Then *if no one dances with her, they're all featherwits.* Then, *even though Paxborough danced with her, he's still a muttonhead, and I'd wager Miss Harcourt knows it.*

None of that rhymed or was separated into aesthetic lines, but it wasn't poetry, so it didn't matter. He was just writing. Something for *himself*, for the first time in years.

Ewan rarely let himself dream of the future; he'd never make it through the present.

But what if he imagined a wee bit? He flipped to a new sheet and sketched out the front page of a newspaper.

Military news? That should be important to the entire country. But the creative arts were just as valuable. Which meant . . . oh, very well, probably something about Lord Byron.

No—Ewan scratched out the name and replaced it with Miss Harcourt's. If he was imagining an alternate reality for himself, he might as well give her one, too. Let her have published a brand-new book of well-received poetry, making her the darling of the *ton*.

No, not the *ton*—of England. Perhaps they'd heard of her all the way to the Continent, the same way Beethoven was famous here. Perhaps her poems . . .

"Are you bored with the music?" came a soft voice near his shoulder.

Ewan jumped as if a tiger had sprung out of nowhere.

It was not a tiger. It was Miss Harcourt. He did not have her pinned to a wall, but she had effectively trapped him in a corner. He could not escape without making a scene.

The edges of her eyes crinkled with a smile. "I didn't mean to startle you."

He tucked the pencil and notebook into his pocket. He did not tell her the whimsical thought about the tiger. She might like it. She might like *him*. This was the perfect opportunity to scowl and grizzle sullenly and claim she was single-handedly destroying his muse.

"I like Bach," his henwitted mouth said instead. "Do you?"

No questions, he told himself firmly. *This is not a conversation. You are not to be friends, no matter what you promised.*

"I adore music." She lowered her gaze. "I hate crowds. I feel lost when there are so many people. The bigger the crush, the lonelier it is."

He stared at her. Partly because that was a very personal thing to say, and partly because he felt the same way. In his case, however, limiting himself to the fringes was a carefully executed stratagem. Not that having an ulterior motive made it any less lonely.

"Where would you prefer to be?" he asked.

Her brow creased briefly, as if confused by the question. Or perhaps no one had bothered to enquire before.

"I love nature." Her tone was wistful. "And solitude,

when surrounded by nature. Without distractions, I can enjoy small things I might not have noticed otherwise."

"I enjoy solitude, too," he admitted. Working on the printing press was magical. Choosing the articles, editing the content, arranging the type . . . it might not seem like poetry to anyone else, but for Ewan those hours flew by as if in a dream. "I'm afraid I am not often in nature."

"Aren't you?" Her eyes filled with sympathy, as if his were the most heart-wrenching confession she'd ever heard. "This property is sizable, and contains splendid walking paths."

She considered the duke's vast, sprawling lands "sizable"? It was an understatement on par with claiming London was a nice village. If Ewan needed any further proof that he and Miss Harcourt were not from the same world . . .

"It's winter," he reminded her. "It's been snowing for days. Even if we could follow the paths, there would be nothing to see."

"Nothing to *see*?" She stared at him in shock. "Have you seen the way snow gathers atop each twig? The way pine needles shiver in the wind? How the warmth from the sun melts the snow like dew, only for twilight to freeze miniature droplets in place, leaving a sprinkle of crystals atop the highest branches?"

Ewan had seen none of that. Not the way Miss Harcourt did. Every word made him wish they were not in this ballroom, but tromping through the snow arm-in-arm. He wanted her to point out everything she could see that others didn't. He yearned to see it, too.

"Oh my heavens, look at these two!" cooed Mrs. Phelps in a voice that carried throughout the entire ballroom. "You're standing right under mistletoe!"

Ewan cast his gaze skyward in dismay. He'd been glowering emotively directly beneath a clump of Christmas cheer? Within wall-pinning distance of Miss Harcourt? What the devil had he been thinking?

He turned to Miss Harcourt. To her credit—and his demerit—it appeared she, too, had failed to properly scan their surroundings before approaching him for conversation. She looked more likely to flee than to flutter her lashes flirtatiously.

"Well?" Mrs. Phelps demanded. "What are you waiting for? You know the rules of the Revelry!"

With an appalling sigh of capitulation, Miss Harcourt visibly collected herself and gave Ewan a good-natured, what-can-we-do shrug.

No. This was not how he wanted to kiss her. He wanted to wrap his arms about that curvy waist, swing her to the wainscoting in order to press every bit of his hardness against her softness, and then deliver one hell of a who-cares-about-the-mistletoe kiss, hot enough to set the entire ballroom aflame.

He needed a different plan.

He didn't have one.

Her face was upturned in question, her lips almost close enough to kiss. He wanted to taste them. He wanted to know her mouth, her tongue, her everything.

He reached his hand toward her cheek.

A painted fan knocked it away before his fingers could graze her skin.

"There you are," Lady Harcourt said briskly, linking elbows with her daughter as if oblivious to interrupting a moment half the guests were watching. "It's our turn to visit the grotto. Come along."

And just like that, Miss Harcourt was whisked out of Ewan's reach without even a chaste peck.

"Oh, well." Lord Clevethorpe cuffed Ewan on the shoulder. "It's not as though Lady Harcourt would allow you to court her daughter." He chortled at the thought. "Not even if you had a barony, like Byron." He leaned closer and lowered his voice. "The mother has loftier goals. The very loftiest, if you know what I mean. Paxborough danced with Miss Harcourt twice tonight. She took a turn with Derham as well."

Once upon a time, Ewan would have whipped out his notebook to capture such a delicious tidbit.

Once upon a time, it would not have felt like a punch to his gut.

A direct strike to his pride. Even if Ewan weren't living a double life, even if he could tell the truth about who and what he was, he still wouldn't be good enough for Miss Harcourt.

Without the mask of poetry to give him a romantic sheen, he was nothing at all.

Chapter Six

On the following morning, Mother was still lecturing Louisa on how a future duchess should behave.

"This is for your own good," she said as she followed Louisa deeper into the duke's well-appointed library. "Greystoke has given his approval—"

"You put an invalid in a position in which it would have been rude to refuse your request," Louisa reminded her.

Mother narrowed her eyes. "Greystoke would not have hesitated to say no if he didn't find you worthy. The man has never bothered with politeness. Your duty is to *be* worthy. That means not kissing any gentleman who is not Viscount Derham—and especially not some common poet!"

"It was *mistletoe*," Louisa burst out. "Not some illicit liaison. Lady Cressida hung the sprigs so that guests *would* kiss. That's part of the tradition of the Revelry!"

"I forbid it," Mother said flatly. "I won't hear another word on the topic."

Louisa swiped at her nose to stop the itching.

Mother glanced about the library. "Please tell me you are not here in search of poetry."

Louisa had absolutely come in search of poems. But first, she had to find a way to make her mother allow contact with Ewan Reid.

He had said they could be friends. She couldn't let her mother ruin the opportunity. Not as long as it was possible that Mr. Ewan Reid might one day decide he wouldn't mind discussing poetry with his temporary friend Louisa Harcourt.

"It's tactical," she blurted out. "Derham hasn't offered for me yet. The only reason he invited me to dance was because he thought Paxborough had caught my eye. If he thinks Mr. Reid has caught my *fancy* . . ."

This was actually not the plan. In fact, if this plan worked—as Louisa's rapidly sinking stomach suspected it would—she might find herself leg-shackled to Derham all the faster. Or, even worse, Paxborough.

Mother's eyes shone with respect and pride. "I daresay you *will* make a formidable duchess. I had no idea such devious stratagems rattled around your flighty little head."

Louisa smiled grimly. Only a mother could make her approval sound like condemnation.

"Just mind you don't take too long." Mother gave her a meaningful look. "The longer you take to bring Derham up to scratch, the more you risk His Grace not being present for the nuptials—and jeopardize a wedding at all. This party is your opportunity, Louisa. Do not disappoint me *or* the duke."

She shook her head. "I won't, Mother. I promise."

"I wonder." Her mother glanced about the empty library, then motioned for Louisa to join her on a sofa in a private corner. Her voice turned wistful. "Did you know that I was almost a duchess?"

Louisa's eyes widened. She could not imagine her mother with anyone but her father.

"I was young." Mother cocked a brow. "Younger than you."

In no danger of spinsterhood, then.

Message received.

"He was dashing and wealthy and heir to a dukedom. He wanted *me*." Mother's cheeks flushed. "And I wanted him."

"What happened?" Louisa asked softly.

Mother lifted an oval locket from beneath her fichu. Louisa had never seen the delicate gold pendant before.

"I wear it next to my heart," Mother explained. "To remind me."

She opened the clasp. Inside was a miniature watercolor of an apple-cheeked baby.

"That's you, of course." Mother ran a loving finger down the plump face. "You were the best thing that ever happened to your father and me. I wouldn't trade you for anything."

Louisa's throat tightened and the backs of her eyes stung.

"This pendant was given to me by the suitor I'd made my entire world," Mother said softly, her tone nostalgic. "I was to be his duchess one day. We would combine our adjoining lands and live like royalty. Or at least we would have, if he hadn't come across a debutante with a larger dowry. I had an estate, but no riches. And it costs a fortune to be the most celebrated host of the *ton*."

"I'm sorry, Mother." Louisa touched the gold pendant. "It must have been dreadful to be tossed aside for a dowry. I cannot imagine what sort of knave—"

Adjoining lands.

The fickle suitor was the current Duke of Greystoke.

The estate they were in was the one Mother had lost.

By marrying Derham, Louisa had the opportunity to put things to rights. To undo her mother's greatest regret. To bring her mother the honor and prestige that she should have had all along. Marrying well wasn't just for Louisa.

It was her chance to grant a decades-old prayer.

Mother reached forward and clasped her necklace about Louisa's throat.

The pendant fell beneath the silk of her gown to nestle just above her breasts. It was warm. It had been nestled next to her mother's heart, and now it nestled next to hers.

Mother cupped her palm to the side of Louisa's face.

"Don't allow a foolish moment to risk your future. You can succeed. I believe in you."

Louisa nodded jerkily. Of course she wouldn't let her mother down. The last thing she wanted was to harm her. They loved each other, wanted the best for each other.

It was too late for Mother, but it was not too late for Louisa.

She kissed her mother's cheek and rose to her feet. Like her mother, Louisa had known the Greystoke family her entire life. At half three in the afternoon, she knew exactly where Viscount Derham would be. She rolled back her shoulders. It was time to start throwing herself in his path.

The sound of the billiard balls snicking against each other carried down the corridor as she drew near. It was not unheard of for ladies to play, but Louisa had no particular talent in this regard.

Her best plan of attack was to be complimentary, but not saccharine. Available, but not clingy. Someone he could imagine sharing this enormous manor with. She straightened her spine. She would secure more invitations to dance, then perhaps a stroll, perhaps a stolen kiss, then voilà: *Duchess.*

Louisa was not nearly as thrilled about the prospect as she ought to be.

Paxborough missed his shot when she entered the room. From the sound of the ribbing, he'd just lost the game. And Derham was nowhere to be seen.

She swallowed hard. Not the best omen.

Paxborough wiggled his eyebrows at her, and thrust his cue backward in blind trust that someone would relieve him of it.

Someone did. Of course.

A prickling on the back of her neck caused her to glance over her shoulder. There was Mr. Reid, staring into an untouched glass of port as if the answers to the universe resided within. Louisa wished she had the answers, too.

She turned her gaze back to the viscount.

He lumbered to her side.

"Gentlemen, if you'll excuse us?" he slurred.

Tippled, then. Louisa hadn't been what caused him to miss his shot after all.

Then she registered his words. *Gentlemen. Privacy.* She should have brought a maid! She'd wanted to seem approachable, not wanton. She'd wanted—

"It seems that everyone at the Revelry knows the truth." The viscount flung himself to the corridor outside the billiards room; out of earshot but still within eyeshot. They weren't alone. Perhaps he wasn't as drunk as she'd thought.

"Er . . ." she said brightly.

"I need an heir; you have the necessary female parts . . ." He waved a hand in the direction of her womb. "But we don't have to start this week, do we?"

"Not at all," she stammered. So much for a fortnight of playing coy and tempting. Paxborough looked faintly horrified by the prospect of marriage and bedding her. He wasn't tempted in the least, and still determined to go through with it.

"Good. Thank you." He closed his eyes and winced, as if the corridor were now spinning.

Perhaps this *was* good, Louisa told herself. Mother would be proud of her for snaring the second-best catch. A disinterested husband would leave her to her own devices, which was exactly what she wanted, was it not? She wouldn't have to give up her poetry. Paxborough was unlikely to notice anything she did.

Her nose itched.

"Why marry me if you don't want to?" she blurted. Why had she asked that? She was self-sabotaging, just as her mother claimed.

Paxborough opened his eyes with obvious surprise. "Same reason as you, I imagine. It's the next step. And marrying you will double the size of my estates."

It was a good thing she wasn't looking for romance.

"Well?" he asked. "Why are *you* doing it?"

"Family, land, parental promises," she mumbled. "The usual."

He sighed. "Let's do this: first and last set at every dance, but no announcement until we chat at the end of the party. That will give us several more days of freedom."

"Splendid plan," she managed. "I concur."

It *was* a splendid plan, she was forced to admit. Everyone ended up happy.

Almost everyone.

Paxborough pushed away from the wall and lurched back into the billiards room without a backward glance.

"Adieu, then," Louisa muttered.

She turned to go.

A shadow fell into step beside her.

"Whatever he said to put that expression on your face, don't believe him," came a warm growl. "Paxborough kisses his cat on the mouth."

"He has a *cat*?" she asked in mock horror.

"A cat and a dog. They don't get along. You should see his scars. Ghastly, really. It wouldn't be half so bad if he didn't share his bed with them. And a muskrat."

"Does he kiss the muskrat?"

"No, no, he's not a *cretin*." Mr. Reid gasped in faux offense. "Milford the Muskrat would never kiss someone who kissed *cats*."

She burst out laughing. "You're ridiculous."

"You are prejudiced against muskrats," he countered.

"No, I'm not." She shook her head. "I am Louisa."

It was a silly joke. She should not have made it.

He looked at her for a long moment, his gold-flecked brown eyes inscrutable.

But when he smiled, she forgot everything but him. "I'm Ewan."

She dipped a little curtsey.

He made an expansive bow, then whispered, "Never tell anyone you saw me being sociable."

She shook her head emphatically. "Your secret is safe with me."

"As is yours," he replied.

For a horrible, awkward moment she thought he had overheard her conversation with Paxborough.

But no, she'd been watching the open door over the viscount's shoulder. Mr. Reid had been in the far corner, engrossed in his notebook. He was referring to her poetry.

Er, *Ewan*. Ewan was referring to her poetry. Ewan who was also a poet.

"Thank you," she whispered. He'd tacitly acknowledged her as a colleague. A poetess. An equal. For that alone, Louisa wished she could kiss him.

"Allow me to accompany you back to the party."

As they walked, a tickle of awareness traveled up her spine. They *could* kiss, if they wanted to. Shouldn't everyone get a Christmas wish? Louisa wasn't betrothed yet, and mistletoe was everywhere. Dozens of couples had already been caught beneath the kissing boughs.

"You're marvelous with words," he said as they wound through the corridors. "I can't stop thinking about trees like teeth. I'd wager the entire poem is splendid."

"I just said . . . they look to me like . . ." she stammered. "I didn't say it was a poem."

He raised his brows. "Isn't it?"

Her cheeks heated. "Yes."

"There you are. I'm sure it's delightfully chilling."

Warmth spread out from her chest.

No one had ever *complimented* her on her poetry before. It was foolish, an embarrassment, something to be hidden. And yet, Ewan hadn't even read her poetry, and already liked it. He could just *tell*. Her breath was shallow, and her heart had never beat so fast.

"Who encouraged you to write?" she asked.

Darkness flashed across his eyes. "My grandfather."

Oh dear, had she said the wrong thing already? Perhaps his grandfather was dead. Or perhaps there had been a falling-out, and here she was dredging up memories he'd hoped to put behind him.

"I'm sorry," she said quickly. "I didn't mean to remind you of a sad occasion."

"I love my grandfather," he replied without hesitation. "There's nothing I wouldn't do for him. He's . . . all I have left in the world."

"I know what that's like," she murmured with sympathy.

He slanted her a surprised glance. "Your mother?"

"Yes." She thought it over. "Well, technically there's a cousin somewhere, but they've not spoken in decades. We lost my father when I was young, and there were no other siblings."

"I had siblings," Ewan said after a long moment. "And parents." He shook his head and put on an overbright smile. "But Christmas isn't the time to talk about accidents and fevers. When do you think they started the pudding this year? It must have been before Stir-Up Day with this many guests, don't you think?"

She tilted her head. "Do you ever talk about your loss?"

"No," he said flatly. "Do you?"

She shook her head. She wasn't even certain what to think about her father anymore.

Mother had been happy with him . . . hadn't she? Had Father sensed her discontent? Or was he oblivious to his wife's internal world?

"Do you believe in love?" she asked.

"Of course." He gave her a quizzical look. "Don't you?"

"I do," she assured him. And she did. But just because

one believed in something, it didn't mean it was in one's future.

Except it was, for Ewan. He had no title to consider, no ancestral land to prioritize. If he fell in love with a woman, he could marry her.

There was no reason for Louisa's stomach to fill with angry bees at the idea. She wasn't jealous of the future Mrs. Reid.

She just envied his ability to choose.

Chapter Seven

The knock sounded on Ewan's bedchamber door shortly after he'd returned from breakfast.

It was a footman bearing a letter on a salver. The familiar writing belonged to Ewan's grandfather.

He closed the door and took the letter over to the window. The day was overcast, but even the clouds could not prevent the sun's rays from refracting brilliantly against the snow. Ewan had to squint and turn away. Leaning one shoulder against the finely mitered windowsill, he broke the wax seal and shook out the letter.

Every few days, there were mundane questions about what to do with this, or how to do that. Ewan had helped with the paper since he was small, but Grandfather had been running it since before Ewan's birth. Had kept it running whilst Ewan was at Eton, then Oxford. But in the last few years, he had started to forget. Small things, at first. Things that Ewan supposed anyone could forget. Then more ordinary things. Something Grandfather had accomplished yesterday, he couldn't recall how to do today.

Not *everything*, mind you. Nor every day. But often enough that Ewan had noticed he was sometimes answering the same questions multiple times.

They'd developed a system. Ewan left a notebook next to each station and machine, with detailed instructions and illustrations. There was also a special basket in the center of the dining table, containing every answer Ewan had sent. Grandfather reread them as he took his meals alone, and consulted the notebooks before beginning any step of the printing process.

The system worked. Grandfather sent far fewer questions, and regained his confidence and pride.

Ewan . . . still worried. He sent home entire articles instead of brief notes. He sketched which should go where, how to set the type so the title would pop. And he wrote to the servants just as often.

Grandfather's house was nothing like Greystoke's vast estate. They had two household staff: a manservant to act as butler, footman, and valet, and a maidservant who served as both housekeeper and cook.

If Ewan lived at home, *he* could take the place of the manservant. But he couldn't, because his efforts supplied their only income. He had to keep moving from country house party to country house party.

It didn't make him feel any less guilty about not being present for his grandfather.

"One more year," he muttered aloud.

Maybe two.

Then Grandfather could retire, and Ewan could turn their scandal sheet into a respectable newspaper with honest-to-God important news. If its profits were slim, who cared?

That's what saving all this money was for. Solvency. The freedom to finally do something he could be proud of, secure in the knowledge that he'd put family first, taken care of his grandfather, and earned a new future for himself.

Today's letter was blessedly mundane. No questions about how to clean type or where the columns should break, just an ordinary request for new content. The more scandalous, the better.

With a sigh, Ewan arranged ink and paper at the escritoire, and set about writing fresh columns for the paper. Things he'd seen; rumors he'd overheard. With every word, his stomach clenched in disgust.

When he started a family, Ewan would raise his children far outside the magnifying glass of Society and its impossible expectations.

At last, he folded the pages and sealed them with wax. For once, he needn't feign his baleful glower. How he resented that idle gossip was the quickest way to profit!

He yanked his journal closer and flattened it to a blank page. What would a poet write? His lips tightened. Wind whistled at the window. Footsteps creaked above stairs. Absolutely nothing resembling poetry sprang to Ewan's mind. His fingers tightened about his quill.

If I were a poet, he scratched across the page, *I'd write about Louisa's eyes.*

Well. Perhaps not a *good* start, but it was certainly . . . words. Ten of them. Surely he could do better than that.

Her eyes are brown. Brown like . . . He paused. They weren't gold-flecked, as she'd said about his, or ringed with this, or streaked with that. They were brown. Brown like dirt, or coffee, or beaver fur. Brown like squirrels.

He slammed the book closed. Poems were *difficult*. He leapt up from the escritoire. If he was to have any hope at all of writing poetry, perhaps he ought to read some first, to see how it was achieved. He was good at research.

What he hadn't expected to find was Louisa.

She was sitting on the cushion of a bay window, out of sight from the main corridor, but visible in silhouette to a reluctant gossip peddler prowling through the shelves in search of poetry.

She hadn't seen him yet. He could come back another time. She was looking out of the window in a way that made him think she wasn't staring at snow or trees, but somewhere deep inside herself. He *could* leave, but didn't. The sight of her made him inexplicably happy, and he wasn't ready yet to return to melancholy. But he wouldn't interrupt. He watched, rapt.

Her slender shoulders relaxed into her cozy corner.

Wisps of dark brown hair kissed her temples and nape. Dusky pink lips parted on a sigh.

Only when she turned to face him without flinching did he realize she'd been just as aware of his presence as he had been of hers.

Her eyes sparkled. Her beautiful . . . squirrel-brown eyes. He winced. He was going to have to find a better metaphor.

"Am I in your spot?" she enquired.

"Yes," he answered at once. "I have brooded extensively out of every window but that one. I cannot hold back any longer."

She swung her legs aside to create room, and patted the cushion beside her. "Far be it from me to stand between a man and his muse."

Louisa wasn't *between* anything. She *was* his muse. Not that Ewan would dare say so, until he at least got the eyes-like-squirrels bit sorted out.

When they were leaning against opposite corners of the bay window, studiously gazing out of the frost-speckled glass, a giggle escaped her lips.

He gave her a quelling stare. "*Shh.* This is a library."

"You're not brooding," she whispered.

His jaw dropped in affront. "I *am.* 'Brooding' is the only expression I have. Ask anyone."

"You're not." She squinted at him. "That's definitely a smile. You haven't stopped doing it since you sat down beside me."

"It's a nice cushion," he admitted. "I may write a sonnet about it. This window is where my soul is meant to be."

"I wish I could find where I was meant to be," she said with a sigh.

He lifted a brow. "I thought you liked expansive views of Mother Nature."

"I do. Views like these inspire me. But if I bring a traveling desk along, someone inevitably wanders by and says,

'What's that you're writing there?' and the words get stuck in my plume."

Stuck in her plume! Yes, that was precisely what had happened to Ewan above stairs. The right words to describe her eyes definitely existed, but the wretched syllables refused to slide out of his quill.

"Don't worry." She turned back to the window. "It's like this every year. I don't even bring my writing slope anymore. I should rid myself of the habit. Perhaps this is the time."

"You shouldn't give up anything that makes you happy," he said. "You *are* a poet. You can't get rid of something that's part of you."

"That's what I'm afraid of." She stared out of the window. "Have you never given up something you desperately wanted, just because it was the right thing to do?"

Only every day of his life.

"Yes," he answered. "That's why I wouldn't wish it on anyone."

Maybe they were more alike than different. Ewan couldn't help but wonder if poetry was the only thing Louisa was giving up. If perhaps she was acting, pretending, just like him.

"What would you do if you *could* do anything you wished?" He leaned forward, pressing his shoulder against the cold pane of the window. "Would you write more poems?"

"I'd publish them," she said at once, then looked adorably surprised at the revelation. "I'd publish them," she said again, slower, as if tasting each word and savoring its flavor. "If I could do anything I pleased."

"Then you should." His blood hummed with excitement. "I could help you."

Her eyes widened. "Would you? Could you?"

"With pleasure."

Because everyone believed Ewan was a poet, he had

contacts with every publisher in England, all of them vying to be the first to print a volume of his work. Even if he were a poet, Ewan did not have the funds to cover the expense of a first printing. He doubted Louisa shared that limitation. Her pin money likely rivaled what Grandfather's scandal sheet earned all year.

Ewan launched into great detail on which editors worked at which publishers, how much they charged for a first printing, how many copies that might mean, and what Louisa stood to gain.

"I could publicly recommend the volume, if you like," he added after a pause. "Your work would stand on its own, of course, but if the idea doesn't offend you, I would be happy to influence everyone I know to give it a try."

"Offended?" A startled chuckle of disbelief escaped her throat. "I would *kiss* you for that."

"Would you?" The words rasped from his throat.

When had she leaned closer to him? Whilst he had been blathering on about publishers and printing and promotional tactics? Louisa was right. Kissing was much more important. A capital idea he intended to put into practice whenever she was amenable.

She angled forward a few more inches.

He did the same.

A hand's width still separated them. Their gazes locked.

"This is a strange sort of kissing." His voice was husky. "I've never done it without touching before. I await your signal."

Her eyes widened. "You intend to make me begin?"

"I shan't make you do anything. You said you wished to kiss me. That sounds delightful. I'm waiting patiently to see if that's truly what you're going to do."

"What if . . ." She licked her lower lip. He wanted to taste it, too. "What if what I really want is for you to kiss me?"

"Ah." He rubbed his thumb against the softness of her cheek. "Then all you had to do was ask."

He slid his fingers into the soft curls at the nape of her neck and drew her closer. Her skin was hot and smelt of lavender. He could not wait to taste her.

He covered her mouth with his, gentle but firm, taking care not to startle her while leaving no doubt how ardently he had longed to pull her into his embrace. He could feel her pulse in her throat. Fast, like his. Uneven, like his.

Her mouth was no longer hesitant beneath his, but open, eager. He touched his tongue to hers. Her fingers clenched about his forearms as if holding on tight. He had no intention of letting go. Her mouth was heaven. He wanted to explore every corner.

It was just a kiss, he reminded himself whenever he managed conscious thought. But it wasn't just a kiss. It was two kisses, three kisses, twelve, twenty. He couldn't keep track because all he could think of was her, all he could taste was the sweetness of her kiss, and all he could feel was the hardening of his loins, the banging of his heart, the pleasure of her willing mouth beneath his.

Even the lavender of her hair drove him wild. He would forever associate the scent with Miss Harcourt naked in a bath. Soapy bubbles, perhaps. Soft petals that invited his touch. Heat and wetness. Bliss.

He would have kept kissing her all morning and night, had she not pulled away from him with a gasp and briefly rested her forehead against his.

"Thank you," she whispered. "For a moment of fantasy as exquisite as poetry."

It didn't have to be just one moment. Or over already. He opened his mouth.

"Of course I won't be publishing my work. Some dreams cannot come true." She leapt to her feet, well out of reach, and strode from the library without looking back.

Chapter Eight

For the rest of the day, Louisa's mother pushed her directly into Viscount Derham's path until Louisa was ready to scream.

She couldn't tell her mother that she and Paxborough had already made a pact to "chat" at the end of the party. Mother would feel as though Louisa wasn't even trying. A chat wasn't a commitment, and Mother would not rest until she had a marriage contract in her hand.

She wanted to make the announcement to the party guests so that the news would spread far and wide, doubly ensuring the match would happen as promised.

Louisa, more than ever, just wanted *Christmas.* One last Yuletide in which she could be herself before she must become a bride, a duchess, a mother. Head of a household bigger than her own, when she had no such experience. All decisions had always passed through her mother.

Writing poems in her journal was the most self-expression and autonomy Louisa had ever had.

Until earlier today. When she'd kissed Ewan Reid, because she wanted to.

"Are you even listening?" her mother said in exasperation. "Don't disappear into your head when I'm talking to you."

"I'm not, Mother," Louisa murmured. "I'm right here."

Every year since her come-out, Louisa had seen firsthand

who made matches and who did not, and which men chose which women. Even if Mother hadn't spent the better part of each day lecturing Louisa on how to dress and act and talk and think, the same messages were continually reinforced just by looking about.

By marrying Derham—or Paxborough—Louisa could prove to her mother that all her effort and sacrifice had not been in vain. That Louisa *was* listening, had always been listening. Of course she would provide for her mother just as her mother had always provided for her. Mother could stop worrying for once. Maybe even for always. Wasn't that what a good daughter should want?

Louisa's nose itched, but she didn't react this time. Ladies did not swipe at their noses as though an invisible fly had perched on the tip. Ladies suffered in silence.

"*Soon*, Louisa," Mother was saying. "What if Greystoke takes a turn for the worse?"

This was a rhetorical question. The duke *was* going to take a turn for the worse. He was in the midst of an inexorable decline, which was why he was putting his affairs in order.

But that didn't negate the point.

Mother pinched her lips. "Act fast, whilst His Grace can still give his blessing."

"He gave his blessing," Louisa reminded her. "We were there."

"His *public* blessing. Do you want him to miss his nephew's wedding?"

Louisa wanted to miss the wedding.

But all she said was, "Of course not, Mother."

"And another thing." Mother narrowed her eyes. "I won't hear another word about this poet, Louisa. Use him as you must, but don't dally any longer in securing Derham's suit. We've less than ten days left. If you haven't an offer by Friday, I will stage a compromise myself."

"No!" The thought made Louisa dizzy with horror.

"Mother, don't. Please do not intervene. I'll . . . I'll work on it now."

She hurried from her mother's chamber, shut the door firmly behind her, and then collapsed against the opposite wall of the corridor with her hands curled into fists.

Why couldn't Mother leave it alone, just for Christmas?

Too many failed Seasons, Louisa supposed sourly. Greystoke's "He could do worse" was the closest Louisa had come to landing a titled suitor.

That she and Derham *weren't* a match was unfortunate. Paxborough would do. She would do what was best and so would he. She would give *birth* to a future peer. Surely that was more noble than dedicating one's life to poetry.

"There you are!" A smile lit Ewan's handsome face as he rounded the corner. "I've been looking all over for you. Do you know how many guest rooms are in this house?"

"Forty-eight," she answered tiredly. Because they were neighbors, Louisa knew this estate as well as her own. It was likely part of why Greystoke thought she'd be a good wife to Derham.

"Come with me." Eyes shining, Ewan held out his elbow with obvious eagerness. "I've a surprise for you."

Her pulse jumped. "You do?"

"But you need boots and warm outerwear. I'll wait out here while you pop back into your chamber."

"That's Mother's room. Mine is adjoining." Louisa doubted Ewan had found something out-of-doors that she didn't know about, but his excitement was infectious. That he *wished* to surprise her was pleasure enough.

She ducked into her chamber for boots, scarf, muff, pelisse, warm gloves. Then, with a jittery pulse and uneven breath, she walked back into the corridor and curled her hand around the crook in Ewan's proffered elbow.

He swept her, not through the front door but out through the back, a servants' exit close to the kitchens. A door Louisa had never used until today.

The snow was up to their ankles, or would have been if they weren't walking a path trod by many other pairs of feet.

At first, she thought he would take her to the gazebo, or the folly, or the frozen pond, but he led her past all of that to a much narrower path where few steps had gone before. So deep in the woods that Greystoke Manor was no longer visible, and the only sounds were their boots crunching in snow.

There was only one structure in this direction. An old caretaker cabin, perhaps the original hunting lodge, before the new ones were constructed decades ago. Nobody used it for anything because it was minuscule and outdated and too far from the main house.

"Voilà!" Ewan flung out his arms in triumph, as if presenting her with the keys to a kingdom.

"I didn't know this was still standing," Louisa said with a laugh.

"Better yet . . ." Ewan pushed open the wooden door and beckoned her inside. "Did you know it was a writing haven for female poets?"

"What?" The word startled out of her, and she rushed forward like a child even though it couldn't possibly be.

It was.

An escritoire sat at the base of the largest window, its smooth surface all but hidden beneath bottles of black ink and stacks of white foolscap. The bed against the opposite wall was large enough for a man, and had obviously been dressed in fresh linens. The small fireplace boasted a modest fire, just bright enough to light the single room and scare the chill back outside where it belonged.

Ewan placed a hand to his chest and assumed the posture of a grand orator.

"Betwixt these narrow, dusty walls," he announced with an expansive gesture, "Miss Louisa Harcourt is free to be the poetess of her dreams."

"What?" she stammered. "How?"

"No one but me knows you're here," he explained. "One of the advantages to being a famously brooding, solitary poet is that hosts often provide me with a private place to work my craft, without fear of interruption by servants or other guests." He beamed at her. "And I'm giving it to you."

Her heart pounded so fiercely she feared it might break free from her chest.

"There's a pitcher of fresh water," he said, pointing out each object, "and plenty of candles, should the hour grow late. Extra kindling for the fire, and a basket of fruit and bread and cheese over on the table. Oh, and a bed, in the event you do your best work napping, as I do. And a kettle, in case you—"

Louisa had no idea what other treasures Ewan had been about to point out, because she threw herself into his arms and hugged him tight.

No one had ever encouraged her poetry. No one had ever arranged a space where she could write poems to her heart's content. Yet it was happening before her eyes, right here, with him.

He looked as proud as if he'd built the cabin himself. "No one knows this old cabin even exists. It's yours, Louisa. Until the Revelry ends."

And possibly forever, if she married Derham instead of Paxborough.

Ewan thought he was giving her a Christmas gift, but in fact he was helping her find a way to survive the rest of her life with some part of herself still intact.

She pushed the thought away. She would not think of either viscount, not here in this beautiful, perfect cabin, and certainly not whilst she was in the company of Ewan Reid. The cabin would still be here after the festivities ended, but Ewan would not. For the duration of the party, it should not be her retreat, but theirs.

"I can share," she said shyly, hesitantly. "I'm not the only resident poet, and there are two writing surfaces in this cabin: a desk, and a table."

"You think I can write poems while you're in the same room as me?" The gold flecks glittered in his eyes like sparks from a fire.

Heat crawled up the back of her neck and spread pleasantly across her skin. "Am I a distraction?"

"The best kind." He moved closer. Only a whisper separated his body from hers. "Thoughts of kissing you consume me."

He looked as if he wanted to consume *her*. Hunt her, capture her, devour her whole. Louisa's shiver had nothing to do with the snow outside. Her breasts tightened. She touched them lightly to his chest, as though by accident.

The heat in his eyes indicated he saw through her.

She licked her lips. "You can kiss me again if you like."

He reached for her.

She covered his mouth with her fingers before he kissed the thoughts right out of her head. There was something important she needed to say, but she found herself wordless.

Louisa was too embarrassed to admit her pact with Paxborough, could not breathe a word of it until there was a public announcement, but nor could she allow Ewan to think their time together could be anything more than a passing fancy.

Full of as many kisses as he wished to give her.

"Whatever happens here, lasts only for the Revelry."

Ewan kissed the pads of the fingers she held against his lips, and she almost forgot what she had meant to say. Her breath was no longer even, but she forced herself to press on.

"When the Revelry ends . . . so do we."

His gaze was hooded, unreadable. Penetrating her as though he could read all of the secret thoughts she kept locked away deep in her heart. Then he nodded.

"I accept your terms." The words were a warm whisper

against her trembling fingers, a promise of heat and perhaps wickedness.

He lowered her fingers to his chest and covered her mouth with his.

Her knees buckled. He caught her. She pressed firmly against him, digging her fingers into the soft superfine of his jacket and the firm muscle beneath.

This kiss was different than the tentative ones in the library. They weren't learning each other's mouths, but reveling in them. Giving, taking, demanding more. His palms skimmed up her body, charting the dip of her midsection, the curve of her spine. She arched into him, helpless.

He lifted his hands and cradled her face as though she were the most precious thing he had ever encountered, but she wanted to rip off her pelisse like a wild thing, have done with clothing altogether. Press her naked flesh to his and feel his warmth. Find out what his clever hands would do then, without stays and muslin to stop him.

Such thoughts were dangerous. As tempting as his drugging kisses, the heat of his strong body. She would happily spend the rest of Christmas lying in the snow, as long as her hot limbs tangled with his and he never stopped kissing her.

If only for the Yuletide.

Louisa broke away from him, panting, her heart rattling in protest. If she didn't stop now, she never would. She searched for something to break the spell. Her gaze fell upon the escritoire he'd arranged for her. "May I touch?"

"Everything you see is yours." His eyes said he didn't only mean the quills and ink.

She ran her fingers over the pristine foolscap, traced the contours of each downy plume, each bottle of ink. She would write many poems here. Some about him.

And then she'd throw them all into the fire when Christmas was over.

"I didn't know what you might like . . ." His voice was hesitant, embarrassed. "But I brought these from the library."

He pulled a basket out from beside the bed and placed it in her lap.

It was heavy and felt like books. It even smelt like books when she lifted the lid. Poetry. He'd brought her poetry. Some that she'd not yet read, and some she'd read a thousand times and could not wait to do so again.

The backs of her eyes stung as she glanced up at him. "Thank you. For all of this."

"I couldn't find the volume of poetry I really wanted." His eyes twinkled.

She frowned. "Whose?"

"Yours." He took her hands. "You should publish your poems. Truly."

"You've never read any," she reminded him. "They could be horrid."

"They're not," he said confidently. "And even if they were, why should that change anything? Dreams are meant to be realized. I meant it when I said I could help you."

"And I meant it when I said that I would never." She took off her coat and hung it on the hook next to his. "If my mother saw my name on such a thing . . ."

"Why should she have to?" His gaze was intense. "You would not be the first to take a nom de plume."

She stared at him. Forced herself to tamp down the flood of happiness threatening to carry her away like the tide. It was a pretty thought, but still not possible.

"Even if I wanted to, I couldn't afford it." She groaned. "All I have is a dowry, which isn't mine at all."

His eyebrows flew skyward. "Have you no pin money?"

"My mother purchases everything. I couldn't even afford . . ." She gestured wordlessly at the pile of paper and ink. "But it doesn't matter."

He frowned. "Why wouldn't it matter?"

"Secrets never stay secret. My name would get bandied about in some damnable scandal sheet, and suddenly—"

His shoulders caved as though he'd just weathered a punch to the sternum.

Louisa touched his arm. She hadn't meant to deflate his optimism, but she hoped he understood how serious the effects of idle gossip could be.

"It shouldn't matter," he said, but his voice no longer held conviction. "You should be able to write and publish whatever you please."

"Young ladies should be able to do a lot of things," she pointed out drily. "If I prioritized a list, poetry wouldn't make the first page."

The corner of his mouth turned up. "What could be more important than poetry?"

"What about you?" she asked as she eased into the chair before the escritoire.

He looked startled. "Me?"

"You've not published a thing, as far as I know."

He was silent for a long moment. "It isn't the right time."

"Why not?"

He pulled over a chair, placed it so he could prop his elbow on the edge of the escritoire and gaze at her.

"I'm helping my grandfather," he said at last. "With the family business."

Ah, that explained his disinclination to answer. The *ton*'s aversion to those who dabbled in "trade" was unforgiving. That a relative should be so tainted was bad enough. Ewan involving himself personally would destroy his reputation as a gentleman of leisure—and dry up a fair percentage of invitations he received to participate in Society events.

"I think helping your grandfather is lovely," she said, and meant it. "Under any circumstances."

"Do you?" The expression on Ewan's face indicated he was far from convinced.

Louisa nodded firmly. "Family is first, no matter what."

"I know." Ewan rubbed a hand over his face. "Grandfather wants to build a nest egg as quickly as possible. He says he didn't spend sufficient time with his family, and doesn't want me to miss out on mine, too."

"That's sweet." She touched his leg. "And . . . a lot of pressure, I imagine."

He inclined his head. "Grandfather relies on me. He wants me to live the life he couldn't."

Louisa's heart ached. She drew his hand into hers.

"I know that feeling all too well," she admitted softly. "Sometimes I think my mother wants me to be *her*, rather than myself. But it's not out of selfishness. She wants me to have everything she couldn't have; the best of the best. Only a churl could argue with that."

"Only a churl," he muttered, and pushed to his feet. "I leave you to your escritoire, Madame Poetess. Shall I return for you at a specific hour?"

I don't want you to return. I want you to stay.

She shook her head. "We shouldn't be seen coming and going together. Besides, if I do start writing, heaven only knows when I'll stop."

"Not 'if.'" This time, his smile reached his eyes. The gold flecks shone with warmth and confidence. "You *must* write. Talent like yours makes the world a better place."

She rolled her eyes. "How would my poems affect the world at all, if I'm the only one who sees them?"

He pressed a hand to his cravat and affected an expression of pure shock. "By Zeus, you're right, Miss Harcourt. The only solution is to publish!"

Before she could toss a plume at him, he was out of the door and gone . . . leaving Louisa to stare at the tantalizing stack of paper and wonder:

What if?

Chapter Nine

Ewan Reid, churl extraordinaire, spent the rest of his afternoon and evening resentfully flitting from tea room to billiards room to the ballroom in search of scandalous morsels with which to fill his journal.

It was abominably easy. The Revelry was a hotbed of intrigue. When Lady Eloise Bennett threw a cup of mulled wine at her husband, Ewan was actually splashed with droplets. The tidbit wrote itself. Which oddly made doing it all the harder.

Grandfather soon would not be able to look after himself. He needed Ewan to persevere, just a little longer.

One more year. He eased the damnable notebook back next to his heart. Its familiar weight felt like coal fresh from the fire. Why couldn't he have had an ordinary cross to bear, like Luddite riots, or uneven whiskers?

He had no idea when Louisa had returned from the cabin, but she was now whirling through the steps of a country dance along with half of the party. After a minuet with Derham to start the evening, she had become a dancing partner in high demand.

Ewan never danced. All of the best gossip was heard on the fringes. That was why he lurked broodingly in the shadows by the refreshment table.

But tonight, he could not tear his gaze from Louisa. She belonged in this world. She was the epitome of Polite Society.

Her soft brown hair was pinned to her head in a profusion of artful ringlets. He knew what it felt like to dip his fingers in that luxurious hair, to cradle her head and crush his mouth to hers. He knew the curve of her spine, the flare of her hips. Not as intimately as he'd like, but his palms could feel those soft curves even now. The heat of her flesh and weight of her breasts had imprinted on him even through their clothes.

But she would never be his.

He did not deserve her.

When Ewan had confessed his lowly connections to trade, she had found it sweet. Would that it were so!

Oh, why did he long to impress her so much? They were friends, but temporary ones at best. She'd been clear that their association ended along with the festivities after Twelfth Night. If he could not keep her, what did it matter what she thought of him?

Because he wanted to have all of her, if only for a fortnight.

He and Louisa were the same in many ways. *I know what duty to family feels like*, she'd said, and he believed her. He also knew the exquisite torture of wanting to write, yearning to publish something of actual value, and knowing it could never be.

His blossoming friendship with Louisa felt like Christmas. Who could ask for a better gift than her kisses? He had an entire fortnight of the sweet warmth of Louisa's embrace. And an opportunity to atone for past mistakes. This time, he wouldn't let her down.

"I hope my Portia brings Lord Clevethorpe up to scratch," came the quavery voice of Mrs. Phelps, from the direction of the ratafia bowl.

Ewan let out a long breath. Enough mooncalfing. He was here to work.

He brooded closer, sending his poetic, unfocused gaze

in the direction of the parquet, and keeping to the shadows in order to remain unnoticed.

"How about your Louisa?" prodded Mrs. Phelps.

"Louisa," came an arch, cultured voice, "is acquitting herself splendidly."

Ewan froze. He didn't need to look. That voice was Lady Harcourt, Louisa's mother.

"Oh?" said her friend. "I didn't think she had ever managed a suitor. Who is interested in her?"

Perhaps *friend* was too strong a word.

"I am not one to gossip," Lady Harcourt responded, in a tone that indicated gossip was imminent. "But I shouldn't be surprised if there's a dukedom or a marquessate in her future. She might have her choice of two suitors."

Ewan's blood drained.

"You don't mean . . ." Mrs. Phelps breathed. "But how?"

Lady Harcourt whispered back, "Paxborough will be marquess one day. Haven't you noticed him slaver over Louisa every time that poet shows her any attention? If she keeps that up, Derham will beg for her hand. They're both jealous of the poet, God knows why."

"That spoilt lad Paxborough will whisk her over his shoulder in a jealous fit, more like."

Lady Harcourt's laugh was calculating. "I'd prefer Derham, but either will do."

Ewan was a fool. No wonder Louisa hadn't blinked when he'd mentioned his connections to trade. She didn't want to be friends. Even the kisses were likely calculated to keep him on the hook. He needed to appear interested, in order for her to ensnare the lord—or lords?—she really wanted. He was a means to an end.

Not anymore.

The moment the country dance ended, he stalked across the parquet to where Louisa stood smiling with friends.

Her smile dimmed slightly when he stepped into her path.

"I'm sorry." She made an apologetic expression. "My dance card is full this evening."

Ewan bet it was.

He had only a few minutes before the musicians would take up their instruments again. Louisa's partner would come to claim her. Ewan had no intention of being present when it happened.

"I hear congratulations are in order." Each controlled syllable was cold as ice.

She frowned. "For what?"

"Rumor has it, a future dukedom. Thanks to Derham's irrational jealousy of a poetic gudgeon. Or is it Paxborough's marquessate you prefer?"

Louisa closed her eyes and grimaced. *"Mother."*

He had not realized how badly he wanted her to deny the charge, to look deep into his eyes and swear that she had been thinking only of Ewan when she kissed him.

But she did not.

"I," he growled, "shall not be your pawn."

Her eyes flew open, and the pained expression proved all his fears true.

"We cannot talk about this here," she whispered. "I must go. I am promised to a waltz."

Ewan's heart flung itself against his ribs.

She was promised to more than a waltz. She was all but promised to a viscount.

He was as disposable as a broadsheet.

Being used as a pawn shouldn't sting. It wasn't even a surprise. She had always planned to walk away at the end of the fortnight.

Now he knew why.

Chapter Ten

Praying unsuccessfully for sleep, Louisa tossed in her lavish canopy bed until dawn. She'd thrown herself in Ewan's arms, kissed him until she was giddy, and failed to mention she intended to marry someone else.

She'd wounded him, which was the last thing she wanted. She liked him more than either of her suitors—and couldn't have him. After he'd spent all day setting up a private poetry retreat for her, just because he knew she would like it, she'd slunk away in shame.

There had to be some way to put things to rights.

He didn't come down to breakfast.

She was the first one there and would have been the last one to leave, had her mother not appeared. Louisa did not want Ewan to walk into the dining room and think Louisa and her mother were cooking up more schemes.

She rose to her feet as her mother made her way toward her.

The baroness raised her brows. "You didn't eat your toast."

Louisa had eaten *loaves* of toast. That was her fourth plate. She hoped never to see toast again.

Her mother sighed as if put-upon. "Why the black look, darling?"

Louisa turned to face her.

"Mr. Reid heard you last night," she hissed.

Mother's brow lined in confusion. "Heard me what?"

"Oh, I don't know. Brag about using him to trap a viscount?"

Her mother had the grace to color.

"It doesn't matter," she said. "He's no one. You don't need him and are better off without him."

"He's someone," Louisa countered. "He's a poet and a grandson and a person."

Mother rubbed her face. "What is it you want me to do?"

Louisa's stomach tightened. *Turn back time* wasn't an answer. But maybe there was something else they could do for him. In the same spirit in which he'd tried to help her.

"Become a patroness of the arts."

Mother blinked. "What?"

Louisa pressed on, gaining confidence in her idea. "It can be anonymous. A donation to a publishing house, which can only be used to publish Mr. Reid's poetry."

"How will that make him forgive you?"

"It won't. He'll not even know it was us."

"Then what is the point?"

"Selflessness is the point. Being kind. Being grateful."

Mother's nose wrinkled. "What has he done for you to be grateful about?"

Louisa pressed her lips together. If Mother knew about the cabin, she'd forbid Louisa from going, and have Greystoke bar the door and windows.

She arched a brow. "You wish your daughter to be a respectable lady one day, do you not?"

"Are you *bribing* your own mother?"

"Is manipulation only acceptable behavior when *you* do it?"

They stared at each other for a long moment.

"This infatuation will go nowhere," Mother said at last, a hint of sympathy in her eyes. "You cannot have Mr. Reid."

Louisa's spine sagged. "I know."

"Gossip columns already send you into a panic. Can

you imagine the scandal if you refused Derham or Paxborough?"

"I *know*," Louisa repeated through clenched teeth.

If it weren't for scandal sheets, she would have married years ago. She'd *had* suitors.

And then came the gossip column.

A certain Miss L—H— was less desirable than the watered-down lemonade at Almack's, it had claimed.

Worst of all, it was almost true. How many peers had stood up with her at that esteemed institution? None. How many routs and soirées did long-suffering Lady H— drag her daughter to in desperation? All of them. Who were the only men that glanced her way? Social climbers and fortune hunters. There was nothing else to recommend her.

After that column, and two more like it, the one gentleman interested in Louisa had ceased looking in her direction if she was in the same room. She became a laughingstock. The *ton*'s youngest spinster. Asking her to dance was an act of boredom or pity. Asking for her hand, unthinkable.

Gossip had ruined her life. Louisa would *not* go through a nightmare like that again.

There was only one path forward.

"I won't be a patroness," Mother said. "My funds are meant for something important. You, darling."

Gritting her teeth, Louisa walked out of the door without further argument.

Despite all his friends, Ewan seemed just as lonely as she was. She couldn't bear to fight with him.

She found him in the conservatory, wandering amongst the greenery.

When he saw her, his expression turned wary.

"I'm sorry," she said before any other words could get in the way. "I never wanted to use you, and I definitely did not wish to harm you. I should have been honest from the beginning. That is my fault. I apologize."

A muscle worked in his jaw.

She forced herself to continue.

"Here's the truth. Greystoke *has* given his blessing to Derham and me. Paxborough *has* indicated willingness to marry me. But no firm proposal been made by either man. I am not promised to anyone. I haven't decided what I'll do. If you want me to leave you alone, I will. If you wish to shout at me, I will listen. And if you wish to be friends . . ." She pushed a small leather-bound book into his hand before her fear could talk her out of it. "Then begin with that."

He stared at the well-worn volume. "What is this?"

"My poetry." Her true self.

His startled gaze met hers. "Do you *want* me to read it?"

"No. Yes." She picked at her gown. "I don't know. I've never revealed myself like this before. But there's no one I'd trust with my poems more than you."

He closed his eyes as if in pain, then ran his fingers over the embossed cover.

L was all it said. Could be *Louisa*. Could be *Love*. Could be, *Let me curl up in a corner and die of mortification before you even open to the first page.*

"Do you want me to read them in front of you?"

"No," she croaked, the word scraping from her dry throat so fast it seemed her soul exited with it. "Please do not."

He nodded and placed her most private, secret journal inside an interior coat pocket, well out of Louisa's sight.

She had to restrain herself from reaching out to take it back.

"I owe you an apology," he said.

She blinked. "*You* do?"

"Several of them. But at the moment I can give only one." He shoved his hands behind his back. "I know what it's like to have to be forced to do something you'd rather not, especially when it hurts someone else. I apologize. I am in no position to judge. You didn't tell me about Derham or Paxborough. I took liberties without intending marriage. I have no claim on you, and I'm sorry. I do value our time together."

"I love the poetry cabin," she said softly. "I wrote the last poem in my book seated at the escritoire you arranged for me, inspired by the liberties you took."

He brightened. "Is it a *lewd* poem?"

She lifted her shoulder. "I suppose it depends upon your definition of 'lewd.'"

"Dear God above . . ." Ewan tilted his face heavenward as if in supplication. "Please let it meet *everyone's* definition of 'lewd.'"

A smile tugged at her lips. "Then we're still friends?"

"Is that what you want?"

"I wouldn't mind being . . . kissing friends."

His eyes glinted. "I would be amenable to that and more. Be your lewdest."

She just wanted to be herself. Did she dare?

"I suffer an itchy nose when I'm doing something I'd rather not. Last night I spent an entire waltz trying not to sneeze into Derham's cravat. When I'm with you, the only thing I want to do with your cravat is take it off."

Her cheeks burned. Was that . . . was that too lewd?

His thumb brushed her cheek. "Then it is fortunate we are in a public conservatory and not in a private poetry cabin, for I would be inclined to let you take off any garment of mine that you please."

He was teasing. Wasn't he? Louisa's entire body was overwarm. She'd never *actually* remove his cravat or anything else. Would she?

Yes.

She was about to play a lead role in her mother's cautionary tale: the heiress who was only chosen for her dowry.

This was her chance to know what it felt like to be desired for who she really was, not for what monetary benefit she could provide. To be appreciated as a person, not a purse. This was also Louisa's opportunity to experience passion, even if it was never more than kisses.

There were separate activities for young ladies and the older generation planned throughout each day, giving Louisa large blocks of time when her mother would not be looking for her.

She was used to wandering off to write or to think—usually in the library, or a quiet corner in an empty parlor. This time, it would be even better.

Whenever her mother and the other guests were busy with the various planned activities, Louisa would cloak herself in her maid's plainest pelisse and disappear to the cabin to write.

And . . . to be with Ewan.

Her voice was surprisingly steady. "Meet me in the cabin whenever you can slip away unseen?"

Ewan's eyes were pools of heat. "I wouldn't miss it."

Chapter Eleven

Ewan sat at the cabin's rough-hewn table, penning a detailed letter to his grandfather. Louisa was at the escritoire, lost in a new poem. It had only been like this for a handful of days, yet Ewan had never felt more comfortable. He thought of this hardback chair as his. And the cabin . . .

This sanctuary was *theirs*. It felt like the home they could have had, if they weren't saddled with other responsibilities.

Sometimes they wrote for hours, without a single spoken word. Other times, they lay head-to-toe on the narrow bed, heads resting on laced fingers, and talked about anything and everything that came to mind.

Despite their increasingly inappropriate banter, they didn't indulge in anything more licentious than stolen kisses. Yet spending every spare moment together in their cozy secret home was more intimate than any embrace. Louisa knew Ewan in a way no one else ever had.

A week might not *sound* like much time, but what was the typical *ton* courtship? A few sets of twenty-minute country dances, in which partners changed constantly. A well-chaperoned jaunt or two in a public park. Perhaps supper at a crowded dinner party, and then a stilted tea under the watchful eye of the young lady's mother.

A gentleman of means could court the object of his affection for the length of an entire Season and not spend half as much time with her as Ewan and Louisa had in a single day. They were as comfortable as an old married couple.

Walking away from her was going to be torture.

Louisa crumpled up a bit of foolscap, and hurled it into the fire. "I believe I'll recline on the thinking couch for a moment."

The thinking couch was the bed. It seemed safer not to call it one. They'd been using it in lieu of a sofa, because there was no other furniture in the small cabin apart from the table and escritoire.

"Do you want me to join you?" he asked.

She always said yes, but he enquired anyway. If she wanted to be alone—inasmuch as was possible in a single-room cabin—he'd give that to her. He suspected he'd give her the world if he could.

"Yes. Come." She scooted closer to the knotted wooden wall and patted the newly unoccupied space beside her. "Lie up here, with me."

Not head-to-toe, then. That had been another prudent measure. In theory, anyway. Ewan liked Louisa's toes and ankles just as much as every other part of her.

This time, they lay shoulder to shoulder. There wasn't quite enough room, so he propped himself on his side and tucked a stray curl behind her ear.

"Poem not going well?"

"Perhaps I just wished to see if I could entice you into bed."

"Always a pleasure." He touched her cheek. "Do you ever wish this cabin was really ours?" He knew it wasn't any more possible for him than it was for her, but it had become his favorite dream. "What if we belonged here? We could spend our days doing nothing but writing and talking."

She arched a brow. "No *kissing?*"

"I thought that bit went without saying." He kissed her on the tip of her nose to prove it.

Her eyes sparkled, then dimmed. "Mother would disown me."

Partly true. All of *Society* would disapprove.

"It's more than Mother, though." Louisa glanced away. "I have a responsibility to my future children."

To choose the best. Which wasn't Ewan.

"I finally have an opportunity to marry well." She swallowed. "When those dreadful scandal columns ruined my Season, they destroyed my chances for a good marriage. Until now."

Ewan's stomach churned with conflicting emotions.

Guilt, for having had an outsized impact on her life.

Sorrow, that he'd hurt her.

Anger, at himself and Society for letting an anonymous opinion carry so much weight.

Shame, because spreading gossip about others was the only way he and his grandfather could put food on the table.

Fear, that one day she might find out.

And a horrible flash of gratefulness that his column *had* ruined everything, because if it hadn't, she wouldn't be here now, with him. She'd be married to another man already.

He claimed her mouth without warning. Infused each kiss with the apologies he couldn't say aloud, the shared future they'd never have. He kissed her as if she were the most splendid thing that had ever happened to him, and life would be meaningless without her in it.

Some things were better unsaid. Even if she had read the truth in his embrace.

"I *would* be content to live as a poetess in a humble cottage far from Polite Society's gaze." Her eyes met his. "But I can't."

"I don't think you'd be relegated to a humble anything, or be far from anyone's mind, once they've seen your work. Have you *read* your poetry? I've told you before that it's brilliant. *You're* brilliant. They'd forget about Byron and Coleridge and Wordsworth, once they had a volume by Louisa Harcourt on their shelves."

"Or my nom de plume, Anne Smith?"

"Or Anne Smith," he agreed. "The most popular and revered Anne Smith who ever existed. You won't even be able to write poetry anymore, what with all of the balls and parties you'll be invited to."

"If I went, they'd notice I wasn't Anne Smith," she pointed out.

"How they'll gasp, and clutch their hands to their bosoms—even the earls and footmen. 'Can you believe Anne Smith was Louisa Harcourt *all along*?' they'll cry, then spend all day in long queues just to beg you to sign both names in their cherished first edition copies."

The corners of Louisa's mouth twitched. "And what will you be doing?"

"Arranging for more copies to be printed, of course. Once you publish, there will never be enough in stock to go around. People will have you autograph handkerchiefs and cravats and the faces of small children."

"Won't the nib scratch their tender skin?"

"Leaving lasting proof of their brush with greatness." Ewan leaned forward. "You could start by publishing one poem. See what kind of reaction it stirs."

She gazed at him for a long moment, her eyes wondering. "I believe you want this as much as I do."

Ewan wanted it because *she* wanted it, because Louisa was talented and deserved every bit of success that could one day be hers, if only she would let it. He would happily be her friend, her lover, her . . . publisher.

"The family business," he began, then stopped.

His family business what? Was the same newspaper that had printed the gossip column that had cost Louisa a suitor and her chance at a successful Season? He *could* publish her poems, would *love* to publish her poems, but she'd probably rather set the printing press on fire once she learned the truth.

She raised her brows with interest, perfectly game to accept what must seem an abrupt change in topic. "Your grandfather's business?"

"I have . . . ideas . . . to make it better," he finished. "But Grandfather is a traditionalist, and my improvements would earn less revenue."

Her nose wrinkled in sympathy. "I wish maximizing income and land and status needn't trump all other concerns."

"Or that 'status' wasn't determined by the patronesses of Almack's?" he said drily.

She made a face. "Would you believe that they didn't renew my voucher after the first few gossip columns?"

Ewan's stomach soured. His neck heated.

I didn't know, he wanted to yell. *I didn't know you, and I didn't know the power of my own words.*

He had to stop.

The thought of disappointing his grandfather, who had sacrificed everything for Ewan, made him want to vomit. But so did casually ruining lives by repeating frivolous gossip.

But if Ewan stopped collecting salacious scandals, the newspaper would barely bring in more money than it cost to print. Grandfather might retire eventually, but Ewan would not even have time to sleep. He'd be utterly exhausted every minute of every day.

Still, he'd be able to meet his own eyes in the looking glass.

"What's wrong?" she asked.

"Nothing could ever be wrong when I'm with you."

He pulled her into his arms, needing her familiar heat, the lush pillow of her breasts, the scent of lavender. She kissed him before he could kiss her. Everything else fell away but the warmth of her soft body and the drugging spice of her kisses.

She was everything he could ever want. Everything he hadn't known he needed. He'd thought connections like these were impossible, yet she not only existed out there somewhere, he'd *found* her. She was right here at his side, in their bed, in his arms.

When Louisa tugged off his cravat, Ewan didn't stop her. They had no future, but he was base enough to take whatever she was willing to give. It would have to sustain him for a life without her.

He kissed the curve of her neck, her shoulder, her bosom. He didn't want to lose her any sooner than he had to; couldn't bear to contemplate the inevitable moment when the fantasy would end.

With luck, they would walk away before she found out the truth.

Chapter Twelve

'Twas the eve before Twelfth Night, and all through the ducal estate . . . Ewan wanted nothing more than to be by Louisa's side. She was waiting for him in the cabin whilst the other young ladies were engaged elsewhere.

He was almost to the rear exit, when—

"I have seen little of you this fortnight." Viscount Derham stopped directly in Ewan's path, a riding whip in one hand. "Been off scribbling rhymes, have you?"

Ewan glared at him, then remembered he'd been off kissing Derham's potential betrothed. Kissing her mouth, her throat, her breasts, albeit through her gowns. Several times, he had barely stopped himself from pulling down her bodice.

"I . . ." Ewan cleared his throat. "What have you been doing?"

"Taking a dressing-down from my uncle." Derham rolled his eyes. "It seems I haven't proposed marriage fast enough to the chit he's picked out for me. I can't find her, for one. I've not glimpsed her this past week. I suppose it doesn't matter, since we'll be seeing each other for the rest of our lives."

Ewan's chest tightened. "You're going to propose?"

"I suspect she's no more eager than I am, though I cannot fathom why. She won't do better than me, that's for certain. Well, she could have Paxborough." Derham swung his riding whip over a shoulder. "Of course, he'll have his lovers."

"Lovers?" Ewan growled in warning.

"Do you think it hedonistic to have several?" Derham asked with amusement. "There are too many to choose from, he says. After the requisite heir and spare, one needn't waste time with one's wife."

Ewan no longer felt like a cad for kissing Louisa. He felt like a prize boxer at Gentleman Jackson's, with Paxborough's arrogant face ripe for the punching.

The woman Ewan loved deserved the life she wished, and she shouldn't need to wed a scoundrel to have it.

Wait . . .

He loved Louisa? A strange warmth filled his bones and set his heart beating faster.

He pushed past Derham without responding.

"Where are you going?" the viscount called in surprise.

Ewan held his notebook aloft and walked faster.

Love. He was in love.

Ewan didn't need a dressing-down by his grandfather to know Louisa was the woman with whom he wished to spend the rest of his life. The challenge was how to make it happen. The Revelry had only one day left.

He'd beg for her hand in the morning. That would give him the evening to dream up the best speech, give her a chance to eat a few eggs and kippers. The last thing he wished was for her to be short-tempered with hunger while he was trying to explain why a commoner who loved her was better than a lord who did not.

It might not be possible. But he wouldn't walk away from what they had without fighting to keep it. Some battles *could* be won—if at great cost. Just that morning, Grandfather had acknowledged Ewan's latest request to discontinue the gossip section. They could estimate the lost subscribers when Ewan returned home.

He detoured through the conservatory to gather a few

flowers for Louisa. He didn't snip the stems; instead, he replanted the roots in a ceramic pot lying against a wall. It was perhaps not the cleanest metaphor, but he was not the poet.

Louisa was. She'd understand that he didn't want their bond to wither and die in a few days' time, but rather to grow, to flourish, to bloom.

He hoped.

When he entered the cabin, her head was bent over a pile of foolscap, her plume flying across the page as if it could not keep time with the speed of her thoughts.

In silence, Ewan placed his offering on the table. He slid into the hard wooden chair to watch the woman he loved creating beauty from her imagination.

When at last she set down her quill, she turned toward Ewan with a joyful grin.

"Sometimes I stare at each blank page in despair, as though its emptiness has robbed all thought from me. Other times, words spring forth too fast to grasp all at once." Her gaze slid to the ceramic pot, and her cheeks turned pink with pleasure. "Speaking of springing forth . . ." She hurried to the flowers and dropped her face to breathe in their sweet scent. "These are beautiful."

Not as beautiful as you was true, but trite, so Ewan settled for leaping to his feet, pulling her into his arms, and kissing her until they were both breathless.

"You should publish them." He kissed the corner of her mouth.

"The flowers?"

"Your poems."

She stepped out of his reach; took the other hard wooden chair on the opposite side of the small table. The flowers blocked his view of her face.

"I told you—"

"I apologize." He pushed the flowerpot to one side so she could see he meant it. "Good intentions are no excuse.

Pressuring you to publish against your will is no better than what my grandfather does to me, or your mother to you."

She ran her finger across the veiny green leaves for a long moment before lifting her gaze to his.

"I *do* want to publish my poems," she said, her voice quiet. "I don't see how I can. Even if I took a pseudonym, I haven't the funds to pay a publisher. And I lack the courage to release a book into the world."

He hesitated. "Do you want ideas?"

She wrinkled her nose, then nodded.

"What if it was just one poem, and free?" He took a deep breath. "My grandfather's business . . . is a newspaper."

It felt like admitting to treason. Shame seeped into his bones. She didn't know about his sordid history. Their scandal columns would close, but the mere thought of the family newspaper still felt like betrayal. He would have to tell her the truth eventually.

What if he could solve Louisa's problems, rather than cause them? What if he could make it be a force of good, rather than evil?

"Grandfather's newspaper has not been as respectable as I'd like," Ewan hedged. "I once wished it were more like the *Morning Chronicle*. Now I'd prefer to deal exclusively with the creative arts. It currently contains nothing of the sort. But if you're brave enough to start with just one poem, so can we."

"A newspaper dedicated to the arts? What a lovely idea! You'd publish, what, a dozen poems every week? A short story or two?"

"Twelve pages of content." The idea was coming into focus. "Poems, short stories, serializations, interviews with actors, dancers, and musicians, reviews of their performances, notices of upcoming plays and art showings, painters seeking patrons and patrons seeking painters, sculptors for hire, tutors for children, models for classes, stained glass makers, architects who . . ." He trailed off.

She was staring at him as if awestruck. "You've *thought* about this."

"Yes," he admitted. Imagining what he would do with his nest egg had kept him sane during the dark days he'd spent collecting gossip. Without the scandal columns, there would be no nest egg, but he could still do something worthwhile.

"I think it's beautiful," Louisa said. "You should do it."

"It's not my paper."

Grandfather was not pleased by Ewan's "financially unsound" decision to strike gossip from their broadsheet. But they *would* have to fill the space with something else. Grandfather wanted news of boxing matches, and chicken fights, and duels.

Ewan would rather see poetry. Words that would bring light into the world rather than reflect its darkness.

"Your grandfather won't let you?" Louisa said in surprise.

"I can do as I please when I inherit, or when I've saved enough for him to retire without fear I'll run the paper into the ground. Until then . . ." He shrugged.

"If I had money of my own, I'd be a founding patroness to your journal of the arts."

"If you had money of your own, I hope you'd spend it on yourself and your poetry."

"Why not both?" She laced her fingers with his. "If we're dreaming, let's dream."

He squeezed her hand. The past two weeks *had* felt like a dream. Ewan loved when he was with Louisa, loved being together, loved being himself, loved *her*. He hoped she could love him, for himself. His new self.

He was no longer a peddler of gossip. The scandal columns would soon be gone. But if he wanted a clean slate going forward, he'd have to give up his double life. Abandon the myth of the smoldering poet.

But first, he would have to think of some way to ease off the mask without causing more scandal himself, once he was exposed as an impostor.

Tomorrow, he would come up with a plan that would solve all of the open threads, and he'd ask Louisa to marry him. For now . . .

He pulled her to her feet and into a slow, silent waltz. An embrace to make up for all of the dances he'd been forced to watch from afar, never joining in. None of those missed dances meant a thing. Only here, now, with Louisa.

"Dancing with you is a dream come true." He gazed down into her beautiful eyes. "Do you have a Christmas wish I could grant?"

Chapter Thirteen

What did Louisa want more than anything?

Ewan.

Dare she have him?

She reached behind her neck and unclasped her mother's locket. It symbolized giving up dreams for duty. But Louisa still had one night left. She set the locket next to the ceramic pot and let the delicate gold chain spill to the scarred table.

There would be no miniature of her time with Ewan to hang about her neck.

All she would have was the memory of what it had felt like to be free, to be herself, to be joyful, here with him. She would savor every moment.

She wrapped her arms about his neck and kissed him. His embrace should be familiar by now, but was still as thrilling as the first time. He cradled her head as he kissed her. She would never tire of being treated as if she were strong yet precious, both admired and desired.

Her chance for passion, her opportunity to feel wanted and cherished, was now.

She adored Ewan's kisses, but kisses weren't enough. Not today. They needed to make their last night together count. A memory strong enough to cocoon inside when the rest of the world was inescapable.

They stumbled to the bed without breaking their kiss. *This* was what kisses should be; passionate, diverting. When the mattress hit the back of Louisa's knees, they tumbled backward atop the blanket and smiled at each other. Shy and bold at the same time.

Her only regret was that the night couldn't last forever.

"Have I mentioned how beautiful you are?" Ewan murmured as he trailed kisses from the curve of her jaw to the shell of her ear.

She shook her head. "Not since you whispered it in the corridor after breakfast."

"An unforgivable oversight." Now his kisses descended the curve of her neck, then traced a shiver-inducing path along the seam where her bodice met her bosom. "Have I told you, you're the cleverest poet in England?"

"Don't need to tell me," she gasped as his teeth gently lowered the delicate linen and he took her bare breast into his mouth. "I'm the cleverest . . ."

She gave up trying to talk and surrendered to sensation. Every part of him was magic; his hands, his mouth, his tongue. She was helpless to resist the pull of arousal and the promise of impending bliss.

But this time, she would not be content with him pleasing her as best they could whilst swathed in winter clothes. This was her chance to see him properly; to know him in every way. To not just bare themselves to each other, but to *give* themselves to each other completely.

She rolled onto her stomach.

He pressed a kiss to the nape of her neck. "Has your bosom tired of my kisses?"

"Never." She gestured to her spine. "It tires of this gown. Would you be a gentleman and kindly divest me of it?"

His hands froze. "Are you sure, Louisa?"

"Yes."

His voice was hoarse. "I thought you'd never ask."

Louisa had never shed a gown so slowly in her life. With every freshly released button, Ewan bared another inch and pressed a kiss to the newly revealed space. A delicious torture that made her want to rend the fabric herself, were she not a puddle of sensation incapable of doing anything that would interrupt his tantalizing progress.

When at last the final button was undone, she pushed off the gown, flung off her stays with trembling fingers, then rose to her knees. She yanked her shift over her head and tossed it to the floor.

She should feel naked and exposed. She wore nothing now save for silk stockings, tied above the knees with pink ribbons. But all she felt was eager. She reached for Ewan's cravat and fumbled it free from his neck, her heart pounding.

"Are you absolutely certain?" His gaze was serious, his gold-flecked brown eyes dark with passion.

She nodded. "Very certain."

When she reached for his jacket, he did the honors himself, tossing his discarded clothing atop hers with a swiftness she had never dreamed possible.

Everything about his body was magnificent. Big, and hard, and strong.

She expected him to cover her, to join their bodies together at once.

Instead, he lifted one of her feet, as though to massage the tension away, as he had done a dozen times before.

This time, he did no such thing. He lowered his body and pressed a soft, worshipful kiss to the tender flesh where the arch of her foot met her inner ankle.

Slowly, tortuously, his kisses marched higher. He tasted her flesh as if savoring it, as though he were mapping every dip and curve with the heat of his mouth and the rasp of his tongue. Devouring her bite by bite until she shivered in want, anticipating each new kiss and dreading its loss until his lips touched her flesh anew.

When he reached the top of her thigh, he did not continue higher to her breasts—as her straining nipples had hoped—but instead followed the sensitive crease with his tongue to the juncture between her legs, where her body pulsed with heat and wanting.

Her breath caught; her pulse flew. He buried his face right where she wanted him most, and she arched into him, gasping. She had not known this pleasure existed. It was buoyant, overwhelming. Her head lolled backward to the pillow.

His palms skated higher, reaching the breasts that had longed for his touch, their peaks hard and eager beneath his talented fingers while his tongue worked its magic between her legs. The pressure was building too fast, the maelstrom too much to contain. Her legs tightened about his shoulders, and she convulsed against him, stuttering wordlessly as the apex took her.

Only then did he fit his body to hers, slowly, carefully. Her body was boneless, sated, and yet hungry for more. The strange new invasion excited her as much as his tongue on her breasts, her nipples.

"I won't spill inside of you," he murmured.

She nodded her agreement and wrapped her legs about him. "I'm ready."

His shaft nudged at her core.

"I'm sorry," he whispered, then jutted his hips. There was a brief stab of pain, quickly replaced by fullness and pleasure.

Her hips rose to meet him as he surged within her, first as gentle and relentless as the tide, then faster, harder, to match the quickening of her pulse and the strange little sounds coming from her throat.

Nothing had ever felt more right. The heat of his kisses, his slick strokes within her, marking her, claiming her, taking her as high as she could soar, his strong arms holding her tight all the while. Was it any wonder she loved him?

The muscles at her core spasmed at the realization.

Love.

That was why they fit perfectly together. Why his breath felt like hers, his racing pulse her own. Their hearts were as entwined as their bodies. She wanted it all, wanted him forever.

No matter what it cost.

Chapter Fourteen

When Louisa awoke, night had fallen. She bolted upright in alarm. Nightfall meant supper time. Mother was used to Louisa sneaking off to write, but if she wasn't seated at her place at the table with the others, Mother would send a search party to find her.

That would be a disaster.

Careful not to wake Ewan, Louisa slid from the bed. She added more wood to the fire so that he would not be chilled when he awoke.

Her heart gave an extra kick as she gazed over at him on the bed.

Ewan had given her more than the freedom to write her poetry. His unflagging encouragement gave her confidence, and restored her faith in her talents. He made her feel proud of herself. She had never felt anything like that before. With him, she didn't have to hide.

She forced herself to turn away in search of her clothes.

Smiling, she sifted through the pile of clothes in search of her shift and stays. Of course hers were on the bottom. There went Ewan's trousers, his linen shirt, his waistcoat, his jacket . . .

A small book fell from somewhere inside the jacket, and landed pages-down atop Louisa's shift.

His poetry notebook.

She wouldn't snoop, Louisa told herself firmly. She

would turn it over, smooth out any bent pages, and place it back on the pile of clothes.

But when she turned over the small book, she could not help but recognize her own name right in the middle of a page.

Had he written a poem about her? She'd written several about him, but that did not give her leave to pry. She would just smooth out the wrinkles, and—

Hers wasn't the only name.

There was her mother's name, and Derham's, and Lady Cressida, and the rest of the guests.

> Lady Harcourt: proud, hovers over Louisa
> Mrs. Phelps: wants Clevethorpe for daughter
> Lord Clevethorpe: more interested in cards than courtship
> Lady Stephen: hunting lodge
> Paxborough: 2 lovers (more?) after wed

She turned the pages too fast to read the hurtful comments, but methodically enough to realize there was no poetry on any of the pages. Just gossip. It was as though he'd been writing the world's most comprehensive . . . scandal sheet . . .

She jerked her gaze toward Ewan.

He was awake, his face ashen.

She held up the notebook, her knuckles white and trembling. "What is this?"

"Notes," he admitted. "I'm not going to use them. I told you I didn't agree with the content in my grandfather's newspaper—"

"'Don't agree' is a far cry from 'I write it myself.'" Her voice was shaking. Her whole body was shaking. "What newspaper?"

"Louisa—"

"What newspaper?"

He told her.

Her heart dropped.

Of course it was the one whose scandal columns had damned her to a life of loneliness and mockery. The column that compared her to Almack's insipid lemonade, and led to her being denied a voucher. The column responsible for the loss of a young man whom she might one day have wed.

All due to gossip *he* had spread!

The book fell from her hand. She could no longer bear to touch it. No longer bear to look at *him*, or to think about what they'd done.

She snatched her linen shift up from the floor. "I suppose I ought to leave you alone so you can add this little interlude to your book as well."

"Louisa, no. I would never—"

"I'm supposed to believe you would *never*?" She yanked her stays about her ribs.

He swung his legs over the side of the bed.

She held up her hand in warning. "If you come near me, I'll scream."

Everything, *everything*, was a lie. He wasn't a kind-hearted fellow poet. He was a blackguard who had spent years mocking the world Louisa belonged to, mocking her in specific.

Ewan wasn't her soul mate. He was her nightmare.

His eyes pleaded with her. "I'm not going to write the column anymore."

"Aren't you?" She kicked the notebook across the room. "There's an entire novel's worth about people at the Revelry alone. When am I supposed to believe you stopped? This morning over tea?"

"It was not well done of me," he admitted. "And I regret—"

She scoffed in disbelief as she tugged her gown over her stays. "Not 'well done'? How many lives have you ruined?"

"It's reprehensible," he said. "I don't blame you for being

angry. You should be angry. I'm angry at myself. But that doesn't mean our relationship isn't real."

She shoved her arms into her pelisse and glared at him. "*Nothing* we had was real."

His eyes were bright. "I'm a blackguard. I admit it. But all you wanted from me was a diverting fortnight, remember? I'm a worse cad than you thought, but I was never good enough for you anyway. This whole time, you've been planning on marrying Paxborough or Derham. Not me. We both know that."

"You've no idea what I intended to do." Her voice was cold and empty. "We don't know each other at all."

"You *do* know me." He scrambled from the bed and scooped up the notebook. "Here's a passage about the sweet scent of your hair." He turned the page. "And here I try to convey the joy of watching you write. And here, did you see this one?" He held the pages out as if begging her to read them.

"Do you really think a platitude or two makes up for destroying lives?"

Without waiting for an answer, she stalked out of the cabin and into the bitter gusts of winter, heedless of the icy snow whipping against her cheeks. She closed her fingers about the gold locket in her pocket.

Ewan wasn't the only one capable of destroying lives.

Louisa had managed to ruin her own all by herself.

THE HEAVY DOOR slammed shut with a hollow *thunk* Ewan felt deep into his bones. He hurled his notebook across the room, then slumped onto the edge of the bed and dropped his face into his hands.

Had he ever believed he could find a way to explain his actions? That Louisa might accept his hand in marriage?

Instead, he'd hurt her terribly.

Again.

He fell backward onto the bed and covered his face

with a pillow. Ewan was worse than the people he'd spread rumors about. Greystoke didn't hide who he was. Lady Harcourt didn't hide who she was. Paxborough didn't hide who he was. *Ewan* was the derisible one, not the Society bucks whose egocentric antics he'd gossiped about.

His duplicity had cost him the woman he loved.

Chapter Fifteen

Louisa did not attend supper.

Her face was too splotchy, and her stomach churned too acidly to even contemplate being on display to the rest of the party.

She could ring for her maid, but she didn't want anyone looking at her. Not like this, with her gown crooked and her hair disheveled, and cheeks streaked with tears.

Breath shaky, she returned her outerwear to her wardrobe, and exchanged her gown and shift for a linen nightrail. She climbed up into the canopy bed, where she could close each velvet panel tight and hide away from the rest of the world.

In Ewan, she'd thought she had found a spiritual kindred.

She'd been wrong.

Perhaps there was no such thing as a kindred. Perhaps she was destined to be lonely, no matter what title she bore or what house she kept.

Perhaps she should have taken her mother's advice from the start.

Her door creaked open, then shut. Louisa froze in the darkness of her bed. It wasn't her lady's maid. Servants always knocked, unless they had been summoned.

It wasn't Ewan, was it? Her heart banged. He knew which guest chamber was hers. He'd stood outside of it whilst she fetched her pelisse and bonnet, before their first trip to the cabin.

Surely he wouldn't barge in uninvited. There was nothing she wanted to hear, nothing she wanted to say. Louisa didn't even want to *feel* anymore.

The velvet panels swung open.

It wasn't Ewan. It was her mother. Looking as fierce as a Viking warrioress at the thought that something untoward had occurred to her daughter.

Louisa burst into tears and threw herself into her mother's arms.

"What is it?" Her mother held her tight, one hand stroking Louisa's hair. "What happened? Did someone—"

"*I* did this to me," she choked out. "I trusted someone I should not have."

Her mother wiped the tears from Louisa's cheeks. "I will drag whoever has hurt you to Tyburn Tree and tie the rope myself."

"He gave me everything I desired," she said softly, resting her forehead against her mother's shoulder. "He said I was talented. He gave me a cabin surrounded by nature with a perfect little escritoire inside and fresh ink to write with."

Her mother's hand stilled in her hair. "And what did you give him?"

Louisa didn't answer.

"Oh, darling," Mother said with a sigh, and then, "No one knows, I hope?"

Louisa let out a humorless chuckle. "He's the very gossip columnist who ruined my chances for a successful Season years ago."

Mother gripped her by both shoulders, forcing Louisa to meet her eyes. "He *what*?"

"Don't worry," Louisa said sarcastically. "He tells me that he doesn't plan to spread gossip any longer."

"Tyburn is too good for this knave." Her mother's eyes flashed with pure rage. "I'd be delighted to turn our wine cellar into a dungeon."

"I don't want him tortured." Louisa swallowed hard. "I love him."

"Oh, darling," her mother said again, her eyes brimming with sympathy. "We do as we must. There is still time."

Louisa's hands trembled. "You still want me to . . ."

"What choice have you got?" Her mother brushed damp wisps of hair from Louisa's face. "Paxborough need never know. With him, you have some leverage. If he doesn't give up his debauchery—"

"Lovers, plural," Louisa bit out. "And I have it on good authority that he is the kind of man to keep them after we marry."

"Then such behavior cancels a single indiscretion that occurred before Paxborough had the good sense to ask for your hand." Mother gripped Louisa's shoulders. "You *can't* say no, darling. Rejecting a wealthy heir will have dire consequences. This is your only chance to control which story is told."

"All right," Louisa said hollowly. "If anyone asks for my hand tomorrow, I'll accept."

It would be a terrible, loveless match, but an honest one. Paxborough drank too much. He was as interested in her as a potted plant was in visiting the moon.

And in return, she'd have all of the wealth and privilege a lady could want.

Huzzah.

"No," she said with a gasp, then louder, firmer. "No. I can't do it."

"Can't be a marchioness?" her mother said in disbelief.

"Can't give up myself." Louisa straightened her spine. "That might have been my fate before, but I no longer want it."

"What, then?" Mother demanded. "Resign yourself to 'fallen spinster'?"

"Yes," Louisa said simply. "I'd rather live in a shack as a disgraced poetess than live in misery high in a castle."

"Shack?" her mother spluttered. "I would never abandon you. You're my *daughter.* You could lie with every man in England, and my home would always be your home, too."

Louisa stared at her mother, heat pricking the corners of her eyes.

"B-but," she stammered. "The scandal . . ."

". . . will be horrid," her mother admitted. "You were so devastated when that gossip column printed those ugly words. The loss of that milquetoast lad left you locked in your bedchamber for weeks. I thought you'd *want* a brilliant match to lord over your peers."

"I don't care about them," Louisa admitted. "I wanted to please you."

Her mother cupped her cheek. "You're a wonderful daughter. I will always choose your happiness over Society's good favor. If it's your dream to live at home as a fallen spinster, you have my blessing. And if what you really want is to live in a shack on a poet's meager coin . . ."

Louisa's heart skipped.

Her mother gave a firm nod. "Then I'm afraid you're to be disappointed, because I intend to give you your dowry money outright to do with as you please. And besides, I'd kill the man before I gave him my only daughter."

"But . . ." Louisa gaped at her. "You never let me have so much as a shilling . . ."

Mother fluttered her hands. "Every penny went to build your dowry, including the land and the home I live in. I would have sacrificed the hair on my head if it would have helped you take Society by storm the way I thought you deserved. My only priority is you. Be *you*, Louisa."

Mother kissed the top of her head.

Louisa gazed at her in wonder.

She didn't need a titled husband to be important. All she

needed was to value herself, instead of allowing others' opinions to rule her.

Having funds of her own meant Louisa could be her *own* patroness of the arts. She was free to be who she wished, to do as she pleased.

She would start at once.

Chapter Sixteen

Ewan didn't see Louisa again until morning. The *last* morning of the Revelry. Since dawn, carriages had been lined up on the drive outside the front door as guests with long journeys ahead of them made an early start.

He had spent a sleepless night in the cabin, gathering the pillow to his chest to breathe in traces of Louisa's scent, praying she might at least return to collect the abandoned poems on the escritoire.

She did not.

Even if she never spoke to him again, he couldn't walk away without giving her the apology she deeply deserved.

He walked into the entryway—and saw her. Bundled, bonneted, but *still here*.

His boots skidded across the decorative floor tiles as he raced toward her. No one else was in the entryway. She was alone.

Her blank face jerked in his direction . . . and did not change expression. No anger, no tears, no flash of recognition. It was as if what they'd shared was nothing. As if Ewan meant nothing.

He held out a bundle of carefully wrapped papers.

"I want no gifts from you." Her eyes and voice were flat.

"It's not from me." He held the twine-bound parcel out further. "These are the poems you left behind."

When it looked as though she still might not accept them, he added, "Do you want me to keep them?"

She took the package.

He handed her the other item he'd been carrying. His breast pocket had hidden journals just like it for years. This one had almost been hurled into a fire. He placed the cursed leather volume in Louisa's hands.

She held it as though it had been doused in plague.

"Why would I want more of your gossip? It already ruined me once."

"And now you can ruin me," he replied without hesitation. "I wrote my name on the first page and signed it. Show it to anyone, and I'll never be welcome in Society again."

She stared down at the journal. With interest? With disgust? With great delight at the hundred ways she could now enact vengeance? He didn't know. Her eyes refused to give any clue.

"I suppose someone like you must have already begun a new book."

"I have not," he said, then clarified. "That is, I keep many notes, but the others are my plans and dreams for when I can start my own paper. I won't live a double life ever again. I did harm, Louisa. That I was trying to help a family member doesn't excuse it. I cruelly and thoughtlessly hurt *you*, and I'm sorry. I do not expect forgiveness. I just thought you deserved to know."

She narrowed her eyes. "Why?"

"Why did I write the column?"

She held up the journal. "Why give me the means to destroy you?"

"Because I am already destroyed." The words scratched from his chest. "There *is* no worse fate than losing you. We agreed to a fortnight together, but a lifetime wouldn't be enough."

She blinked, and her brow furrowed.

This was his only chance.

"I love you, Louisa. I can't prove it with verse, because

my attempts at poetry end up sounding like 'eyes the color of squirrels' and 'at the sight of you my stomach flips like influenza, if influenza were a good thing.' But I love you. I will dedicate the rest of my days to proving you are the most important thing in my life and my heart."

He dropped to one knee.

She didn't turn away.

"What's this nonsense?" Lord Paxborough strode into the entryway with a glass of brandy and a perplexed expression. "Reid, why the deuce are you genuflecting to my betrothed?"

A series of gasps sounded from farther down the corridor. Paxborough was not alone, then. The gentlemen who followed the viscount had heard him lay claim to Louisa.

His stomach fell. He was too late. It was over.

Louisa crossed her arms over her chest and kept her gaze locked on Ewan. "I'm not betrothed yet. Go on."

He stayed on one knee and tried again. "I don't want to lose you. I want to marry you. I want to sharpen your pencils every morning and rub your feet every night and fall asleep in each other's embrace. I want to make you proud."

A new flutter of gasps rippled through their growing audience. His inadvertently public proposal was not only making a spectacle of himself: Louisa would once again be the subject of gossip.

This time, however, the *on dit* would be that Miss Louisa Harcourt had been fought over by two men, one a penniless poet and the other a powerful viscount, in front of the Duke of Greystoke's guests. A story that would only burnish the golden reputation of the Revelry.

There would never be a finer opportunity for Louisa to publicly humiliate Ewan, just as he'd done to her all those years ago.

"I would sacrifice anything at all for a second chance." Ewan's chest was too tight, his stomach in knots. "For one more fortnight with you. One more day. One more hour.

You don't just have my heart. You *are* my heart. Let me prove it to you for the rest of eternity."

She nodded thoughtfully. "All right."

His heart stuttered. "Wh-what?"

"You'll have to prove it for the rest of eternity, and not a second less."

She knelt before him so that they were eye to eye. "You were thoughtless and cruel, but you didn't want to be. You did everything in your power for someone you love. People make mistakes, including dreadful ones. They also can change. Good men are the ones who try to put things right."

"Are they . . . also the ones who marry the poetess they've been in love with since she said the duke's evergreens look like teeth?"

"She said *what*?" Derham barked. He was standing at Paxborough's shoulder.

Louisa set the parcel and notebook to the side and took Ewan's hands. "I love you, too, Ewan Reid, even if my eyes remind you of squirrel fur."

"What?" came a high-pitched squeak that sounded like her mother.

He cleared his throat. "As to the small matter of marriage?"

Louisa grinned. "I accept."

Joy flooded him. "I would sweep you into my arms and twirl you about this room if it wouldn't cause the scandal of the century."

"We've already accomplished that." She laced her fingers with his. "Let's do it anyway."

He twirled her out through the door and into their future.

Epilogue

London, England
The following December

Louisa's heart banged against her ribs. "Is that . . . ?"

"It is." Her husband handed her a pristine broadsheet, fresh from the printing press. "The very first copy."

Louisa's breath caught.

It wasn't the first issue of *The Patroness*, their creative arts newspaper, but it was the first time Louisa had been brave enough to include her name beneath one of her weekly poems.

"It's brilliant." He swooped in to kiss her cheek. "You're brilliant. Everyone loves your poetry."

Louisa's belly fluttered. "They think Anne Smith wrote it. When they find out it's me . . ."

"We'll have invitations again!" Ewan clutched his hands to his chest in faux rapture. "Who shall we turn down first? Lady Jersey? Prinny?"

The Prince Regent was indeed fond of reading, a fact which did nothing to settle Louisa's nervous excitement.

Her name was on the front page of *The Patroness*. Each issue featured different emerging artists, musicians, and actors, taking care to highlight little-known voices.

Established literary journals published men like Byron's poetry, but *The Patroness* published his dear friend, Elizabeth Pigot. And after they published the story—illustrated by Miss Pigot's hand—Byron himself sent them a verse.

Louisa was happy to stay at her escritoire all day with nothing but her plume and a pot of tea. Ewan, on the other hand, visited every theater, studio, and publishing house he could find. Not to fawn over their biggest stars, but to enquire the names and directions of the individuals who had been turned away.

Less than a year later, *The Patroness* had more content than one could dream. In spreading the word about overlooked persons of talent, they connected patrons of the arts with producers of the arts, and helped fill vacant roles with excellent people for any part.

In other words, their paper was still spreading gossip, but the very best kind. Rumors of who was wonderful, who was available, who should be snapped up at the first opportunity. People wrote in, requesting their own names be printed, their letters tied to sample bits of writing, or sketches, or invitations to performances.

The Patroness was also the first to publish the list of guests to the upcoming Christmas Revelry. This year, she and Ewan would be attending as husband and wife.

Louisa no longer minded that he wasn't a fellow poet. Her handsome husband was a tireless promoter of the information he felt Englanders needed most: beauty, music, art, and entertainment.

Things like Louisa's poetry.

And family.

His grandfather had not meant to torture his grandson for the past decade. He'd wished to provide for him, but had wanted to make the most money as quickly as possible to ensure his grandson could live any life he pleased.

It had horrified him to discover that the opposite had occurred.

Mr. Reid wasted no time in discontinuing his old scandal

sheet. He donated his printing press to Louisa and Ewan's new venture instead.

Because Louisa's mother was still prominent in Society, she used her influence to encourage the wealthy to subscribe to the broadsheet and become patrons of the arts themselves.

Louisa and Ewan had refused to accept Lady Harcourt's home as part of Louisa's dowry, but they built a cozy cabin in the rear of the country property to retreat to whenever they weren't in their London lodgings.

"You did it, my love." Ewan danced her about the busy printing press.

"*We* did it. We're still doing it." She wrapped her arms about his neck and kissed him with all of the love in her heart. She'd never been so content or so joyful.

The best poetry of all was the life they'd built together.

Teeth, squirrels, and all.

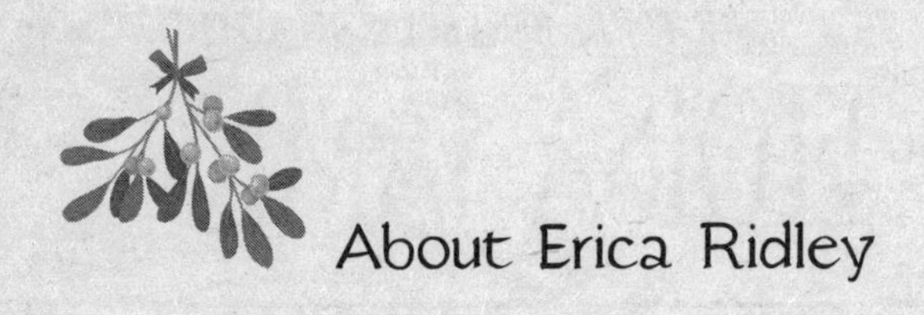

About Erica Ridley

Erica Ridley is a *New York Times* and *USA TODAY* bestselling author of witty, feel-good historical romance novels, including *The Duke Heist*, featuring the Wild Wynchesters. Why seduce a duke the normal way, when you can accidentally kidnap one in an elaborately planned heist?

In the 12 Dukes of Christmas series, enjoy whimsical, heartwarming Regency romps nestled in a picturesque snow-covered village. After all, nothing heats up a winter night quite like finding oneself in the arms of a duke!

Two popular series, the Dukes of War and Rogues to Riches, feature roguish peers and dashing war heroes who find love amongst the splendor and madness of Regency England.

When not reading or writing romances, Erica can be found riding camels in Africa, zip-lining through rain forests in Costa Rica, or getting hopelessly lost in the middle of Budapest.

NEW YORK TIMES BESTSELLING AUTHOR

ELOISA JAMES

The Wildes of Lindow Castle

Wilde in Love

978-0-06-238947-3

Too Wilde to Wed

978-0-06-269246-7

Born to Be Wilde

978-0-06-269247-4

Say No to the Duke

978-0-06-287782-6

Say Yes to the Duke

978-0-06-287806-9

Wilde Child

978-0-06-287807-6